The Girl from Donegal

Carmel Harrington is from Co. Wexford, where she lives with her husband, her children, and their rescue dog, George Bailey. An international bestseller, her warm and emotional storytelling has captured the hearts of readers worldwide.

Carmel's novels have been shortlisted for Irish Book Awards, and her debut, *Beyond Grace's Rainbow*, won several awards, including Kindle Book of the Year. *The Girl from Donegal* was an instant *Irish Times* bestseller.

To keep in touch with Carmel, follow her on social media or visit her website:

Twitter | Facebook | Instagram @HappyMrsH
www.carmelharrington.com

Also by Carmel Harrington

Beyond Grace's Rainbow
The Life You Left
Every Time a Bell Rings
The Things I Should Have Told You
The Woman at 72 Derry Lane
A Thousand Roads Home
My Pear-Shaped Life
The Moon Over Kilmore Quay
A Mother's Heart

Carmel Harrington

The Girl from Donegal

HarperCollins*Publishers*

HarperCollins*Publishers* Ltd
1 London Bridge Street,
London SE1 9GF
www.harpercollins.co.uk

HarperCollins*Publishers*
Macken House,
39/40 Mayor Street Upper,
Dublin 1
D01 C9W8

First published by HarperCollins*Publishers* 2023
This paperback edition published 2024
1

A catalogue record for this book is available from the British Library

ISBN: 978-0-00-852856-0

This novel is entirely a work of fiction.
The names, characters and incidents portrayed in it are
the work of the author's imagination. Any resemblance to
actual persons, living or dead, events or localities is
entirely coincidental.

Set in Sabon LT Std by Palimpsest Book Production Limited, Falkirk, Stirlingshire

Printed and bound in the UK using 100% Renewable Electricity
by CPI Group (UK) Ltd

For *my* last love, Roger

Oh! The heart that has truly loved, never forgets,
But as truly loves on to the close.

'Believe Me, If All Those Endearing Young Charms'
Thomas Moore, Irish Poet, 1779–1852

PROLOGUE

Kate

Palm Tree Cottage, Horseshoe Bay, Bermuda

Kate inched her chair forward and placed her hands on the vintage cookie tin. It was a rich chocolate brown, painted with decorative gold edges surrounding sugared fruit in ochre, russet red and burnt orange. Her fingertips tingled as she traced its contours. She wasn't sure where it originated from, but it served her mother well as a sewing box for years.

Now, it was the gatekeeper to Kate's memories.

Kate closed her eyes and searched her mind, looking for her mother. Ah, there she was. Her mom, with glasses perched on the end of her nose, shoulders rounded as she sat by the fire, the embers dancing behind her. She held the tin on her lap and opened it, ready to fix a patch on the knee of Kate's jeans. Her mother found the end of a navy-blue spool of thread, licked it, and then carefully pushed it through the eye of a needle. Love and care with every stitch.

Kate took a sharp breath as the pain of loss pierced her again, surprising her by its ferocity. Grief was its own mistress, coming and going as she saw fit, no matter how long someone was gone from you. And just when you thought you could bear the unbearable, she came back for more.

Kate's arthritic hands trembled as they clasped the container between them and her breath quickened as she used her thumb to attempt to flick the lid open. It was stubborn and refused to budge. The wear and tear of time.

'Let me do that for you,' Esme said, sneaking up behind her.

She took a seat beside Kate, then took the tin from her, pushing the lid up, millimetre by millimetre, until, finally, it gave way.

Kate breathed in deeply, sighing with pleasure.

Silence fell as they took in the assortment of photographs nestled inside. On top of the pile, a faded black-and-white image of a forlorn young girl in pigtails, standing on the cobbled stones at the Royal Naval Dockyard in Bermuda.

Esme sucked in air through her teeth, then carefully placed a new photograph on to the top of the pile. A grey-haired man with a dapper moustache and goatee smiled for the camera, his eyes crinkling with warmth and merriment.

The room stilled and the silence spoke for Kate. She snapped the lid shut, the sound slicing the air between them.

Kate looked up and locked eyes with Esme – her love,

her confidante, her best friend – and she saw compassion and understanding reflected in her chestnut brown eyes.

'I know you are afraid, Kate,' Esme said, 'but please remember that even bad memories have happy moments tucked away between them. Some of them exist, *because* the sadness led you to them.'

ONE

Saoirse

One week earlier . . .
Palm Tree Cottage, Horseshoe Bay, Bermuda

As Saoirse's flight circled above L.F. Wade International airport, the first glimpse of Bermuda elicited a chorus of gasps from the passengers on board the airbus, the islands appearing through wispy white clouds, surrounded by the deep blue waters of the Atlantic Ocean.

'Paradise once more,' Saoirse whispered, peering out the small passenger window.

She watched the colours change below her. The sea became vibrant turquoise with highlights of emerald dancing through the surf. The landscape was a mix of verdant greens dotted with pastel-coloured buildings. Her heart began to race. Overwhelmed, not from the impact of the view, but from a memory that had pierced her, taking her back to another time, another *her*.

Nine years ago, flying into this same airport, her eyes bloodshot from tears and her heart too broken to acknowledge the beauty of the islands below. On that trip, Saoirse had fled in desperation from Canada, where she'd been working as a ranch hand, to the arms of her aunts Kate and Esme. Her safe refuge as she tried to make sense of her devastation at the break-up of her marriage.

Now, Saoirse shook her head, muttering a quiet 'no' to herself. She would not allow herself to relive those memories. She had moved on with her life.

The plane landed with a gentle bounce, and she instinctively clasped the armrest. As she did so, Saoirse looked down to her ring finger, where a new emerald now sparkled. She slipped it off and looked at the faint white band that had already made its mark. This gem was her future and anchor. It pulled her away from sad memories to her happier *now* – with Finn. Time had moved on, and so had she. As the plane taxied along the runway, Saoirse instead pulled a fresh memory to the front of her mind, a sword to banish unwanted thoughts. She closed her eyes, her mind returning to her favourite trek. She could almost hear the soft thud of Mr Bojangles' hooves as he trotted across the muddy ground, echoing into the air around them.

'Whoa there, boy!' Saoirse had ducked to avoid a low-hanging branch, laughing as an unexpected confetti of green leaves fell upon her and Mr Bojangles.

As she'd pulled on the reins and leaned forward to pat his snow-white soft neck, she'd heard the sound of hooves approaching and turned to see an ebony Irish Draught horse galloping towards her. Saoirse grinned with delight at the familiar sight of Finn and his horse Spirit. Reaching her side, Finn leaned in and kissed Saoirse as Spirit nuzzled Mr Bojangles in greeting. That was the way it was with the four of them.

'You said you couldn't get time off today!'

'How could I miss a chance to see my girl?' Finn replied. Then, clicking his heels into Spirit's side, he shouted over his shoulder with a wink, 'Catch me if you can!'

Saoirse gently squeezed Mr Bojangles' side with her boots, but he needed no encouragement to take off. He was an Irish Sport Horse, fast and athletic, and, luckily for her, had the same competitive streak as his owner. Within seconds, they were neck and neck.

Leaning down low, she whispered, 'Come on, boy, let's show them what you've got.' He rose to the challenge, and as the end of her long lane came into view, Mr Bojangles soared past Spirit.

'One of these days, I'll beat you,' Finn said good-naturedly when he caught up with her again. Then softly, he added, 'It's a good job I love you.'

Saoirse never grew tired of hearing those magical three words.

'I love you too,' she replied as they arrived at her favourite spot on their regular trekking route. 'Oh Finn, look how beautiful it is down there.'

Saoirse had been lucky enough to see some incredible views in her life, but none could ever compare to Ballymastocker Bay which, less than a mile from her home, now stretched out below them. Deservedly named one of the world's most beautiful beaches, its golden sands extending a mile, from Portsalon to the Knockalla Hills.

'The ocean is at peace today,' Finn murmured, his eyes

looking out to the calm waters. His quiet eloquence had instantly stood out to her when she'd met him the previous year, and Finn had continued to surprise her ever since that first meeting.

They moved in comfortable silence until they reached a clearing in a small copse. It had become their place, a quiet beauty spot where they could give their horses a break and take some time for themselves, free of the burdens of running their own businesses. Finn, his cattle farm, and Saoirse, the Anam Cara Stables. Leaving the horses tethered to a tree, nibbling the thick green grass, Saoirse joined Finn on their bench, one he'd carved out of a fallen tree. She leaned into him, kissing him softly on his warm lips. Their bodies moulded themselves together perfectly and she shivered involuntarily. Saoirse looked around her, from the dazzling view of the bay below to the horses standing under the canopy of green leaves, and felt a rush of happiness so acute it almost scared her.

'If this is as good as life gets, that's fine for me,' she said.

'What if life could be even better?' Finn whispered back, looking at her with such intensity it made the hairs on the back of Saoirse's arms rise in response. Taking her hands between his own, he continued, 'I love you. From the moment I saw you, I felt a knowing, a recognition that you would be an important part of my life. But I could never have understood how important you would turn out to be. You are my everything, Saoirse.'

Then he slipped his hand into his jacket pocket and pulled out a small black box.

Saoirse's heart thundered as Finn opened it to reveal,

sitting on a black velvet cushion, a three-stone oval gold ring, the centre stone a large emerald nestled between two diamonds.

'It's said that emeralds signify hope,' Finn explained, his face flushed. 'That's how you make me feel, Saoirse. Hopeful for a beautiful life together. Hopeful for every memory we are yet to make. Hopeful for the family we will raise together. And hopeful that you will say yes to this question . . .' Here he paused, his eyes bright with emotion. Spirit and Mr Bojangles both neighed as if to offer encouragement to him. 'Saoirse, my love, my life, my *hope*, will you do me the honour of marrying me?'

Saoirse's response was to forget how to breathe for a moment, her excitement giving way to a shiver of foreboding.

'Saoirse?' Finn looked at her, his forehead creased in a frown and his voice suddenly nervous. 'Say something, please.'

Saoirse snapped herself out of her daze. She wanted to marry Finn more than anything, of course she did.

'Yes!' she squealed. 'Yes, I will, yes, yes, yes!' But even as she threw her arms around his neck and kissed him, that sense of foreboding remained.

With all her might she pushed her negative thoughts away, determined not to let anything destroy her happiness with Finn.

The sound of the overhead bins opening pulled Saoirse back to the present. Taking one last look at her engagement ring, on impulse she pushed it into the pocket of her jeans rather than back on to her finger. A pang of guilt twisted her stomach and she glanced up uncomfortably, sure she was being judged by fellow passengers. But they were oblivious to her, each standing, eager to disembark and start their holiday. Saoirse stood up too, untangling her long limbs and stretching her arms out.

Within minutes, she was making her way through Customs and then waiting in line for a taxi. As she waited, the warm air wrapped around her, soothing her tired body after the long flight. Saoirse looked up into the blue skies and thought of Finn again. Mixed emotions confused her. She wished he was with her, yet part of her was glad to have some distance. As Finn couldn't take two weeks away from his farm, he was planning to follow her to Bermuda next week. Maybe that would give her time to make sense of her jumbled thoughts.

Pulling her phone from her crossbody handbag, she switched it on, and was immediately greeted with her screensaver, a photo of the two of them out on their horses one grey winter's day. The backdrop was a sheath of icy leaves, and their faces were pink from the frost in the air. Something about the lighting made the photo look magical, and normally every time Saoirse looked at it, she felt grateful for the life they were building together. Now, its perfection irritated her. She'd had perfect before – at least, until it wasn't any more. What if her relationship with Finn was also too good to be true?

A nudge from behind made Saoirse look up from her phone. It was her turn in the queue.

'Sorry,' she mumbled, then placed her suitcase in the boot of the waiting taxi and jumped in the back.

'Welcome to the island, I'm Mr Tucker!' the driver said with a toothy grin.

'Hello. I'm Saoirse.'

He tried to repeat her name.

'Close enough. It's an Irish name and pronounced Sur-Sha,' Saoirse explained with a smile. Then Mr Tucker began a well-practised commentary on their surroundings. Despite her protestations that she'd been to the group of islands that made up Bermuda multiple times, Mr Tucker continued to point out the Crystal and Fantasy caves, as well as all the beaches he felt she should visit that delivered on their promise of pink sands. They passed cottages and villas painted in shades of lemon, green and blue, each connected with their mandatory, sparkling white stepped roofs designed to harvest rain. Until, finally, a little under thirty minutes later, her driver stopped outside her aunts' home, Palm Tree Cottage.

Saoirse exhaled in pleasure as she paid Mr Tucker his fare, happy to be back in her special place. Kate and Esme's three-bedroomed cottage was painted in a burst of vibrant sunshine yellow. It had a colonial feel, with its veranda and white portico fretwork, and was a fifteen-minute walk away from Horseshoe Bay, a stunning pink sandy beach popular with locals and tourists alike.

The cottage sat in the centre of a lush green garden, edged with vibrant hibiscus hedges and filled with swaying palms and casuarinas. Saoirse pulled her case behind her as she walked up the short gravel drive to the front door, practically dancing with excitement at the thought of seeing her aunts again. They weren't related, but that didn't matter. Kate – whose parents had been close friends of Saoirse's great-grandparents, Larry and Eimear O'Donnell – insisted that they were family by choice and by fate. Her aunts had always taken a special interest in Saoirse, and she valued their friendship and support, feeling closer to them than any of her actual relatives. They were the ones who'd instilled her with wanderlust, flying her to Bermuda every summer since she was a teenager.

A moment passed after she rang the bell, but the door remained closed. Saoirse didn't want to be *that* person who had no patience and rang the bell twice, so she jumped over the flowering beds to walk around the side of the cottage, taking the opportunity to pluck a pink hibiscus. She peered in as she passed the white sash window that framed the formal living room at the front of the house. But there was no sign of Kate or Esme. She carried on walking around the side of the house, stopping dead in her tracks when she caught the first glimpse of the stunning Horseshoe Bay.

At the back of the cottage was a row of palm trees, which gave the garden privacy. In the centre, they framed a walkway that had been manufactured by Kate when she'd moved in sixty years before, and led to a path heading in the direction of the sea. Through the canopy of trees, some way into the distance, you could make out the beach in all its majesty. Incredible azure-blue waters lapped on to pink sands. Saoirse longed to run all the way down the path, pushing through the dense trees that separated her and the water, and jump straight in, but instead she continued to the red-brick patio at the rear of the cottage, where a large wooden table surrounded by chairs took centre stage.

And that's when Saoirse saw her. On either side of the dining area were two emerald-green sunloungers, and Aunt Kate was lying on the furthest lounger, her eyes closed and her hands clasped as if in prayer.

'Aunt Kate, it's me. Are you okay?' Saoirse inched her way closer.

Colour disappeared from Saoirse's cheeks when her question met with silence. She reached for the gable wall of the cottage for support. Seeing Kate lying there, so still and peaceful, her fear grew with every passing second. She reached over and gently laid a hand on Kate's bare arm, a flood of relief surging through her when she felt the warmth of Kate's skin. Then she squealed in shock when a hand reached up and grabbed her arm, followed by a bellow of laughter from Aunt Kate as she pulled herself upright, standing to greet her.

'Your face! Oh, you have given me such a laugh. I'm not dead – at least, not yet. Now come here and give me a cuddle.' Kate opened her arms wide, and Saoirse fell into her warm embrace.

'I'm not sure I should be hugging you right now. You frightened me half to death,' Saoirse admonished, shaking with relief. Her aunt had always been a trickster; she should have guessed it was a joke.

'I took a nap, forgot to wake up, that's all. Esme is at the shops, buying treats for us. I woke up when I heard you arrive, but I couldn't resist having a little fun with you. I've got to take my kicks where I can.'

She's shrunk, Saoirse thought. Kate was definitely thinner than when she'd last visited, and her shoulders were stooped. Their video calls of the past few years had told lies, only showing her aunt above her shoulders. Although lined with age and the sun, her pretty oval face still looked at least twenty years younger than the ninetieth birthday she would shortly be celebrating. Age hadn't taken away her high cheekbones either. Her gunmetal grey hair was longer than she usually wore it, which suited her.

Saoirse wrapped her arms around Kate once more, as love for her aunt overcame her. Holding her hand, she followed Kate inside the house, going through the back door into the small white galley kitchen. Saoirse couldn't help but notice that while there were no dirty pots or pans, dust lined the open shelves on either wall. This was troubling. Esme had always been a clean freak. Kate and Saoirse often joked that they would still have a fork in their mouths as Esme whisked their plates away.

The kitchen opened into a large dining and family room, Saoirse's favourite space in the cottage. Terracotta flagstones flowed through the entire house, and original cedar beams made up the ceilings, each room cooled by a wooden ceiling fan. The walls had always been painted white. Kate insisted that it was both simple and practical, offering the perfect backdrop to her lifetime collection of artwork. Some of the paintings were by local artists, others from Kate and Esme's travels worldwide. Two cream sofas were scattered with plump, bright cushions that clashed delightfully, making the room warm and exciting.

'Your bedroom is ready for you. Esme has been fussing, getting it just so. She's like a kid at Christmas, so excited to see you.'

'I told you both not to go to any trouble.'

'You know Esme. I keep telling her she needs to slow down, but she won't listen. Too stubborn for her own good.' Aunt Kate's face creased in worry.

Saoirse thought it was sweet how worried Aunt Kate was about her partner, which was also funny because Esme was fifteen years younger than Kate.

'You go sit down, and I'll make us a nice cup of tea as soon as I've unpacked,' Saoirse said.

'I won't say no. My silly legs get tired so quickly these days. Esme should be home soon. She wanted to get some of that rum cake you love. There's a bakery in Southampton that makes them from scratch.'

Aunt Kate sat at the dining room table as Saoirse moved to retrieve her case, wheeling it to her bedroom, which hadn't changed a bit since the last time she had visited. A pretty rattan double bed dressed in white linen sat under the window. A rattan lampshade hung from the ceiling, mirrored by a smaller rattan bedside lamp on the white locker. A white tallboy sat opposite the bed. Saoirse noticed a long cobweb in the far left corner of the room and as she swiped it away with her hand, the sense of unease she'd felt earlier took root. Her aunts had never seemed to age, remaining much as she remembered them from her childhood. But she could not escape the fact that Aunt Kate looked fragile, birdlike almost.

Saoirse vowed to help her aunts while she was with them. She could do housework and shopping for them at least. But what would happen when she left?

As she unzipped the lid to her suitcase, another unbidden memory hit her so hard that she had to sit down on the edge of the bed.

Overwhelmed by a wave of sadness, she recalled a suitcase lying open on another bed in Mustang Creek Ranch. In her mind's eye she could see herself grabbing clothes and throwing them into the case in a frenzy, packing as fast as she could before her husband Riley returned home from the rodeo. They had fought for hours the night before and again that morning. When he'd left, he had slammed the door so hard that the trailer they called home had rocked from side to side. They'd both been angry, but he had underestimated the depth of her feelings. By the end of their row, Saoirse had made a life-changing decision to leave her husband and their life in Canada.

Damn it. Saoirse shook her head, trying to rid herself of the memory. She hadn't thought about any of this in years. Why now?

Annoyance joined her sadness. She swallowed the ball of acid that had crept its way up her stomach into the back of her throat and stood up. *Enough.*

TWO

Saoirse

Palm Tree Cottage, Horseshoe Bay, Bermuda

Once her bags were unpacked, Saoirse checked her phone, smiling when she saw a new message had pinged its way to her.

Only six more sleeps, and we'll be under the same stars again. Fx

Ireland was four hours ahead of them; she did the mental calculation and felt she could respond and not risk waking him, as it was about 11 p.m. at home. Farmers were early to bed and early to rise. Picking up the hibiscus flower she'd plucked a few minutes before, she placed it behind her ear and then posed for a quick selfie to send him.

Can't wait. Love, your hibiscus girl. Sxx

The previous evening, Saoirse had gone down to her stables to make sure everything was in order before her departure. Breathing in the unique smell of hay, leather and horse that she'd come to love, she smiled as Mr Bojangles stuck his head out of his stall to nuzzle her.

'Will you miss me, boy?' she asked him.

'If he doesn't, I know I will,' a voice had called out behind her.

Saoirse had turned in surprise to see Finn walk into the stables.

'I won't be long,' she said, pulling a penknife from her jacket to cut the twine on a bale of hay, then tearing off a bundle and putting it into the stall of a Connemara pony called Harold. 'You'll need to watch this one,' she cautioned. 'He's a biter.'

'Don't worry,' Finn laughed, coming to stand alongside her. 'We'll all get along just fine.'

'I feel guilty leaving you behind, taking care of everything.'

'I'm happy to do this for you, Saoirse. I want you – I want us – to have a life full of wonder and travel to faraway places.'

Saoirse liked the sound of this. She moved closer to Finn, snuggling into his arms. 'Where will we go?'

'When I dream of our honeymoon, you always have a pink hibiscus flower in your hair, behind your ear.' Finn tucked Saoirse's hair behind her right ear to demonstrate, sending shivers down her spine. 'We're somewhere remote, beautiful, perhaps the South Sea islands.'

'Will there be a blue lagoon?' Saoirse had asked dreamily.

'Oh yes, filled with shoals of rainbow-coloured fish that we'll snorkel amongst in wonder.'

They looked at each other in silence, both lost in Finn's dream, only interrupted when Finn's stomach had rumbled loudly.

'I think I better feed you too!' Saoirse had joked. 'Grilled cheese sandwich and tomato soup combo?'

'Ah, your ultimate comfort food. Why do you need comfort?' Finn looked at her closely. 'I've noticed that you've been quite tense lately, as if you've disappeared from us. Is everything all right with you?'

'Of course.' Afraid the colour staining her cheeks would give her away, Saoirse jumped to her feet and set about filling the water troughs, calling over her shoulder, 'I hate the thought of not seeing you every day, that's all.'

Now, here in Bermuda, Saoirse finally admitted to herself that Finn had been astute in his observations. Ever since he proposed she'd been feeling more and more apprehensive and unsure. She slipped her hand into her pocket, feeling for her ring. Looking at her finger, she paused, deciding her next move. Saoirse carefully placed the ring into a small china bowl that sat on top of the tallboy. She knew she had to pick this apart, but it would have to wait. Right now, she wanted to spend time with her aunts.

Aunt Kate was sitting quietly, her eyes closed again. Saoirse could see her chest's gentle rise and fall as she napped. Was this the new normal? Saoirse moved past her, making her way into the kitchen to prepare the tea. As she waited for the kettle to boil, she did a quick sweep of the kitchen cupboards and fridge, throwing away anything past its use-by date. There wasn't much in any of the cabinets, which was another worry, given that Aunt Kate and Esme were foodies. It was how they'd met:

attending a cookery course in Hamilton, over fifty years ago. For them, mealtimes were an occasion. Whether it was breakfast, lunch or dinner, they always insisted that each meal should be a worthwhile moment.

She quickly wiped down the counters, planning to give them a deeper clean the following day. She looked out the window to the end of the garden, to the gate between the palm trees. This entrance led to a narrow lane that brought you to Horseshoe Bay. The gate had a small painted sign that Aunt Kate had made decades before: *This way to paradise.* Saoirse felt a shiver of excitement, thinking about running to the beach for a swim in the morning. The kettle whistled its readiness. She breathed in the woody scent of her Earl Grey as she spooned two scoops of leaves into the diffuser of the glass teapot and then filled it with the boiled water. Saoirse enjoyed the ceremony of tea making. Watching the water change colour as the leaves steeped soothed her.

'Chingas! When did you get here, child?' a voice called out from the back door, making Saoirse start in surprise.

Saoirse whipped around to see Esme standing at the kitchen door, her arms holding a white cardboard cake box. She placed it on the countertop and opened her arms wide, beckoning Saoirse.

'Aunt Esme!' Saoirse cried out in delight. Unlike Aunt Kate, it was as if time had frozen for Esme, Saoirse thought with relief. She hadn't changed since they'd last seen each other in person, five years previously. Her steel-grey hair fell in soft waves to her shoulder – she never missed her weekly hair appointment. And her russet-brown skin seemed as unlined as it had been when Saoirse first met Esme as a child.

'You look amazing, Esme. How do you do that?'

'Good genes. My mama was the same. And you, child, are as pretty as a picture. Oh, it does my heart good to see you again.' Esme caressed Saoirse's cheek. Then she noticed the dishcloth in Saoirse's hand. 'What in the name of all that's good in the world are you doing cleaning my kitchen?'

'I've made tea,' Saoirse said to distract Esme from her territorial issues.

'Wonderful. And I have cake. But I'll take it from here,' Esme said, shooing her towards Kate.

When Saoirse opened her mouth to object, Esme put a finger to her lips. 'Hush, child. This is my kitchen. Go on out now.'

Aunt Kate sat waiting for them, alert once again, and patted the seat beside her for Saoirse to sit down. She held on to Saoirse's hand tightly. The warmth of Kate and Esme's love for her was evident as always. And it was in stark contrast to anything she'd ever got from her parents, who were staunch objectors to public – and, it had to be said, often private – displays of affection.

'Is it too late to eat if you are on Irish time?' Esme asked as she walked out carrying a large ornate tray.

'It's never too late for treats when they look as good as these,' Saoirse said, her eyes greedily taking in the slices of cake Esme had placed on a white plate.

'Shall I pour?' Saoirse asked when she saw her Aunt Kate's hand shake as she attempted to lift the teapot.

'Yes, thank you,' Aunt Kate replied, sitting back into the seat. 'Darn hands are arthritic and have been giving me some trouble today.'

Esme reached over and gently massaged each of Kate's

hands with her thumbs for a moment. The love in Esme's gentle touch and the smile of gratitude on Kate's face brought a lump to Saoirse's throat. She looked between the two women and felt overwhelmingly protective of them. She'd never thought of them as vulnerable until today.

'Are you taking any medication for the arthritis pain, Aunt Kate?' she asked. 'Mam has arthritis in her back, knees and hands. But she finds her meds do help.'

'She has my sympathy. As for tablets, I have so many to take every day I rattle by the time I've had them. You'll see after breakfast tomorrow,' Kate replied with a wry laugh.

'How are your parents?' Esme asked.

'Same as ever. They rarely leave home these days, they've become quite reclusive.'

'When we invited them to join us for Kate's birthday, we got back a polite but firm no,' Esme said, rolling her eyes.

'Don't take it personally. Finn and I couldn't get them to go on a weekend break to Wexford last summer,' Saoirse replied with a shrug.

Saoirse picked up a slice of the light Bermudian rum cake. She groaned in pleasure as she bit into the sponge and drizzled icing. 'This is a holiday to a tropical island, in one bite.'

'Good. And tomorrow, when you feel refreshed, we need to chat about a certain someone's big birthday. I have plans,' Esme said, tapping her nose conspiratorially.

'I don't want any fuss,' Kate said firmly. 'How is everything at Anam Cara Stables?'

'Busy! I'm now teaching children with special needs every week. They adore the horses, responding to them in ways their teachers cannot believe. The kids have their favourites, forming close bonds with the ponies. It's quite something to see their friendships blossom while they are at my stables.'

'Well, isn't that apt, bearing in mind that Anam Cara means "Soul Friend"!' Kate said approvingly.

'I know. I've always felt that Mr Bojangles was *my* soul friend, so the stables are really named in his honour.' She swiped open her photographs on her phone, handing it to her aunts. 'I took some photos to show you the progress I've made there.' Saoirse's eyes shone bright with pride. She had managed to get a couple of gorgeous shots the previous evening, when the cottage and stables were bathed in an orange glow from the sun as it set.

'It's unrecognizable from the cottage you bought two years ago!' Kate said, taking in the whitewashed walls, with sea-blue painted windows and the door framed with a glorious trellis of purple wisteria.

'We thought you'd lost your mind when you first showed it to us,' Esme said. 'But you could see its potential. I'm proud of you, child.'

Saoirse beamed with the praise. She had worked hard to transform the dilapidated 1950s dwelling she'd bought to the home it was now. The sense of achievement was worth the chipped nails and backache. 'Finn helped with the garden. There's lots more we need to do, but at least we have a small patio now.'

'I look forward to meeting your farmer next week. But, speaking of Finn, we need to know if you've gotten around to telling him that you were married before. We don't want to put our foot in it when he gets here.'

Saoirse's silence was her answer. Damn her aunt for her

directness. Kate and Esme knew that Saoirse had kept her short marriage to Riley a secret from her parents. And in turn, she had made the decision not to tell Finn either. She shoved her hand under the table, its barren ring finger reprimanding her for yet another secret she was holding on to.

'Well now, the plot thickens,' Kate said, picking up her teacup and taking a sip. 'Be careful, Saoirse. Secrets have a way of festering when left in the dark.' Then quietly, almost in a whisper, she asked, 'Do you love him?'

For a minute, Saoirse felt confusion flood her. She wasn't sure who Kate meant. And this hesitation made Kate raise an eyebrow knowingly.

'Of course, I love *Finn*. More than I've ever loved anyone before,' Saoirse said, her voice quivering with emotion.

Kate watched her for a moment, then said, 'I believe you do. But you're playing with fire, keeping your marriage to Riley a secret,' she warned, waving her cake at her.

Saoirse felt a shiver of foreboding at her aunt's words. But she shook them off because they were nonsensical. She knew what she wanted, and Riley had no power over her. Not any more. Saoirse thought about the ring she'd left in her bedroom. She knew that she should run and get it, put it back on where it belonged. But her legs felt like cement, rooting her to the spot. Why couldn't she find the words to tell her aunts about her engagement? They'd be happy for her.

'It's complicated,' she finally replied.

Kate laughed out loud at this, as if Saoirse's comment was the funniest thing she'd ever heard. Esme joined in, but Saoirse had no idea what they were so amused by.

'Affairs of the heart usually are. We don't want to upset

you or open old wounds. But we remember how things were after you and Riley split up. Are you sure you've fully closed that chapter?' Esme asked.

'These things have a habit of biting you, if you turn your back on them,' Kate added.

Saoirse squirmed on her seat, eyeing up the hallway.

'Riley didn't want to end your marriage,' Kate said matter-of-factly as she brushed a flutter of crumbs off the front of her cardigan.

'Nonsense,' Saoirse said.

'Child, the man who came here to our home eight years ago, begging you for another chance, wasn't a man who didn't love you,' Esme chipped in.

'You two had passion. Heat,' Kate continued.

'Aunt Kate!' Saoirse exclaimed.

Kate and Esme laughed as Saoirse pushed her hair back from her forehead and tried to ignore the somersaults in her stomach. This conversation was deeply uncomfortable for her. As she looked around the table, at Kate and then Esme, who knew her better than anyone else, she acknowledged a truth she'd been trying to push down inside of her, ever since Finn proposed.

She wasn't sure she wanted to get married again.

THREE

Kate

Palm Tree Cottage, Horseshoe Bay, Bermuda

Kate stood at the window, watching Saoirse walk back towards the cottage, wrapped in a large beach towel. She'd been swimming. Maybe the cool water would help clear her head, because something was bothering the girl, that was for sure.

'Morning,' Saoirse said, arriving at the kitchen doorway. 'Nice kimono, Aunt Kate!'

'Christmas present from Esme. We both have one,' Kate said, looking down to her long green silk robe. 'Have a quick shower and I'll make the tea. Esme will be out in a minute.'

Saoirse leaned in and, lowering her voice, asked, 'Have you ever considered hiring someone to help out around here?'

'Esme won't hear of it. I've suggested a cleaner many

times. I can't help as much as I used to, and that leaves Esme with the majority of the work. And she's as blind as a bat, you know. But will she go to get her eyes tested? No. Swears she has twenty-twenty vision.'

'I'll have you know that my eyesight is as strong as it was when I was a child!' Esme said, joining them in the kitchen, wearing her own kimono too.

'Nothing wrong with her hearing, word to the wise,' Kate said to Saoirse with a wink.

'Dad has reading glasses,' Saoirse threw in casually. 'It's not a big deal.'

'Bully for him. If I need glasses, I borrow Kate's. That's good enough for me.' Esme's mouth set obstinately.

'How about a trip into Hamilton after breakfast?' Kate asked, deciding it was safer to drop the subject. 'I've a hankering to take the number seven. It's a pretty route along the coast.'

With everyone in agreement, they sat down to eat.

An hour later they strolled arm in arm, Saoirse between her aunts, taking their time to walk to the nearby bus stop. The pink and blue bus arrived on time, and Aunt Esme and Aunt Kate both said a polite 'Good morning!' to the bus at large as they stepped on, Aunt Esme also making sure to stop and chat to a few individuals, checking how they and their families were.

'She knows everyone, and everyone knows her,' Kate said, with pride shining through in her wide smile as she looked at Esme.

Bermuda had narrow and winding roads, but Kate knew that they didn't faze Saoirse. She was a strong kid, resilient and, after Esme, her favourite person to spend time with. As the bus whizzed along, they didn't chat much as they travelled, each lost in their thoughts. When they arrived in Hamilton they stood on the sidewalk opposite the water's edge, where dozens of yachts and boats were docked, the sun beaming on to their white decks.

'This feels a little surreal,' Saoirse said. 'To think I was mucking out horse manure only a few days ago.'

Kate looked up and down the thoroughfare. The colonial buildings looked much the same as they had the first time she stood on this street as a child, although back then the air was filled with the sound of horses and carriages going about their business. She remembered how every sound had made her jump and cling to her mother's hand.

Her gaze turned to Saoirse; she was still puzzled by the younger woman's reluctance the day before to discuss her failed marriage. It seemed her niece was more like her than she had realized. Because Kate never wanted to talk about her past either. The present and future always interested her more. Maybe it was time to lead by example.

'I was five years old the first time I came to this town, a green country girl, scared and awe-struck,' Kate blurted out before she had a chance to change her mind. She felt two pairs of eyes widen with surprise at her unbidden admission.

'What? How did I not know that?' Saoirse asked. 'I thought you were born here.'

'When I'm lucky enough to have you in my company, I'm usually far more interested in hearing about your life than talking about myself,' Kate said.

Esme exchanged a look with Kate, filled with such sadness it made her heart ache with love. 'Don't feel bad, child. I've spent most of my adult life with Kate, but I know little about her early years. She rarely mentions it.'

'Oh that's such a pity! I'd love to hear about your childhood, Aunt Kate,' Saoirse said. 'Where *were* you born then?'

Kate regretted her small admission immediately. Because it would inevitably lead to more questions – questions that she had no intention of answering. She turned away, moving towards Brown and Co., one of Hamilton's oldest department stores. 'Come on, let's do some retail therapy.'

Esme raised her shoulders in defeat and followed Kate as she walked towards the store, using her walking stick to support her.

'I'm not sure I can see Finn wearing these on the farm,' Saoirse joked, holding up a pair of Bermuda shorts a few moments later.

'You've a type, don't you? I never realized that until now,' Kate said, giving her a knowing look.

'What do you mean?'

'Cowboy, farmer, a rugged outdoor man, more at home in tight jeans than a pinstripe suit. That's your type.'

Even though Kate's tone was light and she was clearly teasing, she could see that she'd hit a nerve with Saoirse. Her face clouded.

'Just because they both work on the land doesn't mean they're alike. They are polar opposites,' Saoirse said.

'I'm sure you're right,' Kate replied mildly. *Was that what was bugging the girl? She was afraid she'd met another Riley in her farmer?*

They left the store and walked along the pier, watching the boats coming in and out of the harbour. Then took a seat on a vacant bench, clasping their shopping bags on their laps.

'I sat right in this spot the day after we arrived in Hamilton,' Kate said, surprising herself once again. She laughed as she pointed towards Front Street. 'There was a lunch counter, Richardson's it was called. A carriage, with lanterns on its front, pulled by a white horse. A lot like your Mr Bojangles, now I think of it. And it pulled up, over there. The smell of savoury pies came wafting towards us when the owner tied up the heavy canvas walls. My stomach growled in response to that glorious smell. Mom jumped up and bought two, one for each of us. The flakiest puff pastry encasing the juiciest meat pie. It was one of the best meals of my life. We sat in the hot sun, licking our fingers clean as a soft breeze cooled us.'

Saoirse and Esme laughed with Kate as she demonstrated. 'We'd had our lunch an hour before. That was the wonder of it. The fact that Mom didn't even care that we'd already eaten. She said we could eat for the joy of eating. Not to fill our stomachs, as had been the way up until then.' Kate looked down, falling silent once more.

Saoirse opened her mouth to question her further, but Esme shook her head quickly, indicating that she should remain quiet. 'Would you like to go home?' Esme asked gently. 'Are you tired, my love?'

'I am a little,' Kate admitted. She smiled her thanks to Esme, who always had her back.

An hour later, they were back home again in Palm Tree Cottage. Saoirse went to the beach for another swim, and when she returned to the cottage, Kate and Esme were relaxing in the garden. Kate wore a vibrant red one-piece swimming costume and Esme showed off her curves in a two-piece ochre high-waisted bikini.

'Wowsers,' Saoirse said, whistling at them both. 'I hope I can look as good as you two do when I'm your age.'

'You are never too old to rock a bikini. Remember that, child,' Esme said.

Kate stood up, beaming as she posed, hands on her hips, pouting for an imaginary camera. 'I had my moments back in my day. There was a time when I'd stop traffic.'

'Er, less of the *had*. You are both still having a moment, evidently,' Saoirse replied.

Giving a slight curtsy, Kate sat down beside Esme.

'I made a jug of lemonade.' Esme pointed to a large glass jug on the patio table, with three glasses beside it, ice beginning to melt in the warm sun. It was her speciality, a drink they all enjoyed.

'Thanks, exactly what I need,' Saoirse replied, pouring the drinks.

Kate watched Saoirse take a sip and sigh contentedly. The swim had done her good. Some of her tension seemed to have slipped away in the waves.

'I loved hearing you tell that story earlier, about the pies,' Saoirse said.

'I don't think I have much time left in this world. I feel like it's getting close to the end of this chapter in my life,' Kate said, her voice low, and tears shimmered in her eyes as she spoke. She hadn't meant to speak this truth out loud and only realized she had when she heard Saoirse gasp.

It was as if time paused, the air quelled with the emotion this statement evoked in each of them. The birdsong stopped, the palm trees ceased swaying, and the bees refrained from hunting for pollen.

'Are you sick?' Saoirse managed to whisper.

'There's nothing wrong with me other than old age. Mind you, my head is still as sharp as it was thirty years ago.' Kate tapped her forehead.

'As sharp as it was eighty-five years ago,' Esme corrected, 'to remember the name of the pie carriage earlier. I couldn't have done that.'

'I always remember the food moments,' Kate said, and they all laughed softly at this truth. 'But as you've no doubt noticed, I need to sleep more than I ever did. And I sense that one day I might go to sleep but won't open my eyes again. Which is not a bad way to go, as far as I'm concerned.'

'As long as when you go, I follow on,' Esme said, holding Kate's gaze.

'Come live with me in Ireland,' Saoirse blurted out. 'Let me take care of you both.'

Esme chuckled softly. 'Now look what you've started, Kate.' Then she turned to Saoirse, grabbing her face between her hands. 'Child, you are an angel to make such a generous offer. But we're Onions,' Esme said, referring to the nickname that native Bermudians called themselves. 'Whatever time Kate and I have left, we'll spend it here in the home we've lived in for decades. *Together.*'

'It would be my pleasure to have you in my home. I think you'd like my cottage. I've got a gorgeous spare room ready and waiting for you,' Saoirse carried on, wanting them to know that her offer was genuine.

'We love you for wanting us to be near you. But Esme is right. Bermuda is our home,' Kate said. She stood up and put her arms around Saoirse for a moment, the warmth of her soft body warming her old bones. 'I think I'll take a nap.'

Feeling their eyes on her retreating back, Kate walked to her bedroom. As she lay down on her bed, she closed her eyes and her thoughts went back to another time, another place, another life.

FOUR

Eliza

August 1939
Ballymastocker Bay, Donegal, Ireland

Eliza watched three young boys run from rushing waves as they crashed on to the sandy shores of Ballymastocker Bay. Their screams of delight as the water nipped their feet echoed around the Donegal air. The children were too thin. Bony elbows and knees poked through their clothes. Decades may have passed since Eliza was their age, but families were still struggling to put food on the table, as they had been when she was a child. The boys ran back into the waves again, ready for another game of tag with the ocean.

This beach had been Eliza and Davey's playground when they were kids too. Although it felt like a lifetime ago. Together they would run straight out here whenever they could escape their respective chores. They lived next door to each other, best friends since they were babies sitting on their mammy's hips.

Eliza blinked now as she watched the children playing, noticing that one boy in the water wore a grey tweed cap like Davey himself used to own. Rain or sunshine, it sat on top of his mop of curly brown hair. It had been all he had left from his father, who had died fighting for Ireland with the Irish Volunteers in 1913. If that cap could talk. Eliza had watched Davey grow into it as he moved from child to man, wearing it cheekily tilted to one side.

'If I didn't have you, I'd crack up,' Davey used to say back then. He had it tough at home. His mam had died when he was ten, following his father to an early grave, which left him an orphan at home with his older brother, Paddy. They made the best of things, but as Eliza's mother had often said, the McDaid boys were wild.

When they were thirteen, both on the brink of adulthood, Davey had walked beside her as she collected seaweed from the beach in her apron. A tall girl, all legs, Eliza had always been head and shoulders above Davey, much to his annoyance and her delight. But over the summer months, a growth spurt had finally allowed him to pass her. Oh, how he had strutted with pride. He had several creases on the ends of his trousers, where he had let down the hem many times, but they were still a couple of inches too short. And to confuse matters even more, as he was so lean, Davey's braces were a necessity rather than a fashion statement. His trousers would fall to his ankles without them. It had been a summer evening, and, as the sun was setting over the dark blue ocean, Davey had turned to Eliza and said, 'I'm going to marry you one day.'

Eliza had replied, without hesitation, 'I know you are.'

And that was when he kissed her for the first time. His lips were soft and tasted salty from the sea air. It was no more than a peck, but it was sweet and beautiful, full of the wonder of first love. They had got round to the passionate kisses soon enough after that.

Now, Eliza breathed in the salty air, sighing in pleasure as the soft breeze whipped strands of her black hair from their pins. She loved this beach, visiting it at least once a week. Many of her favourite moments had happened on this exact stretch of white sand.

Eliza reached up to touch her lips, feeling her body yearn for Davey's touch again. They had seven years of beautiful kisses, filled with promise for a future that war had torn to shreds. She wrapped her arms around herself and tried not to think about how long it had been since anyone had embraced her.

'Are you going for a dip yourself?' a voice called out from behind her, startling Eliza.

She turned around quickly, feeling vulnerable. She clenched her fists and braced herself for what she didn't know. These days, you had to treat most with caution.

'Sorry, I didn't mean to scare you.' The stranger took a step back from her, holding his hands up as if in surrender to show her he meant her no harm.

Eliza didn't answer him for a moment, taking a beat to look him up and down. Born and reared in the area, she knew most locals and so was sure this man wasn't from around here. He was stocky and broad-shouldered and about her own height, but at five feet eight, she was used to this. Clean-shaven, with a round, kind face, his dirty blonde hair looked bleached from the sun, and his blue eyes stood out against his tanned skin.

'I'm Matthew.' He offered her his hand, and she shook it.

His hands were smooth and unblemished. Not the hands of a labourer, she deduced. It was a firm shake too, which pleased her. And while he was casually dressed, with an open-necked blue shirt with sleeves rolled up and a matching grey waistcoat and trousers, his attire looked new. Eliza remained silent as she continued to size him up. He had a Northern Irish voice, a Belfast lilt, she guessed, so a little away from home.

'I used to come here with my dad for holidays when I was a lad. We'd book a room in the Pier Hotel in Rathmullan and then we'd head to this beach to do crab fishing. I don't know why, but I got a notion this morning to take a drive here to revisit the place.'

'Where are you from?' Eliza asked, her curiosity getting the better of her.

'Belfast, born and reared. How about you? Are you from the area? And do you have a name?' Matthew asked. His face broke into a wide and friendly smile that Eliza couldn't help returning.

'I lived close by to here as a child, but now I live in Rathmullan, not far from the Pier, as it happens. It's a lovely hotel. Oh, and I'm Eliza.'

'A pretty name for a beautiful woman,' Matthew said.

Eliza acknowledged the compliment with a nod. She'd been told many times that she was beautiful. Not only from Davey, but from the many suitors who called at her house over the years. Thick dark eyelashes framed her emerald-green eyes, her best feature. Her looks were of little consequence to her now, though. She didn't even own a mirror.

'Having this on your doorstep must be wonderful. If I lived locally, I'd walk this beach every day,' Matthew said, looking out to the blue sea.

'Most weeks, I find myself down here too. I almost prefer it in the winter. Few brave the cold, but I find it bracing.' Eliza nodded towards the kids, who were now splashing each other with delight. 'I've many happy memories playing on this beach when I was their age.'

'Do you have brothers or sisters?' Matthew asked.

Eliza winced at the question. She never knew how to answer questions about her family. She looked out to the ocean and said quietly, 'I used to. Two younger brothers that I adored.'

Eliza began to walk along the white sand and Matthew fell into step beside her. And to her surprise, it didn't bother her. There was something about this man that she instinctively trusted and liked. It wasn't how he spoke, with manners and grace; it was also how he held himself. Assured and strong, but with kindness.

'I'm sorry,' Matthew said.

'For what?'

'You said "used to",' Matthew replied.

They walked in silence for a few moments more, and Eliza appreciated that he didn't pry any further.

'Tell me about your family,' Eliza asked, moving the conversation to him.

'I'm an only child, which I know is unheard of. But it wasn't because my parents didn't want children; it didn't happen for them. My mother buried over a dozen babies all in all. And the last pregnancy killed her too.' The pain of his loss was etched in the lines around his eyes.

'I'm so sorry,' it was Eliza's turn to say it now. 'What age were you when she died?'

'I was four years old. My father brought me up on his own, with the help of a couple of good neighbours. He was a good man. But he also died ten years ago.'

'I can hear your love for him in your voice,' Eliza said kindly.

'I suppose I was lucky to have him until I was twenty-three. Plenty of people have seen their entire families wiped out over the last two decades.'

Eliza looked at him, taken aback. But he was looking out to the ocean, unaware that his words had hit a nerve for her.

'I joined the Royal Navy not long after I buried him,' he continued instead. 'There didn't seem much point in hanging around Belfast any longer. I've been overseas pretty much ever since then, travelling the world. And next week, I start a new adventure. I set sail for Bermuda, which will be my new home.'

'Bermuda?' Eliza asked in wonder. 'That's an island on the North Atlantic Ocean, right?'

'Yes!' Matthew exclaimed. 'You know your geography. I'm impressed.'

'I keep abreast of the news. I'm a journalist for the *Rathmullan Gazette*, a local newspaper. Bermuda is a British Overseas Territory, from what I recall. And there's an Allied base there, right? I assume you're going there to be based on that?'

'Now you're showing off! Most people think Bermuda is in the Caribbean or an American island. Not just a pretty face.'

'I can assure you I'm far more than my appearance,'

Eliza replied, curtly. She wasn't interested in receiving flattery from this man, but she *was* still interested in discussing what was happening in the world. 'The rise of fascism and Hitler's tightening grip is beginning to hurt. Do you think we are on the brink of another world war?'

To his credit, Matthew barely reacted to Eliza's swift conversation change. She hated when people, especially men, underestimated her intelligence.

'I'm afraid so. Hitler has been transforming Germany into a war state since he became chancellor. I think everyone in Europe needs to be worried.'

'Even neutral countries like Ireland?'

'We all have a part to play, regardless of our country's stance on war. I, for one, will not be able to ignore what's happening in the world.'

Eliza could see the pride in Matthew's face, and she felt a stab of jealousy. He had a purpose, unlike her. She felt like she had bobbed along the ocean for the longest time, letting the tide take her where it willed.

'I almost envy you,' she said quietly.

Matthew raised one eyebrow, intrigued, so she quickly returned the conversation to him. She didn't like talking about herself if she could help it. It was one of the reasons journalism attracted her. Eliza was the one in control, asking the questions.

'How do you feel about moving so far away from Ireland? I've never been further than Dublin in my travels. Pitiful.'

'Never say never! You can still travel. The Royal Navy has been good to me. It's taken me to places around the world that I'd never even dreamed of visiting. But I feel it's time to put down some roots, so this posting has come at the right time. Not only is Bermuda an Allied base, but it's also the site of a brand-new Royal Navy air station. I was intrigued when it was suggested that I set up a home there. And as I said, there's nothing to keep me here in Ireland now. So in many ways, it was an easy yes.'

'Your role there will be what?'

'I'm there to oversee the formation of transatlantic convoys. Hundreds of ships will be constructed there, getting the British military ready for war.'

Eliza nodded, storing the information in her memory. She would talk to Larry, her editor at the newspaper, about perhaps writing a piece on Bermuda; she was already hooked.

'I read a piece last week in the London *Times* talking about the importance of Bermuda, because of its location on the major transatlantic shipping route,' Eliza told him. She felt a moment of smugness when she saw Matthew's eyes widen in awe. It felt good to flex her awareness of the world's politics. Other than Larry, she rarely discussed her thoughts and worries with anyone.

'I don't think I've ever met a woman quite like you,' he said, staring at her intently.

'Well, thank you, but you barely know me.'

'I know I've enjoyed our short conversation more than any other I've had with a woman. So please accept my sincerity in the compliment.' He stopped, and half bowed to her.

Eliza was charmed with him and stopped walking too, impulsively bowing back to him, making him laugh aloud in delight. 'When do you leave?' she asked.

'In two days. I've checked into the Pier Hotel already. Tonight, I plan to buy the largest steak dinner they serve and drink several pints of porter. I suspect it might be a while before I get the latter again. Then I go back to Belfast tomorrow to pick up the last of my belongings. There's not much left now. When I sold our family home, I only kept a few things as mementoes of my parents and my childhood.'

'You don't need things to remember people. They are always close by once you have your head and heart,' Eliza said, pointing to each.

'That's a nice thought, I'll remember that.' Then he added with a wink, 'I better make sure I take good care of both!'

'You haven't lost your heart yet?' Eliza asked, curious as to why someone as handsome, and clearly charming, as Matthew was still unmarried.

'Not yet. I gave it away a few times over the years for a short period, but somehow it always came back to me,' he said this cheekily. 'I'm hopeful that one day – and soon – I'll find a home for it permanently.'

'I've no doubt you will,' Eliza said, meaning it. She had always thought she had a good instinct for character. It rarely let her down.

'Your own heart is taken, I see,' Matthew said, pointing towards Eliza's left hand.

'Oh, my Claddagh ring,' Eliza said, twisting the gold band once more. 'You know, legend says that the Claddagh ring was invented by a Galway goldsmith called Richard Joyce. Algerians captured and sold him as an enslaved person, and he went on to become an apprentice goldsmith. He was a master craftsman and, while thinking about his love that he left behind in Ireland, he made the first Claddagh ring.'

'You are making this up,' Matthew said, laughing.

'No, honestly. Joyce was eventually freed by his captor, who offered him half his wealth and the hand of his only daughter in marriage.'

'Proof that the Irish can charm anyone,' Matthew said, donning his cap to her.

'Yes!'

'Did he marry the Algerian girl?'

'No, he returned to Ireland and reunited with his sweetheart, giving her the Claddagh ring.' She lifted her hand and pointed to each part of her gold band. 'The heart, hands and crown symbolize love, loyalty and friendship. He became a renowned goldsmith here.'

'You are a wealth of information.'

Eliza was enjoying their back and forth. Matthew was good company.

'You have also dodged my question – with some finesse, I might add. But I shall not be swayed from asking it one more time. Is your heart taken?' Matthew asked, cocking his head to one side inquisitively.

Four words, but loaded with such weight that they made Eliza stop in the sands. She took a deep breath before she spoke again.

'My fiancé, Davey, gave me this ring. He proposed on this beach, actually, just over there.' She pointed to a spot that had a towering backdrop of the Inishowen mountains.

'He's a lucky man,' Matthew said quietly.

'Not so much,' Eliza replied. 'He died.' Then, surprising herself at the admission, she continued, 'They all did.'

'Oh, Eliza. I'm so sorry. What happened?' Matthew asked, his face creased in concern at her words.

Eliza walked over to the rocks on the corner of a small inlet and took a seat. Matthew sat beside her. She glanced at him shyly, chewing her bottom lip as she tried to find the words to explain her sad past.

'It's easier to talk about things with people we are not connected to. I'm leaving soon, so I can take your confidence with me,' Matthew said, sensing her hesitancy.

'Yes. I think that might be it. And you have a kind face. I feel I can trust you with my story.'

'I should be honoured to hear it.' He leaned back as he said this, not pushing any further, letting her tell the story when she felt ready to do so.

'Davey and I were never not in love. I don't remember a time in my childhood that he wasn't there by my side. I think it was inevitable that we would fall for each other. When he proposed, it was the easiest yes I've ever given. I knew that my life and his were entwined, just as the heart and hands were in this ring he gave me,' Eliza's face softened as she surrendered herself to the happy memory of Davey's second, and more formal proposal, on her eighteenth birthday.

'Did you get married?' Matthew asked gently.

'Fate had other plans for us. Davey wanted to wait until the war was ended. He said that, once we were married, he'd never leave my side again.' Eliza closed her eyes for a moment as she remembered the event that changed everything for Davey and her. 'Thomas MacDonagh, one of the Irish Volunteer Leaders, visited Donegal in 1914.'

'I remember hearing about that rally in Ballyliffin,' Matthew replied.

'There were thousands at it. I'd never seen crowds like it. The whole village attended, desperate to hear MacDonagh speak. My parents, brothers and I travelled with Davey and his brother. MacDonagh's words, his passion for a new Ireland free from the shackles of British rule, were hard to ignore. By the time Davey turned fifteen, he had joined the Volunteer movement.'

'What about your father and brothers?'

'No. My mother talked my father into staying home. And my brothers were still wains, too young for anything other than play. After that, Davey was away quite a bit. It wasn't unusual for me not to hear from him for weeks at a time. Then when the Unionist MP William Twaddle was assassinated in 1922, we heard rumours of raids, with hundreds picked up and arrested.'

Matthew listened attentively to Eliza as she spoke, and in a way, she found it cathartic to talk about that time in her life again. It had been a long while since she had.

'Eventually, we heard that Davey and his brother Paddy were among those arrested. It took a while to find out where they were held. In my quest for answers, I met Larry, who owns the *Rathmullan Gazette*. I spent a lot of time at his office, hoping to hear news about Davey. So much so that Larry said he might as well give me a job. I've been there ever since.'

'Ah,' Matthew said, nodding along. 'And did you find out what happened to Davey?'

Eliza kicked a stone, watching it bounce along the sand, before replying with a sigh, 'Davey and Paddy ended up interned as political prisoners on a prison ship in Belfast.'

'The HMS *Argenta*,' Matthew said, instantly understanding. 'No more than hell on earth. I heard they erected wire fencing around it to prevent anyone jumping ship to swim ashore.' His voice was thick with anger.

'They did. Reports said that there were almost four hundred in steel cages on that boat, with little or no food. If they weren't executed, they were lucky to survive the rampant disease from the unsanitary conditions.' Eliza shuddered as she spoke. 'I find it difficult to think that Davey spent his last days in such a place. He, and most others aboard that ship, didn't survive.'

They didn't speak for a moment. Eliza was grateful for Matthew's silence. She hadn't thought about Davey's death for a long time, preferring to lose herself in memories of their happy childhood.

'I'm so sorry,' Matthew eventually said, reaching over to touch Eliza's hand lightly. 'You lost so much, like so many in this country.'

'I lost everything,' Eliza said simply. She looked at Matthew and whispered, 'In the same year that Davey and his brother were arrested, the rest of my family were killed too. My parents and two young brothers died when our home was set on fire in a skirmish.'

Matthew gasped, placing a hand on his face for a moment as he processed Eliza's loss. 'I don't know what to say. That's horrific,' he replied, his face aghast.

'What can anyone say?' Eliza said quietly. She'd heard platitudes offered so many times, but the pain of her loss was hers alone to bear. No words could ease that for her, no matter how well-intentioned.

'How did you manage to escape the fire?'

'Some would say it was dumb luck, I suppose. I wasn't there, simple as that. Mam had asked me to run an errand for her, delivering eggs and blackberry jam to the local shop. My bike got punctured on the way back, so I had to walk the last two miles. I heard gunshots about a mile out, so I ran all the way home, praying that they'd be okay. But somehow I knew that they were gone. I saw the smoke from about half a mile out. By the time I got there, nothing was left.'

There was silence between them. And for that Eliza was grateful. Because silence speaks when there are no words that can.

'God rest their souls,' Matthew finally muttered.

'I don't know where God is, but he hasn't been around these parts for a long time,' Eliza said, bitterness now lacing her voice.

'You survived. That must be God's mercy.'

'Aye. But I can't help thinking that surviving is my punishment. All I'm left with is bittersweet memories of those I've loved and lost.' Eliza stood up. She swallowed down the tears that she refused to allow fall. She had cried for years after her family and Davey died. But what good did that do? It didn't bring any of them back. Now, she focused on her work at the newspaper and did her best to live a quiet and good life. *Alone.*

'I'd better make my way back home,' she said now, briskly. 'It's been a pleasure meeting you, Matthew. And I wish you luck in your adventure in Bermuda.'

This time it was Eliza who held her hand out to shake his, and he clasped it between his own hands.

'The pleasure has been all mine, Eliza. I must admit, I'm reluctant to say goodbye. To that end, I have a motor car, and if you like, it would be my pleasure to give you a lift back to your home in Rathmullan.'

'I cycled here and am happy to cycle home, but thank you.' As soon as she responded, Eliza regretted her refusal. But there was no point dragging this out. He was leaving for the other side of the world. And she would stay here with her ghosts.

'Take care, Matthew.' Eliza began to move away from him, but then she felt his hand reach for her again, stopping her.

'Don't go. I know I'm being bold here, but nothing ventured, nothing gained, I suppose, and time is not on my side. Would you be willing to dine with me this evening, Eliza? It's been a long time since I conversed openly and honestly with anyone. It would make my last evening in Rathmullan much more special if we could continue to get to know each other.'

His words, heartfelt and honest, resonated with Eliza. And she *had* enjoyed their walk as much as he claimed to. To Eliza's own surprise, she found herself saying she would be delighted to accept Matthew's invitation.

With a plan to meet in the lobby of the Pier Hotel at 6 p.m., they left Ballymastocker Bay, each shyly looking at each other as they waved goodbye.

FIVE

Eliza

Rathmullan, Donegal, Ireland

Back at home in her apartment over the *Rathmullan Gazette* offices, Eliza undressed, shivering as a cool breeze ran through her small bedroom. She squeezed the water from a large yellow sponge and began to wash quickly. Then, she dried herself off with a soft towel, wrapping it around herself as she decided what to wear.

She knew her choices were limited even before she opened her wardrobe. Hanging side by side were two cotton mid-calf dresses that she alternated each day for work. Her wide-legged trousers and blouse, while comfortable, would be frowned upon in the restaurant. She pushed all three to one side, ruling them out. She could wear her 'good' dress. It had been months since she had an excuse to give it an outing, last worn for mass on Christmas morning. It was a tailored, chocolate-brown silk dress, cut on the bias, with a belted waist and puff sleeves. Her last option was the only evening gown she owned. Eliza pulled the gown out of the wardrobe and held it up in the evening sun that flooded through the bedroom window, smiling as its rich emerald green seemed to dance in the light. It had a nipped-in waist, capped sleeves and a skirt that flowed to the floor.

It was the last gift that Davey had bought for her not long before he was arrested. He'd arrived unannounced late one autumn evening with a large dress box in his hands. She remembered him bouncing from foot to foot, impatient for her to open it up to reveal its treasure.

'I saw it in a shop window, and I thought, that dress is the same shade as my Eliza's eyes. I had to buy it for you,' he had told her.

He'd blown every shilling he owned to buy it. Eliza had never owned anything so luxurious and glamorous in her life. Davey had promised that they would be together again soon and that, as soon as they were, he'd bring her dancing in that dress. She'd pouted, feeling hard done by that her love was never around any more. But he'd pulled her close and kissed her until everything else disappeared.

She never did get to wear the green dress. Now, in her tiny bedroom, she held it up close to her and danced with it, round and round, imagining she was in Davey's arms with every spin. Exhaling deeply, Eliza placed the dress back in the wardrobe, sliding it across the rail to the far corner. She couldn't wear it tonight, and she probably never would. Instead, she pulled the chocolate-brown dress over her head. It took her two attempts to button the tiny poppers on her back, and as she did, a pang of loneliness hit her. A feeling, she acknowledged, she had experienced a lot recently. Eliza's life had become a solitary one, where, outside of work, she rarely spoke to anyone, which was in stark contrast to the person she used to be. She used to have ambition and fire in her belly, a thirst for exploring the world that could never be quenched. She'd be horrified if her younger self could see how small she'd allowed her world to become.

Eliza and Davey had had so many exciting plans for their future. Davey was a keen photographer, and Eliza wanted to write, so together they'd planned to travel the world, documenting their journey as they went. They plotted and planned endlessly, but both agreeing that once their wanderlust was sated, they would return home to Donegal. They would build a house near their own families. It would be the perfect place to have babies, they thought, close to all that loved them.

In the end, there were no exciting boat trips or plane rides to far-flung destinations. And there were never any babies. Instead, Eliza had become a town spinster, although she hated that word with all her might. So much insult and disappointment laced in those eight letters.

Eliza's only joy was her work with the *Rathmullan Gazette*. She'd started work there a few months before her family home burned to the ground with all she loved inside it. And thank goodness she had, because the newspaper editor, Larry, and his wife, Eimear, rescued Eliza in every sense of that word. They took her into their own home, giving her clothes and food. They had two boys, Larry Junior and Stephen, who reminded her of her own brothers, and in turn, became like brothers to her themselves. Without the gentle care and love that all the members of the

O'Donnell family offered her, she would not have survived in those early months.

Finally, when she came out of her fog of loss, she returned to work, she and Larry making the perfect team. She wrote the copy each week, and Larry would prepare the paper for print and circulation. But he was so much more than a mentor, a boss, or a friend – Larry became her surrogate father. When Eliza finally felt ready to move out of the O'Donnells' home and instead started to look for a place of her own to rent, he suggested that she move into the apartment above the newspaper office. It gave Eliza independence, and space too. Needed, because there were days when her grief all but ate her whole.

Glad to have something to focus on, Eliza turned the once dusty storeroom into a homely place to live, thanks to a bit of elbow grease and a lick of whitewash paint. And as Larry often joked, the daily commute was manageable. The apartment itself had stunning views overlooking the pier, and Eliza could lose hours of her days gazing at the ocean, imagining what it would be like to travel as she'd once hoped to do. The reality was that when she'd lost Davey and her family, she'd lost her nerve too.

Of course, there was a downside to living so close to her job; it wasn't unusual for her to work sixteen hours a day. Larry grumbled that she did too much, that she should get a life, go out and enjoy herself, but Eliza couldn't see the point in dancing at the crossroads. Without Davey, she had lost all interest in being social. Occasionally Eliza went to the local cinema if a movie piqued her interest. She'd sit near the front, as far away as possible from the couples who kissed their way through the shows.

Eliza felt a jolt of merriment as she pictured Larry's face

the following day when she inevitably told him she'd gone on a date with a stranger. A sailor to boot. He might pass out from the shock of it all. She pinned her long black hair into a soft bun at the nape of her neck, then decided to brush a smidgen of powder on her cheeks. That would do, she thought, smiling at her reflection. If Matthew had thought she looked good earlier on the beach, windswept and pale-faced, this should be a pleasant surprise.

As promised, he was waiting for her in the lobby when she arrived at the Pier, wearing a pale brown three-piece suit and a tie, which sat off centre. She resisted the urge to straighten it for him, aware that the receptionist's eyes were on them both.

'You are stunning, Eliza.' Matthew's eyes moved up and down.

'Thank you. And you look pretty good yourself,' Eliza replied, meaning it.

'Shall we?' He offered his arm to her and they walked to the dining room, where he had reserved a table.

A waiter took their order for drinks – porter for Matthew, just as he had been hoping for, and a glass of white wine for Eliza – and they both immersed themselves in their menus. As Eliza looked around her in their formal setting, she felt shy. It had been easier to talk on the beach, somehow.

'They have steak. Good,' Matthew said.

'Sirloin. A nice cut too,' Eliza replied, bowing her head. She tried to add something else but discounted each thought.

'Have you decided what you would like to order?' he asked.

'Lemon sole,' she replied politely.

And then they fell into an uneasy silence, which was

not broken until the waiter arrived with their drinks and to take their food order.

'I normally have far better conversation skills than this, I promise. I think I'm a little out of practice having a meal with a beautiful woman,' Matthew said in a rush once the waiter had walked away.

Eliza noticed a sheen of sweat on his forehead, and he tugged at his shirt collar in discomfort. Matthew was as nervous as she was, Eliza realized, which gave her some comfort, making it easier for her to relax into the evening.

'I fear I've offered little myself. Like you, I'm out of practice. We're a right pair,' Eliza replied kindly.

'That I find difficult to believe. You must be in such demand, every eligible bachelor trying to court you.'

Eliza thought about the many men who had called to her door over the years, none of whom could ever hold a candle to Davey. She had sent each of them on their way with barely a backwards glance.

'I think I've been a bit of a cold fish,' Eliza said, honestly. 'After losing my family and Davey, I preferred my own company.'

Her face flushed pink. Once again, she had opened up to Matthew in a way she hadn't with anyone else in years.

'I'm honoured that you agreed to join me tonight, and even more so now. And from where I'm standing, there doesn't seem to be anything cold about you.'

He raised his pint of porter and toasted her in the traditional Irish way, 'Sláinte.'

'Sláinte,' she replied as he tipped her glass with his own.

The wine was dry and cold, precisely as she liked it. And as she sipped it, she felt herself relax.

The Girl from Donegal

Matthew studied her for a moment, then leaned forward, 'May I say something personal?'

Eliza's eyes widened in surprise. She inclined her head, wondering what he was going to say.

'I know we have only just met. And perhaps I am stepping over a line by saying this, Eliza: you have suffered terrible heartbreak, but you cannot let that define the rest of your life. We all need love in our lives.'

Eliza felt her hand tremble, so she placed her drink down. Matthew's eyes were watching her, waiting for a response.

'Maybe I had all of my love in the first half of my life, and that was all I was destined to have,' she said wistfully.

'I think it would be a great pity if that were the case. But I won't say any more on the subject because I fear I have upset you,' Matthew replied, placing his two hands over his mouth, which made Eliza smile.

He inched his chair in a little closer to the table, leaning in towards Eliza. And she found herself doing the same. They sat silently for a moment, but it didn't feel uneasy this time. A thought struck Eliza, unbidden, but quite wonderful: *I could get used to being in this man's company.*

Matthew took a third of his black porter in one long gulp, smiling in satisfaction when he placed the glass back on the table. 'It tastes as good as I hoped it would.' His words were light now, as he changed the topic.

'I'm not sure you'll find much of that over in Bermuda,' Eliza remarked. 'It will be all rum punch.'

He laughed and then took another long slug of his drink. 'I might have to sneak a few bottles into my luggage.'

Eliza liked how hearty his laughter was. She found herself joining in again. 'Tell me about the places you've visited with the Royal Navy and what you do there,' Eliza asked.

'Well, I joined at the end of the First World War, training in Keyham. Since then, I've done several tours of duty in the Far East and the Indies.'

'I can't imagine how incredible it must feel to travel so far, to experience new and exciting cultures. I'm in awe,' Eliza said, but she also couldn't help feeling a twinge of jealousy and loss for the places she had never visited.

'And I've risen through the ranks over the years. I'm now a lieutenant commander. I hope I'll make my way to commander within the next two years,' Matthew continued, with evident pride in his voice.

Eliza liked that. She, too, took pride in her work and she appreciated it when she recognized that same trait in someone else.

'Your dad would be so proud of you,' Eliza said, remembering how Matthew had spoken so lovingly of his father earlier on the beach.

'Thank you. I like to think so too.'

They shared a smile. For Eliza, it was bittersweet, as she thought about her own parents. Would they be proud of her achievements now? Or disappointed at what she'd done with her life?

'And what will life be like in Bermuda?' she asked, deciding not to dwell on sad topics and instead keep the conversation lively.

'I know Ballymastocker Bay is unparalleled for its beauty, but it has a worthy rival in Bermuda, I have to tell you. We visited the island two years ago, and it was a most welcome pit stop. The sands are pink, unlike anything I've seen anywhere else in the world. The skies are blue, and the ocean changes colour with every wave.' He paused, then continued in a tremulous voice, 'Blues and greens, as pretty as your eyes.'

'I think, perhaps, you're a bit of a charmer, Matthew,' Eliza said, bowing her head and feeling a little off balance by his flattery.

'I only say what I see,' Matthew replied firmly, and Eliza felt butterflies form in her stomach.

She was surprised to acknowledge that she liked being complimented by this man she'd only known a few hours.

'Where will you live? In a barracks with everyone else?' Eliza asked, deciding to move the conversation on to less personal grounds.

'There is accommodation for the officers; some will live there with their families. A community, if you like. There are glamorous and majestic hotels too, where I believe it's not unusual to spot a Hollywood star from time to time. Gary Cooper has been rumoured to visit Bermuda quite a bit.'

'Bermuda sounds like a movie set itself,' Eliza said with a sigh, enraptured by his tales.

Their food arrived, and as they began to eat, the ease they'd enjoyed earlier on the beach was back again. Matthew entertained Eliza with stories of exotic food he'd eaten in the Far East, and Eliza, in turn, shared some of the funnier stories the newspaper had covered over the years. The evening passed by until, without either of them noticing, they were the last remaining guests in the dining room. Their waiter cleared his throat as he hovered nearby – a polite nudge that it was time to leave. He suggested having a nightcap in the residents' lounge instead, which they happily accepted.

As they sipped their brandy, Eliza thought she'd not had this much fun in years. She was enjoying Matthew's company and desperately, against her better judgement, wished they had more time before he left.

'I'm going to have to go shortly,' she said sadly, looking at her watch. 'I'll never get up in time for work in the morning at this rate! And you, sir, have to get back to Belfast.' Eliza half hoped he would try to dissuade her, that, like her, he didn't want the evening to end.

'I wish I had come to Rathmullan sooner. I wasted days of my week's vacation in Belfast, doing nothing but mope in the city.' Here he paused, inching closer to her and looking at her so intently it made Eliza blush. 'All that time I could have – I *should* have – been here with you.'

A rush of elation flooded her. He felt it too.

'Well, if you return to Rathmullan in the future, you know where to find me,' Eliza whispered, raising her glass to her lips. Then, as a wave of dizziness hit her, she put it back down on the table. She'd drunk too much, which wasn't like her. None of this was like her.

'I think it's time I call it a night. I'm afraid the brandy has gone straight to my head.' Eliza stood up, holding on to the table to steady herself.

'I insist on walking you to your apartment.' Matthew stood up too, offering her his arm.

'It's only a few moments' walk along the pier.' Eliza was torn between the urge to run home and fall into bed to sleep off her over-indulgence, and the longing to lean into Matthew's kind offer.

'Maybe, but I'd feel better knowing you reached home safely,' he insisted.

So she took his arm, and they left the hotel side by side. The sea breeze was welcome as they began to amble along the promenade under an inky blue starlit night.

'This is me,' Eliza said a few minutes later when they reached her home.

'Oh, it was as you said,' Matthew sighed, his face falling in obvious disappointment. 'Do you feel well enough to sit on the pier for a moment? I'd like one last look at the ocean before I go. And having you by my side would make it even more special.'

'Yes, I think that would be very nice,' Eliza said, unwilling to let him walk away. 'The sea air has restored me!'

They walked across the road, sitting close beside each other on the wooden bench that faced the water.

'Thank you. Not just for dinner, but for . . .' Eliza paused, waving out towards the ocean, 'helping me realize that I've allowed my world to become very small here. It's time for me to make some changes. Be more adventurous.'

'Come with me,' Matthew blurted out.

Eliza swivelled her body around to look at him in shock, thinking the alcohol had addled her brain. *Had he suggested that she go with him?* But before she had a chance to process that question further, he went on to ask another question, one that she could never have predicted in even a million guesses.

'Marry me, Eliza. Come to live in Bermuda with me.'

This time she was sure that she'd heard him correctly. Her whole body trembled with emotion.

'Are you out of your mind? I can't up sticks and go to the other side of the world with you. I don't know you! As for marrying you, that's the most ridiculous suggestion I've ever heard!' Eliza's voice rose several octaves as her heart began beating so fast that she felt faint again.

'I would argue that you *do* know me,' Matthew replied, all calmness. 'I've spoken more freely and honestly with you over the past few hours than I have with anyone else for years. I feel a connection to you. And I know you will think this sounds crazy, but it's true. I've fallen in love with you, Eliza.'

Eliza's head spun with Matthew's words. How could he possibly love her this fast?

'I know what you're thinking,' he added. 'You think I'm being reckless. Or insincere. Maybe both. But I want to reassure you that I've never said those words to another woman before. I don't want you to think that I go around declaring love at the drop of a hat. Or proposing willy-nilly. But from the moment I saw you on the beach, I felt drawn to you. I couldn't not speak to you, no more than the waves could resist ebbing back towards the ocean.'

Eliza was speechless. She could hear the sincerity of his words, and she believed their truth. But that didn't make them any less crazy.

'If I wasn't leaving for the other side of the world tomorrow, I would stay here and take my time, wooing you, showing you my true intentions. But I don't have that luxury. And Eliza, we both know that the world is on the brink of war. I don't know what the future holds; none of us do. But I do know I want you to be part of whatever it is.'

Eliza's heart thundered so loudly she was worried she might be having a heart attack. She searched his face as he spoke and, for a moment, imagined what it might feel like to say the word 'yes' to him.

But she couldn't. She didn't feel the same way about him. Yes, she liked Matthew, *a lot* even, but that was all.

'You overwhelm me. And I'm flattered. But . . .'

'You don't love me, I know,' Matthew replied, not even needing her to say it. 'But that doesn't mean you can't *grow* to love me. If you say yes to this wild proposal of mine, I will spend the rest of my days proving to you that you made the right choice. And if nothing else, Eliza, think what an adventure it will be. You said you wanted to travel, to see the world. If you say yes, this is your first step into that world.'

He grabbed her hands between his own, bringing them to his lips. And for a crazy heartbeat, she almost threw caution to the wind. But then she saw her Claddagh ring, close to Matthew's mouth, and her stomach plummeted.

'When I lost my family and Davey, I vowed I would never love again,' Eliza whispered. 'My heart cannot take any more pain.'

She felt a tear escape and watched it fall on to Matthew's hand. He didn't move for the longest time, just held her gaze. And then he leaned in and kissed her tenderly on her lips.

It was the first kiss she'd had since Davey. Eliza didn't pull away. She waited for the same butterflies to flutter through her tummy that she used to feel when Davey had kissed her. But they didn't arrive. Whatever this was with Matthew, it was different. She felt none of the passion she had felt for her first love. *Her only love.*

Eliza pulled away from his kiss, her voice barely more than a whisper. 'What if I can never love you in the way you love me?'

'What if you can?' Matthew replied, his eyes dancing with hope.

And it was that question that sent Eliza into free fall.

She didn't *want* to fall in love with anyone else; that would mean she was saying goodbye to Davey. And that could never happen. Despite being outside, Eliza felt claustrophobic. She had to get away. She stood up.

'I'm sorry, Matthew. But I must go. Thank you for your kind, heartfelt proposal, but—'

Matthew put a finger to her lips. 'Ssh. Don't say no. Not yet. I know this is a big risk for you, but it could also be the biggest adventure of your life. Of *our* lives. Sleep on it. And then tomorrow you can give me your final answer. I'll be in the hotel until midday.'

He kissed her cheek so gently she barely felt it. Then Eliza walked across the road towards her apartment, feeling his eyes on her back.

SIX

Eliza

Rathmullan, Donegal, Ireland

Eliza slept fitfully, her night full of contrasting dreams. One minute they were of Matthew, the next of Davey, a constant back and forth from one man to the other. She awoke early, thirsty and groggy from the combination of alcohol and a terrible night's sleep. To add insult to injury, she burned her porridge to the bottom of her skillet pot and then stubbed her toe on the corner of the door.

She washed and dressed, then made her way downstairs to the office, deciding she might as well go in early rather than sit in her kitchen, driving herself mad thinking about Matthew and his insane proposal.

By the time Larry arrived, she had already written a piece about the forthcoming local elections in Rathmullan. Eliza placed it on his desk, muttering a distracted good morning.

'Do you ever sleep? I thought *I* was early today. LJ had a nightmare about Hitler invading Ireland. Some nonsense he heard in the schoolyard. We were all up with his screams.'

'The poor little pet. And I sleep enough,' Eliza said, but a yawn escaped, making a liar of her.

'Is there coffee?'

When Eliza nodded, he walked to the small kitchen and poured a cup for them both. It was dark and strong; he added two spoons of sugar into each, just as they liked it.

'Nice weekend?' he asked from the kitchen as he stirred his drink.

Eliza murmured non-committally.

'Did you go to see that movie in the end?'

'No. I went to Ballymastocker Bay for a walk.'

'Ah,' Larry said, sounding unsurprised. 'Course you did.'

Eliza felt a spark of annoyance at this. Was she that predictable? She decided to shock him, and then he'd be sorry.

'Then I went for dinner in the Pier Hotel last night.'

'Good for you,' Larry said, but his reaction still wasn't shocked enough for Eliza's liking.

'With a sailor!' she added.

At this, Larry walked back through from the kitchen and looked at her, wide-eyed, clearly unable to work out what question to ask next.

'Matthew,' she said simply. 'He's called Matthew. And he asked me to marry him. He wants me to go to Bermuda with him. Start a new life over there.'

Eliza's words fell into stunned silence from Larry. He didn't speak for several moments, spluttered a few 'good God's and then stopped speaking again.

Eliza led him to his desk and put him into his chair.

'I'm sorry, love. You surprised me,' Larry said, his face ashen with shock.

'You should have seen my face when he asked me! My legs turned to jelly. I thought I might faint,' Eliza said, laughing.

'He's a fast worker; I'll give him that.'

'He said he loves me. He said he immediately fell in love with me when he saw me at the water's edge.'

'Well, that I can believe.'

Eliza smiled at this. He always was her biggest supporter, like any father would be.

'But enough about *him*, how do *you* feel about this sailor fella?' Larry asked, finally seeming to get a grip on the conversation.

'I like him,' Eliza replied simply. 'He's kind, intelligent, and good company. But I don't love him. It will always be Davey for me, you know that.'

'But Davey is gone, girl,' Larry said kindly, with a matter-of-factness that only he could get away with. 'You've locked yourself away for over a decade mourning your first love. It can't go on. You have to find a way to move on from your grief. And maybe this is the way?'

'What if I don't want to move on?' Eliza countered. But she wasn't even sure herself if that was true any more. She felt something flicker inside her that felt a lot like excitement.

'If you had died in that fire with your family and Davey had returned from prison, alive and well, would you have wanted him to stay on his own for the rest of his life, mourning a ghost?'

Eliza shook her head vehemently.

Larry looked at her pointedly. She bit back her irritation. She hated it when he was right.

'You know it as well as I do: Davey would want you to move on. And goodness knows you had enough offers to do so over the years, but you turned every one down. Maybe that was for a reason. Maybe fate always had this in store for you.'

'I don't believe in fate,' Eliza said stubbornly. 'Besides which, I can't leave you in the lurch. The newspaper needs me.'

'Yes, you can. I'll find another apprentice.'

'And what am I supposed to do in Bermuda? Be the dutiful wife and bake bread? That's not me. It never would be.'

'Does this Matthew lad expect you to do so? You of all people would never fall for someone who wanted to hold you back. So who says that you can't write in Bermuda? Or find another role that excites you? It's a huge world out there and you've lived over thirty years in this one place. This isn't the life you were meant to have. You were destined for adventure and travel. Okay, it might not be with Davey as you thought, but you have to grab this chance and see where it brings you. You'd be a fool not to.'

'I'm too old to get married,' Eliza protested, although she was weakening.

'Now you're being ridiculous. Nobody is ever too old to fall in love. But I can tell you one thing I know for sure: life is too short for regrets, girl.'

Eliza walked into the kitchen, pulled the stainless steel coffee pot from the stove, and refilled their cups again. She didn't want any more coffee, but she needed to do something to try and quell the onslaught of emotions she was experiencing. Larry's words filled her with a fire she'd not felt since Davey died.

'You know I'm right,' Larry persisted. 'And if you have any sense, you'd stop these shenanigans and go see that man. Talk to him in the cold light of day. Then trust your gut, girl. If you feel it's wrong, say goodbye and come back here to me and our temperamental printing press. But if I'm right – and I believe I am – and you feel that you could be happy with him, then you must say yes.'

When she didn't offer further rebuttals, Larry grabbed Eliza's shawl, carried it over to her, and wrapped it round her. Then, saying nothing more, he ushered her to the door. Eliza set off down the street in a daze. She did not hear the hellos from passing neighbours. A horse and cart trundled beside her, nearly knocking her over when she moved in front of it. It was only the loud bellow of a fishing trawler's horn as it returned to the harbour that shocked her to her senses. She'd walked this pier hundreds of times and knew every nook and cranny, and now she'd grown tired of it. But she did not know how to leave.

Could she let Matthew show her the way?

Barely paying attention to where her feet were taking her, moments later she entered the lobby of the Pier, as she had done the night before, making her way to the reception desk.

'Good morning, ma'am,' the receptionist said. 'How can I help you?'

'I wonder if you could call up to a room for me.' Her voice wobbled as she spoke.

'Of course. What name, please?'

'It's Matthew. Mr Matthew . . .' Eliza paused. Damn it. She didn't even know his second name. The stupidity of her situation came crashing down again. How was it possible that she was even considering a life with a man she knew so little about? She backed away from the receptionist, apologizing for wasting her time. Bloody Larry and his fancies. He had made her look a fool, pushing her out of her office door.

But as she reached the hotel's entrance, she heard her name. She turned, and there was Matthew, rushing towards her.

'I've been watching the street from my room for hours, praying that you'd appear. And then the heavens answered. Goodness, you're a sight for sore eyes! I'm so glad you came.' His voice was full of relief, full of excitement.

'I'm too old for marriage,' Eliza blurted out, her lips pursed.

'What? Then so am I!' he responded.

'I'm thirty-seven. If you want a family, you must marry a younger woman.'

'Well I'm thirty-three, the difference a mere blink of the eye. And I'm not sure I want a family of my own anyway. All I am sure of is that I want you.'

He spoke earnestly, once more making Eliza's stomach flip as she dared to believe his words.

No, she could not allow herself to get carried away by his declarations, for his sake and for her own.

'I can't marry someone whose surname I don't know.'

'Lynch. But I'll change it if you dislike it,' Matthew replied without hesitation, the hint of a smile appearing on his handsome face.

'I don't love you. You should be with someone who adores you. You are a kind and decent man, I can see that.'

'You don't love me . . . yet. There's a difference. I told you last night that I'm willing to take a chance that you can grow to love me as I do you.'

'I don't bake bread!' Eliza almost shouted as she ran out of reasons why she must say no.

Matthew looked startled at this announcement. 'Is that important? We'll buy bread, or I'll learn to make it for us. We can work all of that out.' Then he paused, looking at her with suspicion. 'Hang on, do you think I asked you to marry me because I need a housekeeper?'

Eliza shrugged.

'I don't want or need you to take care of me. I have laundered my clothes for many years and have yet to starve, despite not having a wife to cook for me. I want a life partner. Someone to share adventures with. To be by my side as we conquer new worlds.'

He smiled, and again, Eliza felt a smile light up her own face in response to him. She could feel herself getting swept away with every word he said. She was beginning to think that maybe, despite all her reservations, she should do this. She took a deep breath, running her hands down the side of her skirts, smoothing the fabric as she tried to find the courage to speak.

'Ask me again,' Eliza finally said, surprised at how strong her voice sounded.

Matthew jumped into the air, clicking his heels together in delight and whooping loudly, so that everyone in the busy hotel lobby turned immediately to look at them.

'Quietly! People are staring!' Eliza said, damning the blushes that once again stained her cheeks. But she was grinning, too, unable to hide her own joy.

'Good, I want the world to witness this! I can't believe it. I truly can't.'

Matthew ran his hands through his hair, then, patting it back into place, dropped to one knee. He took a steadying breath, then said, 'My beautiful Eliza, will you do me the honour of becoming my wife?'

The hairs on the back of Eliza's neck rose, and the room swelled with expectation. She closed her eyes for a moment and wished that, whatever choice she made, it would be the right one. She opened her eyes and then looked down at Matthew, who was watching her in agony.

'Yes, I would very much like to marry you, Matthew Lynch.'

He stood up and lifted her into his arms, kissing her as he twirled her around in circles. The lobby erupted into cheers and claps, and when Eliza pulled away from him, she noticed Larry standing a few feet from her, whooping with delight too. He walked over and hugged her tightly.

'I'm so happy for you, girl,' he said, his voice brimming with emotion. Then he turned to Matthew and pumped his hand up and down. 'You better take care of our Eliza, or I'll come looking for you, even if I have to swim the Atlantic to get to that tropical island of yours.'

'I will take the greatest care of her, sir. I give you my word,' Matthew replied solemnly.

Larry rushed off to order a bottle of champagne, and they followed him to take a seat in the lounge together.

'I'm going to ring Eimear; she'll want to come down for this,' Larry said, jumping to his feet and asking them to excuse him for a moment.

When he'd finished pouring the drinks, Matthew sat down next to Eliza. 'I'm glad it's just the two of us for a moment,' he said. 'When my mother died, my father kept her engagement ring. He gave it to me so that one day I could, in turn, give it to my chosen bride. I should have given you this when I was on one knee.'

He pulled a small diamond cluster ring from his inside pocket. His eyes were glassy with emotion as he held it between his fingers. But Eliza moved back into her seat, leaning away from him, feeling panic overtake her. She wasn't prepared for a ring, the thought had not crossed her mind.

'Please know that we can choose another together if you don't like it,' Matthew said evenly, but his brows were knitted in a frown.

Her heart lurched. 'It is not my intention to be rude or ungrateful. Your mother's ring is beautiful, and I would be proud to wear it. It's just . . .' She twisted her Claddagh ring around her finger and felt tears prick her eyes as her voice trailed off.

Matthew nodded in understanding. He put his diamond ring back into his pocket, disappointment clouding his eyes. But he valiantly covered it up, responding with great kindness, 'You do not have to wear it. I understand.'

He shouldn't have to understand, though, Eliza thought. If she could not bear to take Davey's ring off, then maybe she shouldn't marry Matthew.

But before she could process this thought any further, she felt the strangest sensation overcome her. She could sense Davey close by, as if he was urging her to be brave and take the step of removing her Claddagh ring. She looked around the lounge, a shiver passing over her back. Then, before she could change her mind, she yanked the ring off and laid it on the table in front of them both. She held her trembling left hand up and gave it to Matthew.

'I should love to see if that ring fits.'

His answering smile as he slipped the ring on to her finger – a perfect fit – helped ease her sadness. 'I don't expect you to forget about your past. It's part of who you are, and I love all parts of you. I know that Davey was your first love. But I can only hope that, one day, I'll be your last.'

It was at that exact moment that Eliza knew, without a doubt, that marrying Matthew was the best decision she had made in many years.

SEVEN

Eliza

SS Athenia, *Belfast, Northern Ireland*

The first day of September and the first day of the rest of her life, Eliza thought, as she watched the ship that would take her to her new life ease its way into Belfast Lough, anchoring off Black Head. The hull was painted black, and the upper decks were white, with a large black and white striped funnel.

'They say it's like a floating hotel,' a small, thin woman standing to her right said.

Eliza had heard similar and couldn't wait to see inside. She'd read about vessels like these and knew it would have several lounges, smoking rooms, and even a library for the passengers to enjoy. She might even get the opportunity to wear her emerald-green dress, as grand dances would be held on board. Eimear had said that the captain would be sure to ask Eliza to sit at his table and she felt a frisson of excitement at the thought.

It was almost eight p.m. on Friday evening by the time their tender took Eliza and the rest of the one hundred and thirty-five passengers onboard. Dark clouds loomed overhead, and a breeze made her ticket dance in the southerly wind as Eliza waited in line. She noticed that the ship's windows were blacked out. The headlines in all of today's newspapers had spoken of Germany's invasion of Poland and the consequent impending declaration of war. She pushed aside her worries about the state of the world for now. Right now, she wanted to enjoy every part of this new experience, of this new *life*.

Once she'd said yes to Matthew last month, Eliza had barely had a moment to catch her breath. Together, they'd made a plan: Matthew would go to Bermuda to join his crew at the Allied base and from there would make all the necessary arrangements for their wedding, which would take place shortly after Eliza's arrival in Hamilton. In an ideal world, Eliza would have liked to marry Matthew at home in Donegal with Larry, Eimear and their family by her side, but there wasn't any time before he had to set sail.

Before she had left Donegal, she had sent a telegram to Matthew, telling him she would arrive, as planned, in Montreal on 10 September. He would meet her there, and accompany her on the final stage of her journey, onwards to Bermuda. While it had been challenging to say goodbye to Larry and Eimear, leaving Donegal itself was surprisingly easy. She had little to bring with her on the voyage other than two small cases of clothes and her typewriter. Family treasures had all been burned in the fire, and anything accumulated since then held little or no sentimental value.

Matthew assured her that it didn't matter anyway, she wouldn't need much because their accommodation in Bermuda would be fully furnished. Anything she discovered she did need, he had said, they could buy together.

Eimear, though, had joined her on a shopping expedition to Clery's in Dublin, in order to prepare her wedding trousseau. She helped Eliza pick out a wedding dress that was a copy of Wallis Simpson's gown when she married Edward, the Duke of Windsor, two years previously. White silk, with a high neckline and a cinched-in waistline, Eimear had declared it to be 'transcendent'. With Eimear's kind guidance, Eliza had also bought a lace nightgown and matching robe, and, on an indulgent whim, she had purchased a four-piece suit that cost more than one week's wages. It consisted of an electric blue wool coat and matching skirt, a second floral cotton skirt, and a matching blouse. The sales assistant carefully showed Eliza how the four pieces could be worn in different combinations to give different looks. The outfit was completed by emerald-green gloves and a pillbox hat, with two-tone Oxford shoes. Eliza wore the wool skirt and coat right now, the ensemble giving her a much-needed confidence boost.

When a steward began ushering the passengers on to the ship, Eliza laughed out loud with excitement. She was finally on her way.

She reached up to touch Davey's Claddagh ring that she now wore on a chain around her neck. *If you can see this, Davey, from wherever you are, know that every step I take, I do so for both of us. It took me a long time, but I'm going to live our dream.*

She held on to the rope railing as the stairs wobbled with the weight of passengers boarding. And then she stepped on to the ship. This was it. There was no turning back now. She showed her berthing card to a crew member, a fresh-faced young man.

'It's busier than I thought it would be,' Eliza remarked, surprised by the number of people milling around the lobby as well as those she'd seen up on the decks, watching their arrival. The air felt thick with tension as people navigated their luggage, bumping into each other as they went.

'We've more than usual onboard, miss,' he explained. 'We had hundreds turn up at Glasgow this morning, looking to buy a ticket. Americans and Canadians mostly. The captain said we had to turn the gymnasium and the smoking room into dormitories for all the women and children on board. That way, we could fit hundreds more in.'

'Everyone is trying to escape Ireland and England before war breaks out,' Eliza murmured, and he nodded solemnly.

'You have a cabin. Thank your lucky stars for that, miss.' He then gave her directions to her economy tourist accommodation and explained that she would be called to go up on deck for a safety drill shortly and that all passengers needed to attend. 'Captain's orders, miss.'

Thanking him for his help, Eliza moved on, making her way along the narrow hallway, following the signs for her cabin's area. She heard excited voices call out all around her and recognized American or Canadian accents alongside Scottish and English. Then, above the din, she heard an Irish woman's familiar and unmissable lilt calling out to a young girl who was gleefully running ahead of her, excitement etched all over her face.

'Catherine Mary MacShane! Slow down, girleen; you'll fall and break your neck before we even get a chance to reach the shores of Americay!'

'But I want to see what's down here, Mammy!' the little girl responded, ignoring her mother's warning and continuing her journey at speed.

Eliza giggled, finding comfort in their exchange. She had been the same with her mammy too, always running away on the lookout for adventure.

'She's excited, bless her. We all are,' the mother said over her shoulder to Eliza. She carried a sleeping baby in her arms.

'It would gladden any heart to hear her happy cheers,' Eliza responded, stopping when she arrived at her stateroom door.

'Ah, I can hear you're Irish too. Well, it looks like we're neighbours,' the woman replied, also stopping, at the door beside Eliza's. 'They've kept us Irish together, and whether by design or luck, I'm grateful for it. I'm Mary MacShane; my husband Diarmuid will be along any minute, please God. My little sleeping man is Richie, and you've met our firecracker of a daughter.'

Mary pulled the pigtailed little girl towards her, and they both smiled warmly at Eliza, who introduced herself.

'Are you travelling on your own?' Mary asked.

'Yes, I am. But I'll be sharing this room with someone else, I'm sure. The steward said the ship will be at maximum capacity.'

'Well, if your shipmate is any trouble, or you need anything, just knock on the door,' Mary said kindly.

'I appreciate that. And likewise to you. Thank you.'

'I like your coat,' the little girl said suddenly, reaching over to caress the wool.

'Thank you, Catherine. It's new. I thought I'd better get a decent warm coat for the journey.'

'I wish I had a new one,' she replied, gazing down at her own brown coat sorrowfully, which looked like it had seen better days. 'And nobody calls me Catherine, except for Mammy when she's cross. I'm Kate.'

'When we get to America, there'll be new coats for us all,' Mary promised, then blessed herself with the sign of the cross for luck. They said their goodbyes, and each walked into their own room.

Eliza had tried to envision what her cabin might look like. Larry and Eimear had advised her to keep her expectations low, but still, Eliza was pleasantly surprised when she opened the door. On the right, behind heavy brocade curtains, were bunk beds. White linen, clean and pressed, dressed the beds, with a single pillow on each. In front of her was a small mirror above a sink. And then, on the left, opposite the bunk beds, was a narrow, padded bench. A window above the bench gave a view of the harbour.

Eliza placed her green leather handbag on the floor and climbed on to the lower bunk, lying back and sinking into the mattress. It was thin but comfortable. Eliza closed her eyes and happily listened to the sounds of the ship as people walked by, looking for their own cabins. Then she began to laugh, a ripple of merriment flowing through her.

She was moving again. Towards a new life, a new adventure, perhaps even a new love. And for a moment, she saw Davey standing in front of her, smiling encouragingly. Just like Larry had said, Davey would be happy for her.

The sound of the door opening made Eliza jump up, banging her head on the top bunk as she did. A woman strode in, wearing a full-length brown fur coat and matching hat, which to Eliza seemed a little odd, the weather still being quite warm after all. A steward carried three large suitcases into the cabin behind her, with some difficulty. He dropped them on the cabin floor, and the room that Eliza had thought only a short time ago to be spacious suddenly looked tiny.

Eliza watched the woman hand the young man some change, which made him smile and forget his troubles, and then she turned to speak to Eliza.

'I'm afraid you'll have to climb up on to the top bunk, dear. There's no hope in hell that I'll manage to do so. I appreciate you were here first, but it's been several decades since I've hoisted myself anywhere.'

She was American, Eliza realized right away, noting that while her voice was cultured and direct, there was warmth in her request. Eliza immediately moved out of the bed, smoothing the covers down.

'I'm more than happy to change beds. I'm Eliza Lavery. Pleased to meet you.' She walked toward her new room-mate and offered her hand.

'Charmed, Miss Lavery. I'm Mrs Montague. I think you and I will do just fine here.' She took her fur coat and hat off and hung them in the small closet, the bulky coat now taking up every inch of space in there. Eliza noted that the woman, who had appeared rather large when she walked in, was relatively slight under her coat.

'You're Irish, I take it, dear?' Mrs Montague moved to the bed and took a seat at its end.

'Yes. From Donegal,' Eliza said, swapping places with the woman. She moved the suitcases a little in order to take a seat on the bench.

'I've never been to Donegal, but I hear it's beautiful there.

I'm from New York. My dear sister married a doctor from Galway, so I've been visiting her there.'

While Mrs Montague chattered on, Eliza sat down opposite her, instantly liking her.

'But I had to cut my vacation short. My husband insists that war is upon us, and if I don't come home now, I might not get the chance soon enough. And I'm not the only one with that fear, judging by the chaos I've seen over the past twenty-four hours.'

'The steward told me they have a larger number of passengers on board than usual,' Eliza said, keen to share her knowledge. 'I suppose we'll have to make some allowances.'

'Indeed. I spoke with a nice Canadian in the lobby earlier while waiting for someone to bring me to my room. He said that the trains to Glasgow were full of evacuee children. He looked quite emotional as he recalled the sight of them with little knapsacks on their backs and gas masks over their shoulders. And bands with numbers printed on them wrapped around their arms.' Mrs Montague's voice caught as she spoke, and she took a lace handkerchief from her pocket and dabbed her eyes delicately.

Eliza turned away from her, giving her a moment.

'He said some were laughing, maybe with bravado or excitement for an adventure, but most were crying for their parents. I'm afraid I had a little cry myself when he told me. And then I saw a little girl run by me, wearing a darling red beret, which reminded me of my own daughter, Lottie. Well, she's all grown up now, but when she was small, she used to wear a beret almost identical to the one the girl had on. I was filled with such dread it overcame me. What if I never see my family again? My husband, children and grandchildren. I'm so cross with myself. I should never have come on this trip. It was reckless.'

Mrs Montague paled as she spoke and took out her handkerchief to dab her eyes with trembling hands.

Eliza had learned so much about the woman in the space of five minutes, which wasn't a bad thing, as they were going to be in such close quarters with each other. But even so, she felt a little overwhelmed by Mrs Montague's obvious distress.

'You weren't to know what would happen with the world,' Eliza said comfortingly, trying to sound light, even though Mrs Montague's words had alarmed her, too. 'We must do our best not to worry. We'll be on our way shortly, and before you know it, you'll be back with your family again.'

Mrs Montague smiled for a moment, then kicked her legs on to the bed, changing the topic suddenly. 'I don't have the energy to deal with my luggage. I think I'll close my eyes for a moment.'

Eliza, however, knew she couldn't sit still. 'I'm going to and explore the ship and leave you to rest. I'll see you later!'

'Wear your coat, dear. It gets cold up on deck. And reserve two deck chairs for us for tomorrow. One of the stewards will help you. Make sure they are not too close to the entrance so that we don't have to deal with the noise of people banging doors as they move in and out. That becomes most annoying.'

Eliza's funny bone was tickled by Mrs Montague's say-it-like-it-is manner. And while it appeared that Mrs Montague planned on spending a lot of time in Eliza's company while on the trip, the thought didn't upset her. It would be nice to share a meal with a friendly face.

'Leave it with me,' Eliza said, biting back a smile as she closed the door behind her, feeling a shiver of excitement run through her.

Out in the narrow hallway, little Kate was standing in front of her own open door, pleading with her mother to let her explore.

'Please, Mam. I'll be okay. I'll be right back. You won't even miss me.'

'Kate MacShane, you will not go off on your own. We have to wait here for your father to arrive. Lord knows where he has got to. Richie is dead to the world and you know I can't wake him up. I'll bring you up on deck myself soon, I promise.'

Eliza couldn't help but giggle as she watched the impatient little girl hopping up and down from foot to foot. Her mouth formed a perfect pout. She was not happy.

'I can bring Kate for a walkabout if she wants to come with me,' Eliza offered. 'I promise to take great care of her.'

'Please, Mammy, let me go with . . .' the girl paused because she'd forgotten Eliza's name.

'Eliza,' Eliza whispered helpfully.

'Eliza,' Kate finished happily.

'I don't know,' Mary said, looking doubtfully up and down the corridor.

'We'll be back within thirty minutes, promise,' Eliza said, checking the time on her watch. 'She will be quite safe with me.'

'Of that, I don't doubt. It's you I'm worried about. She can be a handful,' Mary replied with a shake of her head.

As if to prove the point, Kate took off at great speed, leaving Eliza no choice but to run after her.

'See you soon, Mary!' Eliza shouted back, then picked up speed to catch up with the little girl.

'How many beds do you have in your room? We have two in ours! But I'm going to sleep in one with my mammy and Richie. Daddy gets to have one to himself because he's bigger, but I told him he can have my teddy bear if he feels lonely,' Kate shouted over her shoulder as she skipped along, chattering relentlessly about her family and baby brother, barely catching her breath.

They weren't the only ones exploring; dozens of others were also wandering around the grand corridors of the *Athenia*. Eliza noticed some were barefoot, and a number were wearing long skirts and headscarves, with bundles of clothing in weaved baskets. The hallways all had wicker benches and chairs lined against the walls and windows were dressed with bright curtains.

Their first stop was the cabin class dining saloon, where the tables were already packed with passengers eating. Kate gasped when she walked in, finally lost for words as she gazed upon the restaurant, the likes of which she had clearly never seen before. Fresh flowers sat in large vases at the centre of each table, and starched white tablecloths and napkins gleamed against the dark wood of the furniture. It was a stark contrast to Eliza's simple life at home in her little apartment by herself. Well, it wasn't her apartment any more, Eliza supposed, as she let her mind wander. Whoever became the next apprentice would move in, no doubt, and, for a moment, as this idea crossed her mind, Eliza felt a stab of nostalgia for Donegal and her old life there. But before she had a chance to become melancholy, Kate was once again tugging Eliza's hand, impatient to move on.

Next, they found the drawing room, which had a baby grand piano in the corner, with clusters of Queen Anne chairs and sofas arranged around it. They were empty now, but ready for guests to sink into when they arrived. They explored the elegant Verandah Café, and the cabin nursery, where teddy bears of all colours sat atop a white table and chairs, forcing Eliza to promise Kate she'd bring her back to play with them the next day.

Finally back on deck upstairs, Eliza remembered her promise to Mrs Montague and went about reserving her a deck chair. To her surprise, they were too late; all the chairs were already booked for the next day.

'We don't have enough for all the passengers, what with all our extras onboard,' a steward explained. 'Hopefully, everyone will be happy to make do. It's extraordinary circumstances.'

Eliza wasn't sure that Mrs Montague was the 'making do' type of person. Realizing the time, she instead turned to Kate, who was finally beginning to look weary.

'Come, child, we'd better find your parents,' Eliza said, pulling the girl towards her. 'It's been nearly thirty minutes.'

They headed to their cabins, where Kate's father waited for her with open arms. The little girl giggled as he tickled her under her chin.

'Nice to meet you,' Diarmuid said to Eliza over his daughter's head. 'And thank you for taking this one out.'

They chatted for a few moments, sharing their stories of how they ended up as neighbours on the ship. The MacShane family were from Downings in North Donegal. They were on their way to Montreal to start a new life. Times had been hard for their families and when Mary's mother had died the previous year, following her father to his grave, they'd decided it was time to leave.

'There's no one left at home now,' Mary said sorrowfully.

'What about your own family?' Eliza asked Diarmuid.

'My parents are long gone too. I've two sisters over in England. Manchester and Liverpool, last I was told. We lost touch once my parents died. I was the baby of the family, so I never knew them.'

'It happens,' Eliza sympathized. 'I know many families who have lost touch due to immigration and circumstance.'

'Maybe just as well when it comes to your sisters,' Mary said, making a face.

'Aye,' Diarmuid agreed with a frown. 'Let's just say that any time spent in my sisters' company tends to be trying. When they came to Ireland for Dad's funeral, it was a difficult few days.'

Eliza murmured her sympathies, but didn't ask any further questions, seeing little point when she was unlikely to ever see them again once they left this ship.

'What about you, Eliza? Are you planning to settle in Canada like us?' Mary asked.

'I've one more stop after we land in Canada, I'm on my way to Bermuda. It's an island close by . . .' Eliza hesitated for a beat. She still found the following words strange to utter. 'I'm engaged to be married. My fiancé is waiting for me there.'

'How romantic!' Mary said, her eyes widening at the story.

Eliza felt like a fraud as they all congratulated her. She wished she shared their enthusiasm about her upcoming marriage. Yes, she was excited about the journey, but she still felt unsure about the final destination as well as what it would mean to be married to Matthew. They all jumped when a loud bang rattled the cabin door. A steward called out in the corridor, telling them to assemble on deck for a muster drill.

'Grab your life jackets from your cabin and follow me,' he shouted out.

Eliza ran back to her room and found Mrs Montague getting back into her fur coat once more.

'I had fallen into a lovely sleep only to be interrupted to go on this safety drill. But one must be grateful for their proactive steps in keeping us safe. We've had a letter delivered too, from Captain Cook himself.'

Eliza picked up the letter from the bench and scanned it quickly. It explained that the *Athenia* was carrying more passengers than normal, given the present emergency and the many urgent appeals made to the ship, and asked for understanding from the passengers in these exceptional circumstances. Sobered by the letter, Eliza offered her arm to Mrs Montague and together they silently made their way up on deck to their predesignated area, should there be an emergency.

'Over here!' Kate called, waving for them. She ran over to clasp Eliza's hand, pulling her towards her family.

Eliza quickly introduced Mrs Montague to the MacShane family before they all listened attentively to a steward as he demonstrated how they should put their life jackets on.

'I'm not sure this will fit over my coat,' Mrs Montague complained.

'Well, if we go down into the water, you won't want that on, missus. The weight of it alone would drown you,' Diarmuid said to her, winking at Mary and Eliza.

'Oh, you may smirk, young man, but wait until we're

out on the Atlantic and you feel its chilly wind whip you. You'll wish you had your own fur then.'

Eliza and Mary exchanged a knowing smile at the woman's retort. She was well able for Diarmuid's teasing.

'The *Athenia* is loaded with lifesaving equipment,' the steward continued despite the crowd's murmurings, 'so there is nothing to worry about, ladies and gentlemen. We have sixteen hundred life jackets – more than enough for all on board.'

'How many boats if we hit an iceberg?' a voice shouted from the crowd. Mary blessed herself and uttered a prayer to Our Lady.

'Don't worry, sir. We have twenty-six lifeboats, which can carry eighteen hundred passengers. There will be no need for anyone to be left behind here. And today's safety drill is simply a precaution.'

Eliza saw Kate move closer to her daddy, her eyes wide as she listened to the steward speak. 'I'm scared, Daddy.'

'We're safer here than we ever were back in Donegal. Don't worry, nothing is going to happen to us,' Diarmuid said firmly, rubbing the top of the little girl's head affectionately.

They stayed on deck after the safety drill to wave goodbye to Belfast and their old lives. They would sail for nine hours through the night, arriving in Liverpool early in the morning. As Eliza stood at the railings, looking out to the departing harbour, she felt a wave of sadness engulf her. Was this the last time she'd see her native home? She uttered a silent prayer that it would not be.

Eliza glanced around her, taking in her fellow passengers' faces. She saw their emotions mirroring her own. Some were in tears, but in the main, the feeling throughout the ship was one of excitement.

'Will we ever see this land again?' Mary asked quietly.

'I don't know, love,' Diarmuid replied. 'But I think the sooner we get out of Europe, the better.'

'There's no doubt about that,' Eliza jumped in, agreeing sadly. 'When Germany invaded Poland, Hitler made it clear what his plan was. There will be consequences.'

'England is getting ready to retaliate. You mark my words,' Mrs Montague added.

Every newspaper and radio broadcast had spoken about ultimatums being issued between countries in the days leading up to the sailing, but with a common consensus that war could not be avoided. Eliza thought about Matthew in Bermuda and felt a frisson of fear on his behalf. While she was apprehensive about her future with him, she found herself caring about his welfare all the same. The closer it got to her departure date, the more she hoped that Matthew was right, that love would follow soon for her.

'Captain Cook is taking no chances. God grant us all his protection for the next ten days,' Mrs Montague said, and they all fell into silence at her words.

As the vessel made its way out on to the ocean, they felt the ship move with the waves, up and down. Kate complained that she felt nauseous, and Eliza herself felt a little queasy. Taking advice from their steward that they should return to their cabins to sleep, they left the deck.

It had been a long day for Eliza since she said goodbye to her friends in Donegal. And no sooner had she lain down on her top bunk than she fell asleep, the motion of the waves lulling her into slumber.

EIGHT

Eliza

SS Athenia, *Liverpool, England*

Eliza awoke early on Saturday morning to the sound of Mrs Montague's snores. She dressed as quietly as possible, grabbed her coat, and then made her way on to the deck. It was overcast, with menacing grey skies.

'I hope that's not a sign of trouble coming our way,' Diarmuid said in an exaggerated voice of doom from behind her.

Eliza laughed along with him. They stood side by side to watch the *Athenia* make its way into Liverpool's Mersey estuary.

'Captain Cook is going to anchor on the river, not the pier, I've been told,' Diarmuid said, lighting up a cigarette. He offered one to Eliza, who declined.

'Is that unusual?' Eliza asked.

'So they said down in the smoking room. The captain

seemingly wants a faster departure, and he'll get that if we anchor out a way.'

'Do you think there's any chance the sailing across the Atlantic will be cancelled if war breaks out?' Eliza wondered out loud. The thought had been troubling her, and not because she wanted to reach Canada sooner rather than later. She was worried that if she were unable to get to Matthew now, she wouldn't have the gumption to prevail a second time.

A frown darkened Diarmuid's face. 'I hope not. Things have been tough for us at home for years, and this feels like our last chance. I can't find work and we've been living hand to mouth for too long. We've run out of options. This is our last hope.'

All traces of his good humour were now gone.

'All will be well. We must have faith,' Eliza said, feeling sympathy for the man. Hearing Diarmuid's vulnerability gave Eliza courage: she wasn't the only one risking everything for a new beginning. She would find a way to get to Bermuda, to Matthew, no matter what.

'It was me who insisted we do this. Mary wasn't as sure at first. But I told her, it's the four of us now, against the world.'

'Well, the world doesn't stand a chance with you four, I warrant, especially with little Kate leading the charge,' Eliza said, smiling, pointing to the girl as she skipped her way towards them, Mary and Richie following on behind.

Eliza turned to look at Diarmuid in surprise when he sucked hard on his smoke as if it might be the last one he'd ever have. 'You're enjoying that!'

'Word is that we will have to travel in darkness at night.

No lights. Not even a cigarette on deck,' Diarmuid explained, holding up the butt.

'Ah! Well, they've already blackened out the cabin windows at night. I noticed that when I boarded,' Eliza said. She wasn't sure if this reassured her that their captain was taking no chances, or made her worry about the possible danger they were sailing into. They stood close together, the start of a new tribe forming as they made their way to the other side of the world.

'Look what I've taught Richie to do!' Kate shouted over to Eliza.

The little girl placed her hands over her face, then yelled 'peekaboo', taking her hands away as Richie giggled with delight.

'I could listen to that sound all day,' Eliza said, charmed by the two children as they interacted. 'What age are they?'

'Kate is five years old going on twenty-five, and Richie is six months next week,' Mary replied, joining them.

By this point, Kate had spotted a group of kids playing hopscotch, so she wandered over to to join in. Diarmuid chatted to fellow passengers on the deck and returned with titbits of news he'd picked up. A Canadian woman and her daughter stopped to talk to them, sharing that they had travelled to Liverpool on a train from London. They explained that it was so overcrowded, many passengers were forced to sit in the aisles, and sleep had been impossible in their hotel room the night before because the air was filled with the sounds of foot soldiers marching. With the new passengers picked up in Liverpool, the *Athenia* was now home to one thousand four hundred and eighteen souls, and around one hundred and fifty of them were Jewish refugees. While the boat wasn't overcrowded, there was definitely a feeling that the space was tighter than usual.

Not long after, Kate came running back to them, pointing upwards to the sky. Eliza looked up to see a barrage of balloons bobbing through the air above them.

'That's a canny trick to fool the Germans,' Diarmuid said. 'The balloons are sent up high into the sky to try and interfere with the enemy bombers' accuracy.'

Eliza felt a sudden shiver coursing down her spine. Someone walked over her grave; that's what her mother used to say when the same thing happened to her. Until this point, the war had felt abstract, as though it was happening somewhere else. Right now though, it felt like this far-off war could begin to affect them, too.

'Let's go inside,' said Mary, pulling Kate towards her and clutching Richie to her chest. 'We'll see if we can find a book for you to read from the library. Come on, Diarmuid,' she said firmly. Perhaps it was her mother's pale face and serious tone, but for once Kate didn't resist.

Finding herself alone, Eliza returned to her cabin and filled Mrs Montague in on the conversation she'd had with the MacShanes.

'Try not to worry, dear,' Mrs Montague said, reaching over to pat Eliza's hand in comfort. 'Dear Captain Cook will take good care of us. Of that, I am sure.'

Despite the doom and gloom of their morning conversation, Eliza and Mrs Montague managed to have a comfortable enough day spent on deck, enjoying the sea breeze. Eventually, several hours later, Mrs Montague declared, 'I'm famished.'

Eliza's stomach rumbled in agreement. The sea air had given her an appetite. So she and Mrs Montague, along with the MacShane family, made their way to the dining room to queue for their place cards. There were three sittings, but luck was on their side. They all managed to get a table at the first sitting, which pleased Mrs Montague and her digestion.

A waiter brought them to their table, and as they were each given a menu, Eliza looked around at her travel mates. They were an unusual motley crew, but she felt affection for them all. Once Mary had secured baby Richie in the wooden Windsor-style high chair, she read the menu aloud to Diarmuid and Kate.

'My stomach is growling like mad; can you hear it?' Diarmuid said, licking his lips. 'I can't remember the last time I ate beef.'

'Our wedding breakfast, I'll warrant,' Mary replied with a wry smile.

'Take my advice, have the consommé and then a light salad. Eat little until you are certain you have found your sea legs,' Mrs Montague said, ordering the salmon and beef for herself.

'Well what about yourself, missus?' Diarmuid asked, laughing as the waiter wrote down her order.

'Oh, I found my sea legs years ago. But I'll warrant this is a first time for you all.'

'I'll take my chances,' Diarmuid declared, rubbing his tummy in anticipation.

Eliza decided to take her cabin mate's advice. A few green-looking passengers had been holding themselves over the railings on deck earlier and she didn't relish the thought of joining them. After dinner, Diarmuid took his coffee in the smoking room while the ladies went to the library. Eliza took the opportunity to read the *Liverpool Echo*, one of the daily newspapers brought on board the ship that day. Ireland had declared their neutrality while entering into a state of emergency. And Italy had proposed a peace conference between Germany, Britain, France and Poland. Could these last-minute attempts to avoid war work? Hearing a whoop from Kate, she looked up to see the child celebrating a six thrown on her dice.

'It's a wonder how quickly children can adjust to their new normal,' Eliza said, nodding at Kate's happy face as she sat cross-legged on the floor, playing a game of Snakes and Ladders with another little girl.

'We can only take our lead from them,' Mary said. She herself was watching Richie closely as he crawled on the carpeted floor beside them. 'I can't help but pray that we're doing the right thing, moving to the other side of the world.'

'You have doubts?' Eliza asked, remembering Diarmuid's worries earlier on.

'No, but it's hard to say goodbye to a country you love,' Mary answered sadly. 'And we're out of options. We want more for Kate and Richie. For ourselves, too. We're hard workers. And from what we're told, there's a good life waiting for us in Canada if we want it.'

'When Matthew – my fiancé – asked me to marry him and follow him to Bermuda, my head spun with many questions. My boss at the newspaper, who is like a father to me, reminded me that I should trust my gut. So I said yes, and here I am, with new friends, sitting in a beautiful library as our ship travels across the Atlantic Ocean. I could not have dreamed of this reality a few short weeks back.' Here, she placed her hand on Mary's. 'You wouldn't be here if your gut didn't tell you it was the right thing to do.'

'Thank you. I needed to hear that,' Mary said, smiling, then groaning as she clutched her stomach. 'I don't mind telling you, Eliza, I hope I don't lose my guts later this evening! I'm beginning to regret all that rich food.'

'I did warn you, dear,' Mrs Montague said, taking a bite of her chocolate tart. She'd found a second wind.

Eliza had to admit that she, too, felt a little ill. And no sooner had Mary complained than Kate came over, ashen, clutching her tummy too.

'I think it's time for sleep for us MacShanes,' Mary said, scooping Richie up and grabbing on to Kate's hand.

Eliza looked at them, mother and children, as they walked away, and felt a pang of regret once again. She'd hoped for a family of her own, once upon a time. Would she and Matthew be lucky enough to have a baby? Or was it too late for them?

'I'm going to go for a short walk before I turn in, the night air might help me sleep. I'll see you back in the cabin, Mrs Montague.'

And before her companion had a chance to suggest that she might come too, Eliza moved swiftly to the exit.

She needed a moment to herself. As much as she was enjoying the company of her new friends, it felt strange for Eliza, who was used to hours of solitude at home in Ireland, and there had already been a lot to get used to in such a short space of time. She walked up on to the deck, welcoming the spray of the salty air as it whipped across her face. Despite the darkness, the deck area was busy, with dozens clearly having the same idea as Eliza, also taking in the night air. Some sat on benches, others strolled arm in arm, but everyone was eerily silent, aware that their voices could carry. Eliza chose to walk to the rear and leaned over the white railing, looking down into the inky blue sea. And as she stood there, she reflected on the headline stories she'd read in the newspaper earlier. Her head spun and she gripped the railings tightly. It was such a strange feeling. One moment she felt exhilarated by the new world she found herself moving towards, the next she was terrified for the unknown future. In the cold night air, Eliza shivered.

NINE

Eliza

SS Athenia, *The Atlantic Ocean*

Eliza woke early on Sunday morning, tired from a broken night's sleep. Leaving her companion to rest, she scribbled a note, promising to meet Mrs Montague for breakfast at 8.30 a.m. Then as she had done the previous day, she went back up to the deck for a walk. She suspected that there would be many days filled with similar moments; it seemed to be par for the course with sailing. It was cloudy and cool again, and Eliza almost stumbled as the sea made itself known, causing the ship to heave.

Clinging on to a handrail, Eliza stopped to chat with a large family travelling together – an older woman, Emile, her two sons, and their wives and children. They explained to Eliza that there were many Jews like themselves in the makeshift dorms on the ship, from all parts of Europe, who all feared what might happen if war broke out.

'If we stay, we face discrimination and persecution. We can see what is coming our way,' Emile said solemnly. 'We left Germany in 1933 when Hitler took power. He quickly isolated our communities. He shut down our family business. It was no life for us. So we came to England. But we still don't feel safe. My brother is in Chicago; he wired us to say that we should make our way to him, so that is what we are doing.'

Eliza had never thought of herself as lucky before, but she realized that she had a choice whether she left Ireland or not, while these poor souls, and many others like them on the ship, had to flee for their lives. She wished them well and then continued her walk.

As she left, she overheard a group of men in a heated discussion, their voices raised in agitation. She moved in closer to them to listen.

'Chamberlain has issued a deadline,' a tall man with a hook nose was saying, waving his arms about animatedly.

'He has no choice but to issue an ultimatum to Hitler,' another older gentleman responded, his lips set in a hard line. 'Hitler has to withdraw his troops from Poland, or a state of war will begin between Great Britain and Germany.'

'How long has he given?' Eliza asked, making herself known.

Nobody answered her at first, surprised to see a woman join in their conversation.

'Two hours, miss,' the tall man replied, with a slight frown. Whether his reaction was directed at Eliza or the news, she wasn't sure.

She had expected this move from Chamberlain, but it

still had the power to shock. She could picture Larry scribbling the information down, ready to report in the *Rathmullan Gazette*. She longed to discuss this with him, tease it apart as they tried to imagine what might happen next.

At breakfast, she found Mrs Montague already seated and tucking into a large plate of bacon and eggs.

'If you like your bacon crispy, you'd best state it. I had to send my first breakfast back,' were the first words she uttered, as soon as Eliza sat down.

'Tea and white toast for me, please,' Eliza asked the waiter politely, unable to stomach anything else. When she shared the latest updates she'd heard on deck, Mrs Montague paled and blessed herself.

'Are you scared we might be torpedoed?' Eliza whispered, leaning forward, panic seeping into her voice.

Mrs Montague closed her eyes, taking her time to answer. 'My dear girl, there is nothing to worry about. The *Athenia* has Americans and Canadians on board; Hitler would not dare to send a torpedo our way. He needs our dear President Roosevelt to remain neutral. Trouble yourself no further; you are quite safe.' But the frown on the woman's forehead made a liar of her. 'Father Joseph O'Connor is holding Mass. Let's go say our prayers for all those poor souls who are about to enter into battle.'

As Eliza sat in the small chapel, listening to Father O'Connor's lilt as he prayed for their soldiers about to go to war, she thought of Matthew. And a familiar ache hit Eliza, one she'd not felt since Davey decided to join the Volunteer Army all those years ago. She was worried. She wished she could call Matthew to talk to him about all this. Was he safe in Bermuda?

Unable to think of anything else, Eliza and Mrs Montague decided to await further updates on Chamberlain's ultimatum in the library after breakfast. The room was already packed by the time they pushed their way in, the atmosphere subdued. No more Snakes and Ladders games for the children present. They sat in silence at their parents' feet. A little after 11.15 a.m., a steward came in and switched on the radio.

'It's Chamberlain addressing the nation on BBC Radio,' he announced soberly.

A hushed silence claimed the room as everyone listened to Chamberlain's sombre English voice. He spoke calmly, but Eliza couldn't help but notice that he sounded disappointed and dispirited.

'I am speaking to you from the cabinet room at 10 Downing Street. This morning the British ambassador in Berlin handed the German Government a final note stating that unless we heard from them by eleven o'clock that they were prepared at once to withdraw their troops from Poland, a state of war would exist between us. I have to tell you now that no such undertaking has been received and that consequently, this country is at war with Germany.'

Mrs Montague reached over to hold Eliza's hand, and the warmth of her touch gave her comfort.

'And now that we have resolved to finish it, I know that you will all play your part with calmness and courage,' Chamberlain finished.

Calmness and courage, Eliza thought to herself.

As she looked around the room at the shocked faces of all who sat there, she could see they were struggling to answer Chamberlain's call. Mothers pulled their children on to their laps. An elderly couple bowed their heads together. And hushed voices filled the room. One common consensus was repeated again and again as they attempted to reassure each other: why would a German submarine attack a ship with predominately American and Canadians on board?

With heavy hearts, Eliza and Mrs Montague returned to their preferred spot on the upper deck. Eliza tried to focus on the children playing around them, their innocent cries of joy as they threw hoops over a pole such a stark contrast to the unfolding drama in the rest of the world. Even Mrs Montague was quieter than usual, looking at a photograph of her family taken at her daughter's wedding a few years previously.

Some kids had formed a choir and sang 'South of the Border, Down Mexico Way'. Mrs Montague joined in, with a surprisingly beautiful voice. The singing and games stopped abruptly when several crew members arrived to make the lifeboats that hung on each side of the ship ready for use. They took the covers off and placed supplies and provisions into each one.

'What are you doing?' Kate asked, eyeing them up suspiciously.

'Nothing for you to worry about, little one. Just in case, that's all,' a steward responded.

Just in case. Three words that sent shivers up and down Eliza's spine. The day's events finally caught up with Mrs Montague's appetite too, and she decided to miss dinner. This suited Eliza, who was feeling queasy. A combination of stress and seasickness, she decided. They sat in their cabin, and Mrs Montague began sorting through her handbag, taking her passport and cash and placing it under her dress.

'I'm not being an alarmist, but I think we should be prudent and ready to leave if our situation changes. Put something warm on over that dress. If you don't have a cardigan, I'll give you one. And anything of sentimental value you can keep on your person, do so.' Mrs Montague took her family photograph from her handbag, folded it in two carefully, and then placed it at her breastbone.

'My family. Close to my heart,' she whispered, her voice trembling.

Feeling close to tears, Eliza did as her new friend suggested, taking her cash and passport and placing them inside her corset. Her hand touched the gold chain she wore around her neck, with Davey's Claddagh ring. That was all she had of value. All photographs of her family had burned in the fire.

'Double-check the life jackets are where they should be, dear,' Mrs Montague commanded from her bottom bunk. She watched, nodding in satisfaction when Eliza held up two cream life jackets.

'And put both our coats beside the jackets.'

Eliza did as she was told, and her sense of unease tripled. 'What would it be like, do you think, having to leave this ship on one of those lifeboats?'

'Cold,' Mrs Montague said. 'But if it happens, we'll be ready. I've survived a world war and the Great Depression. I'll take care of us, you'll see.' Then she closed her eyes and, within minutes, was snoring again.

Leaving the sleeping Mrs Montague, Eliza instead tapped on the next-door cabin. She wanted to let the MacShanes know that they wouldn't join them for dinner. Whispering a hello, Mary pointed to an ashen-faced Kate asleep on the top bunk.

'We'll have to miss tonight ourselves anyway,' Mary said. 'Kate isn't up to it. This fella of course is fine.' She tickled Richie under his chin.

'I know how she feels,' Eliza replied with sympathy. 'It's been a strange day for us all. How are you and Diarmuid feeling?'

'Fit as a fiddle. The water doesn't bother me. Mary's grand too, aren't you love?' Diarmuid said.

Mary nodded.

'It makes no sense that you two miss out on a meal in the dining room. I'll stay here with Kate and Richie while you both go and get something to eat.'

'We can't do that,' Mary said, hesitantly, at the same time that Diarmuid said, 'That's mighty decent of you, Eliza.'

'Yes, you can do it,' Eliza reassured Mary. 'It's my pleasure to stay with the children. Go enjoy a night off, the two of you. Have a walk on the deck before you eat, perhaps. I think after the day's news, we have to take any moment of joy we can find.'

'A date in the moonlight with my love. Now that would be a fine thing,' Diarmuid said. 'What do you say, Mary?'

Mary hovered, a frown on her face. 'I don't like leaving Kate, she looks so pale. And Richie is so clingy with me.'

'Kate's asleep, she won't even know we are gone,' Diarmuid said. 'And you must cut the apron strings to this wee lad one of these days.'

Diarmuid leaned in and kissed his daughter on her forehead, then took Richie from his mammy's arms and placed him in Eliza's.

'We'll be back in no time. We can bring some bread rolls with us, something light for you both, in case your appetite returns,' Diarmuid said.

Mary stood on her tippy toes to reach Kate's side and tenderly brushed an escaped tendril of hair to one side.

'Sleep well, girleen. I'll be back by the time you wake up.' Then she, too, kissed her daughter's brow.

Richie began to howl almost immediately, so Eliza rocked him in her arms as she used to do for her brothers when they were babies. He was having none of it, and his two chubby arms reached over for his mammy.

'He'll settle the second you leave,' Eliza said, trying to usher Mary towards the door as she rocked Richie.

But it was as if he understood Eliza's words and he started to cry louder as soon as she said it. Mary plucked him back into her own arms, and within seconds he was silent, gazing adoringly at his mother.

'Spoiled rotten,' Diarmuid said, but he was smiling indulgently at his son all the same.

'His lordship can have a seat in the high chair again. We'll take him with us,' Mary said.

Eliza could tell there was little point in attempting to change Mary's mind. As they moved to leave the cabin, Eliza saw her falter one more time, looking back at Kate.

'I promise you, Kate will be safe with me,' Eliza said, looking Mary straight in the eyes. 'I'll take care of her as if she were my own.'

Mary clasped Eliza's hand, 'I thank the lord that we ended up as neighbours here. I hope we can stay in touch when we get to Canada.'

'We'll make sure that we do,' Eliza said, meaning it. A few days ago, she'd thought they'd be fleeting acquaintances, but now, she truly hoped they could meet up again at some point in the future.

'Good luck!' Diarmuid said, then they softly closed the cabin door and left.

Eliza's eyes felt heavy, so she climbed into the bunk beneath Kate. The ship hitched to one side again, and her stomach went with it. She lay on top of the bed, closing her eyes, which seemed to help ease her nausea. And as she dozed off, she dreamed of Matthew, and the tropical island that awaited her.

TEN

Eliza

SS Athenia, *The Atlantic Ocean*

Eliza woke as a loud crash exploded into the air around
her. The lights in the cabin were extinguished, and the
room turned pitch black. Kate screamed out in fear, and
Eliza called out to her. The ship seemed to keel over to
one side, and Eliza heard the MacShanes' luggage hit the
wall on the left.

Eliza called out, 'I'm here, Kate. Your mammy and
daddy have gone for food. Come here to me.' She stood
and reached upwards, feeling in the dark for the little
girl's body, then pulled her into her arms.

Eliza heard screams echo outside, allowing panic to
rush over her for a second. But feeling Kate trembling in
her arms galvanized her into action. During the drill
earlier, they had been told what to do in the event of an
emergency. And this most certainly presented itself as one.

'We have to get to the deck to our designated station. Quick, grab your coat. Put it on over your nightdress. Good girl.'

Eliza fastened the buttons on Kate's coat and placed her life jacket over it, then grabbed one for herself and put it on over her own dress and cardigan, feeling her way for the clasps in the darkness.

'I want Mammy and Daddy,' Kate sobbed.

'I know you do. But they will be making their way to the deck, just like we are. Remember how we practised over the last two days at the drill? Course you do. Hold on to my hand and do not let go, not for one second. Promise me, Kate, no running off this time. You must stay right by my side.'

Kate promised she would in a shaky voice, clinging on to Eliza's hand so tightly that it hurt. Holding her breath because she had no clue what lay outside, Eliza opened the cabin door. The fumes struck her first of all. Thick smoke filled the air and burned their eyes. People were rushing by, screaming, and water was coming up from the floor. Then the ship violently shook again, knocking Kate to her knees.

'The water is cold,' Kate wailed, soaked through to her skin.

Eliza did her best to calm the little girl, murmuring endearments to her, telling her that it would all be good. Then she banged on her own cabin door, calling out for Mrs Montague. Eliza heard a groan, and she pushed open the door using her shoulder. She found Mrs Montague on her hands and knees on the floor of their cabin.

'Help me,' Eliza shouted to Kate. The little girl obediently ran over, and together they put their hands under the woman's arms and hoisted her upright. Mrs Montague had a bloody gash on her forehead, the blood streaking its way down her face.

'I think Hitler got us after all, dear,' Mrs Montague said in a dazed voice.

'Not yet, he hasn't,' Eliza replied firmly. 'We're all fine. We have to get to the exit before they lock the doors. Remember they told us they do that, to make the areas watertight.' Eliza was impressed that she was managing to sound calmer than she felt.

She picked up a life jacket from where she had laid them mere hours before and quickly placed it over Mrs Montague's dress.

'I need to get changed. I can't go out like this,' her companion complained, looking down at her wet clothes in dismay.

'No time,' Eliza retorted, but she did at least grab the fur coat and put it around the older woman's shoulders too. She was visibly shaking – from the cold and shock, Eliza guessed. Grabbing her own coat and throwing it on, Eliza held on to each of her companion's hands.

'We stay together, okay?'

They both nodded silently.

They made their way towards the exit and the pre-assigned spot for their lifeboat. The hallway was too tight for the three of them to wade through the water side by side, so Mrs Montague pulled her hand from Eliza's. 'Take care of the child. I'll follow right behind you, I promise.'

Eliza didn't like to let her go, she was worried about her head injury. But she also knew that Mrs Montague was right.

'Hold on to the back of my coat. And tell me if you feel faint,' Eliza said, with no time to argue.

Slowly, they inched forward, following dozens of others in front of them. Something sharp crashed into Eliza's ankle, piercing it. Holding back a groan of pain, she picked Kate up into her arms to try and protect her from the debris hidden under the water.

Eventually, they reached the deck, but relief was short-lived. Cries and screams from passengers could be heard filling the night air. A cloud of black smoke swirled angrily above the ship. Torchlights were flashing, and several men were using cigarette lighters to guide the way. A ship's officer appeared, waving his hands and shouting to his surrounding crew, 'Get the lifeboats out!'

Eliza smelt gas or something similar. She pulled Mrs Montague and Kate towards Lifeboat Station Number 10, their designated area. Frantically, she looked around her, hoping to see Mary, Diarmuid and baby Richie, but there was no sign of them yet.

'Look, there's a submarine!' a woman in a red evening gown shouted, pointing to the dark sea. 'It's the bloody Germans! We've been torpedoed! They're going to fire again!'

Screams of horror came from every side as Eliza followed the direction the woman was pointing. Squinting, she thought she could see a long-shaped object in the distance. Grey smoke snaked its way around its surface. But then it disappeared, and she wasn't sure if it had been a figment of her imagination. The air stilled around Eliza as her mind tried to make sense of the hysteria and panic that surrounded her. She felt nails bite into the palms of her hand as Kate clung to her, desperation etched on to her little face. This brought her back to her senses. Calmness and courage, that's what Chamberlain had called for.

'This way,' Eliza said, leading the way towards a ship's officer.

Huddled together, shivering in their wet clothes, Eliza, Kate and Mrs Montague watched officers and crew shout instructions to each other as they continued to lower the lifeboats into the water. At one point, Kate pointed down to Eliza's leg in horror. A nasty red gash peeped out above her Oxford court shoes, but she reassured the girl it was just a cut and nothing to worry about.

'Women and children, this way!' a steward shouted, directing passengers towards a lifeboat that was now hitched on the ship's side. Mrs Montague began to walk towards him, stopping when she realized that Eliza and Kate were immobile.

'Come on, Miss Lavery! This is no time to dilly-dally,' Mrs Montague said.

'I have to find Kate's parents. We can't leave without them,' Eliza hissed back.

'Yes, you can. If you want to live, you must get on the lifeboat now. They'll be doing the same, wherever they are, if they have any sense,' Mrs Montague said firmly.

People pushed their way around Eliza as she worried about doing the right thing. She had given her word to Mary that Kate would be safe in her care.

'I want my mammy and daddy and Richie,' Kate stuttered out through chattering teeth.

Eliza reached out to steady herself on the ship's metal wall and took three steadying breaths. How could she make this decision?

'We're full here. Lower the lifeboat,' a steward shouted, mercifully taking the decision away from Eliza.

'We're getting on the next one,' Mrs Montague said firmly. 'Please, Miss Lavery, we must take our place before we lose our chance to leave,' her voice pleaded over the wind.

'They said they had enough boats for everyone,' Eliza said, barely even convincing herself.

Mrs Montague tutted loudly. 'Do you trust that they will send all boats full to the water? That in the panic, there will not be some who will be unable to find a space? Or that another torpedo is not on its way to finish this ship off? I for one do not want to take that chance. So, are you joining me?'

When Eliza didn't move, Mrs Montague's face softened for a moment, and then she kissed her cheeks one by one. 'I knew you had a good heart, the moment I saw you. But I must think of my family who still need me. So I shall go on. But if the MacShanes are not here by the time this boat leaves, promise me you will get on the next.'

'We will,' Eliza promised, stroking Kate's hair as she did so.

'May God bless you both,' Mrs Montague said solemnly, then began climbing into her lifeboat, assisted by two stewards.

'I'll see you soon,' Eliza whispered tearfully. She felt Kate's eyes on her, searching for guidance on their next steps. She had no time to mourn the loss of her friend Mrs Montague. The responsibility to ensure that Kate was safe now rested entirely on her shoulders. She grabbed Kate's hand and began searching the deck. Together they called out for Mary and Diarmuid, their eyes scanning left and right. But it was an impossible task; panic was making people run in every direction, losing all sense of what was right. Eliza watched in horror as a father picked up his small son and threw him into a lifeboat, refusing to wait. Others began to do the same, fearing that if they waited their turn to be lowered in, it would be too late.

'There's enough lifeboats for everyone!' a steward shouted desperately, trying to calm people down. But they were too lost in terror to hear him.

Then a thought struck Eliza. *What if Mary and Diarmuid were waiting for Eliza and Kate at the cabin?* She ran back towards the entrance to their hallway, pulling Kate behind her. But the watertight doors were already locked. She prayed with all her might that Kate's mammy and daddy were not on the other side of that door.

A man rushed over to her, his face covered in black soot. 'Have you seen a little boy? He's nine years old but small for his age. He has jet-black hair. And he's wearing a bright red jumper.'

Eliza took in the man's stricken face, her heart lurching in sympathy for him. 'I'm sorry, I haven't seen him, or at least I don't think so. What's his name? I promise I'll keep my eyes peeled.'

'Eric. He's called Eric. I've put his mother and sisters on a lifeboat already. He was right beside me as I helped his mama climb down.' The scared father looked down at his hand, 'I held his hand so tight as we made our way to our lifeboat station. But I had to let him go, you see, to help his mother get down the ladder. I told him, "Don't move, lad, stay right there." And he promised me. But when I turned around to pick him up, he'd disappeared.'

The man was rambling, clearly distraught, but Eliza had to focus on Kate. 'You'll find him, try to keep calm, sir. He's here somewhere. Talk to the stewards at the lifeboats, too. Make sure they know you are looking for him.'

'I want my mammy and daddy,' Kate cried out once again. But there were no more tears, her bloodshot eyes were dry.

'If you see an Irish family, the MacShanes, a mother, father and baby boy, can you tell them that Kate is with me? I don't know whether to leave and take her with me or wait longer.' Eliza said this in desperation, more to herself than the panicking man next to her. She leaned down and lifted Kate up into her arms once more. The little girl threw her arms around her neck and held her so tight she almost choked Eliza.

But something about the distress in her voice, her question, shook the man next to her into action. Firmly, he said, 'Get her off this ship, miss. That's what her parents would want. I can only hope that someone is taking care of Eric for us like you are caring for this one. Take it from me; you need to get on that lifeboat and ensure the girl lives. I'll keep an eye out for them. I promise you.'

'Thank you,' Eliza said, knowing this man had helped her more than she could express. She reached out and shook his hand. 'Good luck. But if you can't find Eric, you must get into a lifeboat too. He might be in one already. And your wife and daughters need you.'

He nodded, then ran off, calling his son's name into the desperate night.

To their left, Eliza saw Father O'Connor, the priest who gave Mass earlier that morning, giving absolution to passengers on the deck. And this sobering image gave her the resolve to make a difficult decision. Eliza's priority was to save Kate. And she knew that the longer they stayed on board the ship, the more at risk the child was. As Mrs Montague pointed out, for all they knew, a further torpedo was aimed at the *Athenia*, ready to strike at this moment.

Taking a deep breath to steady herself, Eliza said to Kate, 'We both need to be brave now. We'll get into the lifeboats like they showed us this afternoon. And we'll meet up with your mammy, daddy and baby Richie later.'

Kate took the news in silence, chewing on her bottom lip as she mulled it over. Then she nodded once before burying her head into Eliza's neck. They made their way to a lifeboat station and queued once again for their turn to climb onboard.

The white wooden lifeboat was about thirty feet long and held by a small crane at each end that lowered them into the sea. The steward in charge of their boat was singing songs to distract the kids. When he saw Kate's tear-stained face, he cuffed her cheek and broke into 'Pack Up Your Troubles in Your Old Kit Bag', making the little girl smile for a moment.

'You go first, miss, then I'll lift the little one over to you,' he said to Eliza when it was finally their turn. He helped hoist Eliza on to the railing and told her to swing her leg over the side, so she could climb down a few steps. Then he did the same for Kate, who clung to the ladder one step above Eliza. The ladder rungs felt slippy under-foot, and Eliza almost lost her footing when she began her descent.

She heard a voice call from below her, she assumed from the steward in her boat, telling her to jump backwards and that he would catch her. But as he spoke, Eliza glanced to her right just in time to see a woman miss the lifeboat she was jumping into, instead landing in the freezing water several metres below. Eliza shuddered at the thought that Kate might fall too. She took a deep breath, trying to calm herself once more, and focused on the little girl now in her care.

'Step down one more rung, Kate. That's it. Now turn around slowly and put your arms around my neck again,' she said, as calmly as she could. Inside, her body trembled with fear.

'I promise I'll catch you, miss. Come on. Jump,' the voice below urged again.

In a leap of utmost faith, Eliza jumped, throwing her arms around the little girl as she fell, and holding Kate tightly as she could. They made it safely into the boat, their fall softened by the promised arms of the steward.

Her first thought was for Kate, but other than being white-faced, the girl was still in one piece. Eliza slipped and fell with a thud, something hard pushing into her side. She rolled over to see what it was. Oily chains. Eliza stood up, wincing in pain. Her ankle was still bleeding and it stung as oil and salt water seeped into the wound. She'd have to find something to bandage it, but first, she turned to thank the steward who'd assisted them. Batting away her thanks as he helped the next person into the lifeboat, he quickly shouted at her that his name was Albert, then encouraged her to find a space to sit. Peering in the dark to make out his features, Eliza could see that he was clean-shaven and fresh-faced, and looked no more than sixteen or seventeen. Regardless of his age, he held authority in the boat, calmly giving orders to passengers and soothing those who were panicking the most.

The lifeboat had benches on either side and five thwarts across the middle for people to sit on while rowing, which the men had filled under Albert's instruction. They held large white oars in their hands, ready to propel the boat. Eliza found a free space on a bench at the front of the lifeboat and sat down, pulling Kate into her arms. They watched people climb into the boat, one by one, until finally, Albert shouted to the officers on board the *Athenia* that they were packed with seventy souls.

As soon as he shouted, they were lowered into the water. People began to pray and weep as the lifeboat scraped and bumped alongside the listing *Athenia*. Two stewards appeared at the edge of the *Athenia*, and began climbing the ropes towards them, but ended up jumping into the cold water. Once their lifeboat was safely launched, the stewards swam over to them, and Eliza helped haul them into their lifeboat. The two men stood up immediately, shook the water off themselves, and then took their places on the thwarts, grabbing an oar, ready to do their bit.

Their lifeboat followed in the direction of dozens of others moving in front of them. As they passed several bodies floating lifeless on the water beside them, fear filled every part of Eliza. She'd seen death before, Lord knew, but this was a new horror. There could be no doubt that they were now caught up in the war.

An hour passed and then it began to rain, and, as it did, the waves began to swell and water sloshed into the boat below them. Eliza called out to Albert, asking him what they should do.

'You need to bale it out!' he shouted back. 'Look beneath your bench; there are pails there.'

Eliza found a pail and immediately began scooping the water up and over the side. Three women did the same and joined in her efforts, all grateful for a chance to help somehow. And then, Eliza heard a voice call out from the darkness. Faint, but definitely a cry for help. She looked over the side and searched the water until she saw movement a few yards away. A woman was in the water, her life jacket keeping her afloat.

'Over there! Albert! Look!' Eliza cried.

As Albert expertly pulled the boat alongside the woman, the two stewards who'd been in the water themselves leaned down and heaved her into the boat by her life jacket. She held a broken arm limply in her lap, crying in pain. An older man with a shock of white hair pulled off his suit jacket and wrapped it round the woman, and someone else rubbed her back, murmuring encouragement while trying to warm her up.

They had only ten men on board, the *Athenia*'s crew having followed the women-and-children-first rule when filling the lifeboats, and they all took turns rowing under Albert's direction. Meanwhile, Eliza and the other women carried on bailing out the water. Despite the horror of their situation, Eliza noticed that people were mostly remaining calm, and there was no hysteria.

'Keep heading into the waves, into the wind. We need to move away from the *Athenia*,' Albert called out encouragingly to the men with oars.

But this was easier said than done. At least six feet tall, the waves crashed into their boat incessantly, throwing them all into each other again and again. At one point,

Eliza felt as if the whole vessel vibrated in fury as it battled its way to safety.

Looking behind them, Eliza could see that the *Athenia* was now noticeably lower at the stern end, its emergency lights on. She shuddered, wondering how many people were still on board, as Kate continued to whimper softly into her shoulder. Then she spotted smoke on the horizon, followed by a vibration that passed underneath. Had another torpedo been fired?

Eliza did her best to comfort those around her, re-assuring them and encouraging them all to stay calm and have courage, borrowing the words she'd heard Chamberlain issue earlier that day. But as the waves continued to pummel the boat, and they were all soaked through to their skin, she found her resolve tested. She held on tight to Kate and thought about Matthew, waiting for her. And somehow, this gave her strength.

ELEVEN

Eliza

Lifeboat No.10, Atlantic Ocean

Several hours passed and Eliza's shoulders ached from her bailing efforts. But she wasn't the only one suffering. The men were constantly wiping beads of sweat from their foreheads with the effort of moving the oars through the waves. Finally, the clouds parted overhead and the moon emerged, offering them some much-needed visibility. The waves continued to play games with them, subsiding every now and then for short respite. But Eliza knew that they'd be back, returning stronger than ever.

'Your leg looks worse,' Kate said, looking down, her eyes wide with shock. Eliza followed her gaze. The gash looked angry, and Eliza knew she needed to bind it. Reaching under her wet coat, she grabbed her dress and ripped a strip from the lining of the underskirt. A flash of her standing in the dressing room of Clery's, trying it on for Eimear, hit her with a pang. She could never have imagined her new dress would end up like this. She scooped some seawater into her pail and poured it over the wound, hoping the salt would help keep it clean and free from infection. Then she wrapped the material of her dress around her ankle and tied a knot to keep it there.

With the help of the moon, Eliza's eyes soon became accustomed to the dark night and she scanned the boat. It was so crowded that she supposed there was a small chance Mary and Diarmuid could be in a dark corner, unseen by her. Even though it was unlikely, she stood up as tall as she could and cupped her hands to her mouth, determined to try all the same.

'Mary and Diarmuid MacShane. Are you there?'

Kate's face lit up in hope for a moment, but collapsed in disappointment almost immediately when silence met Eliza's call. Others followed Eliza's suit, though, calling out for their loved ones. As the shouts echoed around her, Eliza caught sight of a flash of red. Its owner, a dark-haired little boy, wore a red knitted sweater. He was cowering in a corner between two older women in dressing gowns, almost hidden by them.

'Are you Eric?' Eliza shouted to him, hardly daring to hope it might be.

He looked up, surprised, and replied weakly, 'Yes.'

Eliza began to laugh softly, joy engulfing her at this small mercy. She beckoned him over to her, but when he didn't move, she shouted to him, 'Your daddy was looking for you, before we got into the boat. He said that your mother and sisters are on another lifeboat. They are safe.'

With this news Eric stood up and manoeuvred his way through the crowded lifeboat to get to Eliza and Kate.

'I dropped my teddy. I went to look for it, but then I lost my daddy.' Two tracks of tears stained his dusty face.

Eliza didn't think her heart could take much more; it broke a little more in sympathy for the little boy with each quiet word he spoke. She felt protective of him, remembering her promise to his father to watch out for him.

'This is Kate,' Eliza said, turning to the small girl. 'Would you like to stay with us? Kate needs to find her family too. Maybe you can keep each other company.'

Eric nodded shyly through his tears.

People made room to let the little boy move in beside them. Eliza opened her arms and embraced him. He took a moment to return the hug, but then she felt the tension in his body release as he leaned into her.

'Let's cuddle up together, the three of us, so we can keep warm,' Eliza suggested. She didn't know how they were still awake; they must surely be exhausted at this late hour.

Feeling the warmth of the children's bodies as they nestled against her reminded Eliza of a part of herself that she'd thought was gone forever. She'd been the big sister for years, taking care of her younger brothers. When they died, that maternal part of her died too.

Eliza heard shouts in the distance, and looked up. She caught the eye of Albert, who stood at the helm of the lifeboat a few feet from her.

'Thank you for all you're doing for us, Albert,' Eliza called out.

She fancied she saw his chest puff out a little more at the compliment.

'It's my job as a steward.'

'You're a captain now – of this ship, at least,' Eliza said.

This comment made him smile, but he didn't respond otherwise.

'Whereabouts are we?' Eliza asked him instead, looking around. She'd lost all sense of their location.

'By my reckoning, we're off the coast of Scotland, miss.' A cluster of lifeboats came into view in the near distance. Albert called out to them, talking to fellow stewards on board them. He suggested that as a group they release their flares at once. Watching them explode like firecrackers into the sky gave them a glow of hope that energized them to keep going.

But it was only temporary. All thought of rescue vanished because the waves began to make themselves known again, growing by the minute. Eliza reckoned with terror that they reached up to ten feet. The waves towered above their lifeboat, with menace and intent. The boat was lifted so high that several passengers cried out, no doubt fearing they would capsize, and they were taking on more and more seawater with each crash back down. All Eliza could do was hold the children tight. She showed the kids where the ropes were on the outside of the lifeboat, instructing them to cling to them for dear life if the boat capsized. But deep down, she knew that if they ended up in the water for any reason, none of them would survive.

'Look!' someone called out, and they turned to see bright flashes of light coming from the *Athenia*.

'It's SOS signals going out,' Albert explained. 'Help is coming; you mark my words. Don't give up hope.'

And, as if listening to Albert, the waves began to calm down again. As the swell dulled, exhausted, the two children fell asleep across Eliza's lap. She watched the silhouette of the mighty *Athenia* in the skyline as it began to sink lower into the water, and wondered how many would have perished with it. Stroking the children's hair, she repeatedly prayed that their parents and siblings were all spared. She closed her mind to the bodies she'd seen in the water and the whispered accounts from her fellow passengers seated around her, unwilling to know of the people they had witnessed die after the explosion.

Dear Lord, don't let it be Mary and Diarmuid.

By this point, the rowers were getting fatigued, so women who were able took their turn. But it wasn't easy for them, and they often faltered, looking discouraged as they struggled to battle the waves that seemed determined to capsize them. Eliza promised that once the children awoke from their much-needed sleep, she, too, would take a turn at the oar. A woman on the bench opposite Eliza began singing 'How Great Thou Art', and many passengers joined in. And somehow, it helped. The words were a warm blanket of comfort for them as they prayed to their gods for mercy. Hours passed slowly and then, once again, lights were spotted in the distance. Albert said it was too far for them to reach. They were too tired to row that distance. But he also predicted that other ships would be close by too. And he was right. Because almost ten hours after they boarded their lifeboat, they spied a shape on the horizon.

A brightly lit yacht appeared before them, like a gift from the gods. As it got closer, Eliza thought it looked like a floating palace painted in brilliant white with brass trim. Hope rippled its way through the lifeboat, and Eliza allowed herself to believe that maybe their ordeal was finally over. She gently shook the children awake, and they both sat up gingerly, wiping sleep from their eyes. The stewards and Albert lit more flares and waved in its direction. At last, the yacht flashed a light over their lifeboat, and they heard a voice call out, 'Ahoy there!'

Never had Eliza heard a more welcome phrase.

The twenty-two children on board their lifeboat were the first to be rescued. Sailors from the yacht, called the *Southern Cross*, threw ropes down from the glittering white boat and Albert tied these tightly around the children's arms. By the time Eliza had her turn and reached the deck, aided by two strong sailors, daylight had broken. Albert was the last person to leave the lifeboat. As he was hoisted up, Eliza watched their safety vessel drift away, its purpose now served. A school of whales plunged around the boat and this was Eliza's undoing. For the first time since their nightmare began, she allowed herself a moment to surrender to her tears.

'We survived the night,' she choked out in wonder.

Albert put an arm around her. 'Yes, we did, miss.'

Clutching Eric with one hand and Kate with the other, Eliza began walking round the deck, scanning the faces around her, desperately searching for the children's parents. But she could not see Mary and Diarmuid or Eric's father in the bedraggled group onboard. Some were covered in oil, others were in nightwear, and many of the children and babies were naked, shivering with fright and cold. Eliza made her way back to Albert, feeling close to tears again. She had held her emotions in check all night long for the children's sake, but now she felt her courage falter. She was afraid for all of them, especially the children.

'There's hope yet, miss,' Albert said when she explained that she couldn't find the children's families. 'A Norwegian vessel also came to the rescue. And others were picked up by a British destroyer. Keep your faith a little longer.'

Faith. That was all they could hold on to.

The yacht's crew came round with blankets which they handed out to the children. The crew also made hot milk and coffee for everyone and donated their own clothing, what little they had passed around to those who most needed it. Cups of soup and cheese sandwiches were given to all who could manage to eat.

'Here you go. There are a few bits to keep you and your kids warm,' a tall man with a round, kind face said, passing socks and sweaters to Eliza. He tenderly ruffled her surrogate children's hair, telling them that they should ask for Patrick if they needed anything, and that he'd take care of them. His kindness made Eliza's heart swell with gratitude. And there was something about Patrick's smile that reminded her of Matthew. But there was no time to dwell on that. She took the children's wet and oil-soaked clothes off and dressed them in the donated sweaters and socks. She laid their clothes out to dry, and then they all lay down on the stairway under one blanket. They fell into an exhausted sleep in each other's arms on the wooden deck.

Eliza was awoken sometime later by Albert, who gently shook her. News had arrived that an American freighter called *City of Flint* was on its way. Passengers who wished to continue their journey could transfer to that. It would take them to Halifax, Canada. Those that wanted to return home to Britain would be taken aboard the British destroyer.

Eliza ran through both options, once again wishing Mrs Montague was still with her, to help her make the right choice. She'd left Ireland a single woman but now had two young wards to take care of. In the end, she trusted her gut, believing it made the most sense to continue to Canada.

But watching people move on to the destroyer, she couldn't help but worry. She reminded herself again and again that if their parents had made the difficult decision to leave their homes in the first place, it was for a good reason. This was what they would have wanted.

City of Flint was a cargo ship, half the size of the *Athenia*, and had none of the glamour of that or the *Southern Cross*, with room for only six passengers. Now, it had to find a way to accommodate over two hundred. At first it was chaotic, as people looked for a place to drop their weary bones. Half carrying Kate and Eric, Eliza followed a stream of women and children being ushered into a holding area prepared for them. The men were sent in the other direction. Collapsing to the ground, the children once again cuddled into her, putting their heads on her lap for comfort. They had said little in hours and Eliza worried about what must be going through their minds.

'Give me strength, Lord. Show me a sign that I made the right choice for these children,' Eliza whispered.

Two young American students arrived, holding a tray filled with cups of beef broth and sandwiches. To Eliza, as she sipped the warming drink, which she would always remember as the best soup she'd ever had, it felt as though she was dreaming all this. It was less than three days ago that she'd left her home in Donegal, yet it felt like a life-time ago. Now, despite the number of people squeezed into such a tight space, it was eerily quiet, with everyone lost in their thoughts. Eliza found herself daydreaming of walks along pink sands, hand in hand with Matthew. She was about to close her eyes and give in to her tiredness when she heard a voice call out in the distance, 'Eric!'

Was she dreaming? But then the voice continued to call out Eric's name. Eliza laughed out loud when she spied Eric's father running up and down the ship, still frantically looking for his son. Eliza called out to him and he turned towards them, his face streaked with dirt. Eliza would never forget the look on his face – a picture of disbelief and joy. She nudged Eric awake as his father ran towards them, jumping over sleeping passengers, then dropping to his knees with a groan when he reached them.

Eric immediately threw himself into his father's arms. 'Daddy, Daddy, Daddy,' he cried, over and over.

Kate and Eliza watched their reunion, both crying too.

'I thought I'd lost you, son,' the father sobbed.

'Don't be silly, Daddy. Eliza took good care of me,' Eric said.

Eric's father, quickly introducing himself as Charles, pulled Eliza and Kate into a wide embrace, and they all laughed through their tears. As her body shook with relief and joy, Eliza felt gratitude swell inside her for this mercy.

'Where's Mummy?' Eric asked.

'I haven't found her yet. I'm not sure she's on this freighter, but I'll keep looking. There are people huddled in groups in every corner.'

'You keep looking. Find out if your family is on board. We won't move until you get back. I'll take good care of Eric, I promise,' Eliza said.

'Of that, I have no doubt. Thank you,' Charles kissed Eric one more time and then ran, calling out for the rest of his family.

Luck wasn't on their side twice; Charles returned alone, but as he knew at least that his wife and daughters had got on to another lifeboat, he guessed they were now on either the MS *Knute Nelson* or in the care of the Royal Navy, who had also rescued passengers. It was a case of waiting to find out which.

Leaving the children with Charles this time, Eliza searched for Mary and Diarmuid. Every time she heard a voice call out, she turned, hoping it was them, searching for Kate themselves. She heard a baby cry and ran towards the sound, but it wasn't Richie. Eventually, she had to accept that the MacShanes were not on board.

'You have to be brave. Just a little bit longer,' Eliza said to Kate as she wept in her arms, inconsolable.

'I don't have any more brave left,' Kate said.

'Well, I'm going to give you something special. A magic ring bestowed with powers to give bravery to even the meekest.'

Eliza pulled the gold chain from under her dress, with the Claddagh ring hanging from it. Kate looked at it in wonder, her little eyes wide with surprise.

She placed the chain around Kate's neck. 'There you go.'

'I've never had anything pretty like this before.'

'It's a special gift for an extraordinary girl. Can you feel the bravery magic spilling into you?'

As she thought about the question, Kate closed her eyes, scrunching her nose up.

'I can feel it, Eliza!' she cried, smiling for the first time since the *Athenia* was hit.

And as Eliza managed to give calm and courage to Kate, they heard a voice bellow out to them.

'My dear girls. My prayers have been answered!'

Walking towards them, wearing an oversized orange boiler suit borrowed from the crew, was their dear Mrs Montague.

TWELVE

Eliza

City of Flint, *Atlantic Ocean*

And so, the *City of Flint* became their home. Eliza came
to learn that the US freighter had ten officers and thirty
crew members on board, and, following a direct request
from Ambassador Joseph P. Kennedy, also had thirty
stranded Americans that had been picked up earlier in
Glasgow. Captain Gainard had put in place many changes
to accommodate these unexpected guests, but little did
he know that within days of leaving Glasgow he would
welcome hundreds more, also seeking refuge. Before the
freighter left port, Captain Gainard had also instructed
his crew to paint a US flag on the side of their vessel so
it could be identified as American should a German
warship or submarine see it, and they painted one on the
chartroom roof for aeroplanes too.

The early morning sun bounced off the US flag. 'That will

be our saving grace, you see,' Mrs Montague said, pointing to it. 'There is no confusion now. This is an American ship. We will continue our journey in peace, you'll see.'

Luckily for the *Athenia* refugees, a doctor was already on board the freighter. He, along with several nurses who were amongst the survivors all tirelessly tended to the sick, barely taking a moment to recover themselves. Broken bones, burns and bruises were the most common issue. A young Canadian girl named Margaret, only ten years old, needed the most attention. When the *Athenia* was hit, she had been knocked unconscious by flying debris.

A few hours after their arrival on the freighter, an engineer gave Eliza a bucket of seawater, a bar of Wrights Coal Tar soap and a steel comb, so that she could wash her hair. She breathed in the antiseptic scent from the orange bar and smiled in recognition. Matthew had the faintest scent of this soap too.

Eliza had never been a vain woman, but she felt tremendous relief that she could at least attempt to clean herself up a bit. She started with Kate, doing her best to clean the oil from her long brown hair. Then she braided it into two plaits, before she and Mrs Montague helped each other with their own hair. Getting the steel comb to tame their frizzy tangles was difficult, but they made do the best they could and, using a piece of twine, Eliza tied her ebony hair into a low ponytail.

'My dear Cyril would have quite a turn if he could see me now,' Mrs Montague lamented as she tucked her hair behind her ears and looked down at her boiler suit.

Eliza chuckled and couldn't help but think how different her companion looked from the first time they'd met.

'Whatever happened to your fur coat?' Eliza asked.

'I gave it to a mother and child on our lifeboat. They were shivering, God bless them. Last I saw, they were making their way, along with my coat, towards England on a Royal Navy destroyer.'

'You're a good woman,' Eliza said, kissing her on the forehead. 'Your husband is a lucky man.'

'He must be out of his mind with worry for me,' Mrs Montague said. Then she began to cough, a deep racking sound from her chest. When she began to breathe normally again, Eliza suggested a visit to the doctor, but Mrs Montague refused, stating there were others who needed his assistance far more than her, so Eliza allowed the subject to drop.

'Captain Gainard has compiled a list of all survivors on board, then radioed it to the US Maritime Commission offices in London and New York. Other rescue ships will have done the same. Do you think those details have been shared with our loved ones yet?' Eliza asked. And then a thought struck her. Who was her next of kin? Would anyone know to contact Matthew? She felt a sudden ache of longing to see him.

'They won't dilly-dally with that information. Don't worry, your beau will discover that his beloved is not only in one piece but is also a heroine to boot, very soon.'

Eliza smiled her thanks for the compliment, but in truth she didn't feel like a heroine. She was just an ordinary girl who did what everyone else had done when faced with their extraordinary circumstances. The gash on her leg throbbed. In a bit, she'd find a nurse and ask for a dressing. Eliza looked around the freighter, which had groups of people huddled together, some sleeping, others wearing dazed looks.

'I'm impressed that our captain had the foresight to begin preparations for our arrival as soon as he heard the SOS,' Eliza said. 'One of the crew was telling me earlier that while the freighter made its twelve-hour journey to rescue us, he set them all to work. They've been building bunks all night, apparently. It's heartening to see everyone helping out however they can.'

'It certainly is.' Mrs Montague stifled a wide yawn, 'I must confess, I won't need any rocking tonight. I'm bone-tired.'

And she didn't have to wait much longer. Within an hour, Eliza, Kate and Mrs Montague were issued their new quarters for the rest of the voyage. The crew had made tiers of bunks that could hold up to eight people. Heavy canvas had been stretched over boards made from scraps of wood on board and, somehow, they had managed to construct two hundred and fifty-five bunks. An officer had offered Mrs Montague a bed in a cabin, but she had politely declined, choosing to stay with Eliza and Kate in the cargo space, which was now their dormitory. Once again, luck was on their side because there was little cargo on the freighter, so they had room to squeeze everyone in.

Blankets were in short supply, though. Eliza still had hers from the *Southern Cross* yacht, so she gave this to Mrs Montague. Eliza herself shared a bunk with Kate, and their body warmth helped keep them toasty. As they were situated above the engine room, this helped too. They used their life jackets as pillows, and it gave Eliza some comfort to have those life preservers so close by. Someone came up with the idea to give the bunk tiers nicknames based on who was sleeping in them. Mrs Montague suggested Fifth Avenue for theirs, regaling Eliza and Kate with stories about the beautiful shops in her beloved city of New York.

'I'll bring you both to Saks one day and shall treat you to a new dress each. I give you my word on that,' Mrs Montague promised. Her eyes glassing over with emotion, she went on: 'Your company has been my lifeline. I wouldn't have survived this ordeal without your kindness and help.'

'I think you are stronger than you give yourself credit for,' Eliza said firmly. 'But I like the idea of seeing New York one day. I've read so many stories about it.'

As the days passed, and Eliza grew used to watching the crew members go about their everyday duties, it gave her an insight into what life might have been like for Matthew when he first joined the Royal Navy. Somehow, it made her feel closer to him. As they continued towards Halifax, Eliza thought about her fiancé quite a lot, something which surprised her.

The crew somehow found a way to stretch the food to feed everyone in imaginative ways. They received assistance from a Norwegian lumber ship which pulled alongside one morning to transfer provisions for the now overcrowded freighter. In the end, nobody went hungry. They ate three meals in shifts every day, over eight sittings. Scrambled eggs and bacon for breakfast, soup for lunch and meat with vegetables for dinner.

On occasion, the sea would get angry, which terrified them all, and one night there was a particularly fierce storm. As it battered their freighter, the passengers began to cry out in fear. To calm Kate, who was sure she would end up in the water again, Eliza reached for their life jackets and they put them on. Others followed suit, and prayers began as they waited the night out. Mrs Montague was a tower of strength, telling them that freighters like theirs had been built to weather far worse storms than the one they were in. And she was right, of course.

On another night, a loud bang awoke them all. A voice called out, 'It's another torpedo!' and panic ensued. In the end it turned out to have been a crate falling on deck. But Eliza understood why everyone's nerves were so frayed. Fear lurked close by for them all. They knew they would not be safe until they returned to the safety of their homes.

For Eliza, though, the biggest worry was Kate. She had become more and more subdued with every passing hour. She ate little and refused to play with the other children on board. The little girl that Eliza had seen that first day, who'd run ahead of her mammy, excited to explore, was a distant memory. Kate had nightmares every night, waking up sobbing for her mammy, daddy and baby brother Richie. Eliza would take her in her arms and rock her back and forth, promising her that she would help Kate find her family, that she was safe.

Many others on board were in the same situation. They did not know where their loved ones were. Eliza suggested they find ways to occupy themselves and keep their minds off their worries. Mrs Montague rallied some women who were good with a needle, and they began making adjustments to the donated clothes. Mrs Montague made headscarves out of tea towels and stylishly sported a red and white chequered one. One of the officers taught people how to make sandals from rope and canvas as a surprising number of people were shoeless.

Captain Gainard also recognized that, if the passengers were busy, they would have less time to worry. He gave them all tasks to do, helping with the day-to-day running of the ship. Eliza helped create an onboard newspaper. She would listen to the radio with a couple of the passengers, take notes, and then type up the news on a typewriter that belonged to the officers. Falling into her familiar role as a journalist and newspaper reporter steadied Eliza, helping her get through each day.

There were many moments of joy, too. Laughter as children played deck games – I Spy or Animal, Vegetable, Mineral. Jokes, limericks and stories were shared among the adults as they played cards, provided by the crew. There were talent competitions, and costumes made from grain bags were modelled by children in a fashion show. They could almost forget about the danger they were in until late at night. But fear crept back into most heads when darkness swept over the *City of Flint*. None of them knew if another submarine predator was out there, stalking them, ready to strike again.

Four days into their stay on the freighter, another dark cloud fell over the ship when they learned that the ten-year-old Canadian girl, Margaret, was not recovering from her head injury. She developed a high temperature, and Captain Gainard was forced to radio for help. The SS *Scanpenn* sailed towards them on Thursday evening, bringing a doctor and medical supplies. All the rest of the passengers could do was pray that she would recover.

The *Scanpenn* also brought the passengers fresh vegetables, sweets, cigarettes and even some magazines. The children whooped with delight when the captain called them over to show them a package marked, 'For the little ones'. A Swedish grandmother on the *Scanpenn* had donated the gifts she had bought for her grandchildren.

A passenger who was a baker baked cakes and cookies, leading to an impromptu children's birthday party for all the kids on board. A single candle was placed in the centre of a cake. People sang and danced. And as Eliza spun Kate around, the little girl squealed with delight. For a moment, they all managed to forget their circumstances.

THIRTEEN

Eliza

City of Flint, *Atlantic Ocean*

Six days after the sinking of the *Athenia*, devastating news reached them all. As Eliza played cards with Kate and Eric, Mrs Montague beckoned her over and whispered, 'I've just heard that the child has died.' Eliza gasped in shock. How could this have happened? They had been told only the day before that Margaret's fever had broken. She couldn't bear to think of the pain her mother must be feeling. Later, they would hear that pain first-hand. Nobody on board the *City of Flint* would ever forget the sound of the mother's grief as it reverberated around the ship, piercing them.

Eliza slept fitfully that night. Margaret's death was a stark reminder that life could be taken at any time, that war had no prejudice, and all were at risk. She looked down at the sleeping child beside her and felt her heart constrict with love. A realization struck her with such force it made her breathless. She would do anything for this little one, to keep her safe and make her happy.

In the next bunk over, she saw Mrs Montague sit up, rubbing her eyes.

'Can't sleep?' Eliza asked with sympathy.

'Whenever I close my eyes, I think about that little girl. Her poor mother must be wretched with grief.'

Eliza realized that Mrs Montague looked in stark contrast to the woman she first met only one week ago.

'I feel a hundred years old,' Mrs Montague said now. 'It's been quite a week, hasn't it? But I'm so grateful for you, Eliza. You have been so kind to me.'

'And you to me too,' Eliza replied, simply.

She reached across their cots to hold her hand, their bond now unbreakable.

'I don't think I'll sleep again.'

'Me either,' Eliza admitted.

'Indulge your friend and tell me a little more about your forthcoming marriage to your young man. How long have you been together?' Mrs Montague asked.

'I fear you might be quite shocked if I told you the truth,' Eliza answered, to which Mrs Montague raised an eyebrow in delight. Eliza recounted her chance meeting with Matthew and the surprise proposal later that evening.

To Mrs Montague's credit, she took the news as if it were the most normal occurrence.

'I thought my destiny was to remain single, that when my first love died, any romantic future was buried alongside him. But . . .' Eliza paused, a flush forming on her cheeks.

'But now you are beginning to have feelings towards Matthew,' Mrs Montague stated, nodding with approval.

Eliza pondered this and could not deny its truth. The closer they got to Matthew, the more excited she felt. 'For the first time in years, my life feels more expansive. Filled with possibilities. Surviving this, must mean something.'

When they moved to the deck the following morning, they found two US Coast Guard cutters had arrived overnight and taken up stations on either side of the freighter. Eight days into their ten-day journey, they were getting close to their destination. The seriously injured – those with broken bones – were transferred to the US Coast Guard boats and rushed back to land, far more quickly than the freighter could move. They also delivered fresh food and additional crew to assist where needed.

When Mrs Montague was handed a hairbrush, toothpaste and toothbrush by one of the new crew members, she wept with relief. 'How could I ever return to civilized society looking as I do? I never want to see a steel comb for the rest of my life!'

Eliza decided her personal grooming could wait a little longer. She went in search of newspapers, hungry for more news. But there was no joy when she began reading reports about the ill-fated *Athenia*. Her heart quickened as she read the world's reaction to their tragedy. The brutal attack on their ship had far-reaching consequences. When a German U-boat struck the *Athenia*, which had Americans and Canadians on board, it broke all rules. Would Canada and America join the war in retaliation?

But nothing could have prepared Eliza for the moment she came to a two-page spread that listed the survivors of the *Athenia*. She knew already that of the 1,418 people on board the ill-fated ship, 117 had been killed. Some during the explosion, others in accidents on the lifeboats. If the survivors were listed publicly, that meant Matthew was most likely reading the newspaper right now, scanning for her name. And she could picture Larry and Eimear, frantically looking for news about their dear friend, their heads bent low, foreheads touching. Eliza vowed to send them a telegram as soon as she possibly could. As for Matthew, she could only hope he was safe himself as he waited for her to make her way towards him.

Taking a deep breath, she began the task of reading the names listed in black and white. *Dear Lord, let the MacShanes be alive.* She came to her own name first of all, and it was a sobering moment to see it in black and white in the survivors listing: *Miss Eliza Lavery, Irish.*

Eliza trembled as she imagined a different ending for her. For many years, she'd wished death to take her while she slept so she could find Davey and her family once more. But faced with the harsh reality of her own mortality, Eliza realized she was not ready to die after all. Whatever her future held in store for her, she would face it with strength and gratitude.

Continuing to offer prayers to the heavens, Eliza scanned her way down the list of names. When she came to the letter M, Eliza held her breath until she came to a heartbreaking entry: *Miss Kate MacShane, Irish.* There was no Diarmuid, Mary or Richie listed with Kate's name. She looked three times but each time with the same result. Desperate, Eliza then examined the list looking for the MacShanes' forenames instead, thinking that maybe their surnames were listed incorrectly. She knew she was clutching at straws, but how could she ever accept that Kate's beautiful family were gone? Again, no miracle answered her prayers.

Her body ached with fresh pain. Eliza couldn't bear it, and if she couldn't, how could Kate? Still clutching the newspaper in one hand, she began to shake so much that a passing crew member had to take the paper from her and lead her to a crate to sit down. Her legs felt like jelly, and she couldn't even find the strength to return to her bunk.

A few minutes later, she heard her friend's voice calling out for her.

'Are you all right, dear? You look quite ashen. Has something happened?'

With a trembling hand, Eliza pointed to the survivors list and begged Mrs Montague to double-check the names.

When Mrs Montague looked up some minutes later, shaking her head sadly, Eliza asked, 'Do you think there's been a mistake?' Her voice was desperate, almost begging Mrs Montague to lie to her and tell her that they were alive somewhere.

Mrs Montague looked at Eliza with sympathy, shrugging her shoulders. Slowly, her voice filled regret, she replied, 'I would think, dear, that every effort has been made to make this list accurate before it went to press. The eyes of the world are on this. We can always hope and pray for good news, but I fear we must prepare ourselves for the fact that they are lost.'

Mrs Montague's words brought Eliza back to their sombre reality. She had no choice but to be strong. However traumatic this news was for her, Kate was about to lose her whole world. And she would need Eliza as her safe harbour. She was the adult, and there was no room for sentiment here.

'I can't tell her. Not yet. Not until all hope is gone,' Eliza said, sitting up straight. At that exact moment, Eliza noticed Charles running towards them, laughing and kicking his two heels in the air joyfully. He grabbed Mrs Montague and pulled her into an impromptu dance across the deck.

'Unhand me, sir!' Mrs Montague protested, but she was laughing with him all the same.

'You won't believe it!' Charles shouted, returning breathlessly to where Eliza stood. 'They're only in Ireland – all three of them! My wife and daughters, can you credit it?' he cried.

Eliza looked at him in confusion, not understanding for a moment.

'They were rescued by a Norwegian freighter which ended up in Galway. My darling girls. If you'd gone on a different lifeboat, Eliza, you could be back home now!'

That thought did not please Eliza one bit. She was more determined than ever to continue her journey to Matthew and a new life in Bermuda. Not even a torpedoed ship could stop her. But bolstered by Charles's evident joy, she found the strength to stand up. She hugged him close, happy about his good fortune.

'Can you tell Eric about his mama and sisters after I've taken Kate for a walk? I don't want her to hear that. Not yet,' Eliza said. She wanted to feel joy for Charles's good news, but somehow it only served to make Kate's soon-to-be-heard news even starker.

'Of course,' Charles promised, his face clouding in understanding.

The two of them walked together towards the children, following the sounds of their laughter. Eliza watched Kate skip over a long rope that Eric and another boy were turning for her. Her little face was innocent and free from the burden of truth. Before she approached, Eliza walked to the side of the freighter. She looked out to the swell of the waves, offering a prayer for the souls of Mary, Diarmuid and baby Richie MacShane. Then, summoning up resolve from deep inside, she called Kate over.

FOURTEEN

Eliza

City of Flint, *Atlantic Ocean*

Eliza decided honesty was the only policy to use with Kate, and gently explained that her family were not on the survivors list.

'Where are they then?' Kate asked, looking puzzled.

Summoning every ounce of strength she possessed, Eliza gently replied, 'When we get to Canada, we will double-check with the authorities where they might be.'

'But they are not on the other rescue ships?' Kate pressed.

Eliza shook her head sadly.

'Eric said they could be dead,' Kate whispered.

Eliza pushed down a lump in her throat. What world was this, that children discussed death while at play?

'Mammy said that when Granddad died, he was an

143

angel. Do you think Mammy, Daddy and Richie could be angels?'

Eliza had never been more grateful, for this nugget from Mary. 'If they have . . . died, then I have no doubt that your mammy, daddy and Richie are all angels now too, watching over you forever.'

'Where do angels live?'

'In heaven,' Eliza said, biting back tears.

'When we get to Canada, can you take me to heaven?' Kate asked.

Eliza pulled the child into her arms so she could not see her tears. The poor girl hadn't grasped the situation yet. How could she make a five-year-old understand this? When Eliza lost her entire family as an adult, she'd almost drowned in grief.

'Can I go now?' Kate asked politely.

'Of course. And I'm here if you have any questions about any of this.' Eliza kissed her forehead one more time.

As Eliza watched Kate walk away again, Mrs Montague walked over to her with two tin cups of tea. 'I always think tea and scones are the perfect comfort food. I'm afraid in this instance, we'll have to make do with just tea.'

They sat for a moment, sipping the warm drink.

'I don't suppose I need ask how that went,' Mrs Montague said.

'Ever since the sinking, it is as if someone has switched the colour from that vibrant little girl to a muted grey. Kate's voice, her expression . . . they dulled in front of my eyes. And that just made it even worse,' Eliza shivered, taking another drink to try and warm herself up.

'She's too young to comprehend. And I fear she has a lot more to face in the coming weeks. The poor mite is an orphan now.'

Eliza pinched the bridge of her nose.

Orphan, spinster, she'd been called them all. Terms used to describe her position resulting from a cruel twist of fate. But she was so much more than those terms. And so was Kate.

Charles called over to them both, 'Why do you think the Coast Guard cutters are still sailing on either side of us?'

Eliza and Mrs Montague walked over to join Charles and looked down to the water below.

'As a guard of honour because we're getting close to Halifax. And I for one see it as a comfort. We have the protection of our American troops again,' Mrs Montague said.

But Eliza felt unease prickling her. Did the Coast Guard know something that the passengers on board did not? And it appeared that many others felt the same way. The rumour mill was strong on the ship, as snippets picked up from sailors about possible threats were passed on.

A couple of hours later, the news reached them that someone had spotted a submarine off the coast of Newfoundland. Within moments, everyone around them was back to the night of 2 September once again. As Eliza, Mrs Montague and Kate sat on their bunks, the cargo dormitory was gripped by fear.

'We're sitting ducks here,' one passenger cried out.

'We won't get away with our lives the second time,' another replied.

Mrs Montague paled and whispered, 'I can't take it. I

won't survive any more pushing and pulling. If it is to be another torpedo, I can only hope it takes me quickly.'

Eliza took her into her arms and cradled her, as she had done Kate many times. While she had strength in her body, she would ensure this woman survived. And somehow, her frailty gave Eliza the calm and courage she needed.

At some point in the evening, the captain came down to see them, warning them that a further storm was coming that night.

'You mustn't worry. You are perfectly safe in my freighter. We've weathered much worse than this,' he explained.

'You'll see; it's going to be okay,' Eliza said to Mrs Montague.

'We'll take care of you,' Kate added, snuggling into the older woman's lap.

It became perhaps the most harrowing night for them all. Whether it was the crashing waves that flung their boat from side to side, or the threat of another torpedo, there was little sleep for anyone. Eventually, near dawn, the water calmed, and the faint snoring from around Eliza suggested people had drifted off to sleep.

They'd survived another night.

And the morning came with good news, too. Captain Gainard told them they would land at Halifax the following day, shortly after breakfast. Up on deck, as they stood at the railings, searching for the first sights of land, Kate pointed upwards when she heard the sound of an aeroplane overhead. A sailor shouted out to reassure them, 'It's from the newspapers. Look, they're taking your photograph. Wave everyone!'

'Do you think Mammy and Daddy will see me in this picture from heaven?' Kate asked, waving excitedly, blowing kisses for the camera.

'Wherever they are, they can see you, my darling,' Eliza replied sadly.

The nearer they got to land, the more excited the passengers got. As the crew prepared for their imminent arrival, Eliza tidied herself up. But as there was a scarcity of water, it was a quick lick and a spit, as her mam used to say every morning before she sent her to school. When Halifax itself finally appeared on the horizon, the entire boat whooped and cheered, followed by the boom of a gun salute, fired in their honour.

It felt surreal to Eliza. Was it possible that at last they were going to reach safe shores, their ordeal almost over?

FIFTEEN

Eliza

Lord Nelson Hotel, Halifax, Canada

As tugboats brought the *City of Flint* into Pier 21 at the Ocean Terminal in Halifax on Wednesday, 13 September, Eliza felt her body sag with relief. She could not wait to get off the ship and wasn't sure she ever wanted to get back on one in the future. As they were the first of the American and Canadian survivors to return home, there was quite a commotion on the dock waiting for them. Reporters and cameramen wanted to capture every moment, while medical staff and Mounties, dressed in their distinctive red and blue uniforms, stood ready to assist those who needed it.

Like most onboard, Eliza walked around the ship for a final time so she could thank the crew and officers who had been so selfless in their efforts. When she found Captain Gainard, she clasped his hands in her own.

'I don't think you slept once during this trip, did you?'

He smiled and simply replied, 'I slept enough. And I have the best crew that any captain could ask for.'

'God bless you and your crew,' Eliza said, as she took one last look around what had been a safe haven for them all.

As they waited for their turn to leave the ship, Mrs Montague and Kate again held on to Eliza, their fearless leader. They were a united trio and clung to each other for support. Eliza blinked as cameras flashed at them all. She worried for Kate, who must have been overwhelmed.

Reporters continued to shout out questions to them, all clambering to understand what the passengers had been through. But what could any of them say to that? How could Eliza sum it all up in a couple of sentences? Maybe one day, she'd sit down and write about her experiences. But now, it felt too raw.

'Have you any words to share with us?' a reporter shouted at Mrs Montague.

She replied, in typical good humour, 'My dear man, if I ever decide to get on a ship again, please knock me on the head and take me back home. Because it will mean that I have surely lost my mind!'

A ripple of laughter ran through the crowd as dozens of cameras flashed.

They were directed by a group of boy scouts who stood at the end of the gangway to an area where the men were sent in one direction and the women in another. There, the Red Cross waited for them. They gave Eliza toiletries, toothbrushes, new clothes, combs and brushes for their hair. Eliza took Kate's hand and they made their way to the washrooms with bathing facilities that had been cordoned off for them in the port building.

'A little easier to navigate than a bucket of seawater,' Eliza commented, trying to keep her voice light-hearted and cheery for Kate's sake as she washed shampoo suds into her hair in the cast-iron bath.

'You are a natural, you know,' Mrs Montague said, watching the pair of them.

Eliza threw a puzzled look at her. 'Hairdresser?'

'A mother. You always put the child's needs before your own. As any mother would do,' Mrs Montague said with a knowing nod.

Mother. That word had so much power. Happiness trembled inside of Eliza. But she felt immediate guilt at the unguarded emotion. She had no right to feel this way. She was not Kate's mother. Simply her guardian until she could be reunited with her family in Ireland.

'I'm pleased that I can be here for Kate,' Eliza responded simply, giving nothing else away.

Once Kate was towel-dried and clothed in a new dress and cardigan with knee-high socks and shoes, Eliza stepped out of the clothes she'd been wearing for twelve days. Her dress was torn, and her cardigan smudged grey with dirt. As the hot water washed over her face and body, she groaned in pleasure. If it wasn't for the queue of women waiting their turn, she would have stayed in that tub for an hour. Once she too had towel-dried herself, she changed into a pretty red print dress she'd been handed with a matching cardigan, stockings and brown lace-up Oxford shoes. She felt almost human.

'I'd forgotten what colour your hair was. Such a beautiful shade of ebony. And this one, with her lovely blonde curls,' Mrs Montague said when Eliza re-joined her and Kate outside the washroom.

Eliza sniffed the air and laughed as she said, 'No more eau-de-oil either!'

Now clean and dry, the trio were next directed to see a Canadian Red Cross nurse called Carla, who gave them a physical examination.

'You need to see a doctor when you get home about that chest infection,' she told Mrs Montague as she placed a jar of tablets into her hands. 'I don't like the sound of that wheeze. But until then, take one of these, three times a day.'

Kate was given a clean bill of health – her injuries were not the kind that could be solved with tablets or a plaster – but Carla tutted about the gash on Eliza's leg. She dressed the wound and gave Eliza antibiotics, warning her about possible infection. Finally, she declared them well enough to travel on.

'I'm looking for my ward's family. Can you help me?' Eliza asked.

On hearing this conversation start up, Mrs Montague swiftly stepped aside, taking the child with her.

'We've not seen them since the torpedo,' Eliza continued, with Kate now out of earshot.

'Were their names on the list of survivors printed in the newspaper?' Carla answered gently, sympathy on her face as her gaze followed Kate.

Eliza shook her head.

'Then I'm afraid it's unlikely they survived. What are their names? I'll see if I can find anything out. In the meantime, there's a room down the corridor for families to reunite. Plenty of food there too, if you're hungry.'

'I don't know what to do . . .' Eliza said, faltering. She felt ill-equipped to deal with this. And she knew that soon

Mrs Montague would leave for New York. Eliza dreaded that moment when she no longer had her friend's wise counsel and staunch support.

The nurse nodded in sympathy, 'You can leave the little one with the Red Cross. We'll take care of her. Once we can confirm that her parents have perished at sea, we'll sort out what to do next.'

These words were as good as a bucket of cold water thrown over her. Her indecision about what to do with Kate next disappeared. Until a plan was made for Kate's future, she would not leave her. Eliza clenched her fists and shook her head furiously. 'No! Kate stays with me.'

And that's when Eliza felt the little girl's presence. She'd escaped Mrs Montague's clutches and snuck up beside her. Kate threw her arms around Eliza, and clung to her with all her might.

'Don't let them take me from you,' Kate pleaded, her body shaking in fear.

Eliza leaned down and kissed her forehead, 'Don't worry, we're a team, you and I.' Then, looking back at the nurse, she said firmly, 'Her mother and father gave her into my care before the ship was struck. I promised I would look after her, and I intend to hold true to that promise.'

There was no further talk about separating them after that.

Finally, they made their way to Canadian and US Immigration. Tables were set up to deal with each person's paperwork. Thanks to Mrs Montague's wise forward-planning, both Mrs Montague and Eliza had their passports, albeit a little bedraggled now from their own ordeal in the elements. It felt like a lifetime ago that Eliza had stuffed hers inside her bodice. While Mrs Montague walked to a table on the right, Eliza and Kate sat with a round-faced man who looked to be in his forties.

'Aren't you a pretty little girl,' he said to Kate, greeting her warmly. 'What's your name?'

'Kate MacShane. I'm five. And my mammy is Mary, my daddy is Diarmuid, and I have a baby brother Richie. I taught him how to play peekaboo.'

'Aren't you the best big sister? I'm Norman, but most people call me Norm. And you must be Mary then?' He turned to Eliza.

'I'm Eliza Lavery. I was in the cabin next door to the MacShanes. Kate's parents had asked me to take care of Kate at the time . . . that is, when the ship was struck. We haven't been able to find them since.'

Norm looked at the little girl and then back to Eliza and frowned. 'Ah. I see.'

He flipped open a file on his desk and began checking through a list of names.

Kate reached over and clasped Eliza's hand tightly.

Please God, please give us some good news, Eliza prayed as she watched him reading his list.

Clearing his throat, Norm leaned in and said in a low voice, 'I'm afraid we have no record of any MacShane, other than Kate, in the survivor groups.'

Eliza felt Kate's hand slacken its grip.

'Is there a chance that . . .' Eliza let the question hang between them.

Norm shook his head, two spots of colour staining his cheeks. 'Along with 114 others, they are assumed lost at sea. I'm so very sorry.'

Even though she had expected this confirmation, it still winded Eliza. She looked down at Kate, who was ashen

153

white. She didn't cry this time. Maybe her tears had finally run dry. Then her little voice asked, 'Eliza said my mammy, daddy and baby brother might be in heaven. Do you know the way?'

Silence swallowed the room up whole, only broken by the sound of Norm taking a sip from his glass of water.

'I wish I did know the way, sweetheart. Because I promise you, I would bring you there myself,' Norm answered.

Eliza put her arm around Kate, turning the little girl towards her. 'I'm so sorry, but we cannot bring you to see your family. Heaven is a place that only those who have died can go to. And I know that is the most dreadful of news to bear. My parents and brothers are in heaven too. I miss them so much. But I know that even though we cannot see our loved ones, they will always be in our hearts.'

Kate blinked, then nodded silently.

'Do you have any family we can call for you at home in Ireland?' Norm asked.

Kate shook her head.

'No grandparents, aunts or uncles?'

Kate looked down; she'd had enough questions.

'Her parents told me that they had no family in Ireland. But Mr MacShane did say that he had two sisters – one who lived in Manchester and the other in Liverpool. I don't know their names. He mentioned that he didn't know them as there was a big age gap between them.'

'Aunt Hanora and Aunt Constance. I've never met them, but Daddy told me about them, he said they were a right pair of eejits,' Kate said.

'Good girl! That's very helpful,' Eliza praised her, as

she stifled a smile. She could almost hear Diarmuid's voice giving out about his sisters. But then a shiver ran down her spine, as realisation struck her. What would the future hold for Kate, if she ended up in her aunts' care?

The immigration official scribbled the details down. 'I'll make a few calls, see what we can find out. And in the meantime—'

Before he suggested separating Kate from her, Eliza said quickly, 'Kate stays with me. I'll find a hotel and wait for news.'

Norm nodded. 'Very well. The least I can do is book a room for you in the Lord Nelson Hotel in Halifax. In the meantime, Miss Lavery, would you like to make a phone call or send a telegram to anyone?'

Matthew. With her worry for Kate, she'd put all thoughts of him from her mind, but she felt a glimmer of happiness bubble its way inside of her. She was back on solid ground again and that meant she would see her fiancé soon.

'I would like to send a telegram to my fiancé, Lieutenant Commander Matthew Lynch. He's stationed at the Royal Naval Dockyard in Bermuda,' Eliza said proudly, looking down to her engagement ring.

'I'll make sure he knows where you are,' Norm said, writing the details down.

Eliza knew they had much to talk about. Not least the fact that she now had a small child in her care. And she knew that until she found a home for Kate, she could not think about moving on to Bermuda. She could only hope that he understood that.

SIXTEEN

Eliza

The Lord Nelson Hotel, Halifax, Canada

Mrs Montague elected to join Eliza and Kate at their hotel. She was booked on to a train for New York departing later that evening and would wait it out with them rather than at the train station. Eliza was more than happy to delay their goodbyes to someone who had become so important to her in such a short period.

Once they checked into the hotel, they were given a hero's welcome.

'Can I bring you refreshments to your room?' the concierge asked.

Without hesitation, Eliza and Mrs Montague answered in unison, 'Tea and scones!'

Discussing food had been a diversion on board. And scones had been top of their wish list during their escapades.

'I'm travelling home on a special Canadian National

Railway train, with sixteen sleeping and dining cars reserved for *Athenia* survivors. People are decent, aren't they?' Mrs Montague said once they sat down to their feast, placing a thick layer of whipped cream on her strawberry jam-clad scone. She looked much more like herself now, dressed in her new clothes from the Red Cross, although she'd certainly lost weight.

'We've seen the best of human kindness over the past ten days,' Eliza agreed. 'I bet your husband will be relieved to see you. And your children too.'

Mrs Montague took a white hankie from her cuffed sleeve and dabbed her eyes at the mention of her family, 'I can't seem to stop crying since I spoke to him. Hearing his voice was my undoing. Cyril sounded so worried and sobbed the moment the line connected. He was hell-bent on coming here to get me. But that seems a nonsense, waiting for him to get here before I set off. The sooner I leave, the sooner I'm home.'

Eliza was happy for her friend. Even so, she looked at the phone in their hotel bedroom and willed it to ring. Stubbornly, it had remained silent since their arrival. Had Matthew received his telegram? And had Norm, their immigration officer, managed to find Kate's aunts in England? Until Eliza knew that the little girl would be okay, she couldn't think about moving on with her own life. Kate was currently curled up fast asleep in their queen-sized bed. She clutched a small panda teddy bear to her chest that a member of staff gave her when they checked in earlier.

'She'll be fine. She's young. Resilient. Children always surprise us with how adept they are at getting used to new normals,' Mrs Montague said, following her gaze.

'But what about you, dear? Are you looking forward to seeing your handsome beau?'

Eliza took a moment to answer her friend. Yes, she was still excited to see Matthew, but now she was back on solid ground, doubts had once again begun to creep into the corners of her head and heart.

'I'm a little scared, to be honest. It feels like an eternity since I accepted Matthew's proposal. And so much has happened since then . . .'

Mrs Montague nodded in sympathy. 'We will all be forever changed by our near-death experience. It would be silly of us to think otherwise. But your heart is the same as it was when you left Donegal. Trust in the connection you made with Matthew. I am sure it was true, and it will prove as such when you see him again.'

Eliza chewed her bottom lip, then admitted her worst fear, 'What if he's changed his mind? What if he realized he'd been impetuous when he proposed and has decided that he no longer wishes me as his wife?'

Mrs Montague made a loud snorting sound to this. 'Well, if this is the case, he is not worthy of your affections. And you must come to start a new life with my family and me in New York. You can move in with us; I have a spare room you would be most comfortable in. And then I'll help you find a place of your own, a job, a husband too, I dare say. I know several men who would jump at the chance for an introduction to someone as beautiful as you.'

Eliza looked at her friend in wonder. She knew the generous offer was made straight from Mrs Montague's heart and felt overwhelmed with gratitude. But before she had a chance to get sentimental, Mrs Montague stood up, looking at the small gold carriage clock on the dressing table.

'I'm afraid I must start to gather myself and make my way to the train station. I want to ensure I am first in line and get a decent sleeping car. You know I am most particular about my sleeping arrangements.'

Eliza looked at her and raised an eyebrow, a smile hovering on her lips, remembering the first time she met a fur-coat-clad Mrs Montague. Since then she'd seen her friend climb a rope ladder with more finesse than most half her age. Never mind that she'd spent almost a fortnight sleeping in the most appalling conditions Eliza had ever seen and had managed just fine. Mrs Montague raised a hand to her mouth, and then a grin broke out on her face and she began to laugh, which in turn sent Eliza into convulsions. They clung to each other in their mutual merriment. Suddenly they both jumped in shock as the phone shrilled into the room. Immediately pulling herself together, Eliza ran to answer it.

'Hello, Miss Lavery; this is the front desk. A gentleman is looking for you. He says he is your fiancé. I've sent him into the lounge.'

Eliza gasped out loud. *Matthew – here?* In her wildest dreams she hadn't thought he'd come all this way to *her*. She assumed he'd wait in Bermuda until she reached him. Or perhaps send a telegram.

'Oh . . . I'll be . . . right down,' Eliza stammered in response, feeling herself begin to shake in apprehension.

'He's here,' Eliza whispered in wonder, turning back to Mrs Montague. 'I had no idea he'd come *here*.'

'Well of course he would! He loves you,' Mrs Montague replied, clearly delighted. 'What did I tell you?' Picking up a comb, she began smoothing down Eliza's hair. Then she stood back and inspected her critically. 'Too pale.' She pinched Eliza's cheeks sharply, ignoring her yelp of surprise. 'It will have to do. I suppose allowances must be made after all the tribulations you've endured.'

Eliza looked in the mirror that stood over the large mahogany dressing table and frowned as she looked at herself. She hardly recognized who she was any more. She was a little too thin, her face pale with red circles under her eyes. Small changes that would rectify themselves in time with some care and rest. But inside was a different matter. She felt altered.

'My wedding dress and trousseau are lost at sea,' Eliza said wistfully, thinking about it for the first time. And then her green evening dress came to mind. That, too, was now in a watery grave. Was that a sign that it was time to move on from her first love and embrace a new future with Matthew?

'Don't worry about all that for now, and don't frown, dear. It's very ageing. I promise you it will all work out. I just know it. You've had such a rough first half of your life. I believe you are destined for great happiness from now on in.' Mrs Montague smiled fondly at her. 'Now don't keep him waiting. You go ahead, and I'll rouse Kate. We'll come down in . . .' She looked at her watch, 'in fifteen minutes. But I cannot wait one moment longer.'

Giving Mrs Montague a quick hug, Eliza ran out of the room, pausing when she heard her friend call out after her.

'Walk, dear. It's never ladylike to appear too eager.'

Forcing herself to walk at a more sedate pace, but with

her stomach flipping so fast she felt nauseous, Eliza made her way down to the lounge.

She saw Matthew the moment she arrived at the door. Standing by the window, his eyes were darting back and forth as he looked for her. She stopped a few feet from him, and when he finally saw her too they both stared at each other, unable to speak. He wore his naval officer's uniform, and the sight of him took her breath away. A black jacket with gold buttons and braiding, a white shirt and black tie, and black trousers, with shiny shoes, polished to perfection. Eliza had thought he was handsome when she last saw him in his civilian clothes, but now, she felt a jolt of shock.

Matthew called her name out, but it ended on a strangled sob. 'My dear Eliza . . .'

She stepped a few inches closer to him and he followed suit in their shy dance with each other.

'I thought I'd lost you. I couldn't bear it. To find you by chance then to lose you by cruel fate. I've been a shadow of my former self as I awaited news.'

'Oh,' Eliza replied, feeling the heat rise into her cheeks. It was all she could muster. A second look at Matthew revealed dark circles under his blue eyes. Somebody cared for her enough to lose sleep. The thought made her tremble in wonder.

'Thank you for coming,' she added, in a whisper.

Matthew took two long strides and pulled Eliza into his arms. He smelled of spice and tobacco, and Wright's Coal Tar soap too. She leaned into him and the comfort he offered her.

'I was at the pier waiting for you, but somehow we missed

each other. I was frantically looking for you when a kind officer told me I could find you here. Are you unharmed? You look so pale and thin.' He held her at arm's length and looked her up and down, scrutinizing every part of her.

Eliza laughed and reassured him that she was fine.

'I would never have forgiven myself if you were harmed. I should have taken you with me the day I proposed,' Matthew said.

'I think that German U-boat holds a little more responsibility than you do,' Eliza said, still laughing, and now making him smile too.

He took her face in his hands, and he leaned in to kiss her gently on her lips. 'I've dreamed of this, of you, since we said goodbye . . .'

He looked so earnest and sincere that it made Eliza reach up to kiss him again. She only meant it to be a gentle kiss like his was moments before, but it became more urgent, passion moving them closer together, their bodies becoming one. When Eliza heard Matthew groan, she pulled away, flushed and confused.

'My apologies. I got carried away,' Matthew said, his face flushed.

Eliza looked at her fiancé and tried to understand the emotions she was feeling. She'd enjoyed the kiss. Wanted more, even. But then, something stopped her from totally giving into the moment. Or rather, someone.

Davey.

His face flashed into her mind and she felt a stab of guilt that made her wince in pain. She knew it was silly, but she couldn't help feeling that, in allowing herself to respond as she had with Matthew, she'd been disloyal to her beloved Davey.

'Can you forgive me?' Matthew asked worriedly.

Eliza shook her head. 'There's nothing to forgive. We both got carried away in the moment,' she reassured him, aware that he was watching her closely. 'But I would like to sit for a moment. There's something that I need to tell you.'

Matthew took her arm and led her to a table, pulling a chair out for her.

'I can't believe you're here,' he said, still looking at her in wonder. He reached over and touched her arm gently.

'I must look quite frightful. I'm in clothes borrowed from the Red Cross. I'm afraid I lost everything at sea. Including my wedding dress.'

'Clothes, possessions, they can all be replaced. I would marry you in a coal sack if you desired to wear one. But you, my darling, are irreplaceable. We'll buy you everything you need before we continue on to Bermuda. I have passage arranged tomorrow afternoon on a Royal Navy aeroplane. But I'll tell you all about that later on. I thought it would make sense if I booked a room here tonight, or would you prefer to move elsewhere? Is your room comfortable?' Matthew's words rushed out, and Eliza had to put a hand up to stop him. Her feet had barely touched the ground since her arrival, and her head spun with his plans.

'My room here is perfectly fine. But I need to tell you about a little girl that was on the *Athenia* with me. Kate MacShane, from Downings in Donegal. She's five years old and quite alone in the world,' Eliza explained.

Matthew looked at her in surprise. He sat back into his chair, his back ramrod straight, as he remained quiet, giving Eliza his full attention.

'The thing is, I'm not sure I can leave with you tomorrow.' Eliza's hands began to shake so she stuffed them under the table to hide them.

Disappointment and confusion flooded Matthew's face.

'Not because I do not wish to,' Eliza quickly reassured him. 'I'm sorry, that was a clumsy way to start. I promise you, I remain firm in my intention to marry you, Matthew. But Kate's parents are missing, presumed dead. She was with me when the torpedo struck the *Athenia*.'

Eliza shared how Kate ended up in her care, telling Matthew a little of the trauma they'd suffered at sea.

'Oh my darling, you've been so brave. Taking care not only of yourself but a little one too.' Matthew's eyes were filled with admiration.

'I promised her parents that she would be safe with me.'

'And I have no doubt that she has been given the greatest care,' Matthew said warmly. 'So what happens next? Has her family in Ireland been notified?'

'The immigration officials are trying to locate her aunts who live in England. But she has no other family.'

'The poor little thing,' Matthew said, shaking his head. 'Is she with the Red Cross now?'

Eliza drew in a deep breath. A realization struck her. How Matthew responded to her next revelation would determine if they had any chance of a future together. A show of the kind of man she was betrothed to.

'Kate is still with me. She's upstairs in my hotel room sleeping with my cabin mate and dear friend Mrs Montague. I can't wait for you to meet them both. They have been my comfort and only joy in this horrific nightmare.'

And as if the mere mention of her name had conjured

her up, Mrs Montague's voice boomed, 'I hope you know what an amazing young woman you have there, Lieutenant Commander.'

Eliza watched Matthew scrambling to his feet and bowing his head to Mrs Montague, who held Kate by the hand. Kate moved behind Mrs Montague, hiding shyly from the stranger. Eliza looked at Matthew under her thick lashes, trying to gauge what he thought as he took in the duo. But his face was too difficult to read.

Quickly, she scrambled to her feet, standing by his side to make the introductions.

'Lieutenant Commander Matthew Lynch, this is my dear friend and companion, Mrs Montague. Fate made us cabin mates before the *Athenia* was lost, and we have stayed that way ever since. And this' – Eliza bent down and lifted Kate into her arms – 'is Kate. The bravest little girl in the whole world.'

'I am so glad to make your acquaintance, ladies. And any friend of my darling fiancée, I hope, will consider me a friend too.'

Mrs Montague leaned in and pointed to Matthew's row of medals on his breast pocket. 'I've no doubt you are a hero, Lieutenant Lynch, but not all heroes wear shiny medals. I am quite sure that neither Kate nor I would have survived our ordeal without the kindness and strength of our dear Eliza. She was our constant and guiding light in the darkest moments.'

Eliza felt herself blush with embarrassment.

Matthew looked at Eliza with pride in his eyes. 'I look forward to hearing about the adventures you've shared. One thing I knew for sure when I met Eliza was that she is both kind and strong.'

Eliza was unused to attention being focused on her, preferring to stay in the background when she could. 'Have there been any phone calls?' she asked Mrs Montague now, changing the subject quickly.

Mrs Montague shook her head sadly. She took Kate into her own arms and hugged her tight. 'I'm going to miss you, little one. Be strong, my dear. And remember, you always have a friend in me.' Mrs Montague took two folded pieces of paper from inside her coat and handed one to Kate and another to Eliza. 'These are my contact details so you can get in touch with me once you know where your next home is.'

'I'll be wherever Eliza is, so I don't need this,' Kate replied, handing her paper back to Mrs Montague. Then she returned to Eliza's side again.

Eliza felt Matthew's eyes on her, questioning. She had no choice but to ignore them and instead said her good-byes to Mrs Montague. The trio embraced and held on to each other for quite some time, none of them able to break apart, as they reflected on the past couple of weeks.

'Be happy,' Mrs Montague whispered, lightly touching both Eliza and then Kate's faces. Then with a pointed look at Matthew, making sure he was under no illusion that she expected him to make their happiness his prime concern, Mrs Montague left, marching purposefully to the front desk. As Eliza watched her go, with only the clothes she had on her back, she thought of the poor steward carrying her luggage to their cabin that first evening. Had he survived? Eliza would find herself asking that question often over the coming weeks as memories of passengers and crew members came to her.

'I'll warrant that she's a force to be reckoned with,' Matthew remarked, also watching her leave.

'You'll never know how true those words are,' Eliza said. She felt a surge of joy that, despite the horrific ordeal she'd endured, nothing would change Mrs Montague.

A tug on the skirt of her dress made her look down, asking Kate, 'Are you okay?'

The little girl's stomach responded for her when it loudly grumbled.

'Now that's a sound I can identify with,' Matthew said. 'What say we go to the dining room and see about some dinner? Then, little lady, you and I can get to know each other better.'

When Kate didn't respond, Matthew added quickly, 'And of course, dinner wouldn't be complete if we didn't finish it off with a large ice cream sundae.'

Kate perked up at this and gave Matthew her most winning smile. The three of them walked to the dining hall where Matthew asked for a table for three.

'Just one moment, sir,' the maître d' replied. 'Let me find a table for you and your family.'

Family. The word reverberated in Eliza's head. She had been alone for years and had given up on ever being part of a family again. She glanced at Matthew to see if he appeared upset by the inference that Kate was their child but, to his credit, he seemed utterly unfazed. He was pointing out a large aquarium filled with bright, colourful fish to Kate, who oohed and aahed with appreciation. Eliza noted that the young girl had now moved closer to Matthew, stepping out from her shadow.

As they took their seats, Eliza breathed in the wonderful aroma wafting from the kitchen. Her own stomach grumbled, and she realized her appetite had returned too. Perhaps because she was finally used to being on steady ground again. But also, she acknowledged, with Matthew by their side now, the fear she'd held on to for weeks had begun to fade. He had a calming presence about him. One of those people you instinctively trusted with your life.

Eliza listened to him telling Kate stories about his travels to India and the elephants he'd taken rides on. She felt proud of him. This kind man, who made Kate laugh and forget about her parents for a short time, who wanted to marry her. It made her head spin.

By the time Kate had licked her ice-cream bowl clean, she slumped back in her chair, white with exhaustion.

'I'm so sleepy,' she said, yawning widely to emphasize the point.

Eliza looked to Matthew, but he smiled reassuringly. 'How about you take Kate up to your hotel room? I need to sort my own sleeping arrangements either way.'

'That would be great,' Eliza said, rising to her feet. Kate jumped up too and found a sudden burst of energy, running to check out the aquarium again.

'While you settle Kate down for the night, I could make some phone calls. See if I can find out what is planned for the girl, assuming they cannot locate family members for her,' Matthew suggested gently.

'That would be extremely helpful. But I beg you, please don't make any promises about her. She's been through an unimaginable ordeal. And while Kate might seem like she's taking it in her stride, she wakes in terror every night, screaming for her parents.'

'I give you my word that I want only the best for Kate, like you do.' He looked at his wristwatch, 'How about I call up to your room in one hour? I'll tap lightly on your door so as not to disturb the child. I can let you know what, if anything, I've managed to find out.'

'Thank you, that would be so helpful,' Eliza said.

Matthew took her hand and kissed it lightly. They heard a giggle from Kate, who watched them closely, so Matthew reached over and took Kate's hand, kissing it formally too. Eliza felt her heart leap at his gesture. His ease at the change of circumstances he'd walked into made her want to reach out and kiss him again. She settled for a smile of thanks, the most she could offer in the moment, then she took Kate's hand and they walked towards the elevators together.

Once they were back in their hotel room, Eliza ran a bath for Kate, filling it with bubbles, and the little girl smiled delightedly as she sank into the warm water.

'It feels so nice,' Kate said, moving her arms and legs up and down through the silky bubbles. 'I've never had a bath this hot before.'

'Is it too hot?' Eliza said, quickly testing the temperature again.

'It's perfect,' Kate sighed happily. 'At home, I used to get into the bath after Daddy and Mammy were finished in it.'

Kate's face clouded at the memory.

'I remember doing that when I was a little girl too! Mam, Dad, then me, then my two brothers!' Eliza said. 'I was always glad that I was the eldest. Poor little Joe was last. The water would be quite murky by the time it got to him. Dad used to say that he was dirtier when he got out than when he got in!'

Kate giggled as Eliza hoped she would. Then she picked up a large sponge from the sink and dipped it into the water. She sponged the sudsy water down Kate's back like her mam used to do for her many years ago. Her mam was always singing back then, too. They'd hear her pretty voice while she cooked, cleaned, and worked out on the farm. Her favourite song was 'I Love You Truly', a hit by Elise Baker in 1912. But as far as Eliza was concerned, her mother sang it far more beautifully. She began humming the song as she bathed Kate and the words returned to her in a rush.

> I love you truly, truly dear,
> Life with its sorrow, life with its tears
> Fades into darkness when I see you near,
> For I love you truly, truly dear.

Once she was towel-dried and wearing her Red Cross nightdress, Eliza tucked Kate into bed, placing her beloved cuddly panda bear under her arm.

'I know you said that only people who die get to heaven. Do you think that I will see Mammy and Daddy again one day?' Kate asked.

Eliza searched for the kindest words she could use to help make this understandable for a five-year-old. She looked at her Claddagh ring, still hanging from Kate's neck, and thought about Davey. And then her parents and brothers. Her faith that she would see them all again one day had gotten her through her darkest moments. 'I believe we get to see the people we love most of all again. It might not be in this lifetime, though. But if we are patient, we'll see them again somewhere.'

Eliza felt the hairs on her arms rise as she watched the little girl go through an onslaught of emotions. Eliza understood how hard it was to lose the people you love more than anyone else in the world and she feared that nobody had the power to take that horrific grief away. You had to lean into pain and hope that one day you found the strength to stand up tall again.

'My daddy always says that Mammy is like a lioness, that she's so strong and fierce, protecting Richie and me.'

Eliza thought of Mary's face, and in the little time they'd spent together, she could appreciate how accurate that description was.

Kate exhaled, a long, painful breath, 'I know that if Mammy were alive, she'd be with me. She would have found a way to find me.'

Eliza nodded, too choked up with sadness to speak.

'I don't want to be on my own. I'm scared,' Kate whispered, then. A tiny tear escaped her blue eyes and trailed down her cheek.

Eliza brushed it away softly with her thumb. She took a deep breath and leaned down to kiss the little girl softly on her forehead. 'I promise to stay with you as long as you need me to.'

Kate let go of the breath she'd been holding and reached up to put her two little arms around Eliza's neck. Then mimicking the song from earlier, she whispered into Eliza's ear, 'I love you truly, truly dear.'

SEVENTEEN

Eliza

The Lord Nelson Hotel, Halifax, Canada

Matthew tapped lightly on their hotel room door an hour later, as he had promised.

Eliza held her finger to her lips, closing the door softly and moving out into the corridor to talk to him.

'She's fast asleep; it took less than thirty seconds for her to nod off, thank goodness. But I can't stay out here for long. If she wakes up alone . . .'

'Of course,' Matthew said. 'I'm afraid alone is the correct word. The Irish Consulate has officially confirmed that the MacShanes died onboard the *Athenia*. Or perhaps on one of the lifeboats. There were some casualties during the rescues, where people went overboard. We may never know what happened to them, but it is certain they were not picked up by the other rescue ships.'

He waited for a moment as Eliza took in this final

damning sentence. There had been a tiny part of her that hoped a miracle might be possible for the MacShanes. That they were injured somewhere, unable to give their names. She should have known better. Eliza, more than anyone, knew that miracles were in short supply for most people.

'There is some further news, though, this time from England. The authorities were able to locate one of Kate's aunts – Hanora. I took the liberty of calling her myself. She has stated that neither she nor her sister wishes to take Kate in. They barely make ends meet as it is and cannot add another mouth to their tables.'

Eliza shuddered at this unexpected news. How could anyone turn their back on their own flesh and blood? She would give up her last morsel to feed her family. But then she remembered the conversation she'd had with Diarmuid.

'Maybe it's as well. From the little Kate's father said to me about his sisters, I got the impression he was not close to them. So what happens now?'

'The Salvation Army will take Kate and find her a new home. There has been quite a large number of children sent to Canada from England over the past sixty years already. They are known as the British Home Children. I believe many are sent to live on farms. Efforts will be made to find her somewhere to live in the countryside, similar to the life she knew at home in Ireland.'

Eliza felt every nerve in her body rebel against Matthew's plan, so casually outlined. As if it wasn't bad enough that Kate's parents had died, the only relatives she had left didn't want her. And as a result, she was to be sent to a farm in a strange country, to live with strangers. Eliza felt anger begin to bubble its way up inside her. She lifted her chin, getting ready for battle. While she still had breath in her body, she would not allow Kate to be carted off, alone and heartbroken. She still had the money that she had hidden in her undergarments from the *Athenia*. Not much, but enough to get both herself and Kate started in life until she found a job. And she had Mrs Montague, who she knew would take the two of them in.

Matthew watched Eliza, not saying anything for a moment, and it irritated her to see a glint of amusement in his eyes. Had she been so wrong about him all this time?

She looked back at him, not trusting herself to speak, as he adjusted the lapels on his jacket and then brushed off a piece of lint. Finally he cleared his throat. 'Or . . .' He paused again, taking a deep breath, 'I thought we could just adopt Kate ourselves.'

Eliza looked at him in shock. She didn't trust her ears. 'You mean . . . you and me . . . as in *that* us?'

'Yes, *that* us,' Matthew responded, smiling. 'That is, if you think it's a good idea, of course, and assuming Kate agrees. We could take her with us tomorrow afternoon to Bermuda. As a married officer, we are to be given a house for my family in the Royal Naval Dockyard. It needs some work, but nothing we can't cope with. I'm sure we would all be quite comfortable there. And we'd have views of the beach and ocean too. I know it won't be your beloved Ballymastocker Bay, but I assure you it is as beautiful.'

Eliza reached out to hold on to the door, feeling weak as hope flared inside her.

Matthew continued hurriedly, seeming to want to explain all his plans before Eliza had a chance to say no. 'Until then, you and Kate can stay in a hotel. I thought perhaps the Tom Moore's Tavern, once owned by the Irish poet. Or the Princess Hotel, which might be more comfortable—'

'You'd do that?' Eliza interrupted him. Her voice had risen several octaves.

'Of course,' Matthew responded, without hesitation. 'Any fool can see the bond that you both have formed. It would be cruel to take you away from each other. If I'm honest, she stole a little of my heart too earlier. She's such a sweet girl. If Kate would like to throw her lot in with you and me, I think we can give her a nice life.' His voice caught, before he finished in a whisper, 'I know I can never replace her poor father, but I would very much like to care for her, love her, as he no longer can.'

Eliza let out a huge breath, one that she wasn't even aware she'd been holding. Then she threw herself into Matthew's arms for the second time that day, kissing him firmly on his lips.

'Well, if I'd known I would get that reaction, I would have suggested it earlier,' he joked, as she pulled away from him. 'I could get used to you kissing me like that.'

Then, all trace of merriment left his face as his eyes traced over every inch of her. Eliza shivered in anticipation, knowing he would kiss her again. He pulled her close, and she felt his lean, muscular torso pressing against her. Then he kissed her with such passion that she felt her knees weaken, and she had no choice but to cling to him. Only the thought of the sleeping child on the other side of the door brought her back to her senses. She placed her hand on his chest and pushed him away for the second time that day.

'I'm afraid I am not quite myself when I'm with you,' Matthew said. 'I must apologize again.'

But he didn't look sorry. He had a grin as wide as his cap on his face, and Eliza was sure she had a similar one, too. Begrudgingly, they said their goodnights, making plans to meet early the following morning for breakfast.

'We can do some shopping before we make our way to meet our flight to Bermuda,' Matthew suggested. And then they both lingered, each reluctant to say goodbye.

'Don't disappear on me again,' Matthew said softly. 'I could not bear to lose you.'

'Nor I you, Matthew,' Eliza replied shyly. And then with one last touch of his hand, she left him.

Back in her room, as she sank into the starched white bed linen and soft pillows and listened to the soft, slow breathing of the sleeping child next to her, her mind raced with the possibilities of her future. A short month previously, she had not known Matthew existed. Now she was to become his wife, and mother to a five-year-old daughter, all thanks to one glorious leap of faith.

She reached over for Kate's hand and held it while she slept, singing softly, 'I love you truly,' before falling into a deep sleep.

EIGHTEEN

Saoirse

The second day of Saoirse's holiday was quieter. A beach day, swimming and sunbathing, catching up on her latest audiobook. She joined her aunts for lunch at home, where Kate was unusually quiet. Sadness lived behind her eyes now. It was impossible to miss. But when Saoirse questioned her, she waved away their concerns. All was fine. She was tired, that was all. Saoirse wasn't sure she bought that.

Kate suggested that Saoirse and Esme go to the Rum Bum bar on Horseshoe Bay for a drink, then she locked herself away in her bedroom once again.

'I wanted to talk to you alone about Kate's birthday, so this is perfect,' Esme said as they strolled towards the bar.

'She's been quiet since we were in Hamilton yesterday when she dropped the bombshell that she wasn't born on the island, then clammed up,' Saoirse said. 'What was that all about?'

'It's Kate's story to tell in her own time, not mine. And in truth, I know so little about her early childhood, it's better that I don't jump ahead.'

Saoirse agreed and a short walk later, they arrived at the Rum Bum bar, which was busy with tourists. As well as serving drinks and food, the bar rented out sunloungers, parasols and snorkelling kits to the tourists who flocked to spend the day on Horseshoe Bay. They searched the white and blue tables and chairs, scanning the patio area for a free spot. Thinking they were out of luck and would have to stand, Saoirse saw a friendly-looking woman trying to get her attention by waving enthusiastically.

As they approached, she said conspiratorially, 'We're almost finished, you can have our table if you like? We need to get back to our cruise ship shortly anyhow.'

Her companion, a grumpy middle-aged man with a burnt nose and forehead, looked at his watch and said, 'Which will sail without us if we don't hustle. Come on.'

They gathered their belongings, and Saoirse and Esme gratefully took their seats.

'Imagine being stuck on a cruise ship with a grump like him,' Esme said, watching the couple bicker as they walked away.

Saoirse nodded her agreement and thought of Finn, who was the most agreeable person she knew. Rarely a cross word was shared between them. On the other hand, Riley would moan about having to take his cowboy boots off. Damn it, she thought, there she was again, comparing them.

Saoirse looked down to the beach. Blue skies met aqua-blue waters that lapped slowly on to the pink sands. It truly was the view of dreams. Almost every spot was filled with people lying on blue sunloungers, while others still were swimming, with children's laughter echoing into the warm afternoon air.

Esme handed her a menu, and she scanned the long list of cocktails for inspiration. She glanced up and saw Esme squinting as she tried to read it, reminding Saoirse to tackle that particular issue at some point today. A waitress appeared, wearing the bar uniform of a white polo shirt and black trousers, coupled with a megawatt smile.

'Hello ladies, I'm Rene, welcome to Rum Bum bar. What can I get you?'

'What do you recommend?' Esme asked, placing the menu on the table. 'There's so much choice; I'll take forever to make my mind up.'

Saoirse looked at Esme in wonder. She was so smooth in her denial of her eyesight issues.

'I always say you can't leave here without trying at least one Rum Swizzle. Best on the island. And Bermuda's national drink, of course.'

'Done! We'll have two of those, please,' Saoirse said when Esme gave a nod of approval.

Saoirse took her phone out to snap several shots of the postcard-pretty view behind them. They watched a cocktail barman in a bright red tropical shirt as he prepared their drinks. A large group whooped when he began to shake them. The lively atmosphere was precisely what Saoirse needed to distract her from the fact that she was still not wearing her engagement ring and her fiancé would soon be here, and would no doubt wonder why.

The waitress returned within a few minutes with two glasses filled with a tangerine-coloured cocktail, served over ice and garnished with juicy sweet oranges. Saoirse took a sip and sighed with pleasure when her tongue tasted the sweet hit of the Swizzle.

'I could get used to this,' she said, looking down to check out the ingredients listed for the cocktail on the menu. 'Rum, orange, pineapple juice and Falernum. I don't think I've had that before.'

'It's a sugar syrup with spices and almonds,' Esme explained. 'Kate is partial to these too. I remember many years ago having a lively night with friends here, drinking these. For someone so small, Kate sure can hold her liquor.'

'I would never underestimate Aunt Kate. And clearly, she's done a lot in her life that I don't know the half of,' Saoirse remarked as she took another sip of her drink. 'God, this drink is Bermudaful . . .' She grinned as her joke made her aunt smile.

'Word of warning, these bad boys pack a punch. So two will be my limit,' Esme said.

Saoirse took a quick selfie with the cocktail and sent it to Finn.

Tropical paradise, but with one person missing.
Thinking of you. Love you, Sx

Two dots appeared, and Finn responded within seconds.

You're killing me! Fxx

You'll be here too before you know it. Sx

'Do you miss him?' Esme asked, watching her.

Saoirse considered this for a moment before answering. She marvelled that Finn hadn't been part of her life a year ago and yet now he was her waking and final thought of each day. He'd practically moved into Anam Cara Cottage, sleeping over most nights. She'd made space in her wardrobe, and more and more of his possessions were scattered around her home. *Their* home, maybe? She liked that thought. And then an idea snaked its way into her mind. Did they have to get married? Why couldn't they just make it official by moving in together?

'It's strange not seeing him,' Saoirse replied when Esme coughed delicately to bring her thoughts back to their conversation. 'We've gotten into a habit of seeing each other every day.'

'Tell me about him,' Esme said warmly, and Saoirse loved that she could hear genuine interest in her aunt's question. 'I know he's your neighbour, of course, but how did you actually meet?'

'I was fixing a sign to the gate at the entrance to the stables not long after I moved in. Drill in hand, I was totally lost in what I was doing. Then as I stood back to admire my handiwork, I heard movement from behind me. I turned, and there he was.'

Saoirse remembered looking him up and down, first noticing his height. Over six feet with broad shoulders, his muscular physique was undeniable in his T-shirt and cargo pants. He had a shock of messy, ink-black hair, and the kind of stubble that wasn't designer but looked just right on him. And more than that, he had an aura of self-assurance that appealed to Saoirse. Finn had then moved almost instantly, introducing himself and shaking her hand.

'He had a firm shake, and I noticed right away that his hands were calloused and rough from manual labour,' Saoirse said. 'I don't know how to describe it, but there was an honesty about Finn that appealed to me. He told me that he was a local cattle farmer and his farmland nudged my own two acres.'

'You can tell a lot about a person by a handshake,' Esme agreed, and they both clinked their drinks to that. 'Did he ask you out straight away?'

'I asked him how long he'd been standing there, watching me, and he said long enough to see I knew my way around tools. He joked that he knew who to call on if he needed help to fix fences on his farm. He has this crooked grin, and I found myself grinning back. And then I told him that I'd worked on a ranch in Alberta for a year and that one of my regular tasks was fixing broken fencing. He seemed suitably impressed and, before I knew it, he was in my cottage drinking coffee with me.' Saoirse smiled at the memory.

'That's a nice story.' Esme drummed her fingertips on the table as she thought for a moment. 'One thing I'm struggling with,' she continued slowly, 'is that I can't figure out why you haven't told him about Riley.'

'The million-dollar question,' Saoirse replied, trying to dodge the question. She waved at Rene as the waitress walked back past their table, indicating they'd like two more Rum Swizzles.

'Well, I'm going to the bathroom. Maybe you can try to explain why it's so difficult to be honest to the man you love when I get back,' Esme said with a wink.

Saoirse chewed her bottom lip in frustration. She knew she was playing a dangerous game by keeping her marriage to Riley a secret from Finn, especially considering her fiancé had an aversion to lies. After all, that was why she'd ended up in this mess in the first place.

Initially, when she'd started to date Finn, she'd kept her relationship with Riley to herself. It was private, and she had to work out whether she could trust Finn with her heart before she could explain herself to him. And who spills all of their secrets on a first date anyway? But before long, the first date had turned into the fifth, and Saoirse still hadn't found the courage to mention Riley's name.

Instead, she had told herself that it was because she'd been a bit rusty at dating. It had taken several years before Saoirse had dated anyone after her return home to Ireland. And while she'd had a couple of boyfriends since then, none had lasted beyond a few months. She'd guarded her heart with stealth and care: her break-up with Riley had cut her deeply and she wasn't sure she would ever trust herself to love a man again.

But it was different with Finn. He'd crept into her first thoughts every morning, and before she closed her eyes each night, his face had been the only one she wanted to see – and still was. When Finn had started asking her if he could join her on her daily treks, she had known that saying yes would be cracking open her heart a further chink, but as they explored the beautiful Donegal coastline together every day, they had shared their hopes and dreams for a future that might include each other. The air had been filled with possibility.

Saoirse wasn't stupid. She knew she had to find the right time to talk to Finn about Riley. But every time she gathered up the courage to bring it up, something would happen to distract them. One particular evening, as they had sipped beers under the stars on Saoirse's deck patio at the back of her cottage, she was determined to lay everything out in the open.

'We've never spoken about ex-boyfriends or girlfriends, have we?' she had begun, as casually as she could manage.

'No, I don't suppose we have. I fear you might be bored by my admissions on this score,' Finn had responded, entirely at ease.

Saoirse could only hope he would find her story as dull as his. Somehow she didn't think that would be the case.

'Will I start?' Finn had said as Saoirse was about to speak. 'I've nothing to hide; a couple of relationships lasted about six months each. They fizzled out, no big drama. One ex – Sammy – was a little more serious, and I'll admit I dislike talking about that fun time. I went to school with her. We were together for nearly two years in total.'

'Did you love her?' Saoirse whispered, feeling a stab of jealousy that made her stomach flip.

Finn looked away, and for a moment Saoirse panicked that he was about to admit he still did. Finally he answered, 'I thought we were the real deal. But I found out that our whole relationship was based on a bed of lies. I don't think there was a single word she told me that wasn't an untruth.'

'Like what?' Saoirse swallowed down bile at the mention of the word lies.

'Well, for a start, she forgot to tell me that she was also dating someone else on and off throughout our relationship.' Two spots of pink landed on Finn's cheeks at this admission, and his jaw clenched.

Saoirse felt a flash of annoyance at the mere thought

of anyone causing Finn pain. And then her heart began to race as she realized that her confession about Riley had the power to do so much worse to him.

'I swore after we broke up that I'd never allow anyone to cause me pain again. Lies and deceit, I cannot abide. I think that's why I fell in love with you, Saoirse. Your goodness shines so brightly from you.' Finn reached over their beers, and kissed her on her lips. 'Oh, sweetheart, why the sad face?'

Saoirse smiled quickly to reassure him, 'I would never do anything to hurt you, not intentionally at least, I swear it.'

'I know that. You've shown me more honesty and love in these few months together than I had in years with Sammy. I never think about her any more. Truthfully, this is the first time I've given her any thought in months. So come on, kill me with the details of your exes. I'll do my best not to be too pathetic with jealousy. How many times has your heart been broken?'

So many thoughts flashed through Saoirse's mind, she felt dizzy. Should she tell him now about Riley and risk losing his trust? Or keep it a secret, which came with its own risks? Faced with a no-win situation, she made a spur-of-the-moment decision.

'My heart has only been broken once. But that was a long time ago. Unless you count my first love, a cutie called Paul that I went to playschool with. No matter how often I told him I loved him, he refused to look at me.'

'The scoundrel,' Finn said dramatically. 'A curse on him.'

Saoirse giggled, and then Finn kissed her again. And as they always did when they kissed, Saoirse forgot all her good intentions. The moment passed, and the subject of exes was soon forgotten about.

'You were miles away!' Esme said as she sat down again. 'I've asked Rene to bring us some fries. I always get the munchies when I have a cocktail. Go on, tell me why it's so hard to tell Finn about Riley.'

'Finn has a problem with lies.' Saoirse began filling Esme in about his deceitful ex.

'I can see how you ended up in this pickle,' Esme sympathized.

'Thank you!' Saoirse responded, relieved. 'If I told Finn that I'd neglected to mention that I was married before, it could make him doubt everything else I've ever told him. And I'd already fallen for him by the time it was too late. I didn't want to risk him finishing things with me.' Saoirse began chewing her lower lip again. A habit she'd not been able to break since she was a little girl.

'Stop fretting, child. We'll work this out. Although, the way I see it, you have no choice but to come clean, if you plan a future with this man that is.'

Rene reappeared with a, 'Here you go, ladies, enjoy,' dropping two fresh drinks on to the table. Saoirse could see what Esme meant about them being strong. Her limbs had loosened, and her body relaxed as the alcohol hit the spot. Judging by the flush on Esme's cheeks, she felt much the same.

Saoirse knew she should have told Finn, but hindsight was a luxury she did not have back then. And she hadn't deliberately lied, at least not on purpose. It was more of an omission, she told herself. Why, then, did she feel so guilty? She looked down to her empty ring finger. Another omission.

'You look so sad, child,' Esme said, a frown furrowing her brow. 'Next week, when Finn arrives, you'll find the right moment to tell him. But I can't bear looking at that face, so I vote that we forget about your predicament for the time being. Let's have that chat about Kate's birthday.' She clapped her hands in delight. 'I've booked a suite in the Hamilton Princess Hotel for us both, with afternoon tea to be delivered to the room. It's ever so grand. And I've booked a room for you and Finn too. It's Kate's favourite hotel, she's always loved it there.'

'Wow!' Saoirse exclaimed, bouncing up and down on her seat with excitement. She'd always wanted to stay in that hotel. 'Thank you for booking a room for me too. That's so kind. Does Kate know about it, or is it a surprise?'

'The latter. And with you here, it's going to make it easier for me to make the surprise work. I have a couple of projects on the go. I managed to borrow Kate's tin that she keeps family photographs in, for a few hours. I took a bundle of photographs, some dated as far back as 1939, and had them digitally scanned and enhanced. They're with a videographer in Hamilton now. He will make them into a *This Is Your Life* video compilation. I thought we could show it to her at the hotel. I need to figure out how, though.'

'I can sort that out for you. I'm sure the videographer can give us a USB drive that we can plug into the TV in the suite. Leave it with me.'

'Excellent. There's something else I'd like your help on too. I've sent Kate's DNA samples off to one of those heritage sites. I saw a documentary about it a few months ago. Lots of adoptees find their birth mothers. It makes for quite emotional viewing. And it got me thinking: maybe we can find some of Kate's long-lost family that way.' Esme opened her handbag and pulled out a document, handing it to Saoirse.

'I didn't know Kate was looking for long-lost family. How intriguing,' Saoirse said.

'She isn't looking, but that doesn't mean that she shouldn't be. A few years ago she told me that she wished she had photographs of her early childhood. I thought maybe, if we can find a cousin or something, they might have a photograph of her family. But you need to keep this to yourself.' Esme tapped her nose.

'I promise I won't say anything. How did you get a sample without her knowing?' Saoirse asked, as she scanned the information on the sheet. It gave details of an app that could be downloaded to check in on results. She picked up her phone and began to download it.

'Told her I was doing a Covid test. I said I felt a little sick and wanted to double-check we were okay. I used a couple of antigen tests but did an extra swab for the DNA site too. She never even noticed.' Esme smiled triumphantly.

'You sly old thing!' Saoirse looked at Esme in admiration. 'By the way, I'm not being rude using my phone, I'm downloading the app to check Kate's results.'

'Thank goodness you are, for I can't make head nor tail of it all.'

Saoirse tapped in the account details from the document and Kate's information flashed on to the app.

'Right, the results of Kate's test are not through yet. Here, let me show you.' Saoirse showed Esme the screen. 'See, it says that Kate's results are still being compiled.'

Esme looked blankly at the phone. 'You've been honest with me, so I suppose I should return the favour. I can't see a damn thing on the computer screen any more, so I sure as hell can't see anything on your phone.' She exhaled a long breath.

'I figured you were having difficulties with your eyesight. But I can't work out why you want to hide it. Why don't you want Kate to know?'

'I'm a stubborn old fool, that's why.'

Saoirse laughed. They all knew that Esme had a mulish streak in her.

'What are you being stubborn about, though?'

'It's been a difficult couple of years for us. For Kate in particular. Her health issues have made her less independent, and it's harder for her to get out and about and do all the things she used to take for granted. Kate relies on me to take care of her and the household. What happens if I can't do that any more?'

'You are amazing,' Saoirse declared. 'But you can't do everything. Even Spider-man took his costume off at the odd time to rest.'

'I don't have the same energy I had a year ago, that's for sure,' Esme admitted.

'Have you ever considered that, if you take better care of yourself, you'll be able to continue caring for Kate for longer?' Saoirse pointed out.

Esme didn't answer her. She wrung her hands as she pondered Saoirse's words.

'It seems that, apart from your eyesight, you are in excellent health. Seeking help is a sign of strength, not weakness.'

Esme tilted her head and looked at Saoirse for a moment. 'When did you get to be so wise?'

'I'm not sure about that. But I *am* sure I'm making you an appointment with an optician in the morning,' Saoirse said firmly. A small smile began to curl the side of her lips. And to Saoirse's surprise and delight, Esme didn't argue.

A couple walked past their table as they left the bar, holding hands, their bodies moving in sync as they made their way to the beach. And with no control over her mind, Saoirse imagined herself also holding hands with someone.

The only problem was that it wasn't Finn.

Maybe it was the alcohol lowering her defences; perhaps it was the beautiful tropical island they were on, so far from home. Whatever the reason, Saoirse decided to open her own box of secrets a little wider.

'I've been thinking about Riley a lot. Since I arrived here,' she blurted out. She couldn't look Esme in the eye as she spoke. She felt a flush of shame hit her, knowing that this admission was a betrayal of Finn, someone she had thought she loved with all her heart.

'And what kind of thoughts are you having?' Esme asked casually.

Saoirse shrugged, swirling her straw around her drink.

'Are they romantic thoughts, or the I-want-to-kill-that-boy-who-broke-my-heart kind of thoughts?' Esme continued to probe.

'Both. It's so confusing. And I'm riddled with guilt.'

'I sometimes think about my first girlfriend, you know,' Esme said.

Saoirse nearly spat her drink out in shock.

Esme chuckled at her reaction, then continued, 'Occasionally, my mind wanders to the what-ifs. It's natural. Don't feel bad for thinking about your past. We all do it occasionally. It doesn't mean anything. Unless, of course, it does.'

'What do you mean by that?' Saoirse asked.

'Do you still have feelings for Riley?' Esme asked gently. 'No judgement here. You might as well be honest.'

Saoirse took another sip of her drink to buy some time. She'd been asking herself that same question for the past forty-eight hours.

'Truthfully, I'm ninety-nine per cent sure that I don't. I mean, I genuinely haven't thought about Riley at all since I've been with Finn. Surely that wouldn't be the case if I still loved him? I think it's that now I'm here again, somewhere that I spent a lot of time with Riley, well, it brings everything back to me.'

Saoirse watched the couple she'd noticed earlier walking along the shoreline. Even from a distance, they looked good together. And in love too, if she could warrant a guess, the way they kept stopping and kissing every few moments. She and Riley had been like that once: unable to keep their hands off each other. Yes, she had passion with Finn, but it was different somehow. Less intense.

'We've chatted about your first meeting with the farmer. Remind me of how you met the cowboy,' Esme asked.

Saoirse closed her eyes and pulled herself back to ten years ago. 'After college, when I decided to spend a year working on a ranch, I genuinely had no thought of romance. I wanted to learn the ropes, in a working ranch, so that I could bring that knowledge back to Ireland with me to my own stables.'

'You always had such drive and determination,' Esme said, raising her glass to Saoirse in salute.

'Thank you! Well, a few weeks after arriving at Mustang Creek ranch, I went to a rodeo with my bosses, Mitch and Zoey. I'd been waiting for such a long time. Bucket list item. Anyhow, when we arrived, it was one of those scorching days and I realized I'd forgotten to put on sunscreen.'

Saoirse looked down at her pale skin, which went from white to red instantly, grateful that they were sitting under a palm tree in the bar.

'I knew I'd fry if I didn't screen up. So, Mitch and Zoey went on without me, and I returned to the jeep. And that's when I saw Riley for the first time. He walked by me. He was wearing tight blue jeans and a checked blue shirt, with a white cowboy hat perched low. Our eyes met, and as we passed each other by, we held on to the look until the last possible second. I felt . . .' Saoirse flushed at the memory, pausing as Esme raised an eyebrow knowingly. She didn't finish how she felt. 'Anyway, I caught up with Mitch and Zoey; we took our seats and got ready to watch the rodeo. I'd never seen anything like it. The finesse of the riders as they competed in each event. It was the most exciting thing I'd ever seen. The speed of barrel racing took my breath away. The riders raced around barrels against the clock. It was so cool.'

'You used to do that yourself when you were a kid. I remember visiting you all and watching in awe as you fearlessly charged around the paddock behind your house!' Esme remembered.

'I still do it with Bojangles every now and then,' Saoirse admitted. 'Anyhow, after that, it was time for the steer wrestling event, and Zoey got animated because her nephew Riley was competing. As soon as the cowboy moved behind the rope barrier on his horse, I could see it was the guy I'd locked eyes with earlier.'

Esme's eyes widened as she listened.

'I couldn't take my eyes off him . . . again. The steer was released to get a head start. Riley kicked his horse and chased it, then he grabbed the steer's horns. The strength as he latched on to them – it was incredible. We were all on our feet, cheering him on. And when the klaxon sounded, Riley looked up, and I swear, our eyes locked again.'

'Did he win?' Esme whispered, enthralled.

'Yeah. Riley is good at what he does. One of the best. As we drove home that evening, my every thought was of him. I couldn't wait to meet him and was running through ways that I might be able to bump into him. I asked Zoey if she saw Riley much. And she laughed in response, saying he had a trailer on their land that he used when he wasn't away on the rodeo circuit. That he'd be back to Mustang Creek any day. And I had this feeling, this kind of knowing, that it would be important when I met him,' Saoirse finished.

Esme picked up a menu and fanned herself. 'Oh child, that cowboy was something else. When did he roll up at Mustang Creek then?'

'The next day. I was in the stables, rubbing down the horses after a trek, and then he walked in. He has this way of walking. It's more of an amble. You know how some people move with purpose? Riley is the opposite. He moves as if he has all the time in the world. I remember noticing that in particular.'

'I think you noticed a lot more than his walk, by the sounds of it,' Esme said drolly.

Saoirse snorted at this. Esme was right. They had both felt an instant connection.

She had carried on brushing her horse, feeling Riley's eyes on her, wondering what his next move would be. It had felt like hours, but it was only seconds later when he said, 'I'm going to take my horse out for a trek. Would you join me, Saoirse?'

He pronounced the word 'out' like oot, and Saoirse had thought she'd never tire of hearing him speak.

'And that was it,' Saoirse said.

Esme leaned back into her plastic chair. 'Okay, here's what I think. It's natural that being on the island, somewhere that you spent time with Riley, would make you think about him again. But I'm wondering where does that leave your farmer? And more importantly have your feelings for Finn changed?'

Saoirse shook her head vehemently. That her feelings for Finn had not changed was as crystal clear to her as the blue waters on the beach below her. But what was also becoming more and more apparent to her was that her mind kept drifting to Riley of late. Why was that?

'I don't want to think about this any more,' she said, suddenly feeling hot. 'Can we change the subject?'

Esme facepalmed her forehead. 'You and Kate are so alike! She thinks it can't hurt her if she doesn't think about something. But it's the opposite. I keep telling her that hiding pain gives it power.'

The hairs on the back of Saoirse's neck rose at these words. Had she given power to her ex-marriage by hiding it?

'Kate is almost ninety years old and she still won't face her past. Maybe you shouldn't leave it so long yourself.

I'd start by remembering why you and Riley split up in the first place, that might help,' Esme said, then looked up as a figure approached their table again. 'Ah, lucky you, saved by the fries.'

Rene arrived and placed a large bowl of golden fries covered in salt and vinegar in the centre of the table between them.

Saoirse bit into the crunchy, salty fries, moaning in delight at how good they tasted. As they ate their snack, acoustic music began to play. Saoirse moved around in her seat, smiling with delight when she saw a steel band by the bar. The calypso beat made her raise up her arms and wave them in time to the music. She was on a tropical island listening to calypso music.

That was enough for now. She would deal with everything else tomorrow. She called Rene over and asked for two more drinks.

NINETEEN

Saoirse

Eight years ago
Palm Tree Cottage, Horseshoe Bay, Bermuda

Sunlight flooded the small bedroom, warming Saoirse's face, and awakening her from her deep sleep. She stretched her arms above her head and reached to her right, looking for her husband, Riley. But as her hand padded the empty space beside her, the crushing realization that he was no longer part of her life hit her.

She wasn't at the ranch in Alberta any more. Twenty-four hours previously, she had given Riley back her wedding ring, leaving it beside her cowboy hat on the kitchen table. Then she'd fled their home, a trailer that sat at the back of Mustang Creek ranch, and got straight on a plane out of Canada. She knew that the only place she wanted to be now was with her two aunts.

For the first time in her life, Saoirse truly understood

the phrase heartbroken. She could feel her heart splintering into hundreds of pieces as she lay there, cutting her. She didn't know what to do. So for now she was hiding. From Riley, from her family, and from herself too. She could hear Kate and Esme moving around in their cosy kitchen as they prepared breakfast, the sounds of a whistling kettle and china clinking drifting down the hall. But Saoirse's stomach lurched in protest at the thought of food. She couldn't face anything as mundane as eating.

It was difficult to leave her friends at the ranch, not to mention the horses she'd grown to love as she cared for them. But walking away from Riley took every bit of strength she possessed. She couldn't be anywhere near him or the life they'd shared if she was going to stick to her decision.

Saoirse kicked her legs over the side of the bed and stood up, the terracotta flagstones cool under her bare feet. She walked across the hall into the bathroom and splashed cold water on her face. Looking at herself in the mirror above the sink, she was surprised to see her face unchanged. A healthy tan made her blue eyes pop, and there was no longer any sign of the marathon crying session she'd had over the past couple of days.

Sometimes a picture doesn't tell the true story at all.

'Tea's ready,' Kate's voice shouted down the hallway.

Saoirse patted her face dry and then headed to the dining room. Aunt Kate greeted her with open arms, and gratefully she fell into them for a hug.

'Feeling any better, child?' Esme asked, joining them. 'You look a little perkier than last night, at least. The sleep did you good.' She peered at Saoirse closely, then nodded in satisfaction at what she saw.

'I didn't think I would sleep. But I conked out as soon as I hit the pillow last night,' Saoirse admitted. She looked around the comfortable open-plan dining and living room. It had become a second home to her over the years. Esme passed her a cup of tea, and she stirred it distractedly with her teaspoon.

'Do you want to talk about it yet?' Esme asked, her voice gentle.

Saoirse frowned. How could she explain the depth of the anxiety she'd experienced over the past couple of months when she didn't even understand it herself?

'It's too hard. I can't find the words.'

'Well, take all the time you need, child. Since I retired last month, I have all the time in the world,' Esme said. She'd worked for over fifty years in the post office in St George and was still in the adjustment stage of life as a retiree.

As Saoirse watched both her aunts smear creamy golden butter on their toast, she ran through the events of the past couple of months in her head one by one. She'd done this a dozen times but always returned to the same life-changing moment each time.

'Remember when Riley had that accident while riding the rodeo bull, shortly after we got married?' she said now.

'A terrible thing,' Kate said, shaking her head at the memory.

'I thought he was dead,' Saoirse whispered. She squeezed her eyes shut, but that didn't stop the painful memory from returning in full technicolour glory.

Riley lying under the bull, unmoving. Everything deathly silent for Saoirse, as if someone had turned the mute button on in the stadium. She remembered seeing Zoey and Mitch jump to their feet, their mouths wide open in shock, as they called out Riley's name. Zoey had grabbed Saoirse's arm, pulling her to her feet too. But Saoirse had lost the use of her legs. Shock. Terror. And then the manic rush to the hospital, following Riley in his ambulance.

Saoirse shuddered, then pushed away her teacup again as a fresh wave of nausea hit her.

'You were beside yourself, I remember,' Kate said, watching her niece closely. 'And he was in that operating theatre for hours.'

Saoirse nodded. She had called her aunts in tears while she waited in the hospital and had clung to their words of comfort. Aunt Kate and Esme had become her only support system. She couldn't even reach out to her parents: they didn't know she'd married Riley.

They had never understood her passion for horses or how much she adored her life working with mustangs on the ranch. And Saoirse had never managed to find the words to share the feelings she'd developed for Riley, the bronco rodeo cowboy she'd met while living there, during her polite and stilted phone calls home once a month. She told herself that they didn't need to know about her wedding, given that her decision to marry Riley was made predominantly because her visa was running out. But this wasn't strictly true. She'd married Riley because she loved him with all her heart, not because she needed a way to stay in Canada. Her parents would have lost their minds at the thought of Saoirse marrying a cowboy they'd never even met.

Her plan had been to marry in Ireland again over the next year or so. She wanted them to visit Ireland so her family could get to know Riley in person.

But none of that mattered now, she supposed.

'I've found it hard to move on from the terror I felt when I thought he was going to die,' Saoirse said.

Kate and Esme didn't say a word, instead waiting silently for Saoirse to continue.

'And the funniest thing is that Riley returned to his old self within six weeks of that accident, riding and competing again. But for me, every time Riley announces that he has another rodeo, I spin out. It's like I'm lost in a spiral that goes on and on, my mind thinking about losing him to the bull again. But this time for good.' Her brows knitted in pain.

'I can understand that. It's a difficult situation to be in, loving someone who has chosen such a dangerous career for themselves,' Esme said, shrugging her shoulders.

'I used to love watching him compete. I was so proud of him. That was my man, powerful, strong, undefeated,' Saoirse said wistfully.

'The problem was, you thought he was invincible. Which, of course, none of us are,' Kate said, hitting the nail on the head.

Her enthusiasm at the beginning of their relationship was fuelled by her innocence. Now she knew that one mistake could have deadly consequences. At first, she turned a blind eye to the injuries he received from competing; but now, they were all she could see. Every cut and bruise to a competitor's cheek was a siren warning to her.

For good reason, American bull riding was considered one of the most dangerous sports. The rider had to stay on top of the bull for eight seconds, with one hand gripped on a bull rope tied behind the bull's forelegs. After that, the bull would tire, and their bucking ability decreased. That's if you stayed on that long.

'It's eight seconds of pure terror for me each time Riley rides that blasted bull. I can't escape the fear, the worry. It makes me ill, so much so I can't eat for days before a competition.'

'You have lost a lot of weight,' Kate said, frowning, as if just noticing. She buttered a slice of wholemeal toast and then cut it into four triangles, passing the plate to Saoirse. 'Eat a little of this. Please. For me.'

Saoirse nibbled a tiny bite because it was easier to do so than listen to her aunts fussing. She knew she'd dropped at least a stone this year. She felt it in her jeans that now needed an extra two notches on her leather belt.

'This is no way to live,' Esme said, her lips puckered in annoyance. 'What does Riley have to say about all of this?'

'He didn't know how worried I was at first. I tried to hide how I felt, to put a brave face on it. But that didn't work. He could see I was withdrawn and fretting about something. So I came clean. And he was great for a while; he reassured me with all sorts of facts and figures about how safe he was. Promising me that the chances of him being seriously hurt were minuscule. But that didn't help. I live on a ranch . . .' She paused, corrected herself: 'I *lived* on a ranch. I've been to a lot of rodeos. I know what it's like.'

Kate sighed, and the three of them sat in silence, thinking about Saoirse's predicament. The sound of a Longtail's song echoed in the distance, its loud call piercing the air.

'How about you ban yourself from going to the rodeo to see him compete? That way, if he's out of sight, him being in danger is out of mind?' Kate eventually suggested.

'I thought of that myself. But it doesn't work. I still worry just as much while he's not with me. Last month, he didn't call me immediately after his event and I couldn't get Mitch or Zoey on their mobiles. They had gone to watch. Turns out that the phone service was down. By the time they did manage to call me, I'd spent twenty minutes ringing all the hospitals and driving myself into madness with worry.' Saoirse gulped down a mouthful of tea, along with the lump that had taken up residence in her throat.

'Oh, child,' Esme said sadly, 'you have been going through a lot. You should have called us to let us know how scared you've been.'

'I wanted to. I wish I lived closer to you both. I know it's only a short flight, but that can feel like millions of miles away.'

'I'm glad you came to us now. We're always here for you,' Kate said. 'So, what do you want to do?'

Saoirse shrugged. 'I can't see a way out of this. I should be with him when he goes away on the rodeo circuit. He's my husband. What do I do for the rest of our marriage? Spend half of it away from him because I can't watch him compete? Where he goes, I'm supposed to go.'

Kate snorted, 'Or where you go, he's supposed to go too.'

'I didn't tell him I was coming here, I just left,' Saoirse admitted.

'You can't run away from this, child,' Esme said. 'It seems to me that you gave up a lot when you married Riley. You love working on the ranch, but you've lost that now that you spend half your life on the rodeo circuit. I'm not sure that was how you envisioned life for yourself.'

Saoirse couldn't disagree with that. One of her favourite

parts of her job was leading guests on treks along the Bow River. But her full-time job had become a part-time one, now that she was on the road so much. She missed the ranch and her role there.

'And I dare say it's boring at times on the circuit, sitting around watching Riley ride, when that's all you wanted to do in the first place,' Kate said.

As usual, her aunt had grasped the situation without having to be told. Saoirse felt like all she did these days was move from one location to the next, living out of a rucksack day by day. And the excitement of it had begun to wane. She couldn't deny that she was bored.

'I'm living Riley's dream, not my own,' she admitted, bowing her head.

'Yes, you have been. But it's good that you've recognized that. Now you need to work out what *you* want,' Kate replied gently.

'I want to open my own stables, same as I've always wanted to.' She paused. 'And in Donegal. I miss Ireland. But Riley doesn't seem to understand how much I want this. That I have dreamed of nothing else since I was a little girl.'

Kate took a deep breath in response. 'I think that's a great pity. Not to be understood by the person who you love and who is supposed to love you.' A definite edge of irritation laced her words now.

'I think Riley feels let down by me. He says I've moved the goalposts. We had such a big fight two nights ago. We both said things that didn't show us in the best light.' Saoirse shivered and wrapped her arms around herself. 'He'll be home from his rodeo by now, so he knows I'm gone.'

'Then the next move is his,' Esme said, giving a pointed look to Kate.

That thought paralysed Saoirse. The room felt like it was closing in on her.

'I'm going to go for a swim. Maybe it will clear my head,' she said, standing up from the table. She kissed the top of Kate's head and then Esme's, grateful they were always there for her.

'Good idea. We'll be here when you get back.' Esme patted her hand gently as she went, then got up to clear the breakfast items from the table.

Although it was only 10 a.m., a dozen people were already lying on sunloungers. She decided to move away from crowds and turned left, taking the trail at the bay's edge that led east to a more secluded part of the beach. Despite her sadness, she still felt a moment's joy spark when she felt the warm pink sands beneath her feet. Saoirse pulled her hair into a ponytail, hoisted her coverup over her head and dropped it on to her towel and flip-flops.

She ran towards the inviting water and dived into it in one graceful motion. To her face and body, the cold shock of water was everything she needed. In that blessed moment underwater, as she swam out to sea, there was no time to think or worry about anything. She lost herself in the joy of the ocean's embrace. Finally, reluctantly, Saoirse swam towards the surface, gulping in air. She looked around her. The sea was all hers, and she relished it. She swam until her arms ached, flipped on to her back and floated, feeling the sun warm her face. As her body had become accustomed to the water's temperature, she lost track of time, giving herself entirely to the moment's pleasure.

It took a beat for her to recognize that a voice was shouting her name, bringing her out of her daze. She swam back towards the pink sands, standing up to walk the last few feet, pulling her hair from its ponytail and shaking it free.

And that's when she saw him.

Riley, her love, her husband, was standing on the beach watching her. He wore his standard uniform of blue jeans, a white T-shirt and brown boots with his beloved leather cowboy hat. Her heart betrayed her, leaping with joy at the sight of him.

'Only you would wear those to a tropical island,' Saoirse remarked, pointing to his boots when she reached him.

He tipped his hat to her as he always did when she walked up to him. Riley rarely took his cowboy hat off; it was an extension of him. He'd told her early on in their relationship that his father had bought the hat for him and taught him to treat it with respect, as his own father had done for him.

'I didn't have time to pack my Bermuda shorts. I was more worried about finding my wife,' Riley answered, his voice making her shiver.

'Why are you here?' she asked, using her hand to shield her eyes from the sun.

'I told you, I came to see my wife.' His eyes looked down to her left hand, where a white band of skin glared. He reached into his jeans pocket and pulled out her wedding ring. 'You forgot something when you left.'

'Have you seen Aunt Kate and Esme?' Saoirse said, ignoring the ring. If she took that, she'd put it back on and perhaps never take it off again.

He smiled. 'I did. Feisty old dames. I don't think Kate

likes me. She just glared at me. Esme told me I was a fool, then gave my arm a slap – that woman has strength for someone her age – then she kissed me and told me where I'd find you.'

They both laughed for a moment.

Saoirse dropped down to sit on her towel. Riley sat beside her, his two boots like lumps of clay against the pink-hued sands. She moved over and pulled his boots and socks off.

Riley pushed his bare feet into the sands, sighing in pleasure. 'That does feel good.' Then he turned to her, reproach in his voice, as he asked, 'How could you walk out like that?'

'I don't have any energy left to fight, so if that's what you've come for, get back on your horse . . .' Saoirse said.

He held his hands up in mock surrender. 'Me either.' He paused a beat, then continued, 'You hurt me when I got home and found your not-too-subtle message.'

Riley held up her wedding ring again and it glinted in the sunlight. 'I was so angry with you. I decided to drink myself into such a condition that I no longer cared what you said or thought about me. So I went down to High Rollers bar.'

'How'd that work out for you?'

Riley pulled his legs up towards him as he looked out to the sea. 'I couldn't even finish one drink. Logan tried his best to cheer me up, but I'm tormented, Saoirse. I don't know what I can do to save us, but I have to try. And it ain't right, this distance that's come between us over the past couple of months. I don't know what to do about that. But I do know one thing for sure: you're my wife. And I love you.'

Those words never failed to make Saoirse's heart skip a beat. She looked deep into Riley's eyes and saw the truth of his declaration.

'I love you too,' she said.

They moved closer, eyes still locked, and she felt his lips lightly brush hers, sending shivers through her entire body. She almost gave in to the kiss. Instead, using every inch of her willpower, she put her hands against his chest and pushed him away.

'That's our problem, Riley. We don't talk about our issues; we just kiss them away.'

He inclined his head, then said, 'Okay. Talk. I'm listening.'

'I think we did things the wrong way round. We got married for all the wrong reasons. Needing a visa should never be the starting point for a marriage.'

'That need might have sparked the proposal, but I loved you when I asked you to marry me. And I have never regretted proposing, not even for one second.'

Saoirse reached over and found his hand in the sand between them. He inched closer to her, and she leaned her head on his shoulder.

'It was the same for me,' she admitted.

'Then that's all that matters,' he whispered into her hair.

Saoirse wished it were that simple.

'We have to be honest with each other about what we need. I can't carry on the way we've been for the past couple of months. I feel like I've lost myself.'

Riley scrutinized her for a moment, 'You have changed. You don't smile much any more. And I can't remember the last time I heard you snort with laughter.'

'I don't snort,' Saoirse said indignantly, knowing very well that she did. The corners of Riley's eyes crinkled, and she thought, *Damn it, we can make this work*. But out loud she found herself saying, 'I think we want different things.'

Riley made no comment.

'I've not even told my family that we got married. And I've been asking myself why that is.'

'Because we decided we would go to Ireland together. And then we can re-marry for your parents in Ireland.'

'That never happened though, did it?'

Riley kicked the sand with his heel. 'You know I have commitments with the circuit. I can't just take off for a vacation.'

'Oh, I know that.' They hadn't even had a honeymoon because of the damn circuit.

'Let's tell your family. Get it all out in the open. Pick up the phone now, we can let them know straight away.'

Saoirse felt irritation bubble up again. He just didn't get it. 'I can't drop that kind of news on the phone.'

Riley sighed; his eyes flashed a spark of anger. 'Okay then, I'll prioritize a time for us to travel over there.'

Was this her future? Riley getting annoyed because he had to make time for them to do something important for her? She remembered a joke Zoey had made after they married – that Saoirse would have to make sure to time any pregnancies so her babies would be born in the winter when there were fewer competitions. At the time, Saoirse had laughed along, but now that joke felt like a premonition of her future. Not that they'd ever discussed having a family. Damn fools that they both were, they let themselves follow their hearts without talking about the important stuff.

'Do you want kids, Riley?'

He looked surprised by the change of subject. 'At some point. Not for a while, though. Is that what's bothering you? You want a baby?'

'No! But I'm trying to look forward to our future. If we have kids, what happens then?'

'Well, you and the kids would come with me on tour. A lot of the wives do that. Or you can stay at the ranch.' Again, that spark of irritation in his eyes.

'I don't think either of those options will work for me. I want to have a husband who shares parenting with me so I can have a career.'

'Can we worry about this when we have kids? Why are we talking about this now?'

'Because we have to!' Saoirse said sharply. She twisted her body to face him. 'We had this romantic notion – or rather, *I* did – about what our life could be. But it's nothing like I envisioned. The trailer doesn't feel like a home. It's somewhere to throw our heads at night. I want a *house*. I want stables where I can keep my own horses. I'm bored, Riley. You have a career you love, and I've got nothing.'

Riley smiled, slapping the sand with his fist, making the pink pebbles jump into the air. 'But that's easy. We'll talk to Mitch. Get you back working with him and Zoey, teaching again. You should have said you missed it so much. And look, we don't have to live in the trailer. You know there's an open invitation to move back into the homestead with Zoey and Mitch.'

His face broke out in a big grin.

Saoirse rolled her eyes. As far as Riley was concerned, problem solved.

'That isn't our home either, though.'

Riley exhaled angrily. 'You know I'm only earning about

a thousand dollars per rodeo right now. I can't afford to buy yet.'

'I understand that. But you refuse to discuss our future. You shut me down the second I dare to raise the subject.'

Riley muttered under his breath and kicked the sand with his heels. Through gritted teeth, he said, 'If I keep going the way I am, I can go professional. And that's where big money comes in. Last year, Trip Donnelly earned nearly one hundred thousand dollars. With that kind of money, we could buy our own ranch in a couple of years.'

Saoirse bit back the response that jumped into her mind. *That's if you're still alive, Riley.*

And there it was again. Within minutes of talking, she was back to the same old sticking point. She wished that her love for Riley was enough, that she was willing to sacrifice her own happiness for his. And maybe it said more about her than it did about him, that she found she couldn't. But even if she was happy to wait for Riley to have his big break and start making decent money, that didn't solve the issue of her out-of-control anxiety. She took a deep breath and decided to give it one more try.

'Have you ever been afraid?'

He looked at the blue ocean thoughtfully. 'Yes. When my mama first got sick, I've never felt so terrified. And not being able to do anything other than wait for news when she had that biopsy. Well, it was cruel. So yeah, I do understand what it is to be afraid.'

Saoirse pulled his face back towards her so they were looking into each other's eyes. 'That fear you felt then, well, that's how I feel every time you ride the bull.'

His mouth opened and closed. He shook his head as if trying to deny her words.

Saoirse looked at him and felt her heart constrict in shared pain. 'You are a risk-taker, always have been. A daredevil. It's one of the things that attracted me to you, if I'm honest.'

'I can't explain it. But it's a rush, knowing that you've beaten the clock, the bull, the horse, the cowboys I'm competing with. I can't live without that challenge, that adrenaline.'

'And I can't live *with* it,' Saoirse replied sadly. 'Every time you go into that ring, I say goodbye to you and think, *This is the last time I'll see him.*'

That hung in the air between them, damning them both forever.

'I'm not strong enough, Riley. It's killing me,' she added when he didn't respond.

Sounds of children laughing echoed in the air. A family appeared around the rocks. Two toddlers ran towards the water as it crashed into the bay. They squealed when the water hit their little toes, making the family laugh in unison.

Saoirse tried to imagine Riley and her doing the same with their own kids one day. But the image was grainy and unclear.

'What do you want?' Riley whispered.

'I want to start living my life again.'

'And what about us?'

'Can you walk away from the rodeo?' Saoirse crossed her fingers in the pink sand, pleading silently that Riley would choose her.

She saw his response in his grey eyes. His pain was etched, mirroring her own heartache. In one swift move, Riley pulled Saoirse into him, telling her repeatedly how sorry he was.

It was over. Finally, they both accepted that love wasn't enough.

TWENTY

Saoirse

Saoirse awoke with a start. With a sense of déjà-vu, she sat upright in bed and looked around in confusion. Heart racing, she took several deep breaths to calm herself down. She'd been dreaming about Riley, about the last time she'd seen him. Esme's words from last night, suggesting she confront her hidden pain, must have penetrated her subconscious. Saoirse swung her legs down from the bed, feeling the dull ache of a headache begin to make itself known.

What was it about this place that brought back so much she thought she'd already dealt with? Was it the location, and the fact that her first marriage had finally ended right here? Or was it more than that?

Saoirse decided to leave those questions for now and

212

made her way towards the kitchen. She found Esme and Kate at the dining-room table, eating breakfast.

'You look how I feel,' Esme commented, two bloodshot eyes peering at Saoirse as she sat beside her.

'Rehydrate,' Kate advised, nodding towards the teapot.

'I blame the calypso music. We were ready to go home after our second drink, but before I knew it, we'd ordered another round.' Esme shook her head sorrowfully.

'And another! I don't remember coming home,' Saoirse admitted. 'Those swizzles really got to me.'

'You wanted to ring Finn when we got home. I had to wrestle the phone off you! You were quite insistent. But I thought it best not to disturb him,' Esme said.

Saoirse felt a flood of warmth move from the pit of her stomach up to her body and on to her face. What an idiot she was.

'Thank you,' she whispered. Something nagged her, a buried memory of the night before, that she couldn't quite hold on to. She had been so drunk, worse than she could ever remember being.

'Was I limbo-dancing?' Saoirse asked, not sure if she could trust that flash that had just popped into her mind.

'Oh yeah. How low can you go? Very!' Esme cackled laughter. 'Did you sleep well? I was out as soon as I hit the pillow.'

'Weird dreams. I've had better nights,' Saoirse admitted.

'Must have been the night for them. I had a restless night, my mind was racing with many things,' Kate said. Her forehead creased in a frown, and she shook her head as if trying to dislodge her thoughts.

'You were tossing and turning when I got in,' Esme said.

Kate nodded. 'I can't seem to switch off memories. It's

as if I've opened a floodgate, and now I'm awash with unbidden thoughts.'

Saoirse nodded in sympathy. This was how she felt right now. Riley was her past, yet she was struggling to leave him there. But this wasn't about her. 'Anything you want to talk about, Aunt Kate?'

'Maybe. But not right now. What I will tell you is that I was adopted when I was five years old. And I was lucky that when my parents died, I gained a new set almost immediately, who could not have loved me more had I been born into their arms. But my dad never wanted me to discuss life before Bermuda. "Don't look back; it's not the direction you're going in," he'd say. "Leave the past where it belongs."' Kate's face twisted in pain as she spoke.

They sat silently for a beat, each drinking their tea as they pondered Kate's words.

'I'm glad you had great adoptive parents,' Saoirse said eventually. She had so many questions, but Kate made it nearly impossible to ask them.

'I've told you many a time that you remind me of Eliza, my mother. You might not be blood-related, but you could be. You even have her build and similar colouring. Like you, Eliza had great courage to take steps of change. I've always thought you moving to the ranch when you were so young was brave.'

'I take that as a huge compliment. But I'm not sure me spending a gap year on a ranch was all that brave.'

Saoirse remembered that first day in Alberta, Canada, arriving wide-eyed and green from Donegal. It was a world away from her home in Ireland. From the large wooden sign hung over the wide entranceway to the tall fir trees that lined the road, the ranch looked like a movie set. There were green fields with horses grazing in them and a white mustang had galloped straight towards the gate to check out who was coming in. She'd never thought about that trip in terms of her bravery before, it was simply something she felt she had to experience. She had a plan and went for it. But maybe Kate had a point.

Saoirse wondered if she could channel some of that bravado into her future.

Esme coughed, and then Kate and she exchanged a look. 'I wasn't prying, but when I brought you to your room last night and left your phone on the dresser, I couldn't help noticing a ring . . .'

Saoirse felt her aunt's eyes upon her, and she knew that she could no longer hide her engagement. It was getting silly. Not to mention that in four days Finn was due to arrive. She still couldn't pinpoint why she'd been feeling so anxious about the engagement since she touched down in Bermuda. But the longer she was away from Finn, the less certain she felt about the easy yes she'd given only a week ago.

If she was back home, she wouldn't feel like this. *Would she?* Saoirse closed her eyes and thought about Finn and their special bench in the copse overlooking Ballymastocker Bay. And as if she'd conjured him up somehow, her phone buzzed.

Saoirse moved the sound to silent and turned the phone face down.

'You don't want to get that?' Esme asked.

'Not right now,' Saoirse said. At last, the phone stopped vibrating, and Saoirse waited for the voicemail notification to ping. It didn't come. She pushed that aside and told her aunts she would be back in a moment. A colossal event had happened to her, and she didn't want to keep the news to herself one more moment. Saoirse returned and held out her hand, now with the ring sitting prettily on it.

'Finn and I are getting married,' Saoirse said, shyly showing Kate and Esme her ring. Kate raised an eyebrow, then reached for her glasses that hung from a gold chain around her neck and took a closer look.

'That's a beauty. I like it,' Kate said. 'You kept that quiet.'

Saoirse flushed. How could she explain her reluctance to share her good news? She decided to say nothing.

Kate handed her glasses to Esme, who was peering at the ring with scrunched eyes. 'The ring is exquisite. Your farmer did well choosing an emerald. A perfect choice for you. Congratulations,' Esme said, clapping her hands together in delight. 'We are so happy you shared this with us. Now tell us everything, do not leave out a single detail!'

'The ring is vintage. His great aunt left it to Finn years ago to one day give to a future bride,' Saoirse said with great pride. She twirled her hand, looking at the ring from every angle.

'He knows you well. You'd never want a new diamond,' Kate said with approval.

Saoirse acknowledged this with a nod. You only had to look around her cottage in Donegal to see that she loved all things pre-loved. She'd filled her home with antique finds from auctions and charity shops.

'And there's a nice energy about the ring,' Esme decided. 'It feels like it's filled with love.'

Saoirse couldn't help spluttering out in a burst of laughter, 'By all accounts, his aunt was very loving. She was married four times. This was her first engagement ring.'

'Ha! Well, it's filled with love now. That I know for sure.

And this will be your first and only engagement ring. That's what matters,' Esme said. Then in realization at her words, she put a hand to her mouth, 'Sorry, child! You know what I mean.'

A flash of silver from a beer can tab placed tenderly on her finger. A temporary engagement ring that she'd loved until a small diamond ring was bought. Saoirse pushed that memory away. Maybe she could pretend her disastrous first marriage never happened if she didn't think about it.

'When is the wedding?' Kate asked, moving the conversation to safer ground again.

'No date set,' Saoirse replied, twisting the ring on her finger, feeling shy and awkward with the attention. When she told her parents, they'd been happy, but their enthusiasm for her news had been far more restrained than her aunts'. Now, she could feel Kate's eyes on her, watching her face closely, and Saoirse felt a blush creep its way over her cheeks.

'I'm a little confused why you have not been wearing the ring,' Kate said.

Saoirse looked down at her sparkling emerald, avoiding the knowing eyes of her aunt, and tried to come up with a plausible excuse. She stuttered and stammered about wanting to wait for the right moment. But the look on her aunts' faces left her in no doubt that they didn't buy one word.

'Do you both feel up to a short trip? I haven't been to the dockyard in a long time. And last night, it was in my dreams again. I'd like to see it, if your hangover can cope, that is,' Kate said, rescuing Saoirse.

'The tea has cured me. I'm in!' Saoirse said, then whispered 'Thank you,' to her aunt for letting her off the hook. For now, at least.

TWENTY-ONE

Kate

Royal Naval Dockyard, Bermuda

They took a taxi, agreeing that comfort was in need for them all today. Kate refused to be drawn on why she wanted to visit the Royal Naval Dockyard. Esme had accused her of enjoying keeping them in suspense earlier. And if she was honest, there was a truth to that. So much of her life was out of her control now. Her inability to stay awake for more than five hours in a row was the most annoying. Her legs often refused to cooperate unless they had something to lean on. Her arthritic hands, which were twisted in pain and age, were useless for most tasks. So yes, she'd take her wins where she could.

In truth though, Kate wanted to bring them to the Royal Naval Dockyard, as Matthew had brought her and Eliza back in 1939. She watched the island pass her by through the taxi window. The landscape was much unchanged through the decades. Palm trees danced against the blue skies now, as they had back then. Out on the water in the distance, she watched two cruise ships appear as they turned towards the dockyard. Kate blinked as her eyes played tricks on her, turning the cruise liners into naval battleships for a split second.

Kate directed the driver to stop near the museum, and they got out into the warm Bermudian air. The driver promised to return in two hours to bring them home again.

She watched Saoirse spin around in a 360-degree twirl, taking in everything from the walled perimeter to the cannon guns that sat under a canopy of palm trees. 'This is pretty awesome, Aunt Kate.'

'It looked a little different when I first saw it. This area here is the Keep. It was the final line of defence for the dockyard during the war. I remember people milling about everywhere. It was a hive of activity in 1939, with hundreds of naval officers and volunteers stationed here. The dockyard was a strategic outpost during both the First and Second World Wars,' Kate said. She looked out to the Atlantic Ocean and pointed to the distance. 'Bermuda is at the centre of Europe and the New World, so it was the perfect spot for the headquarters of the Royal Navy.'

'It was often referred to as the Gibraltar of the West, a symbol of the British Empire's might,' Esme added. 'My father was a volunteer, he worked here too, in the kitchens.'

Saoirse pointed toward two clocktowers that stood tall and proud at over one hundred feet tall, their grey steeples resplendent against the blue skies. 'Were they here then?'

'Oh yes. They're a shopping mall nowadays, but in

1939 they housed administration offices,' Kate said. She pointed to a row of terraced buildings that were now souvenir shops. 'These used to be houses for the naval officers and their families.'

She ambled into one of the shops, and Saoirse and Esme followed her in. It had open brick walls with old cedar beams supporting the ceiling and cedar boards on the floor, with knots ingrained into the wood. Kate tried to reimagine it as it had been when she was five.

'This is where the kitchen was,' she said, pivoting around as she found her bearings. In its place now, the wall had floor-to-ceiling shelving displaying bucket hats and flat caps, T-shirts and tote bags for sale.

'My first home in Bermuda. Boxes arrived, stacked high, ready for Mom. I remember she was so excited when she opened a box with an electric mixer in it. She'd never had one before. I was mesmerized by an electric fan. I'd stand in front of it for ages, feeling the air whip through my hair.'

'I can't believe that they had electricity,' Saoirse marvelled.

'Oh yes. We had all the mod cons. And over there, by the till, that was where the kitchen table and chairs sat. We bought them in Hamilton. And a large crystal vase sat on top of the table.'

Kate looked around again, looking right and left until she found what she was looking for. 'Through that door was the master bedroom. And off that room, there was a more modest room that was mine, filled with more toys and teddy bears than I'd ever had in my entire life.'

Kate closed her eyes and imagined herself falling back into a pile of soft velvet cushions and cuddly toys that nestled on the single bed, waiting to catch her. She had loved that bedroom. In Ireland, before, she had shared a single room with her mammy, daddy and Richie. So this terraced home had felt like a mansion. That was until she saw the Commissioner's House.

Kate walked into the courtyard again and pointed to a residential house that sat atop a hill overlooking the Atlantic Ocean. A grand Georgian House with a distinctive cast-iron facade and limestone walls.

'I went to a party in the Commissioner's House once. What a night that was! Mom bought me a new dress. It was incredibly exciting.'

Saoirse muttered a little more about knowing nothing about Kate's life. She clearly had questions, but was doing a valiant job at respecting Kate's boundaries. Kate remembered it all like it was yesterday, how it was when they arrived in Bermuda. As survivors of the *Athenia*, they found themselves thrust into the limelight. People wanted to talk to them both, to hear their first-hand experiences. The problem was, neither Eliza nor Kate were comfortable discussing the horrors they'd experienced. Kate clutched her chest as a sharp pain pierced it.

Matthew had done his best to shield them from the unsought fame. She remembered him explaining that people were born with morbid curiosity – and he wasn't wrong about that. It was evident every time rubberneckers caused a traffic jam by slowing down to stare at a car crash.

'Do you want to go up to see the house?' Saoirse asked, looking doubtful as she took in the steep hill it sat on.

Kate looked down at her legs, which were already fatigued from their short walk to the house. Could she manage it?

She firmly believed that she was still alive today because she rarely sat still. The more she moved, the stronger her body was. But she was also a realist. Her body had moved on to a new stage. Her skin was thinner. There was a large conker-shaped bruise from a knock she didn't remember on the back of her hand. Her nails were short, and she couldn't recall the last time she'd needed to file them. Every part of her was slowing down. Kate took in the faint beads of sweat on both Saoirse and Esme's foreheads from the midday sun. Her sweat glands had given up too. That was no loss, she supposed.

Kate knew that, no matter how much she willed herself to do it, she could not walk up that hill.

Saoirse and Esme shared a glance, understanding.

'It's too far, love,' Esme said. 'I dare say for me too. Let's sit in the Frog and Onion and have a cold drink. You can paint a picture of life here at the dockyard for us. Colour in the grey, so we understand what it was like for you.'

'One minute. I'm not having this! There must be a way,' Saoirse said, running towards the shop.

Five minutes later, she returned, triumphantly telling Kate to 'wait and see'. Kate supposed she was getting revenge for all her own secrecy. Good for her. Then a man appeared in the distance, pushing a wheelchair.

'I asked the shopkeeper if we could hire a wheelchair. It turns out we can't, but when I explained why you wanted to go up, she made a phone call. She knew that a shop owner in the Clocktower Mall had a wheelchair in storage. And, long story short, a deal was agreed upon, and we've hired it! So I can wheel you up that hill. I'll be your legs.'

'I'd never manage the steps,' Kate said, afraid to get her hopes up, yet feeling a buzz of excitement.

'There's a lift – I checked.' Saoirse beamed with delight.

Kate watched her pass a folded wodge of cash into the man's hands. Kate's eyes filled with tears of gratitude as she took her seat in her new wheels, but they were soon forgotten as Esme pretended to climb aboard on her lap. Giggling, the trio made their way towards the Commissioner's House. Saoirse took off with great speed, and Kate whooped with delight as the wind whipped her hair from her face. She wasn't running, but she was moving with speed. Alive. Living.

The hill slowed them down, but credit had to be given to Saoirse, who tackled it without complaint. They stopped several times to give her and Esme a chance to catch their breath.

'Where do you want to go?' Saoirse asked when they finally arrived.

'Up to the top floor, out on to the veranda. I want to see the same view I saw that night at the party.'

They moved into the elevator and headed up to the North Reception Room. Polished mahogany floors shone, with glass cabinets in rows displaying memorabilia of the house's past. The high vaulted ceiling had a large wooden fan at its centre.

'This room was full the night of the party. The Commissioner and all the officers were in full dress uniform. Their medals were worn proudly, as shiny as their black shoes. And the women, mostly officer's wives, the best of society, were all there in evening gowns that sparkled like the stars in the sky. I had never seen anything like it. I clung to Mom's hand as we walked into this very room. And then we went outside.' Kate pointed to the large patio doors, and Saoirse took the hint, pushing her through them.

They moved out to the wrap-around porch, which offered panoramic views of the island. Shutters framed the long windows, open atop golden flagstones.

'You know what, I bet my father worked here the night of that event. He often helped out in the kitchens when the Commissioner entertained,' Esme said, in wonder.

'It appears that ghosts of both our pasts are here,' Kate said, patting Esme's hand. Then she gripped either side of her wheelchair and pushed herself up. She walked over to the cast-iron railing and looked down to the gardens below.

'I stood here that night, watching bright-hued little birds dart in and out of the hibiscus bushes below,' Kate pointed downwards.

A seagull swooped by, cawing as it moved, the complete opposite of the dainty birds Kate had just spoken off. They looked at each other, the juxtaposition so absurd it made them burst into peals of laughter.

Then Kate walked back to her wheelchair and retook her seat. For a moment she saw the ghost of her mom and Matthew standing in front of her, talking animatedly.

She didn't know why, but that night, Mom had been on edge. Kate had never seen her anything but calm. Even as the ship went down, she'd been unflappable. But as she watched her speak to Matthew's friends and colleagues, she'd been distracted. Now, of course, Kate knew why. And she marvelled at how she'd held it all together.

TWENTY-TWO

Eliza

October 1939
Hamilton, Bermuda

Eliza applied the brakes on her bike, resting it against the post office wall. Wearing wide-legged trousers and a blouse, with a headscarf to keep her hair pinned, she breathed in the perfumed scent of the flowers that lined the winding street. She had fallen in love with the tropical isle of Bermuda within moments of her arrival. The air here was deliciously pure, with no factories on the island and cars banned from the streets.

'Can I wait out here while you go in?' Kate asked, using her Mary Jane black shoes to bring her own bike to a skidded stop beside Eliza. They had borrowed the bikes from the hotel concierge.

They had been out running errands for the past hour, the last of which was to post some letters, one to Larry and Eimear in Donegal and another to Mrs Montague in New York. Eliza felt another stab of pride as she looked down at the two white envelopes, where she had neatly written, in the top right corner, her new address at the Royal Naval Dockyard. By the time these letters reached her friends, she would not only be a married woman, but would also be living in her new home.

Their new home.

Over the previous month, since their arrival in Bermuda, Eliza and Kate had adjusted to many changes. As promised, Matthew had arranged lodgings for Eliza and Kate at the Tom Moore's Tavern in Hamilton Parish. It was once a private house, but when the Irish poet came to Bermuda in 1804, he fell in love with it. The seventeenth-century building stood alone in a wooded conclave of cedar trees, with the sea on one side and a mangrove-bordered lake on the other. The gabled tavern was handsome, with casement windows, and Eliza loved the simplicity of their double room, with white linens and comfortable bedding.

When Matthew brought them both to view their new home at the Royal Naval Dockyard, though, Eliza felt a rush of conflicting emotions. His officer's house was in a row of terraced cottages and, while Matthew had always warned her that work might be necessary to make it a home, upon inspection, she realized this was a big understatement. It was dark and dismal, needing a lot of work before it would be suitable for them to even move in. And this in turn meant that their wedding would have to wait a further few weeks too.

Matthew worried, though, that she was using this as an excuse.

Was she?

Admittedly, she could acknowledge that there was some truth to that. But rather than avoiding the wedding, Eliza was sure she just felt grateful for their time in the tavern, which allowed her and Kate a moment to acclimate to Bermudian life – and to each other – before their lives changed dramatically one more time.

The cottage wasn't all bad, though. It had a lot going for it, too, with a fish pond within the grounds ensuring a plentiful supply of fresh fish for their table, and, a short walk away from the ocean. While the house was damp, at least this could be forgiven thanks to the pretty gardens at the rear of the terraces.

Eliza had spent over two weeks cleaning the cottage from top to bottom with the help of a friendly Bermudian lady called Delta, who was to be their housemaid. Delta's brother also pitched in and painted the walls inside bright white. Eliza bought new curtains, bed linen and soft furnishings, and soon they had transformed the dark cottage into a home she now looked forward to living in. They could have a happy home here, she was sure of it. One filled with laughter, kindness and love too.

And when Matthew told Eliza that he would buy her fresh flowers every week for the rest of their lives, to place in a vase that sat on the kitchen table, she threw her arms around him and kissed him on his lips, not caring that they had an audience watching. He was such a romantic and she couldn't quite believe that this was her life now. For years, the only romance she saw was in the movies, at the cinema in Rathmullan, or in novels. Now, every day Matthew proved his promise to her on the day he proposed, through his actions. He loved her. And she was falling in love with him too.

But no matter how content Eliza was in her new life with her new lodgings, Kate continued to be a worry. She was withdrawn and too quiet as she mourned the loss of her family. There seemed to be nothing Eliza could do to get through to her.

To try to cheer the little girl up, Matthew had insisted that no money be spared on the house, particularly when decorating Kate's bedroom. It was painted a pretty lemon, and her bed was filled with soft toys and gifts from many of the nearby officers' wives. And yet, for every time she played happily with them, another time they would find her sobbing her little heart out, clutching the teddies tight to her chest.

The other officers' wives who lived at the dockyard were kind and would call over to visit with a cake fresh from the oven. But this also came with a multitude of questions about the experience Kate and Eliza had endured on board the *Athenia*. As the newspapers had been filled with survivor stories, having two people who had walked away from the sinking ship was big news in the dockyard. Eliza found this uncomfortable, partly because she had never felt comfortable being the centre of attention, but mostly because she knew the subject was harrowing for Kate. No matter how often Eliza tried to get her to open up about it and talk through her feelings, Kate refused. Matthew believed they should let her move through her grief in her own way. And maybe he was right.

Now, Eliza regarded the little girl as she leaned the child-size bike beside her own at the post office. Kate looked adorable in a new blue gingham summer dress, long white socks and black Mary Jane shoes. Her hair was tied back in two pigtails secured with bright red bows and she was clinging to a pretty doll that Matthew had bought her. To a casual observer she might seem no different to any other five-year-old, but when you looked closely into her eyes, you could see the hurt and pain of her losses, and not a night went by without her crying out in her sleep as a new nightmare overtook her.

'I can sit here,' Kate said, pointing to a bench a few feet from the post office. 'I don't want to go inside.' She tilted her chin obstinately.

Eliza looked around her, searching for potential dangers. Yes, the street was busy with shoppers, but she wouldn't be long. She had to learn to trust the girl. Matthew had said more than once that she was mollycoddling Kate. It was difficult, though. Eliza's first instinct was to keep her close. Keep her safe.

'Okay, but do not move from here. I'll be back soon,' Eliza kissed her lightly on her forehead and watched until Kate was safely ensconced on the bench. She walked into the large, bright shop and made her way to join the queue at the cashier.

Eliza listened to the locals in front of her chat about their days. She loved their accents, clipped and polite, British but with a slight American twang. In front of her, a gentleman wore shorts to his knees, with socks almost reaching their hem. Traditional attire for Bermudian men. Two women discussed the ocean and whether the sounds of the waves that morning signalled a storm. Eliza shivered at the thought, although she was on safe ground. Maybe it wasn't just Kate who had her demons.

When it was Eliza's turn, the cashier greeted her warmly. This was another thing that Eliza loved about the island: there was genuine warmth from the locals.

She had felt welcomed and included by everyone from the get-go.

'Two first-class stamps please, one for Ireland and one for New York,' Eliza said to the cashier, then started when she felt a tug on her dress. Kate was beside her, jumping up and down with delight. Eliza's own heart leapt with joy seeing the girl so animated.

'I met someone from Ireland,' Kate said, excited by this exchange.

'Oh, how nice for you. One second, you can tell me everything once I've paid.' She opened her handbag, took out her purse, and handed a dollar to the cashier.

'Can I lick the stamps?' Kate asked, sticking her tongue out.

Eliza dabbed the stamps on her tongue one by one, and then placed them on the envelopes.

'Now, you can put them in that box over there.' She directed Kate to the postbox. Once the letters were safely on their way, Eliza took Kate by the hand and left the shop.

'Tell me about the person you met before we make our way back to the tavern. I'd like us to have a quiet afternoon, perhaps even a nap, before the reception at the Commissioner's House this evening,' Eliza said.

Kate wasn't interested in any of that. 'The Irish man sat on the bench beside me to tie his shoelace. He said that he was forever tripping up over his laces. He was funny. He had a huge camera, and he took my photograph!' Kate said, grinning. 'Do you think I'll be in a magazine?'

Eliza wasn't sure she liked the sound of that. A stranger taking a snap of her child? She looked around, squinting in the bright sun, looking for the man.

'Let's go,' Eliza said hurriedly, grabbing her bicycle.

'Can we go for a walk on the beach first, like you promised?' Kate seemed unfazed by Eliza's unease.

'Of course, we can,' Eliza said, smiling at this unexpected enthusiasm. 'We might see turtles if we're lucky. Hop on your bike, and let's get going.'

They were back at the tavern within minutes, giving their borrowed bikes back to the concierge. Matthew had promised them that he would buy them each a bike of their own once they moved into their cottage. He'd seen how much Eliza and Kate enjoyed whizzing around the island and, as he kept telling them both, his joy was making them happy.

He was, unfortunately, also swamped, which was understandable now that the country was at war. He oversaw a new base called RN Air Station, Bermuda, located on Boaz Island. It had two large hangars and slipways to the sea on both sides. Eliza and Kate had visited once in their first week, and had both been open-mouthed at its immense size. It was a hive of activity, the teams there working round the clock to replenish and restore warships and work on the merchant ships of each Allied nation.

This evening, though, they would see Matthew for the last time before the wedding. Eliza's heart jumped at the thought. She was looking forward to joining him at the party. Perhaps they could even steal a kiss when Kate was not looking.

After a restorative cold drink in the lobby, Eliza and Kate strolled to the nearby beach, with Kate excitedly talking about turtles.

'At home, when I used to go to Ballymastocker Bay, I would always take my shoes off and chase the waves. Do you want to give it a go?' Eliza asked when they arrived at the sandy shore. She pulled her headscarf off and let her long ebony hair dance in the sea breeze.

Kate had already removed her shoes and pulled off her stockings, throwing them to the ground. Eliza bent down to gather the child's things, and they began walking to the water's edge.

'The man said he liked my necklace. That's why he wanted to take a photograph of me. He said it reminded him of Ireland,' Kate said, pointing to the Claddagh ring she still wore on a chain around her neck. 'He pulled a funny face when he looked at it.'

'Claddagh rings are popular at home in Ireland. Maybe he remembered someone from his past,' Eliza said, as she rolled up her own trousers to paddle alongside Kate.

Eliza had hinted the previous week that Kate might give her back her Claddagh ring, but the little girl had been adamant that she wanted to keep it. She truly believed in its magic. For a long time, Eliza would never have dreamed that she would let the ring out of her sight. But so much had changed since then.

'Look, over there, it's a turtle!' Kate exclaimed, distracted again already.

A group of turtles were lazily swimming into their sightline. Eliza watched them for a moment, then from the corner of her eye she saw a figure standing with his back to her in the distance. She stopped, feeling her heartbeat accelerate. His broad shoulders reminded her of . . .

The man turned, and Eliza felt her legs give way. She dropped Kate's shoes and stockings into the sand.

Kate called out hello to the man and waved enthusiastically as if she were meeting an old friend.

'Look, it's the camera man! Did you see the turtles?'

Eliza closed her eyes and reopened them, sure that the tropical heat had made her hallucinate.

But there was no doubt – standing a few feet from her was Davey.

TWENTY-THREE

Eliza

Tom Moore's Tavern, Hamilton Parish, Bermuda

The man standing before Eliza looked as confused as she felt. He raised a hand, then dropped it again. Dazed, almost, Eliza moved closer. For years after his death, she had imagined that she saw Davey on the street, on the bus, on the beach. But each time it was a trick of her imagination. She knew that this must be the case now. A cruel trick of her mind. She closed her eyes, opening them slowly. But he was still there.

The man had a mop of curly brown hair, just like Davey's, and his eyes were steel grey. He wore an open-necked white shirt with the sleeves rolled up, revealing muscled, tanned arms. A camera hung low across his chest. And most heartrending of all, perched at an impossible angle on his head was a grey cap.

It was this that made Eliza gasp out loud. There was no doubt that cap was Davey's, and his father's before him.

As Eliza tried to make sense of these details, telling herself that it was a coincidence, nothing more, she heard the ghost call out her name on a strangled sob. 'Eliza!'

And then he was running towards her. But no matter how hard she tried, she could not make herself move to him.

'I thought you were dead . . .' she cried, at the exact moment he said, 'They said you died.'

Everything else on the beach disappeared for Eliza, Kate included, as he reached her, finally stopping close enough so she could touch him. All she could see was Davey, *her* Davey, standing before her. And then, finally, her agonizing wait was over, and she was in his arms once more. He called her name repeatedly, holding her face between his hands and kissing her tear-stained cheeks.

'I can't believe this is true. Am I dreaming? My darling, my sweetheart, *mo grá*,' Davey was saying now, as she struggled to believe what was right in front of her. He took a step back to look at her but didn't let go of her shoulders, as if afraid she might disappear again.

'If you are dreaming, then I am too,' Eliza said through her tears.

Her body felt light and heavy at once. Her head spun with questions. She didn't trust that what she was seeing was true. The heat of the Bermudian sun beat down on her face, and this time, instead of leaning into the warmth, she felt a wave of dizziness overcome her. 'I need to sit.'

'Of course,' Davey said, his face creasing in worry. He looked around him for a suitable place.

But Eliza crumpled on to the pink sands right where she had been standing. She half sat, half lay, in an undignified slump, having lost all use of herself.

Then she heard a voice, filled with fear, whisper from behind her, 'Eliza? What's wrong?'

Kate, white with worry, stood above her, trying to understand what was going on.

Hearing her voice brought Eliza back to some sensibility. She sat up straight and said to the girl, 'I'm okay, Kate, I promise. I got a fright, that's all. Davey – Mr McDaid, is an old friend from Donegal.'

'He's my friend too. He's the man I told you about on the bench with the camera,' Kate said. 'Hello again.' She smiled at Davey.

'That's my ring,' he said, pointing to Kate's necklace.

'Yes. That's your ring,' Eliza said weakly. She couldn't think of anything else she could add.

'There's a tavern a few minutes' walk from here. Do you think you could manage that?' Davey suggested, concern in his voice. 'I could get you some tea? Or perhaps something stronger.'

'Your voice sounds different,' Eliza said, ignoring his questions. 'Is it really you?'

'Aye. It's me,' he said, and then his face broke out into a wide grin. It was Davey, all right, his face now reverting to the one she'd grown up with. His voice was definitely different, though. It still had echoes of the soft Donegal lilt, but there was also a definite American twang in it.

'We are staying in Tom Moore's Tavern. Perhaps that would be a good place to go,' Eliza said.

Davey held his hand out to her, and Eliza looked at it in wonder. He had done this a hundred times in their past while walking the sands of Ballymastocker Bay and a hundred times more in her dreams. And now, again, unbelievably, after all this time, here he was doing it again.

'I know,' Davey said, looking down at their clasped hands, his voice trembling in instant understanding.

'I like tea too,' Kate said, unaware of the emotional undercurrent between Eliza and Davey. 'But I like mine with two spoons of sugar.'

'And do you like cake or ice cream?' Davey asked, turning to her, as Eliza pulled her hand back.

'Both!' Kate exclaimed, skipping along in front of them.

'Well, we shall have to have both with our tea then,' Davey replied. He offered Eliza the crook of his arm as they began to walk, but Eliza pretended she didn't notice and instead walked by his side, a few inches apart. Her engagement ring burned on her finger, and she glanced at Davey's hand, but couldn't see if he wore a band of gold himself. The thought that he might be married pierced her so deep she almost expected to see blood stain her cream blouse.

'I have so many questions. My head is spinning,' Davey said.

'Can they wait until we're seated? I'm not sure I can take any further shocks,' Eliza said.

'We have all the time in the world,' Davey replied, looking sideways at her.

But they didn't, did they? Tomorrow, Eliza would marry Matthew. And at that thought, a lump grew in her throat, so big that she almost cried aloud.

The concierge found them a booth in the lounge, in a quiet corner, as requested by Davey. With ease, he placed an order with their waiter. He was no longer the young man she'd last spent time with, unused to restaurants. There was an air of assurance radiating from him. Eliza couldn't take her eyes off him. And it seemed to be the same for Davey. They looked at each other, taking in every new line on their faces, and every now and then, they laughed with joy. Kate watched them constantly, agog with interest.

Shortly after they sat down, the waiter arrived with a large pot of tea and cakes for everyone. 'There's a box of books and games in the corner by the bookshelf, that my daughter plays with when she's in the restaurant. Your little one is welcome to play with them when she's finished her cake.'

'Thank you,' Eliza replied, smiling at the waiter.

She felt Davey's eyes watching her again. Flushed, she placed the strainer on a china cup and poured their tea, one by one.

'Do you still take one sugar and lots of milk?' Eliza asked.

'You remembered,' he smiled.

'I remember everything,' Eliza said. She decided to add two spoons of sugar to her own drink. Her mam always used to say it was suitable for shock.

'Can I take my cake over there to play?' Kate asked, now bored with the adults' chit-chat.

'Yes, darling,' Eliza replied. She helped Kate settle into her nook in the corner, placing her cake, a bowl of ice cream and a milky tea in front of her. Eliza gave her a quick hug and then returned to her seat.

'You have a daughter,' Davey said. Then his eyes dropped to Eliza's left hand, taking in the diamond ring. 'And you're married.'

His voice was soft, but his smile slipped, his eyes filled with new pain.

Eliza looked down at his hand and felt joy course through her when she saw his fingers were bare from gold.

'I'm engaged. Not married. Yet,' Eliza replied, holding her breath as she waited for his reaction.

Shock filled his face at this news as he looked between Kate to Eliza's engagement ring.

'Kate is my adopted daughter. Or will be, anyway, once I'm married. We were both on the *Athenia* last month. And her family were killed, making her my ward,' Eliza explained.

Immediately, the tone of his voice switched to concern. 'Were you hurt?' he asked, reaching over the table for her hand. Worried that Kate might be confused if she saw her holding hands with another man, Eliza pulled back.

'I'm fine. We're fine,' Eliza said.

'I am sure that's not true. I cannot imagine what you must have both been through. Was your fiancé with you?' he asked.

'No. I was on my way to meet him here when the *Athenia* went down. Chance put Kate in my path.' She looked over to Kate, who was trying to fit a heaped spoon of ice cream into her mouth. 'But I love her with my heart as if she were my own.'

Eliza picked up her cup and took a sip. The hot drink was calming; drinking tea somehow made the situation feel less surreal.

She looked at Davey. Her first love. And suddenly she was consumed by the need to find out where he'd been all this time. It was unbearable to think that he'd left her alone all these years.

'You never came back,' she said, her voice trembling.

Davey's voice was quiet when he responded. 'Not because

I didn't want to. We were arrested, my brother Paddy and I. And we ended up in the *Argenta* prison ship in Belfast.'

'I knew that much. I used my contacts at the *Rathmullan Gazette* to trace you there.'

He acknowledged this with another smile. 'It was hell on earth on that ship. We watched fellow prisoners die from the conditions or be marched outside for execution. But I never gave up hope. Because I had you to go home to. My darling, beautiful Eliza.'

His words washed over her like a balm. He'd thought of her as much as she had of him.

'I don't understand,' she said, still confused. 'Then why didn't you come back to me?'

'Johnjo Quigley was arrested and joined us on the ship. You know, from up Knockalla way.'

She nodded. She knew of the man, but he wasn't a close acquaintance.

'He brought news from home. And he told me you had *died*, Eliza.' Pain flashed across Davey's face with his words. He reached over and grabbed her hands between her own as if checking once more that she was real. 'Johnjo was adamant that a fire had killed your whole family. He swore that he knew it to be true. And yet here you are, and I am at a loss why he would say such a thing to me.'

'There was a fire. It took Mam, Dad and the boys,' Eliza said, her voice trembling. 'But I was down in the village on an errand. When I came back, only burned ashes remained of my home.'

A muscle in Davey's jaw twitched as he took this news in. 'My darling. I am so sorry. I cannot imagine the pain that must have been for you, losing your whole family,' Davey said, tears filling his eyes.

'It was the most horrific time of my life,' Eliza said, bowing her head.

'Please understand that I thought I had nothing to go home to Donegal for. Without you, Eliza, I couldn't face going back. It would have been a reminder of all that I had lost. Or so I thought.' He banged the table with his fist.

Eliza felt a flash of anger too. Years of pain, for what? 'So where did you go?' She tried to keep her voice level now, as she took it all in.

'When we were released from HMS *Argenta* in 1924, Paddy decided to try his luck in America and talked me into joining him. In truth, I was a shell of my former self back then. If Paddy hadn't taken me under his wing, pulling me physically on board the ship that brought us to New York, I would be dead now, I'm convinced of it. Without you, I had no will to live.'

His eyes blazed with sorrow and anger at the cruel twist of fate that had conspired to keep them apart for so long.

'When you didn't come home, I waited for years, never believing that you were truly gone. But then I had no choice but to accept that you had died. My editor made enquiries for me and he was told that it was most likely that you and your brother had been executed. I mourned you, Davey, for years; I mourned your death and lost myself in my grief.' A tear escaped her emerald-green eyes.

'And I mourned yours. What a waste. All this time, we could have been together.'

They sat in silence drinking their tea, both lost in their thoughts of what-ifs and what might have been.

'Tell me about your life now,' Eliza asked. She nodded towards his camera, smiling. 'You're a photographer, as you always dreamed?'

241

Davey smiled, 'I am. Freelance mostly, but I've been featured in *National Geographic*. I make a decent living from it and have a house in Boston, which is my base. It's near to Paddy and his family. He married an Italian girl – Rosa. They've five kids, who I adore. They own a pub. I've been known to do a few shifts at the bar between photography gigs.'

'You travel?' Eliza said in awe. 'I am so proud of you. You did it, Davey.'

'Every place I've been to, I told myself, this is for Eliza. I took you with me on each journey. You may not have been by my side, but you were always here.' He pointed to his heart.

Suddenly not caring who might be watching, Eliza reached over and took his hands in hers.

'You've been in my heart every day, too. I've never stopped loving you.'

The waiter returned to see if they needed anything further, raising an eyebrow when he saw them leaning in close together. Eliza pulled back her hands, and as she did, she caught sight of Matthew's engagement ring. It was as good as a bucket of ice-cold water. She was no longer a free woman. She could not hold hands with another man, no matter how much she longed to.

Davey picked up his camera from the mahogany table, and, looking through his lens at Eliza, he fired several shots.

'If you knew how many times I have longed to take your photograph. Or wished I had taken one before I left, to carry with me always. One day, I should like to do so properly.'

He grinned, looking like he used to as a kid when he'd done something he was pleased about.

'You should have given me notice. I must look a mess,' Eliza said, brushing her hair behind her ears and wishing she'd worn powder on her face this morning.

'Eliza Lavery, you are the most beautiful woman I've ever known, with a mind so quick, I spent my youth trying to keep up. If you could only see yourself as I see you.'

'Tell me,' Eliza whispered.

'Emerald-green eyes which are more oval than round, and when the sun hits them, you can see flecks of moss green. Your face, shaped like a heart, is as beautiful as the heart inside you. You have a dimple on one side when you smile, like now. And your rosebud lips are the colour of the pink sands here in Bermuda. Lips that I've dreamed of every night . . . Forgive me, but you are perfect as you are. My best friend, my first love, my *only* love.'

Eliza had never felt more loved. 'Your only love . . .' she repeated in awe.

'Yes. I've never met anyone else who stood a chance of taking the place in my heart that you've had for all this time.'

With imperfect timing, Kate wandered back over to their table, her eyes darting between the two of them.

'What time is Matthew coming at?' she asked.

The question felt loaded, and Eliza's face coloured. She was behaving inappropriately; even a five-year-old could see it.

'We shall have to say goodbye,' Eliza said feebly to Davey. Her eyes searched his, imploring him to understand how much it cost her to say those words. She knew she would spend the rest of her days reliving this moment and wishing it could be another way.

'I can't do that,' Davey replied evenly. 'How can I let you go, now that I've found you?'

Eliza turned to Kate, ushering her back to her jigsaw. 'Five more minutes, then we will go back to our room. Go on now.'

Then she turned back to Davey. 'I am to be married tomorrow. To a good man, who has only shown love and affection to Kate and me.'

'Here on the island?' Davey asked. He pulled his hands through his hair, sucking air in through his teeth.

'Yes. Here. St Theresa's. The Church of the Little Flower. It's a pretty chapel.'

Davey held his hands over his face for a moment, then, slowly taking his hands away, he asked in a low voice, 'Do you love him?'

It was a question Eliza had asked herself so many times over the previous month. And yet it was still filled with many complications.

'When he proposed, I told him I didn't love him. That I had never stopped loving you.'

Davey exhaled deeply, hope fluttering in his eyes.

'But, I have developed feelings for Matthew over the past month. I didn't expect it to happen, but he's a kind man. Someone I could have a good life with.'

'You deserve more than a good life!' Davey exclaimed. 'You deserve *love* and joy and excitement!'

'He'll be here shortly,' Eliza continued curtly, ignoring Davey's words, 'and it would be cruel for him to find us together like this. I cannot hurt him. He doesn't deserve that.'

In truth, she wouldn't be seeing Matthew until later, when they'd arranged to meet at the dockyard. But Eliza needed the excuse to put some distance between her and Davey. If she remained in his company for another minute, she feared she would forget altogether that she was betrothed to another.

'We've done nothing wrong,' Davey protested. 'Let me talk to him. Man to man.'

'No!' Eliza said, holding her hand up. 'Whatever I decide to say to Matthew will be my own words. I do not need any man to talk on my behalf.' Her eyes flashed with anger.

'There's the Eliza I remember,' Davey said, grinning again. Then, leaning towards her, he said quietly, 'If you tell me you passionately love this man, I will walk away and respect your decision. Knowing you are alive and happy will be enough for me. I will endeavour to move on. But if you love me as I love you, I have no choice but to fight for us. Please do not expect me to do otherwise.'

It was as if Eliza's heart was splitting into two. It pulsated and raced as she tried to work out what to do. She looked over to Kate, who was frowning as she watched them from afar. She had to think about her, too. The child had been through so much.

'I have to go,' Eliza said, standing up. 'You will never know how much I wish you'd come back to Donegal. Or that I'd come here a single woman, so we could walk a different path. But *I am* getting married tomorrow.'

Davey stood up too and walked two paces to her side. He came so close to her that she could feel his breath on her cheeks. She breathed in his scent and, for a moment, almost gave in to kiss him.

He stepped back, but not before whispering, 'I love you, Eliza. It's not too late for us. And I will never give up hope that we can find a way back to each other.'

TWENTY-FOUR

Eliza

*The Commissioner's House, Royal Naval Dockyard,
Bermuda*

Eliza had insisted that Kate take a nap, if for nothing else
but to halt her constant stream of questions about Davey.
She herself sat at the bedroom window, watching the
comings and goings of the hotel grounds. Her mind was
spiralling as she pondered her next move.

Run to Davey.

*Accept that he was your past. Be happy that he's alive
and move on with your life with Matthew.*

Then back to *Run to Davey.*

Eventually, she bathed and dressed in the evening gown
Matthew had insisted on buying her, trying to prepare
for the evening ahead. It was black silk, with polychrome
sequins designed in spiralling fireworks. The bodice was
fitted, moulding to her curves as if it had been tailor-made

for her. She pinned her hair into a soft chignon with bobby pins and then powdered her face.

'You look like a movie star,' Kate's voice said dreamily from behind her as she woke up, sitting up in their bed.

Eliza twirled for her little girl, and there was no doubt that she'd never felt more glamorous in her life. It was a far cry from the ink-stained dresses she used to wear in the office in Rathmullan.

She helped Kate, who also had a new dress, get ready. It was similar to one worn by the actress Shirley Temple in the movie, *A Little Princess*. Black velvet knee-length, with a cream lace cape and sleeves.

'Now you look like a movie star too,' Eliza told her.

They travelled by boat to the dockyard, as arranged by Matthew. Eliza and Kate were used to this journey, as it was far quicker than horse and carriage. When they arrived at the port side, Matthew was standing waiting for them, smiling enthusiastically. He looked dashing in his dress uniform, and when she saw Kate skip to him, Eliza marvelled at how close the two had become already.

'My beautiful princess, you could give Shirley Temple a run for her money!' he declared, making Kate beam. 'And you, my darling Eliza, are a vision. I am the luckiest man alive to have you by my side.' He offered her his arm, and the three of them headed up the hill towards the Commissioner's House.

Eliza had never felt more like a fraud in her entire life. What would Matthew say if he could read her mind right now?

Lanterns shimmered on the cast-iron veranda, setting the house aglow, and the sounds of a string quartet filled the early evening air. Matthew greeted his friends warmly as they walked into the reception room. He was a social soul and obviously well-liked by his peers.

Waiters walked around the room with gold trays filled with coupes of sparkling champagne. Eliza sipped hers, hoping it might quell the butterflies that had taken up residence in her stomach. She had to find a way to talk to Matthew about Davey. Her head and heart were at odds. But opportunities were scarce as Eliza and Kate were introduced to prominent members of Bermudian society, making their way to meet them in a constant stream. When the admiral's wife, Lady Kennedy Purvis, joined them, she looked Eliza up and down.

'So you are the mysterious Irish woman who has captured Lieutenant Commander Lynch's heart? Many ladies here tonight are a little broken-hearted that such an eligible bachelor is about to marry.'

Matthew shuffled uncomfortably, 'I'm sure that's not true.'

Eliza's heart swelled at his obvious embarrassment. He had no idea how incredible he was.

'I'm sure it is,' Eliza retaliated. 'And I know how lucky I am. Ever since I met Matthew, he's shown me his generosity and love, through his every action.'

'Well, I will always counter that it is me who is the lucky one,' Matthew insisted, gently lifting Eliza's hand to his and kissing it. 'Did you know that Eliza is a journalist? She puts me through my paces daily with her knowledge of world politics.'

'Now that *is* interesting,' Lady Kennedy Purvis replied. 'Eliza, do tell me more.'

Eliza inclined her head in acknowledgement of the

compliment. 'I worked for the *Rathmullan Gazette* at home in Donegal for the past fifteen years as assistant editor. And I'd like to continue working after we marry. I hope to find a way to put my skills to good use. I believe that as well as being a helpmate to my husband, I can also have an active role in society.'

'Go on. Do tell me what you'd write about if given the chance,' Lady Kennedy Purvis encouraged.

Eliza took a moment to gather her thoughts. 'Yesterday, I had an interesting conversation with the owner of Tom Moore's Tavern about the decline in tourism on the island. I thought it would make an interesting piece to explore the war's impact on visitors coming to Bermuda. Perhaps an article for the local paper.'

'Good for you,' Lady Kennedy Purvis said. 'You must come for tea. The Ladies Hospitality Organization could use someone like you in our ranks. We have plans to play our part in the war effort too.'

Then she walked away, leaving Eliza and Matthew open-mouthed. 'You made quite an impression there,' Matthew said.

A waiter approached at that moment with a tray of hors d'oeuvres. Kate stuffed one whole in her mouth, then made a face when she discovered she didn't care for the taste. Matthew reached to take one, but Eliza had little appetite. Instead, she tried to broach the subject of Davey, but quickly lost courage as Matthew began to speak about his work at the naval base. It had been a particularly stressful day for him, he explained. Dozens of local Bermudians had been recruited into a newly established Royal Naval Volunteer Reserve, and there was much to do to prepare them for their new roles.

'I can only imagine how difficult it is for you right now,' Eliza sympathized. How could she add to Matthew's stress?

'I can handle anything, with you and Kate by my side. And I have good news, too. I have booked a photographer to take our formal wedding photograph tomorrow,' Matthew said, beaming.

Kate chimed in, 'We met Eliza's friend today. He's a photographer. He could take your picture if you invite him to the wedding.'

Matthew looked at Eliza in surprise. 'You never mentioned anything. Oh, I'm so pleased you have met someone you know here. It's true, the world is but a village.'

'I didn't get a chance to tell you yet,' Eliza said, feeling a flush form in her cheeks, giving her away.

'Who is this friend?' Matthew asked, and as if he could sense the answer to his question could only bring trouble, a frown creased his forehead.

'Can we go outside? I'd like to get some air,' Eliza said.

'Of course.' Matthew took her arm, and reached down to clasp Kate's hand in his own. Together they moved out to the veranda.

'His name is Davey,' Kate chirped happily, determined to be the news bearer.

Eliza had not wished to discuss such an important matter in front of Kate, but now she was left with little choice. She stopped as they reached the veranda and turned to look at her fiancé, taking a deep breath.

'At the beach earlier today, we met . . .' Eliza paused, unsure how to finish the sentence that she knew would cause Matthew pain.

She didn't need to, because recognition and shock moved across Matthew's face as he repeated the name. 'Davey, as in . . .'

'Yes. The man I believed to be dead,' Eliza said. Her words, calmly spoken, belied the maelstrom of emotions she felt inside.

A muscle clenched in Matthew's jawline. He placed his drink on a nearby table, then forced a smile on to his face as he turned to Kate.

'Will you go outside and tell me if it looks like it may rain later on?'

'We're already outside,' Kate said, confused. But something in Matthew's face made her walk away without further questioning.

Once she'd left on her errand, Matthew said, 'Tell me everything.'

Taking a steadying breath, Eliza relayed her conversation with Davey, careful to omit how she felt. She also refrained from telling Matthew about Davey's declaration of love. He listened quietly as she spoke, but he could not hide the flicker of pain in his eyes.

'That must have been upsetting for you,' he said, matter-of-factly, when she had finished.

She nodded. 'But it was also joyful. I'm happy to see that Davey is not only well but has thrived since we last saw each other.'

He accepted this with a slight incline of his head. 'And did you tell him of our wedding?'

Eliza nodded, 'But of course.'

'Then I only have one further question.'

Eliza braced herself, expecting him to ask her if she still loved Davey. And she knew that she could not deny her feelings, any more than the sun could be prevented from setting at the end of each day.

She held her breath, watching Matthew as he closed his eyes for a moment, as if in prayer. She hated that she was causing him pain, but could see no way to avoid it.

'Do you still . . .' Matthew stumbled on his words, unable to continue his question for a moment. Then, he seemed to change his mind and instead pulled a small box from his inside jacket pocket. 'I was going to arrange with the concierge to drop this to your room later as a surprise. But I think I'll give it to you now. I hope that you like it.'

He opened the lid to reveal a diamond charm bracelet, the gems glittering from the velvet bed they sat on.

Eliza gasped, she couldn't help herself. 'It's breathtaking,' she said.

Matthew closed the lid and pushed the box towards her, across the table. They both looked at it for a moment, but Eliza did not pick the bracelet up.

'You were going to ask me a question?' Eliza prompted.

'Forgive me. It's been a long day, and I want to be fully rested before tomorrow's wedding. Would you mind terribly if we said our goodbyes now? I'll arrange for an escort to take you back to the hotel.'

'Matthew . . .' Eliza began, but he cut her off, kissing her cheek softly.

'We'll have the rest of our lives to talk once we are married. I love you with all my heart, Eliza. You do know that, don't you? I'm not sure what I'd do if anything came between us.'

Then he turned on his heel, leaving Eliza reeling in his wake.

TWENTY-FIVE

Eliza

Tom Moore's Tavern, Hamilton Parish, Bermuda

On the morning of her wedding day, Eliza awoke to birdsong and the golden glow of the sun's first rays. She stretched in their double bed and tried to imagine what it might be like to wake up beside Matthew, rather than having the warm little body of Kate beside her. Unfortunately, every time she did, it was Davey's face she saw, not her fiancé's.

Her heart leapt at the thought of Davey, but she valiantly pushed it aside. She could not even think about him today; she feared she would not have the strength to go through with her wedding if she did. Matthew had made it clear last night that, as far as he was concerned, nothing had changed with the reappearance of Davey. And she was determined to do the same.

Their wedding would take place at 10 a.m. Afterwards,

they would travel to the Hamilton Princess hotel for a wedding breakfast. They'd both decided their wedding should be a simple affair, with no guests. They were not having a honeymoon, which was impossible now that they were at war, but Matthew had nevertheless insisted they spend their first night as a married couple in luxury, so he had booked a suite in the Hamilton Princess with adjoining bedrooms. To Matthew's credit, he had not complained when Eliza pointed out that Kate would have to go with them.

The wedding dress that Eliza had bought in Ireland was lost with the sinking of the *Athenia*, so she had no choice but to buy a second dress. She stood up now and looked at it, hanging on the back of the wardrobe door. A sleeveless white silk dress, with a short button-up crop jacket and a cap veil. It felt like a better choice in the warm Bermudian sun than the first one she'd bought in Ireland anyway.

Kate had said she looked like a princess in it when she'd first tried it on. Eliza didn't feel much like a princess now, though. Her heart ached. What she needed now was a friend. At this moment, all she wished was that Mrs Montague were by her side again to offer her forthright and wise counsel. What would she say?

Eliza walked to the dressing table and picked up the small jewellery box Matthew had given her the night before. Such a beautiful piece. She knew life with Matthew would be filled with more expensive trinkets and gowns, like those she'd been given in the past month. Constant declarations of his adoration. But more than that, his kindness, his strength of character, his fun nature, were all evident in his interactions with Kate too. He would be a great father, and she knew that the three of them could be happy together.

'Morning, Eliza!' Kate called out then, bringing her back to their room now.

'Good morning, little one,' Eliza called back. 'It's time to get ready, sleepyhead. We shall need to leave for the church within the hour.'

There was a knock on the door, and as Eliza went to open it, she told Kate over her shoulder, 'As a special treat, I've ordered room service to be delivered. Tea and hot buttered toast with strawberry jam!'

Once their breakfast was devoured, it was time to get ready. Eliza brushed Kate's hair into soft curls and tied it into pretty bunches. She carefully placed her white knee-length chiffon dress over her head.

'You look as pretty as a picture,' Eliza said as the little girl twirled around in circles, curtsying to her reflection in the mirror.

'Do we have to give the dresses back after the wedding?' Kate asked.

'No, my darling. They're ours to keep.'

Eliza then began her final preparations for herself. She styled her long hair into a chignon at the nape of her neck, then tweaked soft waves to frame her face. The dress, tailored to fit perfectly, accentuated her slim figure. With Kate's assistance, she pinned her cap veil to her hair, and finally they were ready.

'We need to put our jewellery on, silly!' Kate said. She ran to the dresser and returned with the diamond bracelet for Eliza and the Claddagh ring and chain for herself.

Her past and her present, side by side.

As Kate pulled the chain over her head, letting the ring

drop to her chest, Eliza felt a moment of dizziness. She was in a situation she felt she could not escape. As she closed the clasp on the bracelet around her wrist, it pinched her skin. Tears stung her eyes, and she could not stem them.

'Eliza, what's wrong?' Kate asked, her little nose scrunched up in worry.

'Nothing, dear. Just a wee nip that took me by surprise.'

But once the tears began, they released an avalanche of emotion. Everything from the past month came tumbling out, devastating her. As Eliza wept into her hands, Kate rubbed her back, the small child unsure how to help.

Then came another knock on the door, a voice calling out that their carriage had arrived to take them to the church.

'One moment,' Eliza called in response.

She rinsed a facecloth in cold water and patted her face to repair the damage of her tears. Her eyes were red, and her cheeks blotchy. She blew her nose and then used powder to attempt to even out her skin tone.

'It's as good as I can make it,' Eliza said, taking the little girl's hand. 'It's time for me to be brave now. No more tears.'

'No more tears,' Kate agreed, nodding solemnly.

And together, they made their way to the waiting horse and carriage below.

TWENTY-SIX

Saoirse

Present day
The Commissioner's House, Royal Naval Dockyard,
Bermuda

They'd arranged for their taxi driver to wait for them at the souvenir shop and, as promised, he was there by the time Saoirse wheeled Kate back down the hill. Soon, they were on their way home. Kate had become withdrawn again while on the veranda. Ghosts of her past catching up with her, was all she said. And this had struck a nerve with Saoirse. She too felt ghosts nipping at her, demanding attention. A wave of sadness overcame her, and tears threatened to fall.

Saoirse sat between her two aunts, and as the car trundled along, she could feel the warmth of their love encompass her. And she had never needed them more than she did now. She laid her head on Kate's shoulder, then reached over to hold Esme's hand.

'I love you both very much, I hope you know that,' she said, tears filling her eyes.

'We know, child,' Esme said, bringing Saoirse's hands to her soft lips for a kiss.

'And we love you too. And we're here to listen if you are ready to talk about whatever it is that is clearly bothering you,' Kate said.

Saoirse didn't know where to start. There were so many things flying around her mind. But she surprised herself by responding in a whisper, 'I'm afraid.'

'Of what, child?' Esme asked gently.

'Of making a mistake again. I've already got one failed marriage under my belt; what if I'm not the marrying kind?'

Kate and Esme shared a glance, nodding as if they'd been waiting for Saoirse's admission.

'Not everyone is, remember. We've all had relationships that didn't work out. The trick is to learn from them. And if you don't want to marry Finn, that doesn't mean you don't love him,' Kate said.

'I *do* love Finn. Our life together is important to me. But I loved Riley too, and look what happened there. What if love isn't enough?'

'Maybe you still love Riley. Perhaps that's the question you are most afraid of asking yourself,' Esme said quietly.

Saoirse acknowledged the truth in Esme's words with an incline of her head.

'Ring him,' Kate said then, looking at her determinedly.

'That's a crazy idea,' Saoirse replied, shaking her head, just as Esme exclaimed, 'Great suggestion!'

'You should,' Esme continued insistently, as Saoirse turned to look at her, wide-eyed. 'By talking to Riley, you might get some closure.'

'What if it opens up something instead?' Saoirse asked.

'Then you'll still get the answer you need: you'll know that you shouldn't marry Finn,' Kate said wisely.

Esme leaned across Saoirse to talk to Kate, conspiratorially. 'What if she doesn't ring Riley, but instead flies over to see him?'

Saoirse might have fallen down at that suggestion if she hadn't been already sitting down.

'Don't be ridiculous,' Saoirse began, only to be cut off by Kate, who held up a hand to stop her.

'It's not a bad idea.' She was speaking directly back to Esme, both of them pretending Saoirse wasn't even there as they plotted. 'She could get the first flight out, look Riley square in the eye and see what she feels, then get the first flight back the next day.'

Saoirse looked from Kate to Esme, both of them beaming back at her, thrilled with the genius of their suggestion.

'Get your phone out!' Kate ordered, delightedly. 'See if there's still room on some flights that will take you there and back. I'll give you the money if you need it.'

'I have money,' Saoirse replied, her heart beginning to race at the mere thought of following through with this madness.

'Well, what's stopping you then? Go on,' Esme said, picking up Saoirse's handbag from the footwell and shoving it in her lap. 'Get your phone out!'

Saoirse did as she was told, deciding it was easier to pretend she was at least considering their plan.

'There may not be a flight available,' she reminded them, wondering if she should tell them that was the case regardless, so they would drop this entire idea. But when she looked, she discovered that there were still some seats free to fly in and out, and she didn't even need to remortgage her stables to do so. She would need to overnight in an airport hotel when she arrived in Calgary, then hire a car to drive to the ranch the next morning, but it was doable.

'It would be unfair on Finn if I do this,' Saoirse said, unsure who she was trying to convince: herself or her aunts.

'Just tell him you're taking a very quick trip to Canada to catch up with old friends. That you'll explain all when he gets here in a few days. That way, you're not telling any lies. It's more of an omission, like the one you've already made,' Esme said, as though it was the simplest thing in the world.

Saoirse considered this for a moment.

'Book it,' Kate pushed again.

'I need to check Riley is even at Mustang Creek and not at a rodeo first,' Saoirse said, thinking of the practicalities. She sent a text to Zoey, who responded immediately to confirm that Riley was indeed at the ranch this week.

Saoirse texted back, warning her not to tell him she had asked. She couldn't be sure that Riley wouldn't disappear if he knew she was on her way. Did he hate her? Maybe. There were times she'd convinced herself she hated him, too, over the years. She closed her mind to that for now. Her nerves were in tatters as it was, worrying about her own feelings, without also worrying about what went on in Riley's head.

Before she could talk herself out of it, with a trembling

hand, Saoirse pushed the button to confirm her purchase. Esme clapped her hands with delight, as Kate beamed her approval. But Saoirse felt her stomach somersault as she registered the magnitude of what she'd been talked into doing. Had she lost her mind?

They sat in silence for the rest of the journey. Saoirse tried to work through what she needed to do next, but her mind refused to cooperate, flitting from Finn to Riley in an endless loop.

When they arrived at the cottage, Saoirse excused herself so she could ring her fiancé. But the phone rang out and went to voicemail. Hearing his soft Donegal lilt made her heart constrict.

Taking a deep breath, Saoirse said into the phone, 'Hello Finn. Having such a wonderful time here with Kate and Esme. I've got so much to share with you when I see you. I miss you.' She paused for a moment, almost chickening out. 'Finn, I'm going to Alberta for a quick trip, leaving tomorrow. To see some people I worked with at the ranch. There's something I need to do. I promise to explain everything when I see you. Give Mr Bojangles a carrot from me.'

Saoirse pressed end to the call, exhaling deeply. She hated keeping secrets from Finn, which she knew was laced with so much irony.

But as she began looking through her clothes and working out what to wear tomorrow, she realized she finally felt a little more in control of her life. And alongside the nerves she felt about the trip tomorrow, she also felt relief. Perhaps her aunts knew her best after all.

It was time to determine why she felt so confused about Finn and Riley.

TWENTY-SEVEN

Saoirse

Mustang Creek Ranch, Banff, Canada

With every passing mile, as Saoirse drove from the airport to the ranch in her hire car, a rush of memories returned. Most of which included Riley. His hand on her thigh as they drove this same route in and out of Banff. Sometimes on provision runs, others to socialize with Logan, Riley's best friend, at the High Rollers bar down the road. Saoirse could almost feel the warmth of Riley's arm, slung casually over her shoulder, as they sat in a booth watching a hockey match.

And before she knew it, she was back on the avenue that led to Mustang Creek ranch. Once in the driveway, she parked and sucked in her breath as she took in the view. The majesty of the snow-capped Rockies behind the rustic homestead took her breath away. Saoirse had spent years pushing aside all unhappy memories of her time here, but in doing so, she'd buried all thoughts about the spectacular parts. She'd fallen in love with the ranch almost immediately when she first arrived and for a long while had thought this beautiful part of the world would be her forever home.

Now, she was just another tourist passing through.

She glanced in the rear-view mirror to check she looked okay. She reached for a tissue from her handbag and wiped off the lip gloss she'd only put on after landing at the airport. She didn't want Riley to get any ideas that she was trying to impress him.

Zoey and Mitch walked out the wooden front door of their two-storey homestead. They stood, arms around each other, as united as Saoirse remembered them, looking out to her car. She appreciated them giving her the time and space she needed to collect her thoughts. Scanning the surrounding area, Saoirse could see no sign of Riley. She breathed a temporary sigh of relief. Clenching her hands by her sides, she climbed out of her car and then took a beat to look at them properly. Zoey was unchanged, her frizzy mop of greying blonde hair pulled back into a ponytail tied with a rainbow-coloured scrunchie. She was a little rounder now, but otherwise looked the same. Mitch had aged, though, completely grey now, and shoulders a little stooped. Finally, Zoey ran down the wooden steps to greet her, opening her arms wide. They embraced warmly, with Saoirse breathing in Zoey's unique scent, a mix of sugar and cinnamon. While Mitch took care of the ranch, Zoey ran her kitchen like a sergeant major and cooked all meals for the family, ranch hands and guests in the lodges from her range cooker.

'It's been too long. But my goodness, don't you look great!' Zoey exclaimed.

'You too. You've not changed a bit.' Saoirse turned to greet Mitch next, hugging him close. 'Silver fox! I like it.'

'All looks the same under my cowboy hat,' he said in his gravelly drawl. 'It's good to see you, kid.' It was the nickname he'd called her by when she lived with them all those years ago.

'Come on inside. There's a pot of coffee brewed; I thought we could catch up for a bit. What brings you here on such short notice? We assume you want to go see Riley? He's almost finished with a group from Calgary staying in the lodges. They're off on a four-hour trek into Banff National Park with one of the new guides.' Zoey looked over to the stables to their left.

'Coffee sounds good. I'm visiting my aunts in Bermuda. And as I was close by, I thought it would be nice to see you all,' Saoirse said, wrapping her arms around herself. She could see the doubt on Zoey and Mitch's faces, her explanation lame. Riley could wait twenty minutes. She was a little surprised to hear that he was involved in the treks and tours. When Saoirse worked here, Riley left all guest management to Mitch and the ranch staff.

'D'you know, you were one of our best tour guides? After you left, we had people return to the ranch and ask for you. That Irish charm leaves a lasting memory,' Zoey said.

Saoirse smiled at the compliment. She'd loved bringing tourists out on treks through Banff National Park. Seeing their reactions to the scenery made it new and fresh for her, too, each and every time. And she'd learned so much from Mitch and Zoey that she'd taken back to her own stables.

Following Zoey and Mitch inside, Saoirse's stomach flipped as she took a step back in time. The floor-to-ceiling brick fireplace boasted a blazing fire, just as she remembered, and the mantel above the fireplace was made of one long piece of wood shaped into bull horns. With its wooden ceilings and walls, and large windows to take advantage of the views outside, the immense space seemed as cosy as ever. Saoirse took a spot at the long rectangular oak table, carved by Mitch's grandfather many years previously.

She ran her hands over the grooves in wonder. How many meals had she shared at this table? Loud, noisy, fun and happy dinners, a stark contrast to the quiet suppers at home with her parents, where the conversation was typically muted and polite. There was no ceremony with Zoey and Mitch. Everyone was welcome and treated the same, whether staff or paying guests.

'I can remember the first day I arrived as if it was yesterday,' Saoirse said as she sat down. 'I was so nervous.'

She had walked into the kitchen, following the chatter sounds, and found a large group seated around this same table. She had taken a free seat between Zoey and one of the ranch hands, a New Yorker called Luke, and immediately everyone had begun passing food around in big bowls. Saoirse had instantly felt at home.

'You were like a little mouse when you arrived,' Mitch said. 'Hardly opened your mouth, except to squeak yes or no.' He had joined her at the table with a plate of cinnamon buns, and Zoey, just behind him, placed cups of steaming black coffee next to them.

'You'll find cream and sugar on the table, you know how it is here,' she said. 'As always, just help yourself.'

Saoirse took a bun and bit into the soft dough, white icing dribbling down her chin.

'Even better than I remembered.'

'So tell us a bit more about your stables at home,' Mitch said, wiping crumbs off his shirt.

As Saoirse sipped her coffee, she told them about Anam Cara Stables and her cottage. Talking about a place that she loved, and one that she had built thanks in part to the influence of the two people sitting right in front of her, helped her relax. Saoirse told them about the horses she stabled at home, about Colm and Amy, her part-time staff, and about how much she loved teaching kids and adults alike how to ride.

'So you like teaching the young 'uns,' Zoey said, sounding unsurprised.

'One of my favourite things to do,' Saoirse replied. 'The school is for kids with disabilities. Most of the kids who attend are on the spectrum. It's hard to explain, but within half an hour of being in the company of the horses, they become calmer.'

'Horses can do that. I've seen people walk into this ranch, their backs curled up with tension. But after a few days with our horses, I can see them unfurl in front of my eyes,' Mitch said.

'Exactly!' Saoirse agreed. 'They come once a week. Some like to groom the horses and feed them. Others are taking riding lessons. Last week, one kid – Jacqueline, a nine-year girl – had a big breakthrough. She's non-verbal ninety per cent of the time, but she started to speak to Ed, the pony she's been riding. It was a big moment for everyone. Her parents were so excited when they heard. They called me that evening and tried to buy Ed!'

Everyone laughed at this.

Zoey reached over and patted Saoirse's hand. 'You

always had a way with kids. Whenever we had families at the ranch, they would gravitate towards you. We've missed having you around the place,' she added, almost sadly.

'I had to go. But I'm so sorry about the way I went. I couldn't see any other way at the time.'

'We understand. And you're here now, albeit briefly. That's all we need,' Zoey said. 'It does my heart good to hear how well you are doing in Donegal.'

'I wouldn't be doing half so well if I hadn't spent my time here with you both. I learned so much at Mustang Creek, which I have applied in my own business. It was one of the best years of my life.'

'Mine too,' a voice said from the doorway. The hairs on the back of Saoirse's neck stood up.

That voice. Slow and deep, unmistakable.

TWENTY-EIGHT

Saoirse

Mustang Creek, Banff, Canada

Saoirse placed her mug back on the table shakily. She turned slowly in her chair to see Riley leaning against the kitchen door wearing his beloved white cowboy hat. He seemed leaner than she remembered, but his blue jeans still melded to his hips and legs almost indecently and a fitted black T-shirt showed off his muscular frame.

He looked good.

'Hey, Saoirse,' Riley said, walking into the kitchen. He moved in the same manner as he spoke. Measured, half a beat too slow, but with undeniable purpose.

'Hey,' Saoirse managed to reply. She stood up too quickly, almost toppling over her chair as she did.

'You never said you were visiting,' Riley said, almost accusingly. When he took off his hat, his dirty blonde hair was shorter than he used to wear it. It suited him, showcasing his strong jawline. Saoirse allowed herself to lock eyes with him and instantly felt a jolt of recognition. She wanted to pull away from that gaze, but it was as if something otherworldly held her to him, to the moment.

'What do you want?' Riley asked.

Saoirse almost smiled. This was the Riley she remembered: direct and to the point. There were times this hurt her, but at least you always knew where you stood with him.

'Nothing. Just a chat,' Saoirse replied, moving a step closer.

Riley, too, moved closer. He was right beside her in two strides, so close she could feel his breath on her cheek. Saoirse took a step backwards, colliding with the table, jabbing her hip sharply. She retook her seat and had another slug of coffee. Then she put the mug down quickly, unable to work out what to do with herself and afraid it would make her even more jittery. Zoey and Mitch clearly understood this was not something they should be involved with. Hurriedly, they made excuses and then left the kitchen, but Saoirse and Riley barely acknowledged their departure.

Instead, Riley poured himself a cup of coffee and sat opposite Saoirse. He took his time adding sugar and cream to his mug. Every nerve in Saoirse's body felt on fire as she waited for him to show his hand. Suddenly, the sound of her phone rang shrill in the room, making her jump. She stared down at it sitting on the table for a minute, willing it to stop.

'You not going to get that?' Riley asked.

'It can go to voicemail.'

He raised his eyebrow at that.

Saoirse rolled her eyes in frustration. She picked up her phone, more to give herself a moment to steady than to see who'd called. It was Finn. This was the second missed call; he'd rung while she was driving too. Her stomach plummeted.

'Let me send a quick text,' Saoirse said, twisting her body away from Riley so he couldn't see what she was typing.

'I've all the time in the world,' Riley answered, his eyes never leaving her, a smirk hovering on his face.

So sorry I missed you. Can't talk at the minute, but will call later. Love you. Sx

Fine.

Saoirse frowned. Finn seemed short with her. Admittedly, she would be, too, if it were the other way around. Her stomach clenched again as she remembered that, while she was ignoring him, she was sitting in front of an ex he knew nothing of. She felt shame rise through her. But there was no time to worry about Finn now.

'I've met someone else. We're getting married,' Saoirse blurted out.

This wiped the smile from Riley's face. But seeing the hurt that replaced it didn't feel as good as Saoirse thought it would.

In a softer voice, she said, 'Sorry, I didn't mean to tell you like that. I'm visiting Aunt Kate and Esme. It's brought back some stuff.'

Riley nodded, watching her closely. He downed the last of his coffee. Then, placing his mug back on the table, he said, 'Why don't you come for a trek with me? One hour, just you and me. We'll head out to our favourite spot by the Bow River, like we used to.'

'There is no more "our", Riley,' Saoirse said evenly as her mind played a trick on her and flashed a memory of the two of them galloping along the Bow River at the foothills of the Rockies. Happy. United.

His mouth tightened. A flash of annoyance flew across his face. Time stretched between them. Then finally, he said, softer, 'Maybe so. But I'll always think of that trail as ours.'

Riley stood up and walked towards the door, not waiting for an answer. Perhaps he knew that she would follow him. She hadn't come all this way for nothing, after all. She thought about Finn on his farm, working hard. Missing her. An innocent party in all of this. She began to doubt her decision to fly here. Bile rose in her throat, burning.

But she had to see this through, had to try and work out why Riley was in her head since Finn's proposal. Defiantly shoving her phone into her jeans pocket, she followed Riley outside. Together, they walked towards the stables, passing a group of six riders tentatively clinging to their horses on what looked like their first vacation trek.

'A work retreat for a company from Calgary. Team-building nonsense. None of them ever in the saddle before,' Riley explained as they moved aside to let the group pass.

'Nice money, so don't knock it. It's something I'm thinking of exploring more, actually.' She glanced at him. 'I was surprised to hear you help out with the guests now.'

'A lot has changed at the ranch since you've been gone.'

In the training ring, a young red-haired woman was working a horse with a rope. She shouted hello to them both. In the distance, Saoirse spotted a sizeable horse-drawn wagon heading towards them with what looked like a whole load of passengers inside.

'It's busy as ever here,' Saoirse noted.

'Flat out. Come on, let's get out before that crew come back in. The Kelleher family. Nice, but full-on. Had to pose for dozens of photographs yesterday.'

Riley was a good-looking man, the quintessential sexy cowboy, and she guessed there were dozens of framed photographs of him with his arm around a former guest sitting on mantelpieces around the world. People liked posing with him.

'You love all the attention, really,' Saoirse joked.

Riley threw his eyes upwards, but he grinned all the same. Then, he responded suddenly, 'I'll tell you what I loved, hearing you talk about your stables earlier. It was good to hear how happy you are. And that you've continued working with horses. It would have been a waste if you'd ended up in an office.' Saoirse was touched by this. She hadn't even realized he'd been listening earlier when she'd mentioned Anam Cara.

She looked around her, at the green paddocks with horses grazing, the red wooden stables and barns. Anam Cara was smaller, of course, but otherwise not that different. She felt a dart of pride at all she'd achieved.

'Thank you. The time I spent here changed me. Yes, of course, I loved horses before that. But by the time I left here, they were in my blood. I could never have sat at a desk in an office from nine to five.'

They had arrived at the stables. And as Saoirse walked through the red wooden barn doors, she might as well have stepped back in time. Nothing had changed. Bridles and ropes hung side by side above a row of American-style saddles on her right. Heavier and more ornate than the simple ones used at home in Ireland. Just next to them, a shelf had about a dozen hard riding hats, all with a layer of dust atop them. They didn't get much use then, she thought, with a wry smile. Most of the riders here preferred to wear cowboy hats.

Saoirse hadn't had her own horse when she worked here; she rode whatever horse needed exercising or was free. Riley had wanted to buy her a horse after they got married, but she'd put him off each time he suggested it. It felt wrong to have a horse that she would be unable to ride for long periods at a time, while she followed Riley on his rodeo circuit. Nevertheless, she'd always had a special place in her heart for a chocolate-brown horse called Nessie. If she could, Saoirse would have chosen her every time.

Riley moved closer to her. 'Looking for Nessie?' he asked.

Saoirse nodded, looking at him in surprise. Riley could still read her mind.

'She died about two years back. She was a good age, almost thirty, and went in her sleep.' Saoirse felt him watching her face closely. 'I know you liked her. I'm sorry.' His voice was kind again, not blunt this time.

'I'd guessed that she might be gone. I'm glad she died peacefully, though.'

Then Saoirse saw Dakota, Riley's Appaloosa. His coat, glossy caramel brown with white and brown spots, shone in the afternoon sun. And as Saoirse walked closer to his stall in the stable, he whinnied.

'He remembers you,' Riley said.

Dakota leaned in to nuzzle Saoirse, and she wrapped her arms around his neck, whispering, 'good boy, good boy' into his ear.

'Do you still compete with him?'

Riley grabbed a couple of bridles, ignoring her question and instead asking one of his own, 'Do you think you can still remember how to ride with a western saddle? Or do I need to use one of the English-style ones?'

'I can remember fine,' Saoirse took the tack from Riley, colder now, aware that he was dodging her questions.

The weight of the more oversized western saddle caught her by surprise. She'd forgotten how much heavier they were than those they used at home in Ireland. Ignoring the amusement on Riley's face, she instead asked which horse she could use, and he directed her to a black American quarter horse called Blaze.

As she readied Blaze for their trek, she felt a bubble of excitement creep up inside her, partly because it had been several days since she'd been out with Mr Bojangles, but mostly because she couldn't wait to once again see up close the majesty and beauty of the Banff National Park. Being atop a horse gave a unique vantage point.

Once Blaze was ready, she grabbed the reins and brought him outside. Then she swung herself up into the saddle in one fluid movement. As she settled into the soft cushioned leather, it felt like coming home to an old friend.

Riley followed her, leading Dakota, then chucked her a black cowboy hat.

She looked at it in shock as she caught it. Was that hers?

'I couldn't throw it out,' Riley said simply. 'It's been here, waiting for you. I knew you would come home one day.'

Saoirse placed it on her head and grinned in delight. Riley tipped his hat towards her, and then with a kick of their heels, they were off.

TWENTY-NINE

Saoirse

Banff National Park, Canada

They left the ranch behind and trekked alongside the Bow River. Thick marshes and grassy meadows surrounded them, and the Rockies, majestic and tall, pierced the blue skies with their snow-capped tops. When she'd lived with Riley at Mustang Creek, it had been the most romantic time of her life. Up to that point, that was. The terrain was rustic, but Blaze was surefooted and obviously well used to this trail. Saoirse leaned down and whispered in his ear, 'Fancy a run, boy?'

When she squeezed her heels gently into his side, he responded immediately, and they galloped past Riley and Dakota. It took her a moment to get used to Blaze's stride, which was different to Mr Bojangles. But soon they moved as one, rushing past the lush alpine forests towards the base of the river. As the warm breeze whipped Saoirse's face, she felt an explosion of joy and whooped with pleasure. A few moments later, Riley appeared beside her and told her to slow down. She pulled the reins and Blaze responded immediately, changing to a slow trot.

Grinning, she turned to Riley. 'Nothing feels as good as that.'

'Nothing?' he asked, raising an eyebrow suggestively.

Saoirse blushed, remembering how his hands felt when they traced her neck, her arms, her . . . Saoirse had to stop this. She turned away from him.

'It felt good, you know, watching you get lost in the trek. I've missed this. Us,' Riley said. As she looked back at him, she realized his eyes were glassing over, and she thought he might break into tears. In all the time they'd been together, she'd never seen him cry. It was disconcerting. He opened his mouth to speak but shut it again, clenching his jaw.

Saoirse heard movement ahead of her. She felt Blaze stiffen; he'd heard it too.

'Over there,' Riley whispered, pointing to the far left. 'It's why I wanted us to stop here.'

Saoirse gasped when she saw that standing amongst the brush was a large elk. The Canadian deer was reddish-brown in colour with large antlers. He paused, eating his twigs, alert to his new companions watching him. Saoirse peered through the bush, searching for more elk. From her experience, where there was one elk, there was always a gang of friends close by too. Sure enough, a cluster of about five elks stood a few feet to their left.

'I'd forgotten how gorgeous they are,' Saoirse whispered. She committed every detail to memory so that she could tell Kate and Esme later, from the velvety covering on the elk's tree-like antlers to his black hooves. Losing interest in his voyeurs, the elk soon went back to his twigs.

'No elks in Donegal then?' Riley asked.

'Not so much, no.'

'A win for Canada,' he remarked, and they both laughed.

And in their shared moment, echoes of hundreds of similarly shared moments from their past came forth in Saoirse's mind. Picnics in the sun. Sledging in the snow. Mountain hikes. Waking up in a tangle of each other in the small double bed in Riley's trailer. It seemed impossible that their life could be any bigger than it was back then. Saoirse felt Riley's eyes on hers once again, his face impossible to read.

Together, they continued on their trek, crossing the Bow River, the cold water splashing the horses' legs, then they doubled back to begin the return trek home. They rode in silence for some time, each lost in their own thoughts. Saoirse had half expected Riley to pull a stunt of some kind, to extend their outing somehow. And she felt an ache that seemed a lot like disappointment when he didn't.

'You haven't asked me about the circuit,' Riley said.

That was true. Saoirse couldn't see the point in getting into a discussion with him on it. Their views were so different that it would only cause another argument, something she was sure neither of them wished for.

'I've retired,' he continued, without waiting for her to respond, but he spoke so quietly she almost didn't hear him.

Saoirse looked at him in shock. Riley was the same age as her, and last time they'd discussed this, back when they were still married, he had planned on working the circuit until he was at least forty.

'What do you mean?' Her heart sank. When she left him, she did so 100 per cent secure in the knowledge that he would never give up his passion. She'd been convinced that he would get seriously injured, or much worse, have a fatal accident, while riding the bronco bull. And now he'd given it all up?

'I quit a few months ago, actually. I work full-time at the ranch with Mitch and Zoey. They've made me a full partner, and the ranch will be mine one day.'

This explained a lot. Saoirse wasn't surprised at the partnership news. Zoey had confided to her long ago that the ranch would be Riley's one day. In fact, what she'd said, was that it would be Riley and Saoirse's too. But still, the timing seemed odd.

'What changed?' Saoirse asked, her voice tight. 'What,' she paused, 'or who, I suppose, had the power to make you give up the greatest love of your life?'

His face clouded, and his eyes watered. This time she was sure of it; he was trying to hold back tears.

'Can we stop for a minute?' His voice was strangled.

'Of course,' Saoirse nodded.

They both swung their legs up and over the saddles, jumping to the dusty ground. Tying the horses' reins to a tree, they sat down on a pair of rocks, facing each other.

Riley looked deep in thought and didn't speak for a moment. Saoirse remained quiet, sensing that she needed to let him share whatever was bothering him in his own time.

'Logan . . .' he began, then faltered.

Saoirse felt the hairs on her arms rise as a flicker of panic set in. Logan was Riley's rodeo buddy. Best friends since high school, they'd competed together and shared a trailer for years. And for a time, Logan had been an important part of Saoirse's life too, with their weekly trips out to the High Rollers bar, where Logan would always sing Garth Brooks songs in karaoke.

Steel laced Riley's voice when he spoke again: 'Logan died a few months ago.'

Saoirse put her hands over her face as she gasped in shock. Logan was as close as a brother to Riley. Her hand shook as she reached over to clasp his hand.

'I'm so sorry.' It was all she could muster, but her words felt inadequate.

Then her thoughts immediately went to Logan's wife. They hadn't been close, but had watched their men compete several times together, which had bonded them. But when Riley had his accident, the catalyst for their break-up, Lizzie had not understood Saoirse's point of view. She kept saying that Saoirse had no business being a cowboy's wife if she couldn't take the stress of rodeo, which of course was quite right.

'How's Lizzie?'

'She's pregnant. Eight months,' Riley said.

They sat in silence as the sadness of this further news sank in.

'What happened?' Saoirse asked as gently as she could.

Riley looked at her, and the pain in his eyes hurt her.

'We were at a rodeo in Toronto. I'd already competed, and it was Logan's turn to ride the bull. He was having the ride of his life. He got to eight seconds and dismounted, winking at Lizzie and me. Ever since discovering her pregnancy, he'd been strutting about the place; he was so proud and happy. "King of the world," he told me. "King of the rodeo," I replied.'

He stopped and kicked the dirt with the toe of his cowboy boot. 'Then the bull turned and rammed him with his horn. It happened so quick. Ushers ran into the arena, and I climbed over the rails, trying to get to him. I kept telling myself that we'd all been through a lot worse than that. Nothing to worry about.'

Saoirse trembled as Riley shared the story. Every single worry she'd locked up inside of herself came rushing back in a torrent.

'The bull ran off. And as I ran towards Logan, I could see that he was lying in the dirt, face down. The ushers got to him before me and flipped him right side up. But I could see he was gone then. There was no breath. Just stillness. Goddamn stillness.'

Saoirse could see the pain of loss etched into every part of Riley. She reached out to him and cradled his head in her arms, and he sobbed into her embrace. He only stopped crying when the horses made a noise as they rustled the marshy grasses. He wiped his face with the back of his arm hurriedly and pulled himself together.

'Thank you,' he said. 'I haven't cried for Logan until now. I've been bottling it up inside of me.'

'I wish I'd known. I would have . . . I don't know, sent flowers or something.'

'I thought about ringing you. I had a couple of rodeo tours to finish, but then I decided I'd tell you in person. And you won't believe this, but I have a flight to Ireland booked. Next week, I had planned to go to see you. You beat me to it.'

This took Saoirse's breath away. Riley was coming to see her? Why? It took a moment for her to respond.

'Are you out of your mind? You can't arrive at someone's house on the other side of the world out of the blue!'

Riley looked at her, raising one of his eyebrows. And she realized the irony of what she'd said.

'Don't make me laugh,' she demanded. But it was too late. Soon they were giggling away.

Suddenly Riley's face changed; all merriment disappeared as he looked at Saoirse with such intensity it made her stomach flip. 'I was coming to Ireland to ask you for another chance. I know I've screwed everything up. And I know I've no right to expect you to give me one. But I'm asking for it all the same.'

This was not the closure that Saoirse had wished for. Confused, she stood up abruptly, intending to walk away, to put some distance between them. But Riley grabbed her arm, holding her close to him.

'I'm sorry that Logan died. And I'm sorry that you are grieving. But that doesn't change anything,' Saoirse said. 'We've been over for a long time. Almost a decade, Riley. We can't just pick up where we left off. And anyway, I'm in love with someone else. I'm getting *married* to someone else.'

'Earlier, you said that the greatest love of my life was rodeo. That's on me that I made you feel that way. Because the greatest love of my life has always been you. Only you. And Saoirse, I still love you.'

His words fizzed between them. Saoirse felt her heart begin to race. Riley leaned in, and before she knew it, his lips were on hers.

It was for a second only, the briefest of kisses. But that one moment was enough to make her doubt everything she thought she knew to be true. She pulled away and looked over to Blaze. She had to get away from Riley. From whatever this was. It was too much. She ran over towards the horses.

'Wait!' Riley called out. 'Please. Let me finish this. I've been planning what to say to you for weeks. I need you to know that I understand now that I never saw it from your side. But after Logan died, all I could think of was you, Saoirse. What it must have been like for you to watch me, especially at that moment when I went down hard and broke my collarbone. I'm sorry I never tried to understand your perspective.'

Saoirse had waited a long time to hear this admission. And yes, it felt good to be understood. But it was too late. Riley couldn't start saying all of this now. It wasn't fair. Even so, she turned back to let him finish.

'Listen, we all knew it was dangerous when we took up this way of life. I'd always felt invincible. But it's hard to push aside the death of a best friend. That's stayed with me for every ride since. It gave me second thoughts.'

'Logan's death made you decide to stop competing?'

'That's part of it. I was broken after he died. And I realized the one person who could put me back together, I'd let slip through my fingers. I'm so angry that I didn't fight more for you, Saoirse. That we didn't find a way to stay together.'

'So what are you saying? That you've given up rodeo for me, now, after all this time, even though we're no longer together?' Saoirse reeled from this admission, her heart racing as she tried to compute Riley's words.

'That's exactly what I'm saying. I want to show you that I'm serious about settling down. We can build our own homestead on the land. We can have a family. We can have the life that you always dreamed of, Saoirse. *You and me.'*

Saoirse knew that she should respond, but her emotions were in turmoil. She felt confused, angry, sad, and, if she were honest, there was a part of her that was jubilant. Her ego liked that Riley still loved her. And that he was willing to change his life for her.

'I know I can't ask you to make a decision here and now. But will you at least consider what I've said? We could have such a great life together; I feel it here.' Riley thumped his chest.

Her head spun, and her heart rammed so hard against her chest she thought she might be having a heart attack. She backed away as if standing close to him might cause a ricochet effect that she couldn't control. She steadied herself against Blaze for a moment, then she put her foot in the stirrup and swung her leg back over the saddle.

'I need time to think,' was all she could respond. With one last glance at Riley, she galloped back towards the ranch.

THIRTY

Saoirse

Mustang Creek, Banff, Canada

With the wind whipping through her hair, Saoirse gave herself to Blaze, allowing him to take her back to the ranch. As she moved in time with her horse, a rush of memories flooded her.

But they were not of Riley this time. They were of Finn and their life together, their *current* life together, not something that was over. Side by side in their spot above Ballymastocker Bay. Snuggled up in each other's arms, watching Netflix. In their local pub, having a drink with friends. Watching Finn play hurling at the weekend. Trying not to laugh when he made a face at her while they sat silently at her parents' house for Sunday lunch. The mundane, day-by-day moments of their life. Did she want to give that up for this?

She passed a fallen tree, aged and gnarly. At once it sparked another memory.

Six months previously, a savage storm had hit Ireland, the kind that knocked trees down and flooded the roads. They'd had a red alert warning that it was on its way, so Finn battened down the hatches at his farm in preparation for the bad weather and, with Colm and Amy's help, Saoirse had locked away anything at the stables that might get blown away in the storm. Her main priority was to keep the horses safe.

But the storm was even worse than any of them could have envisioned. Despite all their preparations, the grounds around the stables had begun to flood. Moving slowly through the wind as it tried to lift her off her feet, Saoirse had made her way to her terrified horses. They were pacing anxiously in their stalls, eyes wide with fear as they heard the wind batter their home. As the water began trickling inside the barn, she knew she had to find a way to stop it. She'd been struggling to drag a bale of hay towards the door when, suddenly, standing beside her was Finn. He'd left his own farm to come to her, instinctively knowing she needed him.

As she threw herself into his arms, grateful for his support, he told her, 'I had to make sure you and the horses were okay. I know these stables are everything to you.'

Then they had set about lifting bales of hay one by one and stacking them inside the door to form a dam. Afterwards, they'd gone from stall to stall, calming the horses down. And that night the two of them had bedded down in the barn to keep vigil, Finn taking off his coat and placing it over Saoirse as a blanket.

Now, as she galloped through Banff National Park, she had an epiphany. Finn had been wrong about one thing that night: Anam Cara meant the world to her, yes. But it was *Finn* who was her everything. How had she ever doubted that, even for a second?

By the time she had arrived back at the ranch and de-tacked Blaze, wiped him down and refilled his water bucket, Saoirse felt calm again. Whatever momentary madness had overtaken her earlier, when she accepted Riley's kiss, was now gone. As she left the stall, she hesitated, then sucked in a deep breath. Her body was reeling with another round of conflicting emotions. Relief, that she had finally got what she'd travelled all this way for, but also sadness. Her marriage to Riley had failed and she had to take ownership of her part in that. Saoirse knew that she could no longer hide from that fact. It was time to acknowledge and accept it.

When she stepped out of the stables, Riley was standing right outside, waiting for her, leaning against the barn door. Looking up, he locked eyes with her for one last time.

'Thank you for the happy times we had together,' Saoirse said, and while she spoke warmly, there was a finality to her words.

Riley sighed, seemingly understanding the fact that it was over between them, not putting up a fight. 'It wasn't all bad then?'

'On the contrary, it was mostly good,' Saoirse replied. 'We loved each other, of course we did, but there are times that love isn't enough. And I'm so glad I came to see you, Riley. I think I needed to say goodbye to you so I can say hello to my future with Finn. I hope you can understand that.'

He didn't respond.

'I've got to go.' She turned to leave, but he grabbed her arm, stopping her.

'I meant every word that I said back there. I'll be here, waiting for you. For as long as it takes. We can start again. And this time we can get married properly, in Ireland, with all your family. Exactly as you wanted. We can have it all, Saoirse.'

She saw a look in his eyes that she remembered well. It was the look of steely determination he had before competing at rodeos. Nothing was going to stand in his way. Riley always had been a force to reckon with.

Back then, Saoirse had gone along with whatever he wanted, telling herself that it was what she, too, wanted.

But that was then, and she was a different person now. She had a mind of her own. She knew what she wanted.

'It's over, Riley.'

And then she ran. Out of the barn, past the training ring, up the gravel driveway to the homestead. But she wasn't running away from Riley. This time, she was running towards her future.

Towards *Finn*.

Zoey and Mitch were in the kitchen when she arrived. Out of breath, Saoirse explained that she needed to go, apologizing for making yet another hasty exit.

But Zoey held her hand up. 'No need for explanations. We figured this would be a difficult visit for you. If you need to go, you do that, honey. Mitch and I will be here when and if you need us.'

'Maybe we'll come to Ireland one day,' Mitch said, giving her a big bear hug.

'I'd like that,' Saoirse replied, meaning it.

Saoirse left the ranch and didn't look back. She felt exhausted as she took her seat on the plane. She ordered a whiskey on ice from the stewardess as soon as the bar service began. Her hand shook as she lifted the plastic cup to her mouth. In fact, it felt like her whole body was trembling in protest at her emotions. The alcohol burned the back of her throat as she sipped it, but the shock of it made her shoulders loosen as the tension seeped away.

It was late afternoon the next day when Saoirse arrived back at Palm Tree Cottage. She found her aunts watching a Hercule Poirot drama. They quickly switched off the TV when she walked in.

'Did he look good?' Esme asked cheekily.

'He hasn't changed. So yes, he looked good.' There was no point pretending their age-old chemistry had faded. The room had fizzled with it the second Riley walked in. The moment they locked eyes, there had been a heat between them.

'Well, were doors closed or opened?' Kate said, an eyebrow raised in question.

'Seeing him today, being out by Bow River again, brought back so many memories and feelings I thought I'd thrown away.' Saoirse could hear the weariness in her own voice. It felt like a lifetime since she'd left on her flight the evening before.

'I can understand that. Remember, he wasn't just a boyfriend; he was your husband child,' Esme said.

Saoirse pressed on. 'Zoey and Mitch have given Riley

Mustang Creek. He's finally given up professional rodeo to take it over as a full partner now.'

Esme and Kate exchanged a worried look. Saoirse could tell this wasn't going in the direction they had thought.

'And Riley wants me to come over and help him run Mustang Creek.'

'Like you used to ten years ago,' Kate said, in a whisper.

'Kind of. But back then, I was a paid ranch hand. This would be different. He wants to get married and start a family. Everything I said wanted before.'

'And how do you feel about that?' Kate asked.

Saoirse took a deep breath. 'I love the ranch, I love Banff; being back reminded me how much I adore that part of the world. But Riley never asked me how I felt about leaving Anam Cara. Not once did he even broach the subject or acknowledge how much he expects me to give up at the drop of a hat.'

'A cowboy hat,' Kate threw in, giggling at her own joke.

'Ssh,' Esme chided, but also unable to hide her own grin at the joke.

Saoirse wasn't in the mood, though. She felt a snap of anger crackle inside her.

'Why should I be the one to give up my life? Why couldn't he leave all this behind and come to Ireland? And why has it taken him until now to say all this to me?'

Kate smiled. 'That's my girl. Now you're thinking with this' – she tapped her head – 'and not that –' she pointed in the direction of Saoirse's nether regions.

Her aunt was incorrigible. But Saoirse had to acknowledge that there was some truth in what she'd said. One look from Riley, and she used to melt, ready to do whatever he wanted.

When he proposed, she'd wanted to travel to Ireland to get married. But he'd knocked that on the head because it would have interfered with his rodeo competitions. And Saoirse had allowed herself to be swayed.

'It took me years, working two jobs, to get Anam Cara Stables!' Saoirse said, remembering the slog and dedication.

'You have poured your heart and soul into it. Not to mention your darling cottage,' Esme agreed.

The cottage she wanted to spend the rest of her life in, with Finn by her side.

'You needed this trip, child. When you ran away from Canada, you buried your feelings about Riley. And as you never told anyone in Ireland about your marriage, you didn't have the chance to talk it through, as people normally do when relationships break up,' Esme said.

This made a lot of sense. Maybe Saoirse had to go through all these feelings to reach the other side. Where she hoped Finn would be standing waiting for her.

'I miss Finn,' Saoirse said tremulously. 'It feels like forever since I've seen him.'

'So not the cowboy?' Kate asked, a grin appearing on her face.

'Not the cowboy,' Saoirse was also grinning. 'It's Finn. Only Finn. Today made it even clearer how much he means to me. So, to answer your question, Aunt Kate, the door is closed.'

'Good on the farmer,' Kate said, laughing now.

THIRTY-ONE

Saoirse

Palm Tree Cottage, Horseshoe Bay, Bermuda

As another wave of fatigue hit Saoirse, she excused herself and went upstairs, where she fell into a deep sleep within moments of lying down on her bed. But a nightmare awoke her before the alarm went off the following day. In her dreams, she was on Mr Bojangles in Ballymastocker Bay, trying to get to Finn, who was a few hundred metres from them. No matter how fast they galloped, she could not reach him. She called Finn's name, over and over, but he kept his back to her, always out of her reach. Saoirse sat up in a start, crying out for him. She looked around her bedroom in confusion, forgetting for a moment where she was.

She felt a prickle of annoyance run through her when she remembered. All directed at herself for the mess she'd made, and with Riley for his ill-timed declarations. She didn't want him. He was her past. They'd broken up for good reasons. She could never go back. Riley had fallen in love with a young girl with stars in her eyes. But she was a woman now.

Saoirse looked at her watch and worked out the time difference. It was early, but she knew she wouldn't go back to sleep, so she decided to put her time to good use. She could call Finn, but it was a conversation she needed to have with him in person. She wanted him to know about every part of her before they married. She could only hope that he understood why she had lied to him. If he couldn't forgive her, she'd never forgive herself.

Instead, she opened Esme's laptop and fired it up, logging into Kate's DNA account. Her DNA results were finally uploaded, and hundreds of blood relatives were linked to Kate. She punched the air in delight.

Most of the results were third and fourth cousins, but there was also a close relative – a second cousin of Kate's called Adrian Keeler. Saoirse took a deep breath, clicking on to his family tree. Time to try and work out how he was connected to her aunt.

A keen archivist, he had an extensive family tree, which took a while for Saoirse to get to grips with, scrolling up and down, side to side, to see all members in it. He had photographs attached to many family members, which looked promising. Then, finally, Saoirse found a possible match. There was a Kate listed, with the same year of birth as her aunt. A coincidence? Saoirse shivered at the possibilities.

She looked at Kate's immediate family. A Diarmaid MacShane had been married to Mary, with two children, Kate and a brother Richie. Three of the four names had the letter D in brackets beside them, which Saoirse gathered meant they were dead, but there was a question mark beside Kate's name. *Well, Adrian, assuming this is my aunt you're referring to, I'm happy to share that Kate is very much alive.*

The hairs on Saoirse's arms rose. This felt huge. She worked her way across the screen again and saw photographs attached to Adrian Keller's mother – a woman called Constance. Saoirse took a minute to work out that would make this woman Kate's aunt. Looking at her photograph, Saoirse could see the resemblance to her Kate. They had the same eyes and mouth.

She scrolled upwards and almost whooped for joy when she saw a further photograph attached to Adrian's paternal grandparents. She opened it and zoomed in on a couple standing in front of a whitewashed gable wall. Of a cottage, perhaps? They were dressed in layers, their clothes shabby with age. But it was their faces that stopped Saoirse short. Saoirse searched for a word to describe how they looked. The couple looked defeated.

How would Kate react when she saw all this? Would she even know how she was connected to these people? And if she did, would she be happy to share how with Saoirse and Esme?

Saoirse noticed a small inbox icon flashing on the top of the screen. She opened it and saw there was an email from Adrian Keller.

Dear UserKate9011

It appears we are related! I see we are second cousins. I'd love to chat a little about our connection.

Kind regards

Her heart racing, Saoirse replied that she was acting on behalf of her aunt, sharing who she thought Kate might be in his family tree, and explaining that she hoped to find family photographs. In particular, she'd love to find one of Kate's parents. Adrian immediately responded with attachments of several pictures of his own mother Constance and her sister, Hanora, who he agreed were most likely to be Kate's aunts. He said that they had left Ireland in their late teens, starting a new life in Liverpool and Manchester. And he expressed how much his mother and aunt would have loved to have known about Kate, had they still been alive.

He also attached the photograph of Kate's grandparents and another of his mother and aunt as children, standing beside a young boy, who he believed was Diarmuid. Tears sprang into Saoirse's eyes as she looked at the man who could be Kate's birth father.

Entranced by the photos, Saoirse jumped when she heard footsteps outside her bedroom door. She pulled herself out of bed and peeked out her door to see Esme shuffling her way down the hall in her dressing gown.

'Come in here,' Saoirse hissed. Closing the door behind them softly, she quickly told Esme about Adrian.

Esme listened in stunned silence as Saoirse brought her through the family tree and read the email exchange from Kate's second cousin.

'Well, I'll be damned,' Esme eventually said, sinking on to the bed beside Saoirse. 'Can you download those photographs? If we can confirm that they are Kate's family, we can email them to the videographer.'

'Absolutely. Oh, hang on, here's another email from Adrian.'

Saoirse clicked it open and read it out loud:

Dear Saoirse,

Another possible avenue to find a photograph of Mary and Diarmuid is through a Facebook page called the Downings Chronicles. A cousin sent me a link to it, and it's where I found that photograph of the grandparents. There are photographs dating back to the 1930s. A long shot, but you never know, you might find Mary or Diarmuid in one of them.

All the best,

Adrian

'Oh my, isn't that something?' Esme declared. 'Well done, child. I'll put the kettle on and we'll work out how best to broach this with Kate. Best get yourself ready.'

Saoirse felt a new, invigorating energy within her. She sang to herself as the warm water from the shower cascaded over her, relieved that things were back on track again. All her angst about her engagement to Finn seemed silly now. She held up her engagement ring and laughed out loud in delight. And when Finn arrived tomorrow, she knew he would help her and Esme make Kate's ninetieth birthday incredible for her. He was always so interested in hearing about her aunts, and was good to Saoirse's parents when he visited them with her. Family was important to Finn, as it was to her.

After breakfast, Saoirse began ticking off items on her to-do list. She made an appointment for Esme at the opticians in Hamilton, she emailed the videographer, called the hotel to double-check all Esme's arrangements, and then messaged the administrator on the Downings Chronicles Facebook page. She even managed to talk Esme into letting her give the kitchen a deep clean. Saoirse felt like she'd accomplished a lot in one morning by the time Kate emerged from her room at midday.

They were contemplating what to eat when the doorbell chimed. Esme walked out to the front door to answer it.

'You expecting anyone?' Saoirse asked Kate while Esme was out of the room.

'Not as far as I know,' Kate replied, confused.

Esme returned moments later, her eyes wide. She pointed theatrically over her shoulder, indicating that she wasn't alone.

Following her into the room was Finn.

'The farmer,' Esme whispered to Kate as she sat back down beside her.

Saoirse could hardly believe her eyes. She felt disorientated at first, but then her heart leapt with joy. Her gorgeous Finn was *here*, in Bermuda, at her aunts' house. She ran towards him, her arms open wide. But he did not return her embrace. His body felt stiff in her open arms. She stepped back, seeing an expression on his face that she'd never seen before. His eyes flashed with pain, and his lips were set in a grim line.

'What a surprise! I can't believe you are here a day early,' Saoirse said, her voice sounding unnaturally bright to her ears. 'Did you know about this?' She turned to her aunts, hoping it was one of their tricks. But they shook their heads in unison. Saoirse began to think this wasn't one of the good surprises.

Finally, after an agonizing minute, Finn spoke.

'You left me a voicemail.' His voice was ice cold. He'd

never spoken to her like that before. And she shivered, despite the heat of the early afternoon sun.

'I know. About my trip to Canada,' Saoirse replied slowly, trying to work out why he was so cross about that.

'Not that one. The one before it,' Finn replied, still icy cold.

Saoirse was puzzled. She'd not left any other messages. And then, in an agonizing flashback, she had a vision of herself calling Finn the night she'd been drunk on Rum Swizzles. With a sudden clarity, she remembered how his phone had gone to voicemail, and she must have left him a message. What she said to him was still a blank.

'Oh.' The pitiful response was all she could utter. She could feel her aunts' eyes on them both. Saoirse felt exposed. She didn't want to hash this out with an audience. She tried to steer Finn towards the garden, but his body was unyielding.

'Tell me you didn't keep from me the fact that you were married before?' Finn asked, the pain and hurt now etched on to every line on his face.

'I'm so sorry,' Saoirse whispered. She could barely look at him.

Finn's face crumpled. 'Why did you do that, Saoirse?'

Saoirse heard Esme tut, and Kate mutter something under her breath. Her mind reeled as she tried to remember what she'd said to him on that voicemail.

'Let me explain. I can't imagine what you must be thinking,' Saoirse begged, taking his arm.

He shook her off and said, 'No, you have no idea.'

She supposed she didn't.

'I've worked out that you got married when you were

in Canada. Then it seems you accepted my proposal, keeping a huge fact about your life a secret from me. And then you came to Bermuda, under the subterfuge of seeing Kate and Esme . . .' he paused and nodded apologetically in their direction, his manners catching up with him, '. . . when really you were here to see your husband. Am I all caught up? Tell me if I have missed anything?'

Her gorgeous, innocent, loving fiancé looked devastated and angry at once. It was as if an enormous chasm had opened up beneath Saoirse, and she was now free-falling deep into it.

'He's not my husband. He's my ex,' Saoirse said feebly. 'And it's over. It's been over with us for years.'

'Not according to your voice message, it's not,' Finn responded. 'The voice message where you told me not to worry, that you were probably only confused, and not still *in love* with him!'

Saoirse gasped and covered her face in shame. *What had she done?* She turned to her aunts, who looked at her with sympathy, but could do nothing to help her. This was her own mess to clear up.

'I was drunk, Finn. And briefly confused. I promise I don't love Riley.'

Saoirse had a second of hope when relief flashed over Finn's face. But it disappeared as fast as it came, leaving that unrecognizable steely cold stance in its place.

'Saoirse was going to tell you about all this when you arrived, Finn,' Esme said, desperately trying to help. 'That was her plan.'

But Finn continued to glower. 'What a fool I've been,' he said.

'You are the furthest person from a fool,' Saoirse

responded, pleading with him. 'Please, will you come for a walk with me? Give me a chance to at least explain my actions?'

He didn't say no, but he didn't move to follow her either. Regardless, she left the cottage and began to walk down the garden towards the path beneath the palm trees that led to Horseshoe Bay. She doubled over when she reached the gate, holding on to it as panic made her stomach ache. *What if I've lost him?* she repeated in her head over and over. *What have I done?*

Saoirse held her breath and wished with all her might that Finn would choose to follow her.

THIRTY-TWO

Saoirse

Horseshoe Bay, Bermuda

Finn never said a word, not when she opened the gate nor as they walked down the winding tree-lined path, or when the first glorious vista of Horseshoe Bay came into view.

If she inched closer to him, he moved away. The agony of being so near, but feeling oceans apart, made her heart constrict in pain. They'd never walked on their beach at home in any other way than hand in hand. But as they finally reached the pink sands, fifteen minutes later, she knew she had lost the right to reach out and hold his any more. Her mind scrambled with words, but they all felt wrong. Saoirse didn't want it to seem like she was making excuses for herself, but she had to make him see that, in keeping things from him, she'd acted with the best, albeit misguided, intentions.

A few feet from the ocean, Finn stopped. He bent

down and picked up a handful of the sand, examining it closely.

'It really is pink sand. You can see the tiny pink crystals mixed up with the yellow grains. Wow.' He exhaled, letting the sand fall between his fingers below.

Saoirse felt a rush of relief that he was being civil. She quickly responded, her words tumbling out in a rush, 'There are so many beautiful beaches in Bermuda. And you can see turtles swimming in Turtle Bay. The reef on Tobacco Beach is perfect for snorkelling, and there's a tiny cove a short walk from here with gorgeous rainbows of fish,' Saoirse paused for breath, then cursed herself because she knew she sounded like a lame tour guide.

Finn ran his hands through his hair and stifled a yawn.

'You must be tired. You must have been up early for the flight. Do you want to sit down? I can rent us a couple of sunloungers from the Rum Bum bar. Or we can have a drink up there if you prefer.'

He looked at her in surprise, and she smiled, 'It *is* called the Rum Bum bar. It's where I got so drunk the other night. I didn't even remember ringing you . . .' Her voice trailed off as she noticed Finn's face had become dark once again.

'I was just the poor schmuck at home in Ireland, missing his fiancée who turns out to be nothing but a liar.' His voice was flat.

That hurt, but Saoirse took the hit without complaint. She deserved that at the very least.

'Let's walk. I'm not in the mood for a drink,' Finn said.

He kicked off his trainers, so Saoirse did the same. Then they walked to the shoreline, dipping their feet in the warm water. Waves lapped over their feet and ankles, and Saoirse was grateful for the warm blanket.

Taking a deep breath, she said, 'I'm sorry. Unequivocally. There's no excuse for how I've handled everything. But please know that I would do anything to avoid hurting you.'

'Yet you did all the same.'

Again, another hit that stung.

Finn carried on walking along the beach, so Saoirse followed him. He usually slowed his pace because his stride was longer than hers. But this time, he steamed ahead. She had to half jog to keep up.

'Start with why you lied in the first place.'

'I never planned to lie to you. The problem was that I had never told my parents about Riley. You know my relationship with them has its issues. We're not the kind of family who discusses the messy parts of life, and my marriage fell into that category. And to be honest, Finn, until I knew that we were serious, I couldn't tell you something I'd not trusted anyone else with.'

Finn nodded, almost to himself, then said, 'I can see that.'

Saoirse almost tripped up on her own feet, she felt so relieved by this acknowledgement. Feeling buoyed by this unexpected early understanding, she continued, 'I don't know if you remember that night in my garden, a few months after we started to date. I asked you if we could talk about our previous relationships.'

A look over his shoulder. He remembered.

'I intended to tell you that night, I swear. But then you began to share about Sammy, your ex. And how she'd lied to you. You kept talking about how my honesty was one reason you'd fallen for me, and that you could never date anyone who could be as dishonest as Sammy was. I panicked. By telling you about Riley, I thought you wouldn't be able to look past my omission, that you would only see it as a lie. And I didn't want to lose you . . .' her voice trailed off.

Finn's only answer was to kick a wave that crashed into them. But he didn't dispute what she said, again giving her hope.

'I told myself I'd wait until we were sure of each other. I knew I was falling in love with you, but I needed to know you loved me too.' Saoirse's voice trembled with emotion. She pinched the palms of her hands with her nails to stop herself from crying. She was determined not to play the victim card. If anyone should be allowed to cry here, it was Finn.

'Okay, I'll buy all of that,' Finn replied. 'But it wasn't long after that that we both told each other how we felt. And yet you still didn't tell me then.'

Saoirse could see how damning this looked. 'I'd dug myself into a hole. I was scared to tell you then. I thought you'd start to question everything else I'd ever told you.'

Without missing a beat, Finn replied, 'Well, you were right about that part, at least.'

Saoirse stopped walking. She felt a tear escape despite her best efforts. She brushed it aside, held on to Finn's arm, and whispered, 'Have I lost you?'

He shrugged. Never had such a slight movement caused such pain to Saoirse.

'Tell me about the wedding to him. What's his name even?'

'His name is Riley. We dated for almost a year and then

when the subject of me returning home came up – I was there on a one-year visa – Riley joked we should get married.'

'You got married to stay in Canada?'

Saoirse sighed, knowing she had to come clean. There was no point holding back now. 'I got married so I could stay with Riley. I was in love with him. We were married by Mitch, the guy who owns Mustang Creek, who has a celebrant's licence. You'd be surprised how many people want to get married on a ranch.'

He snorted at this, unimpressed.

'It wasn't a big wedding. Just Mitch and Zoey – that's his wife – as our witnesses,' Saoirse said. She decided to keep to herself that, while it wasn't a big wedding, it was lovely. She had arrived atop Nessie, side-saddle, in her white sundress, with yellow flowers pinned into her long hair, which sailed out behind her as she moved. Saoirse had felt beautiful and powerful that day. And Riley had thought so too, groaning at the first glimpse of her, his eyes bright with love and emotion.

No, best to keep all of that to herself.

Finn continued walking. 'When I proposed, did you consider telling me then?'

'Truthfully, I was conflicted. By then, I was in too deep. I didn't know what to do for the best . . . I've been so worried about it.' She let the sentence hang.

Finn's face was hard to read. He looked desperately unhappy, in a way that Saoirse had never been witness to before. But could he come back from his anger and sadness?

'I always felt that you were holding back a little, you know,' Finn said.

304

This admission shocked her. Had she been? She supposed that it was possible.

'When Riley and I split up, it was difficult for me. Aunt Kate thinks that because our relationship was shrouded in secrecy, I didn't have a chance to give it the closure it needed.'

'Break-ups are hard,' Finn agreed, simply.

Was he thinking about his ex, Sammy, now? Worse, was he putting Saoirse into the same category as her?

'Finn, I'm not Sammy. I would never cheat. I would never . . .' She stopped.

'Lie?' He finished for her. 'That's the part I find hard to get past: the deceit. If you'd only trusted me, trusted *us* with this, I would have supported you.'

Saoirse stopped walking. Finn's words were as good as a slap to her face. She could see the truth in them. Why *hadn't* she trusted him? Shame, a feeling she was getting too used to, came crushing back again.

'Why did you come here, Finn?'

'I don't know,' Finn replied, seemingly truthfully. 'I didn't believe your second voicemail. Then throughout the whole flight, I kept telling myself that it didn't matter. We all have pasts; it's part of who we are. But I played second best with Sammy, and I refuse to do that with you. You said you had feelings for this Riley. And the pain, the searing pain, nearly floored me. And then when I walked into your aunts' cottage and saw you standing there, I wanted to rush over to you and shake you. I wanted you to feel the same pain that I felt. You did that to me, Saoirse.'

Saoirse wiped tears away as fast as they splashed on to her cheeks. 'If I could change all of this, I would. I never wanted to hurt you. But I'm glad that I went to Canada. I'm happy I saw Riley. Because I know without a doubt that I don't love him any more.' She ran her hands through her hair, as she tried to find the right words to make Finn understand. 'I needed to do this, *for me*. I feel like I've been running away from my past for so long, and I'm done running now. He's not half the man you are, Finn, and I know that. My relationship with him was no more than a holiday romance that went on way past its return flight home. I was young, naive, and caught up in a situation that my youth and inexperience couldn't get me out of.'

She watched him as he took in her words, and she was sure she saw a softening in his jawline, his eyes glassing over with unshed tears. She stepped closer.

'Your past has left you with demons, Finn. And so has mine. They made me question your proposal because I was afraid of failing again. Everything got messed up in my head. That's why I went to Canada. To see Riley, to confront the fact that I'd been married before, but that it had failed.'

He watched her closely, remaining silent as she spoke.

'Seeing Riley clarified everything for me. I remembered what was important to me, and that was our life that we created together. When we fell in love, I realized how easy love felt when it was with the right person. I know I've screwed things up. But please don't throw us away because of this. Please.' Her voice trembled as she looked up at Finn, waiting for his response.

THIRTY-THREE

Saoirse

Palm Tree Cottage, Horseshoe Bay, Bermuda

Saoirse tried to wrap her head around the possibility that she may have lost Finn. And for what? She'd blown it because she'd allowed lies and secrecy to bleed from her first marriage into her life with Finn. There was only one fool in their relationship, and it wasn't him.

Finn paused when they reached the entrance to Kate's garden, then said, 'We could have had such a great life, you know.'

He wrapped his arms around himself, and the fact that he had to take comfort in this way, rather than from her, broke Saoirse's heart.

'We still can . . .' she whispered, reaching out to him. But her words fell into nothing. He'd already moved away.

'I need some space,' he said.

So he was leaving. Saoirse's shoulders slumped as disappointment crushed her.

'Where will you go?'

'I saw a hotel not far from here. I'll walk to that.'

'It's a nice hotel,' Saoirse said, then winced at their polite exchange, far removed from how they usually spoke. After an uncomfortable silence, she walked inside, and Finn followed her.

Esme rushed towards them, her face questioning. When Saoirse shook her head, Esme's forehead creased in a frown. The air was filled with their disappointment and sorrow.

'Finn is leaving,' Saoirse whispered.

Using her stick for support, Kate walked over to him. 'We've not had a chance to speak, young man. And that's not good. You've come all this way; you must at least stay for a glass of lemonade.' Kate made her way to her favourite spot at the dining room table, and when Finn didn't follow, she added, 'That wasn't a request, young man. Come along. You can sit beside Esme and me while Saoirse prepares some drinks.'

Saoirse wanted to run across the room to hug her aunt, who she knew was doing this for her.

Esme softly added, 'Please stay. We are so happy to meet you. We've heard so much about you, we feel we almost know you.'

Saoirse saw him working through his next move. His eyes followed her aunts, then glanced at his bag, currently sitting in the hall. She knew that if he walked out now, that was it. There would be no more Saoirse and Finn. And she'd spend the rest of her life regretting the mess she made of everything.

When Finn finally walked towards Kate, pulling a chair out to sit beside her, Saoirse exhaled with relief.

'Good man,' Kate said, patting his arm. 'Did you know that I'm ninety in two days?'

'I did know that. And I hope I look as good as you when I get to that age.'

'Ah, there's that Irish charm.' Kate's eyes crinkled with pleasure.

This warm exchange was painful for Saoirse. She'd wanted her aunts and Finn to meet for ages. She figured they'd get on well, and it looked like she was right. But Saoirse felt like she was an awkward observer, outside of everything. She wasn't sure where to sit. Or even if she should. She moved back into the kitchen to prepare the drinks.

When she returned to the dining room with a jug of fresh lemonade a few minutes later, Finn was gone.

'He's freshening up,' Esme reassured her, seeing Saoirse's face whiten.

'What have I done? I can't bear the look of hurt and disappointment on his face.'

'He's a broken man,' Kate agreed, then quickly added, 'But it's a good sign that he's here. Focus on that.'

'You have to have patience, child,' Esme agreed. 'He'll get back to you when he's had a beat to calm down. It's been a shock for him to find out that you kept something so big from him. And his ego will be bruised. But if your love is as true as you say it is, he'll forgive you.'

'And if he doesn't, you'll recover from that too. We women are made of strong stuff. We endure. We know no other way,' Kate added. 'Now grab the gin from the cabinet over the sink while you're at it. I think we all need something a little extra.'

Saoirse did as she was asked while Esme filled the tall glasses with ice, then poured the lemonade. She took the gin from Saoirse and added a shot to each glass.

There was a buzzing sound from Saoirse's phone. She glanced at the screen and saw a notification for Kate's DNA page. Perhaps Adrian Keller had further news. She turned the phone face down. It would have to wait for now.

Finn returned and sat opposite Saoirse, making a point to avoid eye contact. And then they all sat in uncomfortable silence.

Saoirse looked over to her aunt when she coughed, 'Are you okay, Aunt Kate? You have the strangest look on your face.'

Kate looked thoughtfully at Saoirse and then Finn. 'I know things are difficult for you both right now. You're hurting, and who can blame you,' she said, pointing to Finn. 'But maybe I can take your minds off yourselves for a bit. I've been thinking a lot about how I ended up in this beautiful paradise. And I'd like to tell you about that. But first of all, I have to go back to 1939. And across the Atlantic Ocean to where you both live in Ballymastocker Bay.'

'Are you telling me that you are originally from Donegal too?' Saoirse asked, her voice coming out in a squeal.

'Yes. But further north. Downings.'

'I went to uni with a guy from Downings. Nice fella,' Finn said, smiling.

Kate gave them both a withering look and they got the message and stopped talking. She cleared her throat and continued, 'A chance meeting happened on Ballymastocker Bay beach that would change so many lives. Not least of all mine. Because I'm quite sure that I wouldn't be alive if it wasn't for what happened there and the chain reaction that followed.'

THIRTY-FOUR

Kate

Palm Tree Cottage, Horseshoe Bay, Bermuda

Kate spared no details as she recounted Matthew's proposal on Ballymastocker Bay, Eliza and Kate's fateful trip on the *Athenia* and their arrival in Halifax. They all sat in silence as they listened, their faces mirroring Kate's own sorrow as the story of her early life unfolded. Once or twice, Kate's voice faltered, and her grey eyes clouded with emotion. But she held up a hand each time to ward Esme and Saoirse off. She hoped they understood that a gesture of comfort might derail her from sharing the story she was determined to get out.

Eventually, Kate slumped forward on to the table, resting her head on her arms. She had so much more to share, she hadn't even got as far as Davey's arrival yet. And Kate especially wanted to share this part with young Finn. She had a feeling that he'd find it useful, as he tried to work out how he felt about Saoirse's actions. But for now she needed a moment to recover; every part of her body ached, bone-tired. Nobody spoke for several minutes as the ghosts from the *Athenia* danced around them.

'Are you all right, my love?' Esme was the first to break the silence. She placed a hand on Kate's back as she spoke.

A small smile of reassurance played on Kate's lips when she looked up. But it didn't stick. This had cost her deeply. While her body may have aged as eighty-five years moved on, inside her heart, her grief was as raw as it had been when she was a child. Kate was surprised when a shadow darkened the wooden table as the sun shifted positions. She had been talking for over an hour.

'You were so young to lose so much,' Finn said, his voice coated with emotion.

'It is a harrowing story, which is why I rarely discuss it. And it's private too. I've never wanted it thrown around at dinner parties as an anecdotal tale,' Kate replied.

'I didn't think it was possible to love or respect you more than I did, but I was wrong,' Saoirse said softly.

Kate acknowledged this with a slight incline of her head. She pulled herself up straight away, shoulders back. It wouldn't do, giving in to her fatigue.

'I wish I'd known the level of the ordeal you endured,' Esme said, her voice trembling as she spoke.

Kate felt a stab of regret as she looked at Esme. Had she hurt her by keeping so much to herself? She hadn't meant to. Kate reached for Esme's hand and held it between her own for a moment. She searched for the words to explain herself.

'It feels almost as if it happened to someone else, not me.' Kate tapped her head with a finger and continued,

'I'm not sure if my memories are mine or the ones that Mom shared with me over the years. But sometimes, I wake up in the middle of the night feeling confused and panicked. Much like I felt when the torpedo hit our ship. And no matter how much I pull the blankets over myself, I'm shivering with cold, as if icy water is again trying to claim me. Maybe that's why I've never liked being cold.'

Kate heard a sniffle from Saoirse. She hated that her story was upsetting for the girl. That wasn't her intent.

'I feel you shivering beside me some nights and hear you whimpering in your sleep. Maybe that's why you chose to live here in Bermuda, where our winters are so mild,' Esme commented.

'Maybe,' Kate agreed. She wrapped her arms around herself and tried to quell the rising feeling of panic that rushed about her. This was why she hated dredging up the past. It bloody well hurt. Physical pain, as fresh fear and terror gnawed at her insides, nipped at her, ready to inflict new wounds. She clenched her fists into two tight balls, her nails piercing her palms.

Esme stood up and moved behind Kate, leaning down to hug her. The warmth of her soft embrace sent gratitude soaring through Kate. Some would say that Kate had had an unlucky life. But she couldn't disagree more. The people in this room and those that had gone now were all testament to a life well-lived and loved.

Saoirse inched her seat a little closer to Kate and spoke with such tenderness it almost finished her off. 'If you need a break, I can make you tea or help you to your room for a nap.'

'You're a kind girl. It's been a long time since I took such a long trip into my memories. I have to admit, it's taken a lot out of me,' Kate replied, taking in her niece's pale face. 'You look a little shell-shocked too. I don't suppose you ever guessed any of this, did you?'

'No! I thought I knew *you*. I can't believe you kept this to yourself all this time,' Saoirse said.

'It was different when we were your age. Your generation are a bunch of oversharers. Stub your toe, and it's straight to Instagram to tell the world,' Esme said, rolling her eyes.

'Exactly, back in my day, it wasn't the done thing to talk about painful memories. There were too many of them, I suppose. My parents had lived through two world wars, not to mention a civil war in Ireland. And in some ways, it was as if my life restarted when we got off the *Athenia*. I shoved the part of me before that voyage into a tiny box up here that I rarely opened.' Kate pointed to her head again.

'And whenever you did revisit, it hurt too much,' Esme said. Kate took a sip from her lemonade, making a face because it was now lukewarm and watery from the melted ice.

'Will I make a fresh jug?' Saoirse asked, pushing back her chair to stand up.

'No, that's okay. I'm tired and will need to go for a nap soon enough. I'll finish this part of my story, and Eliza's, and then I'll leave it for a while. Now, where was I?' She looked at Esme for a prompt.

'The morning after you arrived in Halifax. You woke up in bed beside Eliza,' Esme said quickly.

'That's right.' Kate began to giggle. 'I remember waking up in that hotel bed in Halifax, feeling confused by my whereabouts. It wasn't at home in Ireland. It wasn't the cabin on the *Athenia*, the lifeboat, or the makeshift bunkbed on the *City of Flint*. But then I looked to my right and saw Eliza sleeping beside me. That calmed me immediately. I felt safe when she was near.' Kate pushed her lemonade away from her. 'Eliza – or Mom as she went on to become for me – was in such a deep sleep. I'm not surprised, after everything she'd been through. I pinched her nose to wake her up. I was a little minx, full of devilment back then.'

'You still are,' Saoirse said. 'I've still not recovered from your prank the day I arrived.'

They all laughed for a moment, as Saoirse told Finn how she'd found her aunt playing dead on the sunlounger, and it was a welcome relief to Kate, a respite from the flood of emotions still assaulting her. She could call a halt to all of this, she supposed. Saoirse and Esme loved her. Of that, she was sure. So if she said it was too much, they'd be disappointed, but they would also understand. Then Saoirse smiled at her, her face alight with kindness. Kate could not love that girl more. And deep inside of her she felt that, by sharing Eliza's story, she could help Saoirse and her farmer.

Clearing her throat, she continued: 'While Eliza brushed my hair – one hundred brushes, that was her way – she asked me if I'd like to live in Bermuda with her. She said that she and Matthew wanted me to. But only if it was something that I could be happy with. I was confused by the question.'

'Why?' Esme asked.

'Because I had already decided to follow Eliza no matter where she went. When I realized that my mammy, daddy and Richie had died, I knew I had nowhere to go. And there was only one place that I wanted to be. All my love for my family had to go somewhere. And I chose to give it to Eliza. One of two best choices I've ever made in my life.'

Kate looked at Esme, smiling at her. She was the second one.

'It's hearing you say, my mammy and daddy died – it gets me. You were so little,' Saoirse sobbed.

Finn stood up and walked into the kitchen, returning a moment later with a kitchen roll. 'All I could find.' He handed a wad of the tissue to Saoirse and his hand touched hers for the briefest moment.

That's more like it, Kate thought. She could tell that Finn was a good man. And a much better fit for Saoirse than Riley ever had been.

'Were you upset with your aunties in England when they said they didn't want you?' Saoirse asked gently.

Kate felt a splinter of anger spark its way inside her. 'They had no interest in me, so I do not trouble myself thinking about them.' She pursed her lips tightly and refused to discuss her father's extended family further. 'Young man, will you get me that tin, please, the one on the shelf. Flip it open for me, thank you.'

Finn placed the open tin in front of her. Kate searched for a moment, smiling when she found the photograph she was looking for. With her long black hair blowing softly in the breeze, there was her mom Eliza, gazing lovingly at a young pigtailed Kate as they stood on the pink sands of Bermuda.

'Matthew took this photograph the week we arrived here. I'd never seen sand that colour before. It felt like we'd fallen into a fantasy world,' Kate murmured.

'You were so cute,' Saoirse said, her eyes wide in awe.

'I can't remember what I had for dinner yesterday, but I can remember how I felt that day,' Kate remarked, pointing to her younger self. 'We had passed a family on the promenade just before the photograph was taken. A young girl my age was playing peekaboo with her baby brother. And his laughter, his joy at the game, sounded like my Richie. I pulled my hand away from Mom's and ran away from her and from them, that happy family. I was fast. It took Mom several minutes to catch up with me. I thought she'd be so cross with me. Because even though I couldn't stop running, I knew it was wrong. I waited for a cuff across the ear or the belt. But Eliza pulled me into her arms and rocked away my grief for another while.'

Kate wrapped her arms around herself, a part of her still reliving her five-year-old self's grief. 'I've often wondered what life might have been like, growing up with a little brother by my side.'

'You would have been a wonderful big sister,' Esme said, patting Kate's hand.

Kate's face changed as a smile lit up her face. 'Richie was a bonny little baby, and his giggle had magic. Could change humour with one note of his joy. He couldn't get enough of that silly peekaboo game.' Kate held her hands over her face as if she were playing the game again for Richie. 'I can't remember his face, but the sound of his laughter . . .' Kate sighed in frustration. 'I keep trying to conjure up his face, but it's blurry, unfinished. Maybe that's for the best, though. My subconscious telling me that the past is where it should be.'

Kate pulled a second photograph from the tin, of a young man wearing a naval officer's uniform.

'This is Matthew. He cut quite the dashing officer, didn't he?' Kate said with a smile.

'He is exactly as I pictured him in my mind when you spoke about him. He's not only handsome as hell, he just radiates goodness,' Saoirse said.

'I'm glad you can see that. Because it's true. I've never known a kinder man than Matthew,' Kate replied.

'Did you like him straight away? I know you loved Eliza. You had that bond from the ship. But he was a stranger to you,' Saoirse said.

'Yes, it was confusing because, while I liked him, I also wanted Mom all to myself. I suppose I struggled to come to terms with the many changes in my life for a long time. One minute I'd be fine, excited by a new experience. Like the day Matthew brought Mom and me shopping in Halifax before we set off to Bermuda. He called a taxi cab, and we arrived in style at Kay's Clothing Store. I'd never been in a store like it before. Four floors filled with everything we could possibly desire. It had two big glass window displays on either side of its entrance, filled with mannequins wearing brightly coloured dresses. Matthew said to us, "Spare no expense, ladies." He was determined to spoil us. For an hour, as Mom helped me choose a new wardrobe; everything from shoes, underwear, and dresses to a new coat, I felt excitement bubble up inside me. And I forgot about my loss.'

'You've always enjoyed a spot of retail therapy,' Esme said.

'That's fair,' Kate agreed with a grin. 'Well, all was good until Mom paused to look at a table filled with folded nightdresses in pretty pastel colours of lemons, pinks and blues, all with little lace trimming at the breast. I felt uncontrollable anger course its way through me, and I swiped the whole display on to the floor in my rage.' Kate paused for a moment. 'Mammy had a pink nightdress, like the one Mom had picked up. It was folded under her pillow in our cabin, waiting for her to wear it each night. And I'd fall asleep in her arms, feeling that fabric against me. As I saw those nightdresses fall on to the floor, in my head, it was Mammy's nightdress sinking into the ocean, dancing its way amongst the debris. It was too much. The excitement of new clothes was gone, as I relived losing my family again. That's grief for you. Happy to ruin every good day if you let it. I went on to have many more moments like that. Until I found a way to lock the grief away.'

Saoirse was crying again; but Finn had placed his arm across the back of her chair. Kate caught his eye and nodded approvingly at him. She cleared her throat, then continued her story. And to her surprise found that this part of the tale, she looked forward to telling.

THIRTY-FIVE

Saoirse

Palm Tree Cottage, Horseshoe Bay, Bermuda

It took Saoirse a moment to register that Kate had stopped speaking. Because within moments of her aunt picking up Eliza's story again, Saoirse was swept back to 1939. Her heart raced as Eliza's impossible decision was outlined. Her shock that Davey was alive echoed in the gasps from the room. Saoirse's heart broke thinking about the years Eliza and Davey had lost, living apart, grieving for each other.

But Matthew! Oh, how Saoirse's heart swelled for him. He loved Eliza with his all. That was evident. Both men wanted to give Eliza the best possible life and a loving marriage.

'I cannot imagine the emotions Eliza must have felt. How could she marry Matthew, knowing she loved Davey, but equally, how could she ever *not* marry Matthew?'

Saoirse said, her heart racing at Eliza's dilemma. 'I need to know what happened next!'

'It's possible to love two people at once,' Kate said pointedly to Saoirse. 'But I'm happy to see you enjoy hearing about Mom's life. It's been special for me to share it with you. Let me take a moment to catch my breath, then I'll tell what happened next.'

'It's all ever so romantic, Eliza's love triangle. If I had been Eliza, I don't think I could have chosen between them,' Esme said dreamily.

When the words love triangle were mentioned, Saoirse felt Finn's eyes on her. Her face flamed, and she ducked her head, staring at the chipped nail polish on her thumb.

Finn turned to Kate and asked, 'Who did *you* want Eliza to pick?'

'It all went over my head. I didn't understand what was happening. All I knew was that I wanted to be wherever Mom was. I liked Matthew and Davey; they were both kind to me. And I got a lot of ice cream that first month in Bermuda. Looking back now, I can see that Mom did a sterling job keeping all the drama from me. When she told me the full story years later, like you all, I was wonderstruck by it.'

'Eliza sounds like she took great care to make sure you were not affected by her situation,' Finn said, then he looked over to Saoirse. 'You know what, I'd love to hear which "team" you support?'

'What a great question,' Kate said, grinning.

Saoirse felt the weight of that loaded question. Of course Finn must see the parallels between Eliza's love triangle and theirs. Eliza's past and present clashed together, just as Saoirse's had. Saoirse made an educated guess that Finn was rooting for Matthew, the new love. And if Saoirse answered anything else but Matthew too, she felt Finn would see it as an indication of her own heart. Taking a deep breath, she replied, 'I'm on the team of love. I hope Eliza makes the right choice for *her*, not out of loyalty to anyone.'

'Quite right,' Kate said, beaming with approval at Saoirse's words.

Saoirse couldn't work out whether Finn approved of her words or not. His face was difficult to read. She decided it was best to change the subject for a bit to safer ground. 'Did you ever see Mrs Montague again? She sounded like such a character.'

With a smile, Kate said, 'Mrs Montague remained in our lives until she died in 1975. We visited her in New York many times, and she visited us too, with her own family. The bond we made on those perilous waters never waned with time. Mom thought of her as a surrogate mother, and she became a grandmother to me too.' Her voice softened, 'I loved her. And I became great friends with her youngest granddaughter Matilda, who was the same age as me. Tilly and I spent a summer in Paris when we turned twenty-one. That was a lot of fun, I can tell you!'

'I've never wanted to know what happened there. In this case, I agree with your dad that the past should be left exactly where it is!' Esme said with a sniff.

Kate cackled with laughter.

'Is Matilda still . . .' Saoirse paused, unsure how to finish her question.

'Alive? Yes! She's in Florida now and has been for years. We've not managed a visit to see each other for a while.

She's in a retirement community there. Assisted living. But we write to each other most months. The old-fashioned way, mind, none of that texting and emailing.'

Kate passed Saoirse some other snaps of her and Matilda, their outfits an often hysterical nod to the era they were in. In the first, Kate and her friend were around ten years old with arms slung around each other's shoulders. In knee-length tartan skirts and crisp cotton blouses, they had matching Colgate smiles as they posed on the top of the Empire State Building.

'The day after that photograph was taken, a B-25 Mitchell bomber flew into the Empire State Building. Killed quite a few people. Mom said we had used another of our lives by missing that by twenty-four hours.'

'Your guardian angels were looking after you,' Esme said.

The next photograph was of Kate and Matilda wearing high-waisted flared trousers, with bright, high-necked blouses and large, covered buttons. Eliza and Mrs Montague stood on either side of the girls in pretty cotton midi dresses. Saoirse could see Kate's sass and style evident in how she tilted her chin upward and the curve of her hip.

'That must have been 1945 or 1946. We were twelve years old and thought we knew it all,' Kate said, smiling at the photograph. 'I like this one a lot. This is us that summer in Paris.'

Kate, Matilda and three other women sat in what looked like a bar or cafe. They were all wearing slim-fitted trousers, flat pumps, turtle-neck sweaters, and smoking cigarettes.

'You look glamorous. Your expression is one that says

it has life sussed,' Saoirse said, her eyes taking in every detail, from the coiffed soft wave in Kate's hair to the full red lips.

'I was in love. Or thought I was, at least, with the woman sitting beside me.' She pointed to a lady with short dark hair and big eyes, heavily blackened with eyeliner. 'We were always in that bar in Montmartre. The summer of 1957. I was twenty-one years old and on a tour of Europe. We loved Paris so much; we stayed there for the summer.'

'I'm sensing you weren't a dress girl back then,' Saoirse said.

'Trousers were so much easier. And I was heavily influenced by Katharine Hepburn. One second, wait till you see this one.' Kate rifled through her photographs until she found the one she wanted.

Saoirse whistled in delight when she saw Kate in wide, low-rise bell-bottom jeans and platform shoes, with a knitted vest top and matching cap, but this time she was standing beside Esme, who looked like she belonged on a fashion runway.

'I'm. Not. Able,' Saoirse said, looking between Kate and Esme in the now and then. 'You two are iconic. No other word for it.'

'We turned heads when we walked into a room,' Esme said.

'You still do,' Saoirse confirmed, thinking about their swimsuits the day before. She made a face at Esme, throwing a silent question: *Please say you've got this on the video compilation.* A little wink from Esme was all the confirmation she needed.

Saoirse watched her aunt showing Finn more of her

photographs, and her heart broke that Kate did not have a single one of her birth family. At least she now knew that the family connection they'd found on the DNA app was true. Saoirse made a vow to herself: if there was a photograph of Richie in the world, she'd find a way to discover it. Maybe she could use social media to reach out to possible family members who might have a photograph of the MacShanes. She knew cameras and photography were common in 1939 because she'd seen plenty of photos from the Second World War, but would families like the MacShanes, who were poverty-stricken, have had access to such a thing?

Saoirse couldn't help but wonder at the events that ultimately brought her aunt into her life. So many perfect acts of fate. She shivered as she realized that had even one strand been different, she would not be here today. And if her great-grandfather Larry hadn't hired Eliza years ago, then she'd never have met Kate or Esme. And then another horrible thought struck her. Had Matthew not impulsively proposed to Eliza, Kate would likely not even be here today, but would instead have probably died on the *Athenia* with her parents and brother. She reached out and squeezed each of her aunts' hands.

'Saoirse?' Aunt Kate said, interrupting her thoughts.

'Sorry, I was miles away. Thinking about you, actually. And how your family and Eliza were so brave to leave Ireland to start a new life in America and Bermuda.'

'Mom could have stayed in her safe world working for your great-grandfather Larry. Instead' – Kate patted her tiny round tummy – 'she followed her gut. You would both do well to follow her example.' She ended by pointing her finger at Saoirse and Finn.

This time Saoirse found her courage and looked at Finn directly. She lifted her chin and held his gaze. Yes, she'd made a mistake keeping something from him, but it had been with the best intentions. And if he couldn't learn to accept that, then maybe he wasn't for her. Finn didn't look away, holding her gaze too. And it was only when they heard the snap of the tin's lid that they looked away.

'Let's get back to 1939, shall we? Eliza and Kate were on their way to the church in a grand horse and carriage. Two bouquets of orange blossoms sat waiting for us on the seats when we stepped inside. I can remember the scent as if it were yesterday. Eliza was quiet; she didn't say much on the journey. And then we arrived, and it was time for us both to walk down the aisle . . .'

THIRTY-SIX

Eliza

October 1939
St Theresa's Church, Hamilton, Bermuda

Eliza and Kate stood outside the large chapel on Cedar Avenue, which contrasted majestically against the blue skies. Its Spanish architecture looked far removed from any church Eliza had ever attended in Ireland, but it made little difference what the building looked like, she supposed; it was the prayers said inside that mattered.

'Go on into the church, Kate,' she said, looking down at the pretty little girl clutching her skirts. 'Matthew will be at the altar waiting for you. I need a moment, then I'll follow you in.'

Giving her a smile of encouragement that contrasted entirely with the lack of confidence she felt inside, Eliza watched Kate walk through the front entrance. She leaned over, taking deep breaths in and out, trying to calm herself.

She thought of her mam and dad, missing them more today than ever. If ever she needed her family, it was now, on her wedding day.

Her father often said, 'It takes a person with good character to keep their promises.' She so wanted to be that person, to make her family proud. And she wanted to make Matthew happy too. She looked towards the chapel door, knowing he was waiting for her on the other side.

How was *he* feeling? Had he given her revelation about Davey a second thought, or was it already forgotten? He'd barely said anything last night.

She closed her eyes and tried to find Mrs Montague in her mind. What about her? What would she say if she were here now? Would she tell Eliza to keep her good character and marry Matthew? As an officer's wife, she could have a good life here in Bermuda. Or would she tell her to pick up her silk dress and run, run as fast as she could into the arms of Davey?

Kate peeked her head out the door, calling over, 'Eliza! Matthew is waiting!'

There was nothing more Eliza could do but go to him.

She made her way into the chapel, each step bringing her closer to a future that she suddenly realized, there and then, she no longer wanted. She looked from left to right at the empty wooden pews on a polished wooden floor, as if searching for a way out. The priest, Father Kelly, was standing on the altar, smiling encouragingly. And then Matthew himself turned to face her. His face softened into a wide smile as he watched her make her way towards him.

In the way they'd rehearsed, Kate began walking down

the aisle in front of Eliza, tightly clutching her flowers in her tiny hands. When she reached the top, Matthew pulled Kate into his arms, giving her a warm hug.

It was Eliza's turn. She held her bouquet before her and focused her eyes on the cross above the altar. She moved with elegance, one step at a time, until, finally, she was by Matthew's side.

'You look more beautiful than I could have imagined,' he said, his eyes taking in every part of her. His smile was hesitant, though, as he looked at her, his eyes questioning.

She inclined her head in acknowledgement and, seeing the uncertainty fill his expression, she damned herself for making him feel like that. This was his wedding day too, and she would not hurt him by making him feel any less than the incredible man he was. So she did as she knew best, gathered her strength, and smiled as brightly as she could.

'You look handsome,' Eliza said, taking in his Royal Navy dress uniform. Gold brocade and buttons gleamed against the ebony black suit he wore proudly. Pinned to his chest was his row of medals, badges of honour befitting the man he was.

'Shall we begin then?' Father Kelly asked, smiling.

Eliza nodded, then looked at Matthew, who she felt tense beside her. A bead of sweat had formed on his brow, and he closed his eyes, as if he was praying.

'Are you quite all right, Matthew?' Father Kelly asked.

An interminable silence followed.

Matthew finally spoke, 'No,' panic surged through Eliza as she heard his words. 'I'm afraid I'm not. And I am also sure that Eliza is not either.'

What was going on?

'What is wrong, Matthew? Are you unwell?' Father Kelly asked, concern furrowing his brow.

'I told myself last night that we could all pretend that he was still dead if we didn't talk about him,' Matthew said.

'Pretend who was dead?' Father Kelly gasped. 'I'm afraid I don't understand.'

'Davey. He's Eliza's fiancé. She believed him to have died many years before, but yesterday she found out that he was very much alive.' He said this evenly, his eyes not leaving Eliza's for a split second.

'Oh my goodness,' Father Kelly replied, looking from one to the other in shock.

Colour drained from Matthew's face, and he continued. He was speaking as though to Father Kelly, but still looking directly at Eliza. 'I was so angry that I wished that Davey was still dead. What kind of monster does that make me, Father? I am not proud of that.'

Eliza winced as he spoke. She tried to utter some reassurance, but her mouth was dry. No words came.

'It makes you human, son,' Father Kelly said, understanding. 'I think you both should take a moment to have an honest discussion before we proceed further.' He stepped towards Kate, reassuringly placing a hand on her shoulder.

Matthew took Eliza's arm and walked with her a few steps to the corner of the church. As she waited for Matthew to speak, Eliza felt hope circle her heavy heart.

'I was too cowardly to ask you if you still wanted to marry me at the party last night, because in my heart, I knew what the answer would be,' he said eventually, pressing a hand to his chest. He looked at her with such sorrow that Eliza felt blinded by it. 'And I told myself repeatedly that you were falling in love with me. I felt the start of something wonderful over these past few weeks, and if we could have a little more time together, I truly believe that you would grow to care about me as much as I do about you.'

'I do care about you. I . . . I love you, Matthew,' Eliza said fervently, realizing its truth as she spoke the words. 'I have been happier since arriving in Bermuda than I have in many years.'

'Since Davey died.'

Eliza nodded.

'The fact that you are here now proves that I was right all along about you. You are everything I thought you to be. Kind, brave, loving. Willing to marry me because you made a promise. And if Kate hadn't said something to me just then, bringing me to my senses . . .' He stopped speaking, looking towards the little girl, who stood by Father Kelly still, twirling her hair between her fingers.

'What did she say?' Eliza whispered.

'I asked her when she walked into the church how you were, and she said that you were sad. Then I asked her what did she think of your friend Davey, and she said she liked him a lot. And that . . .' here, Matthew's voice trembled, '. . . and that you and he looked at each other the same way that her mammy and daddy used to look at each other.'

Eliza trembled as Matthew held his head in torment. She touched his arm gently, wishing she could take away his pain. He gazed at her, then pulled his shoulders back.

'It would be my greatest honour to marry you, Eliza. But I will not stand in your way if you still love Davey as much as I believe you do. You have lost so much in your life, yet fate conspired to bring you to the other side of the world to find Davey again. That has to mean something.' He took a deep breath and stood tall, 'I'm setting you free, my darling Eliza, if that is what you wish.'

Eliza fought to breathe through the swell of emotions flooding her head and heart. Matthew's generosity and selflessness were all-encompassing. She truly loved two men. But who did she love the most? The answer came crashing into her, with barely a need to think about it.

'I never meant to hurt you,' she whispered.

'I know,' he replied sadly.

'You have made me so happy.'

She closed her eyes and prayed for guidance to make the right choice for her and Kate. Then a voice, one that sounded like Mrs Montague's, popped into her mind: *Be selfish, Miss Lavery. Choose the life you want, not the one you think is best for others.*

'If Davey had not returned . . .' Eliza continued. 'But knowing he's alive, it's eating me up inside. I cannot fathom not being with him. I am truly sorry, Matthew.'

'Don't be. Our world is at war, and our futures are uncertain. This is not the time for regrets. So go to Davey with my blessing and be happy. Promise me that you will make this decision mean something. Live a happy and full life, explore the world as you once dreamed you would.'

'I give you my word.' Eliza stood on tiptoes and kissed his cheek, whispering her thanks to him. She would forever be indebted for his kindness. She pulled his mother's ring from her finger and placed it in his hands.

'One day, you'll find the right person to wear this. I promise you.'

'Maybe. But if you ever need me, Eliza, come to find me. I'll always be here for you.'

Then with one last look of sorrow, Eliza held out her hand to Kate, and together they walked back down the aisle.

THIRTY-SEVEN

Eliza

St Theresa's Church, Hamilton, Bermuda

They pushed open the church's doors, running down the steps towards the road.

'What's happening, Eliza?' Kate asked, giggling as they ran, thinking they were on another adventure.

Eliza stopped and asked, 'Did your mammy and daddy love each other?'

Kate's face broke into a huge smile, 'Oh yes. They loved each other. They were always kissing and laughing and singing and dancing together. Daddy said that Mammy was the light of his life.'

'Well, my darling, that's how I feel about Davey. And how Davey feels about me.'

'But not about Matthew?' Kate asked, mulling this over.

'No, I'm afraid not. And I bet that sounds confusing for you.'

Kate made a face. 'Not really. It would be silly to marry someone you didn't love properly.'

'You're a clever girl.'

'Will we still live in our cottage at the dockyard?' Kate asked.

'No, darling. That's Matthew's cottage, not ours. I'm not sure where we will go yet, but will you trust that I'll take good care of you, wherever it may be?'

Kate nodded, her big blue eyes wide with innocence and love.

Their horse and carriage stood outside the church, waiting for the bride and groom to arrive. Hoping Matthew would forgive her one last time, Eliza took it for herself and Kate because she did not want to walk around Hamilton in her wedding dress. They got into the carriage, and she asked the driver to take them back to Tom Moore's Tavern.

'Not the Hamilton Princess?' the driver asked, confused by the change of plans.

'Not today, thank you.'

'Surely we should wait for the groom?' The driver scratched his head as he looked up to the church steps.

'Best not to,' Eliza replied.

He made a face, then gee'd the horses to move on. They had only plodded a few feet when a figure appeared around the corner, running so fast he knocked over a flower pot.

'Look, it's the camera man!' Kate said, pointing out the carriage window.

Davey stopped, doubling over to catch his breath. He watched as the carriage moved away from the church towards him, then kicked the dusty road in frustration.

'Stop, please!' Eliza called out to the driver. Barely waiting for it to do so, she jumped down from the carriage and, picking up her white silk skirt in her hand, ran towards Davey, faster than she'd ever moved before.

'I got here too late,' he cried out breathlessly.

'I would say you're just in time,' Eliza replied, throwing herself into his arms.

'You didn't get married?' he whispered.

And when she shook her head, he screamed out loud, swinging her around in his arms, 'You didn't get married!'

Then, letting her slide back down to the ground, he took her face between his hands. As he gently caressed her cheeks, shivers ran down her spine.

His eyes locked on hers, and he murmured, 'My first love. My last love. My everything.'

Eliza tilted her head to one side, and he leaned in to kiss her. At first, a gentle, tentative brush of their lips together, echoing their first kiss many years ago on Ballymastocker Bay. But Eliza wanted more now. She placed her hands around his shoulders, pulling him closer to her; his hands moved down her back, making her body tremble as their kiss intensified. They pulled apart, breathless, looking at each other in wonder.

'What now?' Davey asked as he gazed at his love.

'We start the rest of our lives,' Eliza replied, then, laughing with abandon and joy, she grabbed Davey's hand and led him towards the carriage, where Kate was waiting.

THIRTY-EIGHT

Saoirse

Present day
Palm Tree Cottage, Horseshoe Bay, Bermuda

As Kate reached the end of Eliza's story, she began to cry. In fact, the only sounds in the dining room were the muffled sobs from each woman present. Even Finn looked suspiciously teary-eyed.

'Not tears of sadness this time. Of joy,' Kate explained. 'It felt so good to talk about that day again.'

'Eliza's last love,' Esme said with a sigh. 'I knew how it ended, but it gets me every time I think about it.'

'My heart was in my mouth, the whole way through that story. I had no idea what Eliza was going to do! But my heart breaks for Matthew. What a great guy,' Saoirse said.

Finn passed around more kitchen roll. Saoirse dabbed the trailing mascara from under her eyes and then blew her nose. Her heart hurt from all the emotion.

'Did Eliza and Davey get married in Bermuda that day?' Saoirse asked.

'No, they waited until we arrived in Boston. We left the island the following day; there wasn't much to hang around for. Dad wanted to give Mom the wedding they'd always dreamed about. So once we got to Boston, we moved into his home, and he bunked down at Uncle Paddy's house. They waited a few weeks so he could organize the wedding properly, then they got married in front of family and friends, old and new. The party went on for days.' Kate grinned at the memory. 'Not long afterwards, they formally adopted me.'

'And I thought it was Matthew who was your dad throughout your telling of the story,' Saoirse said, shaking her head in amazement.

A grin lit up Kate's face. 'I had to keep you guessing,' she teased. 'I loved them both so much. And what a childhood they gave me. Idyllic, filled with laughter and warm embraces.' Kate's voice trembled as she spoke.

'If anyone deserved that, you did, my love,' Esme said, kissing Kate's hand tenderly.

Saoirse desperately wanted to ask her next question but was almost afraid to do so. So much seemed to hang on its response.

'Were they happy? Did Eliza make the right choice in the end?' she finally whispered.

Everyone's eyes were locked on Kate, who reached over and clasped Saoirse's hand between her own.

'Eliza followed her heart, and it did not let her down. Mom and Dad both believed that something or someone bigger than them had brought them together. Dad would hold court at Uncle Paddy's bar, telling people about the missteps of their relationship and how they almost didn't end up together, and I never tired of hearing him tell that story. He had a way with words, my dad. The bar would quieten and people would listen, enthralled.' Kate was smiling through her tears.

'I think perhaps you might have inherited some of his storytelling skills,' Finn said.

'That's a nice thought,' Kate said gratefully, dabbing her eyes again with a tissue.

'Have you got a photograph of them together?' Saoirse asked. 'I have this image of Davey in my head, I'd love to see if it matches up!'

Kate nodded, had a quick search through the tin, pulling out another group of photographs. 'These ones are my favourites.'

She pushed the first one to the centre of the table. It was of Eliza and Davey on their wedding day. 'Mom used to joke that she was the spinster from Donegal who ended up with three wedding dresses!'

They all smiled as they took in Eliza's third choice. In the photo she was wearing a simple white silk dress with long sleeves and a train, and tiny pearl buttons running down the front bodice. She held a trailing bouquet of white roses and standing beside her, his arm around her back, was Davey, handsome in his formal grey suit, and rose boutonniere.

'He's exactly as I imagine him! Only item missing is his cap. What a good-looking couple. Eliza is stunning, I've never seen anyone more beautiful in my life. That dress is . . . flawless,' Saoirse said, in awe.

'They look so happy; it radiates from them,' Finn added, pointing to their matching Colgate smiles.

'Those smiles never left them,' Kate said knowingly. 'They knew how lucky they were that fate put them back in each other's arms. They fulfilled their dream and worked together on a couple of pieces for *National Geographic*, then Mom became an editor with the *Boston Daily*. They also travelled the world side-by-side many times. With me, of course. We visited Donegal often, to see your great-grandparents Larry and Eimear, before you came along, Saoirse.' Kate scrunched her nose up, as she thought for a moment. 'All in all, Mom and Dad had fifty-one years together and never spent one night apart again.'

Kate paused and smiled as a memory came to her. 'One time, Mom had an operation on her gallbladder and Dad slept on the chair by her bed for three nights. He refused to leave her side. He would say that he made the mistake once of letting Eliza out of his sight and now he would never do it again.'

A strangled sob escaped Saoirse, she couldn't help it. But as it did, she felt the warmth of a hand touch hers. Unbelieving, she looked down. Finn's thumb was gently caressing her hand as he held it. Kate then placed the second photograph on the table.

'This is the photograph Dad took of Mom, the day they found each other again in Bermuda.'

Eliza's ebony hair was windswept, falling in soft waves around her tanned face. She wasn't looking directly at the lens, unaware that the shot was being taken. But it was her eyes that captivated the camera and all who were looking at the photograph now. They shimmered with emotion, emerald-green pools filled with awe and love.

'That's how I remember my mother when I close my eyes every night,' Kate said.

Saoirse gulped down a lump as emotion hit her again. She grabbed her glass and took a sip of her gin cocktail.

Kate rifled through the photos and placed a final one on the table.

'I threw a party for them on their fiftieth wedding anniversary. I get so much pleasure looking at this photo, every line on their face, their white hair, their eyes knowing and wise, a roadmap of their life together.'

Everyone leaned in close to see an older, distinguished Davey, sitting with his arm, once again around his elegant Eliza's shoulder, as they smiled for the camera. This time, wearing his cap, which made Saoirse whoop with delight.

'They didn't make their next anniversary, so I'm glad I could give them that celebration. Dad died first, which was his wish. He made it clear that he did not want to be alive without his beloved wife. And it appears Mom felt the same. Because a few weeks later, I found her in bed, clasping his cap in her arms, wearing his favourite sweater. She'd died peacefully in her sleep. There was a smile on her face too. I like to think it was because Dad came to get her.'

Life and love were precious and should never be taken for granted, Saoirse thought, looking over to Finn. *If he gives me another chance, I'll take that into our future.*

'I think I'd like a walk around the garden. I need some fresh air,' Kate instructed, breaking the spell of the photo. 'Come on, let's all go.'

They all stood up in agreement and made their way outside. Finn offered Kate his arm, and Saoirse took Esme's, following on behind them. She took extra care to commit every detail to her memory. If this was the last time Finn spent with her aunts, she wanted to remember it.

'Did you ever see Matthew again?' Finn asked Kate as they moved on to the lush green grass.

It was as if Finn had taken the thought from Saoirse's head. 'I was wondering the same thing,' she said to him, smiling. And as they walked past bright rows of hibiscus, he smiled back. Was he thinking about how they had planned their own honeymoon a few weeks earlier, like she was?

'Eventually. But I didn't see Matthew for a long time,' Kate replied. 'I was so young then, and life was so different in Boston, that I forgot a lot of my early life. But that was a shame, because in that short but happy time I spent in Matthew's care, he embraced fatherhood with his all. I can remember feeling loved and protected when we were together.'

Saoirse watched Finn look down to Kate, and put his arm around her. His kindness, now, even with his own sadness, made her want to run over to him and pull him into her arms.

Kate continued, her voice a little breathless, 'Now, with the hindsight of age, I think I made a conscious decision to let my past go. It was easier to pretend that life began when Mom and Dad adopted me. Less painful. And for obvious reasons, Mom and Dad didn't like to talk about Matthew either.'

'Did they ever talk to you about your MacShane family?' Saoirse asked.

Kate nodded. 'On my eighteenth birthday, they sat me down and brought up the subject. Mom shared with me all she remembered from her couple of days at sea with them.'

'That must have been difficult,' Finn remarked.

'It was surreal. Almost as if she was talking about a

movie I'd watched years before, rather than something I'd experienced.'

Kate paused to catch her breath and they all stood quietly by her side, waiting for her to continue. 'With Mom and Dad's encouragement, I reached out to my relatives in the UK again and . . . let's just say that it didn't go well. But I know now I would not have wanted my life to be anything other than the way it turned out.'

They all smiled with Kate at this admission.

'After that chat with my parents though, it was strange; all sorts of memories began to resurface. And a lot of them were about Matthew. He gave great piggyback rides. He taught me how to snorkel. And he read stories to me, always with pirates in them, although I don't now remember why.'

They made their way back to the patio. Kate took her favourite seat, putting on her large sun hat that lay on the table.

'It took me a few years, but with Mom's blessing, I wrote to Matthew and asked him if he remembered me and if so, whether he'd like to meet. He responded immediately that it would give him great pleasure. So I flew over to Bermuda from Boston after my thirtieth birthday, and we went for afternoon tea in the Hamilton Princess. It's such a grand hotel, you know, they don't make them like that any more. You must find the time to go there before you leave.' Her face was a picture of innocence as she looked at Saoirse and Finn.

Saoirse had to look away, to make sure her face didn't betray her in any way.

'I recognized Matthew immediately. As soon as he walked into the lobby, I became a little girl again. He hadn't changed;

he was still handsome, but with temples greying. And when I walked over to him, he was incredulous that it was me. He kept saying over and over, "my little Kate, all grown up". It was so good to see him and have the chance to thank him for his kindness to me. He told me that he'd never forgotten me. That it wasn't just Eliza he mourned after we left, but me too. That meant a great deal to me.'

'Did Matthew ever get married?' Saoirse asked, crossing her fingers under the table that he had found his own happy ever after too.

'Yes, and he had two teenage boys at the time we met up. But the marriage didn't work out and they had divorced shortly before I wrote to him. We stayed in touch after that, mainly through Christmas cards, but we'd have a drink together if we were in each other's vicinity. He did get married a second time. He left Bermuda in the seventies when the Royal Naval Dockyard closed down and then settled with his second wife in Virginia. I will always be grateful to him.' Here, Kate paused, looking deep in thought. 'Most of all, of course, because meeting him brought me back to this beautiful island. I fell hard for its charms, and I decided to start a new chapter in my own life here, going on to buy this cottage. And shortly after that decision, I met my own great love, Esme.'

She looked at Esme, who was staring back at her, the beautiful views of the azure blue ocean behind her, and contentment on every line of her face. Saoirse could only hope that one day, she could look back on a lifetime of love like these two.

But something else had struck her.

'What about Eliza? Did *she* ever see Matthew again?'

Kate shook her head. 'Mom never told me this herself,

but Matthew said at her funeral that she wrote to him before she died. I've no idea what she said, but I know he was emotional about it.'

'Did he regret not fighting for Eliza, I wonder? He stepped aside so graciously, but if he hadn't, Eliza would have married him,' Finn said.

'He could have done that, yes. But regret would have eaten them both up, I think, ruining what they had together. When you know what your heart wants, you feel it with every part of you. Remember that,' Kate said, waving a hand in Saoirse's direction.

Finn didn't respond, but looked thoughtful as he digested Kate's words. 'Excuse me,' he said when a loud yawn suddenly escaped him.

'You need to go to bed, young man. And there's no need to go to a hotel,' Kate said. 'There's a spare room with your name on it. Get a good night's sleep, then you can tackle the day with fresh eyes tomorrow.'

'Follow me, and I'll show you the way,' Esme added, already standing up to take him.

'Okay. I think I will. Thank you,' Finn replied, the hint of a smile finally returning to his face as he said goodnight to them all. He paused as he came to Saoirse, and for a moment she thought he was going to lean down to kiss her. But he moved away, leaving Saoirse's stomach flipping, as disappointment crushed her.

'Remember what my dad said to Mom: "I will never give up hope that you and I can find a way back to each other." Food for thought, that,' Kate said reassuringly.

After Finn went to bed, Kate followed on shortly herself. As Saoirse and Esme sat outside in comfortable silence, watching the sun go down, Saoirse remembered the notification she had received earlier from the DNA app regarding Kate.

'I bet it's from Adrian,' Saoirse said as she opened the app. She wondered if Adrian knew his aunts had rejected Kate when she was five, orphaned and alone. 'When you asked me to follow up on the DNA testing, I thought it was exciting. But I didn't know Kate's story. It's so sad.'

'It is, child. We are reaching into her past in a way that we never could before. I hope Kate is happy that I did this for her.' Esme's face clouded with worry.

The app opened and Saoirse gasped when she read the message. It wasn't from Kate's cousin, as she'd expected.

Instead, there was a different alert altogether on her phone screen.

NEW MATCH – NOAH2710 – SHARED DNA 48.7% – PREDICTED RELATIONSHIP – SIBLING it read, in bold letters.

Slowly, her voice trembling, Saoirse read the alert aloud to her aunt. Esme clutched her chest as if in pain.

They gripped each other's hands tightly as they desperately tried to process the information they'd just gleaned.

'What does it mean?' Saoirse asked, turning in shock to look at Esme.

'It must be a mistake,' Esme replied, incredulous.

Saoirse began googling the risk percentage of error matches on DNA sites. Low. She shook her head as she responded. 'It's unlikely that there's an error.'

'You don't think that's . . .' Esme asked.

'Yes. I do,' Saoirse was amazed at her own certainty. 'But we need to learn more about this before we say anything to Aunt Kate.'

'What age is this Noah?'

Saoirse's hand shook as she tried to open the profile of Noah2710.

'It's private, damnit. I can't see anything other than that he is listed in the Blau family tree. But that's private too.'

'That's a Jewish name, how curious,' Esme said, frowning. She began to pace the floor as she tried to grapple with the turn of events.

'I could send him a private message?' Saoirse suggested.

'I don't know. Let me think for a minute, child. Why did I do that blasted DNA test?' Esme cried out.

Saoirse got up, went into the house, and pulled a bottle of Irish whiskey from the dresser, pouring a measure into two shot glasses. 'Here, drink this,' she commanded, emerging back on to the patio shortly after. 'You've had a shock.'

The alcohol did the trick, calming them both. Enough to make a decision that a message should be sent. They spent nearly an hour writing and then rewriting a three-sentence email.

Dear Noah,
   My name is Saoirse, and I manage my aunt Kate's DNA account. I cannot understand your connection to Kate, and I would like to discuss this further with you,
   Best wishes
   Saoirse

'What do we do now?' Saoirse whispered.

'Now we wait,' Esme replied, as they both stared at the phone, willing it to ping with an answer.

THIRTY-NINE

Kate

Palm Tree Cottage, Horseshoe Bay, Bermuda

Kate had awoken at midday, as she did most days now, and joined her family, who were sitting on the patio. As she moved downstairs, she wondered if the farmer would still be there, hoping he'd decided to stick around to talk to Saoirse. She saw immediately that he *was* there, which pleased her, but, less pleasingly, her two girls were looking at her with faces drawn with worry. The air around them felt thick with tension and the unsaid.

'You'd swear someone had died, the looks on all your faces,' Kate remarked.

A look passed between them at that.

'Okay, spit it out; whatever is going on, tell me.' Kate watched their eyes flit to the laptop that sat on the patio table.

Esme fussed, making sure Kate was comfortable in her

seat. Saoirse hung her head low. Kate heard a motorbike thundering down the road, its roar echoing toward them. The sound ominous, as if to forewarn her that a storm was coming.

Esme cleared her throat and then began to speak. Kate listened to Esme as she shared stories of undercover DNA samples and genetic matching for secret birthday reasons. Kate knew they had plans for a big surprise, but in her wildest imagination, she'd not thought this was in the pipeline.

'A degree of secrecy is of course essential for any surprise birthday celebrations,' Kate said to Esme, not under-standing why they were telling her this now, before her birthday. And why did they all look so stressed?

Suddenly, the answer dawned on her. 'You've found some of my family, haven't you?' she said.

They all nodded, even the farmer.

'My father's side or mother's?' Kate asked.

'Both,' Saoirse replied quietly. She flipped open the laptop and switched it on.

As Kate listened to it whirl its way to life, she wondered what secrets it held.

'Initially, we found many distant cousins,' Saoirse was explaining now, 'and then one second cousin appeared. The son of your aunt Constance.'

Ah, that was why they all looked so worried, Kate thought. She had intimated that no love was lost between her and her aunts. 'Well, that's good, isn't it? Is he a nice guy?' she asked, still confused.

'Seems to be friendly,' Saoirse confirmed. She looked over to Esme again. 'Will I continue?'

Esme nodded her consent.

Kate felt a shiver run across her back. The leaves of the palm trees rustled in a gust of wind. It appeared that the storm had arrived.

'Last night, we had a notification that an even closer family relative had been matched to you. Aunt Kate,' Saoirse placed her hand on her aunt's knee, 'it said that the match was a sibling.' She moved the laptop so that it was tilted towards Kate, then Saoirse began to read out loud the notification message.

'*You have a new DNA match with User Noah2710,*' Saoirse read. '*It is 99.9 per cent probable that he is a full brother.*'

Kate felt her body stiffen as she grappled with Saoirse's words. *A brother?* That was impossible.

'We were shocked too. We thought it best to message the person you have been matched with. His name is Noah. We reached out to him last night, to try and find out more about him,' Saoirse continued.

As Saoirse spoke, Kate felt Esme's eyes watching her, but she refused to look in her direction. She squared her shoulders and prepared herself for the next hit she knew was on its way.

'About an hour ago, Noah responded,' Saoirse said.

Whatever this Noah person had said, Kate figured it had the power to damage. Her instinct was to stand up and walk away. And whatever this uncomfortable truth was, she wanted no part of it.

'Shall I read Noah's message to you? Or would you prefer to read it yourself?' Saoirse asked.

Neither, Kate thought. But her eyes were locked on the computer, and she knew there was no running away from this. She gestured to Saoirse to pass the laptop to her,

351

then pulled her reading glasses from her pocket, and put them on, steadying herself with a deep breath.

Dear Saoirse,

Thank you for your message last night. I apologize that it has taken me a while to respond. I must confess that I, too, am reeling at this news. When my wife Leah suggested that I undertake DNA testing to see if I could discover my unknown heritage, my hope was that I might connect with cousins who could give me some clues about my birth parents.

Discovering a sibling is beyond my wildest dreams.

I didn't sleep much last night as I tried to understand the possible implications. I'm sure, like me, she has questions. I shall endeavour to answer hers by telling you a little about me.

My name is Noah Blau. I am eighty-five years old. I have lived in Connecticut my entire life. Or at least, the life that I am aware of. I was adopted as a baby by a Jewish family who emigrated to America from England many years ago. I am part of a large and happy family with siblings, nieces and nephews. Leah and I have been married for sixty years and we have five children and, at last count, eighteen grandchildren.

I've lived a good life. I am loved, and I love many with my whole heart.

I'm attaching two photographs for you. One was taken on my first birthday. The date of which was guessed by my adoptive family, with guidance from a family doctor. I didn't have a birth certificate when they welcomed me into their lives. The circumstances of my arrival are quite a story, but that's for another time. And

*the second photograph was taken earlier this year at
my grandson's bar mitzvah.*

*I would like to meet your aunt Kate to try and make
sense of all this. I hope she would like to, also.*

Until then,

Noah

Underneath his name, he'd left his phone number.

'How do I see the photographs?' Kate asked. She marvelled that her voice sounded so strong and sure. Inside, her body trembled and shook.

Saoirse leaned in and clicked a button. Immediately, a picture of a smiling baby wearing a white and blue sailor suit and bonnet appeared on the screen.

Time stopped. The air stretched so thin that it almost snapped in two.

In one moment, everything Kate understood about her past turned upside down. She put her hand to her mouth and looked at Esme in confusion.

'I thought I'd forgotten his face, that it was grainy. But that baby looks just like Richie, my baby brother. He's a little older than I remember, though, and his hair is longer. And he's dressed differently.' Kate lifted her hand to trace the photograph on the screen, but it shook so much, she had to let it drop to her lap. She couldn't trust her eyes, nor her heart.

'We think it's probable that the baby in that photograph *is* your Richie,' Esme said gently.

'No!' Kate shouted, making Esme flinch. Her body recoiled from that suggestion. If this Noah was her brother Richie, what did that mean for her eighty-five years of grief and loss?

Nobody spoke and the only sound in the air was Kate's ravaged breaths. Saoirse touched the screen again and a second photo filled it. This time, an image appeared of a grey-haired man with a dapper moustache and goatee, wearing a three-piece tweed suit and dickie bow. Kate's confusion grew as she looked at the man in front of her. She knew his face. Every line looked familiar to her.

'Why do I know him?' Kate whispered. A face flickered into her mind, then it was doused in darkness once more. She stared at the photograph again until a memory punched her.

A little girl having a piggyback ride on a man's strong shoulders around a field with long green grass and yellow dandelions. Squealing with delight. A chipped teacup, filled with milky, sugary tea. Watching a woman nurse a baby. This Noah looked exactly like her grandfather.

The skies darkened overhead and a cool breeze rushed over them, as Kate rocked back and forth in her chair. Finn pulled his denim jacket off, then gently placed it around Kate's shoulders. She realized that she was shivering. She was so damn cold again.

'Aunt Kate,' Saoirse said slowly and carefully, 'would you like to call Noah? Or I can do it for you if you'd prefer?' Saoirse reached over to touch Kate's hand.

'You've done more than enough!' Kate screamed at her, brushing her hand away. 'I do not want to call or email this person. My family died on the *Athenia*. My brother Richie is dead. And this man is playing a cruel, twisted trick I will have no part of.'

'I don't think it's a trick, my love,' Esme said, her brown eyes brimming with tears.

'I kept telling you. Let me leave the past where it belongs.

But you kept pushing me to unburden and share, and now look where we are!' Kate pushed the laptop away from her. 'You've torn me apart, both of you. I hope you're happy.'

Kate could see the impact her words were having on the two people she loved more than anyone else in the world. But at this point, she did not care.

FORTY

Kate

Palm Tree Cottage, Horseshoe Bay, Bermuda

Anger turned to despair in an instant. Kate began to cry, great wracking sobs that shook her small frame.

It was Finn who stood up and walked over to Kate, taking her into his arms. And while she didn't know this man very well, Kate found herself leaning into him, taking strength from him, as he murmured soothing sounds of comfort.

How long did she stay like that, keening and lamenting? Kate lost track of time. A dram of whiskey appeared in front of her at one point, accompanied by a box of tissues.

'I'm sorry,' Kate said to Finn when she finally managed to pull away from him. She dabbed at a sodden patch on his T-shirt.

He brushed aside her apologies. Eventually, Esme walked over and swapped places with him. When Kate looked up at her, she noticed her face was twisted with pain.

'I don't want or need your apologies,' Kate said firmly. 'I know you acted with love.'

'I'm not here to say sorry actually,' Esme said. She had a glint in her eye that Kate recognized. The woman had something to say and would not be swayed until she got it out.

'Do not try to talk me into anything,' Kate commanded.

'In almost sixty years together, I've never managed to do that with any success. I am not about to try now,' Esme said firmly. But then, gentler, and with a small smile tugging at the corners of her mouth: 'First of all, are you feeling okay? I don't want you keeling over on me with the shock of it all.'

'I will be perfectly fine once you all agree to put this DNA nonsense away. Right?' Kate said.

'You want us to keep the fact that you have a brother a secret,' Esme stated, warily.

Kate looked at her in irritation. 'Correct. And do not try and manipulate me with that tone.'

Esme lifted her chin in defiance, 'You can huff and puff all you want, Kate McDaid, but I am not afraid of you. And you'll hear me out. I seem to remember you telling someone not so long ago that secrets fester when you keep them in the dark. They grow, larger and larger, until they are so strong, they have taken all the good from you.'

Esme looked over to Saoirse, who bounced up on her chair as she remembered that same pearl of wisdom Kate had shared with her only a few days ago.

'But when we shine a light on our secrets, we take back the power again,' Esme continued. She reached up and tenderly brushed a tendril of Kate's hair from her face. 'You've been so brave, telling us about your early life. I know it has been painful. I've seen the toll it's taken. But surely it's been worth it?'

Kate couldn't deny there had been joy in talking about her family.

'But I didn't ask or want any of this,' Kate insisted. She reached for her whiskey, but her hand shook so much that she splashed it in her lap. Esme took the glass from her, then tenderly brought it to Kate's lips, so she could take a sip.

'You've had a traumatic shock, Kate. Take a moment until the world stops spinning for you and then think about it again,' Esme said.

'I'm afraid,' Kate admitted.

'Of what, my love?'

'That it will be like it was in Liverpool.'

'Liverpool? When did you go to Liverpool?'

'When I was eighteen,' Kate admitted softly.

'You've never spoken about that. Maybe it's time to shine a light on that too,' Esme said.

Kate wasn't sure she had the strength. Her shoulders slumped in defeat.

'I've got you,' Esme said, clasping her hand.

'We've all got you, Aunt Kate,' Saoirse added, placing her hand over Esme's and Kate's.

Then Finn placed his hand on top of their solidarity tower. 'I'm here too, to support in any way you need me too.' A faint blush crept up his face, as all three women turned to smile at him.

Maybe it was time to throw in the towel. What did Kate have to lose now? They knew almost everything, they might as well hear this.

'We were in Ireland, visiting your great-grandparents,

Saoirse – Larry and Eimear. A family holiday that Dad said would probably be our last for a while, as I had turned eighteen, was going to university and would start travelling with friends soon enough.'

'He wasn't wrong,' Esme said, trying to get a smile from her partner.

'The vacation was shortly after Mom and Dad spoke to me about my MacShane heritage. At first, I had little interest in learning about them. I have always been my father's daughter. But being in Ireland, questions began to dance in my mind. I wondered whether Mary or Diarmuid had ever walked on the soil I was treading. I strived to remember their faces, but they were my ghost family. The longer I was in Ireland, the more I craved information about them. I questioned Eliza relentlessly, looking for new hidden nuggets from her short acquaintance with them on the *Athenia*. But Eliza's well of information dried up pretty fast. So that's when I came up with the idea to go to Liverpool to find my aunts, a short ferry ride across the Irish Sea.'

'Did Eliza mind?' Saoirse asked.

'No. She encouraged me to go. But Dad wasn't happy.'

'Did he feel undermined?' Esme asked.

'I don't think it was that. Or at least, if it was, that was only a small part of it. Dad knew I loved him. We never left "I love you" unsaid in our family. He was simply worried. He had a bad feeling that it wouldn't end well. I should have listened to him.'

Kate took another sip from her whiskey, closing her eyes, remembering. And within seconds she was back to 1959 again.

FORTY-ONE

Kate

July 1959
Belle Vale, Liverpool

Davey stopped the car on the edge of Belle Vale. He turned the key, and the engine shuddered to a halt. He glanced to his left at Eliza, and then they turned to face Kate.

'Don't look so worried!' Kate said to them, taking in their matching frowns.

Eliza rearranged her face and gave Kate a bright smile. 'Me? Not a care in the world. The question is, are you ready?'

Kate gave her two thumbs up. Since she'd decided to reach out to her two aunts, she had felt excitement course its way through her. Larry had helped them locate Aunt Hanora, who lived in Liverpool. And then, after an evening of once more running through the pros and cons of reaching out, plans were made for their trip.

'I've read about these prefab estates, built after the Blitz. Seen photographs of them. But they're quite impressive when you look at them all in a row,' Davey said, picking up his pipe and sucking on it.

They followed his gaze, taking in the purpose-built prefabricated bungalows that made up the community of Belle Vale. Well-kept gardens sat neatly in front of each one. A couple of kids were skipping rope out front, and two women were chatting over their fence.

'Do you think they will remember Daddy and Mammy?' Kate asked for the dozenth time since they'd set off on the ferry from Dublin's Holyhead to Liverpool. Kate had told her parents that she was happy to travel alone, but when they insisted that they join her, she felt relief. Larry had thankfully even loaned them his Ford Prefect car to make the journey less arduous.

Eliza glanced at her wristwatch. 'They weren't close to your parents, we know that. But I can't see how Hanora won't remember some details about her brother. And I distinctly remember Mary telling me that they had seen them at your grandfather's funeral.' A small frown wrinkled her forehead, but she smoothed it away with a smile. 'Try not to worry. It's time. We agreed two p.m.'

'Do I look okay?' Kate asked, tucking her hair behind her ears.

'Two prettiest ladies in the land,' Davey said, giving her a little wink.

Kate had chosen her favourite red-and-black tartan cropped trousers with a red crew-neck sweater. She wanted to make the right first impression with Aunt Hanora.

'What do I call her, do you think? Aunt Hanora or just

Hanora?' Kate pondered as her dad pulled the front seat forward so she could climb out.

'Why don't we play that by ear,' Eliza replied, as she smoothed down her own pleated plaid skirt that she wore coupled with a cream twin set.

'Try not to get your hopes up too much, honey,' Davey said as Kate walked a little ahead of them.

'I'm not!' Kate insisted.

But that wasn't true. She had daydreamed her way through the five-hour crossing across the Irish Sea. Daydreamed that she would become best friends with her cousins. That her aunts would tell her stories about her father when he was a boy. That they might even have photographs. And that she'd find her lost family again. Kate hadn't told her mom and dad this, but she'd come with half a plan to stay in Liverpool with her aunt for a few weeks, if she was asked.

In the distance, Kate saw one garden stand out like a sore thumb. An unkempt lawn, with litter strewn all the way from the cracked front steps to the entrance. Kate crossed her fingers and hoped this wasn't her aunt's. But as she checked the piece of paper she held in her gloved hand, her heart dropped. She stopped in front of the bedraggled bungalow. 'This is it.'

A prickle of apprehension ran through her, but she smiled brightly through it. What difference did the state of one's garden make?

Davey did a rat-tat-tat on the window pane of the red front door, as there was no doorbell. And then, as the door opened, Kate came face to face with her aunt for the first time. All thoughts that this woman could be a visual reminder of her father vanished as Kate stared at her aunt. From the grey hair that hung lankly around her lined face to the cigarette that hung from her blistered lips, she felt not one jolt of recognition.

'You're here then,' Hanora said bluntly through a cloud of smoke as she eyed them up and down.

'Hello. Are you Hanora?' Eliza jumped in, clearly as puzzled as Kate. The toothless woman before them looked as though she was old enough to be Kate's grandmother.

'Who else would I be?' she replied. 'You'd better come in.'

Kate took a step backwards, faltering at the last minute. But she felt the warmth of her mom and dad's hands on the small of her back, gently ushering her into the narrow hallway. The door to the living room was open, revealing a man asleep on the couch with his feet up, the television blaring. Hanora led them past it, through to the kitchen, at the back of the house.

Kate could feel her mom and dad watching her, then flitting around the room, observing the mess in the kitchen. There wasn't a clean counter space, and the sink was overflowing with dirty pots and pans. This jarred with the image she'd built up in her mind of her aunt's home. Kate felt a flash of guilt at how shallow that made her.

'I can make you tea, but I don't have no biscuits,' Hanora stated.

Eliza held her hand up, 'Thank you for your kindness, but we have had something to eat and wouldn't dream of putting you to any trouble.'

Hanora took another long drag from her cigarette until it was smoked down to the butt. Then she squeezed it between her fingers before flicking it in the sink. Without missing a beat, she reached into her cardigan pocket and pulled out a pack of Marlboros. She tapped the box and then lit a new cigarette.

'So you're Diarmuid's daughter.'

Kate held her hand out, 'I'm Kate,' she said brightly. 'It's nice to meet you.'

Hanora cackled laughter. 'Look at you, Miss La-De-Da!'

Kate's hand dropped to her side, immediately crestfallen.

Davey and Eliza each took a step closer to their daughter, flanking her.

'We're proud of our daughter's manners,' Eliza said, her voice now with a slight edge.

Hanora shrugged, unimpressed. She walked over to the kitchen table and took a seat. 'If you're looking for an apology from me about not wanting you after the ship went down, you're barking up the wrong tree.'

'I'm not,' Kate said. She walked over to take a seat beside her aunt. 'When my mom explained that you couldn't take me in, I understood. I wanted to meet you. And I hoped you might be able to tell me a little about my parents.'

Hanora took another drag on her cigarette and then coughed into the sleeve of her cardigan. 'Spoiled rotten, your dad was. The only boy. Our father doted on him, of course.'

Kate felt a shiver of hope bubble back again; at last, some new information. 'I think I can remember my grandfather. He used to give me piggyback rides. He lived with us.'

'You lived with him, you mean. Your lot never left home. Not like Constance and me. We had no choice but to go and earn a living. There wasn't a thing for us in that house. Two rooms. This place is a palace compared to that.'

'It sounds a lot like the home I grew up in,' Eliza said.

'Mine too,' Davey added.

Hanora looked at the two of them, her eyes slowly moving up and down. 'Well, I bet you're not in two rooms any more. Got a few bob, by the looks of it.'

Davey's jaw tightened visibly and he threw a wary look at Eliza.

'I know you left Ireland when you were quite young. But did you see much of Diarmuid when you went home for visits?' Eliza asked, helpfully changing the topic.

Kate threw a look of gratitude to her mom.

'I never wanted to go back to that hellhole. But after Mam died, Constance and I went to the funeral. Your mammy had her feet under the table nicely by then.' Bitterness laced Hanora's voice. 'All my father could do was talk about how great Mary was. Sick to my teeth listening to it, I was.'

Kate felt deflated from her aunt's words. She clearly didn't like either Diarmuid or his young wife, by the sounds of it.

'It's not nice to speak ill of the dead,' Eliza said diplomatically. 'Perhaps you have some kinder memories to share?'

'It's my house, and I'll say what I want,' Hanora replied with a huff. Then, narrowing her eyes, she said, 'I never asked you to come. And if you don't like what I'm saying, you know where to go.' She pointed her cigarette in the direction of the front door.

Davey didn't need to be asked twice, and walked over to grab Kate's hand. 'Come on, love. You've nothing to gain by staying here. Let's go.'

But Kate wasn't ready yet. Her dreams of being

welcomed into the bosom of her birth family were falling to the ground like dead leaves from a tree, but she was sure there had to be a way to make this trip, this visit, worthwhile.

'Do you have any photographs of my parents?' she asked, pulling her hand free from Davey's.

A sly look flashed over Hanora's face. 'For the right price, I might.'

Eliza gasped, but Davey didn't flinch. He barked at her, 'How much?'

'Fifty pounds,' Hanora replied immediately.

Without hesitation, Davey reached into the inside pocket of his jacket and pulled out his chequebook. Hanora licked her lips, unable to keep the glee off her face. Kate watched the interchange take place with her mouth wide open. Was this really happening?

'Photographs first,' Davey said, every word clipped in annoyance.

'I don't have them here. My sister Constance has them. But I'll post them to you. You have my word.'

Davey snorted, 'You're a gas woman, I'll give you that. Tell you what, I'll post the cheque to you after you send us the photographs. How about that?'

Hanora cackled laughter at that, then narrowed her eyes as she said, 'No cheque, no photographs. Your choice.'

Her mom and dad looked at Kate for guidance. They would follow her lead here.

Kate had dreamed of her mammy and daddy occasionally, snapshots of happy moments with them in Ireland. Now, as she studied her aunt's face and tried to find a trace of that daddy from her dreams in the woman in front of her – of his family, his blood – her stomach plummeted. She realized that what she'd been looking for would never be found in this woman.

'You know what, I *would* like to know why you didn't take me in when Mammy, Daddy and Richie died?' Kate asked, her voice colder now.

Hanora looked at her in surprise, then sighed as if the trouble of the world was on her shoulders. 'Look around you.' She indicated the broken pane in the window above the sink, the lino beneath their feet, ripped and torn. Then for a moment her face changed, softened as she whispered, 'I did you a favour, kid.'

Kate acknowledged this with an incline of her head. She didn't doubt that one bit. Then she locked eyes with her aunt. Kate lifted her chin, 'You haven't answered my question. Did you even consider taking in your only brother's child?'

Hanora waved her cigarette in Kate's direction. 'I got a phone call from some lieutenant, a Belfast man. He asked me if I would take you in. So I said to him, sure, but what's in it for me? I told him I wasn't a charity. Tight bastard said he didn't care for my tone and wouldn't give me a penny.'

'That must have been Matthew,' Eliza said. Then she walked over to Kate's side, laying a hand on her shoulder and squeezing it. She looked over to Hanora and said firmly, 'Diarmuid told me he wasn't close to you and now I can see why.'

'Don't start on me, lady muck,' Hanora retorted, her eyes flashing with a spark of anger.

It was all going wrong. Kate's disappointment crushed her as she realized her fantasy of how this would turn out was precisely that. She slumped into a chair, hiding her head in her arms the way she used to do as a child when she was in trouble for some misdeed. She felt Eliza's hands gently stroke her hair. And then a sensation overcame her, a wave of warmth bathing her from head to toe.

Kate was not a fanciful girl, but at that moment, she could have sworn she could feel Mary and Diarmuid's love wrapping around her, joining her mom and dad, providing a shield against the ugliness of her aunt. It lasted mere seconds, but Kate felt stronger and more sure in its wake. She stood up and looked at her dad, repeating softly the words he'd uttered so many times: 'I think I need to leave the past where it belongs.'

Davey's eyes filled with tears, but he blinked them away. 'Aye, love.'

Hanora shouted to Davey, not liking the direction the conversation seemed to be taking, 'You can make the cheque out for cash, please and thank you.'

Kate moved closer to Hanora, recoiling as a waft of smoke burned her eyes. 'I thought that by meeting you, you'd bring me back to my MacShane family in some way. But that's never going to happen, is it? I don't suppose you grieved even for a moment when they died. Or cared how I might fare.'

Hanora paled slightly and her mouth twitched, but she played a good game and shrugged at Kate's words.

'I don't need anything from you after all. Mammy, Daddy and Richie are in here,' Kate touched her chest, patting it lightly.

Hanora stood up. 'Oh, there she is, her mammy's child. Just like Mary, you think you're better than the rest of us. Well, fancy clothes don't change the fact that you're a girl from a mud shack born without a shilling to her name.'

Eliza moved between Kate and her aunt. 'How exhausting it must be for you to carry so much bitterness in your heart,' she snapped. 'Your brother was a good man who wanted a better life for his family. But I will thank the heavens for the rest of my days that you said no to Matthew when he called you, because in doing so, you gave my husband and me the greatest gift of our lives – our daughter.' Eliza held out her hand to Kate, 'Let's go.'

Kate looked around the tired kitchen. If fate had played another card, she might have ended up living here. What would that life look like now? And then another thought hit her. Matthew could have given Hanora money so that he could start his life with Eliza without the encumbrance of an orphan, but he'd recognized instinctively that this should not be the home for a little girl.

All these years, Kate had rarely given Matthew a passing thought. But now, she wanted to run into his arms and thank him for his part in ensuring she stayed with Eliza.

'Keep your photographs,' Kate said. Then she took Eliza's hand and, together, they followed Davey into the summer sunshine.

FORTY-TWO

Saoirse

Present day
Palm Tree Cottage, Horseshoe Bay, Bermuda

'I'm so sorry that happened to you,' Finn said, as soon as Kate had finished talking. 'To have your first experience of meeting your birth family be that hurtful, must be difficult to get past.'

Kate looked at him gratefully. 'Thank you for understanding. Can you all see now, why I cannot allow myself to get excited about this Noah person? For all we know, he's a scammer looking for money.'

While this explained her aunt's reluctance to Saoirse, her every instinct told her that, regardless, it would be a good thing for Kate to respond to Noah.

'You truly don't want to pursue this any further?' Esme asked, clearly agreeing with Saoirse.

'That's what I said,' Kate replied, then pressed her lips tight together.

'Fine,' Esme said, in a tone that implied it was anything but.

Saoirse and Esme locked eyes. *What should their next move be?* Esme shook her head. She was at a loss too. They sat in uncomfortable silence, trying to find a way to push through it. But then Finn surprised them by leaning into Kate, his voice calm as he asked, 'If you walk away from this, are you sure you will be able to forget about it? Or will the unknown stay with you, eating you away? I'm not saying it's the same, but I've been thinking about walking away from something too. You said earlier today that you wanted to share your story with us because it might help me. And you were right. You've helped me enormously,' Finn paused and glanced at Saoirse, who was holding her breath as she listened to him speak. Then, Finn continued, 'I can't ignore what's happened in my life any more than you can ignore this. Because you said it yourself, when you leave things in the dark, they fester.'

Kate opened her mouth to respond, but closed it as the unmistakable sound of footsteps approaching from the side of the house made their way towards them. Kate and Esme turned to look at each other, their faces clearly questioning whether the other was expecting anyone. And when they turned back to the path, just as the figure came into view, their mouths both dropped open.

Saoirse, too, could not believe her eyes as Riley, a rucksack slung over one shoulder, walked on to the patio. He stopped upon seeing everyone there waiting, and shuffled from one foot to the other, the only sign that he felt unsure. Then he tipped his hat towards them all, ever solicitous.

'That's the cowboy,' Kate stage-whispered to Finn.

'I figured,' Finn replied. 'But thanks.' His voice was wary.

'I did ring the bell, but there was no answer, so I thought I'd try around here,' Riley said, as though this was the strange part, and not his arrival in Bermuda at all. His eyes passed from each person on the patio to the next, finally resting on Saoirse.

'I half expected you, you know. You always were one for dramatic entrances,' Kate replied, barely hiding a smirk as she looked at Riley.

'Well, I didn't expect him!' Saoirse said incredulously. 'What are you doing here, Riley?' She looked over to Finn, panicked, but his face was impassive. She needed to get rid of Riley before he extinguished whatever hope she and Finn had to move on.

'I couldn't leave things like they were. I had more to say,' Riley replied. 'Can we have a word in private?'

Everyone turned to look at Saoirse, waiting for her response. She was damned if she did and damned if she didn't. But a slight shake of Kate's head helped her decide how to respond.

'You can say whatever you need to, here. I've nothing to hide,' Saoirse replied firmly, staying seated.

He shrugged. 'Well, I'll come out and say it then. After you left, I talked through everything with Zoey and Mitch, and they helped me see that I had been presumptuous with you. You've made a life in Ireland, and you might not want to give that up.'

'Damn right, she doesn't want to give it up,' Kate interrupted.

Riley ignored her and continued, 'The thing is, I don't care where we live, as long as we are together.' He threw his rucksack on to the patio and then, with a smile, said, 'I'll come to Ireland with you.' When Saoirse didn't respond, a frown creased his forehead, and he said, a little louder this time, 'I'm saying I'll live with you in Donegal.'

Before Saoirse could digest or answer this statement, she heard a chair scrape the patio cobbles beside her. Finn was on his feet now too, and he looked over to Riley with a steely stare, then walked purposefully over to him. Riley tipped his hat, puffed his chest out, and they sized each other up. Saoirse wasn't sure what would happen, but from how they looked at each other, a friendly chat wasn't on the cards.

'Riley, I told you we were over,' Saoirse cried out. 'It's not fair, arriving here like this.'

'I know, and I'm sorry. But what was I supposed to do? Let you walk out of my life?'

Finn took a step closer to Riley. 'From what Saoirse has told me, that's exactly what she's asked you to do. You need to get on that horse of yours and trot on home.'

Riley took his cowboy hat off, clenching his jaw. That wasn't a good sign.

'I'm mighty sorry that you got caught up in our mess. This must be hard for you.' Riley thumbed towards Saoirse and himself as he spoke.

'I keep telling you that there is no more "our"!' Saoirse snapped.

But Riley ignored her and continued speaking to Finn, 'I have no issue with you; you seem like a decent bloke.

But I love Saoirse. Always have done. And I'm willing to do anything to be with her, even if that means moving my ranch to Ireland.'

'We have farms in Ireland, not ranches,' Finn shouted, his composure now gone, as two spots of red flashed on his cheeks.

Saoirse could have sworn she heard Kate snigger behind her, and, for one moment, as Finn clenched his fists into two balls, she thought he would hit Riley. Instead, he shrugged, then took a step back to the patio table and chairs. What did that mean? Saoirse's eyes moved between the two men, trying to work out what they were thinking.

Kate reached up and tugged his arm. 'You do not have to step aside like Matthew did. Fight for Saoirse, if you want her, that is. But from where I'm sitting, you'd be a damn fool to let her go from stubborn pride.'

Finn smiled at Kate and said, 'I have never stood on the sidelines in my entire life and I don't intend to do so now.' He turned back to Saoirse, her face crumpled in agony. She yearned to reach out, touch his cheek, kiss him, find a way to erase the pain he was in. 'You need to be honest with me, Saoirse. No more hiding the truth. Is there any part of you that still loves him?' Finn's voice had softened, he sounded like her lovely boyfriend again.

'I stopped loving Riley a long time ago,' Saoirse answered, without hesitation.

As Finn exhaled a sigh of relief, Saoirse continued, 'And you don't need to fight for me. You've already got me, Finn, if you will still have me. I want to grow old with you like Eliza and Davey did. I don't ever want to spend another day without you. I love *you*.'

Finn didn't answer her, but his fists unclenched. That was good enough for now.

Saoirse turned to Riley and spoke slowly, ensuring every word was understood, 'I told you in Canada that it was over between us. What we had has to remain in the past, and we can't get it back. And even if we could, I don't want to. I'm sorry if this hurts you, but you have to let this go. Let *me* go.'

Riley smiled, one of those bittersweet smiles that held so much pain.

'There's not much more to say then, I suppose,' he said quietly. 'I'm sorry that me coming here has upset you, Saoirse. But I'm not sorry I came. I had to try.' He looked towards Kate and continued, 'As your aunt said, only a damn fool would let you go.'

Saoirse felt her anger towards him disappear. But even so, she wanted him to leave so that she could find a way to make Finn understand that they had to be together, just as Eliza and Davey had done. 'I hope you find happiness in your life,' she said definitively. Then she lowered her eyes.

Riley put his hat back on, tipping it one last time to Saoirse. Then he walked round the corner and disappeared. Silence fell over that small patio. Nobody moved or spoke; the only sound was the soft rustling of palm tree leaves in the sea breeze.

Kate and Esme stood up without speaking and walked inside, leaving Saoirse and Finn alone.

Saoirse's stomach stopped its somersaults. She felt calm again, ready to face whatever was coming her way. If Finn could not get past this, she supposed they were not meant to be. As Kate said before, she was a strong woman and would endure.

'Finn . . .' she began, but he held his hand up to silence her.

'No more talking.'

Then he took two steps towards Saoirse, took her into his arms and kissed her.

FORTY-THREE

Saoirse

Palm Tree Cottage, Horseshoe Bay, Bermuda

Saoirse stretched her arms over her head languorously. She rolled on to her side and rested her head on her hands while watching Finn sleep. Once Riley had left, it was as if the clouds of suspicion and mistrust that hung over them had disappeared.

Kate had almost immediately gone for a nap, declaring herself exhausted from all the drama. Esme, meanwhile, had practically pushed Finn and Saoirse out the door, insisting they go out for dinner, just the two of them. It was precisely what they needed. In a rush of apologies over comforting pasta at a local Italian, they shared their regrets and love for each other. And later that night, when they'd made love, it had felt like a new beginning.

Finn stirred, opening his eyes sleepily. 'Hey, you.'

Saoirse leaned in and kissed him. She vowed never again

to take the warmth of his lips on hers for granted. 'I couldn't bear it if I lost you.'

'You don't have to keep saying that,' Finn said, reaching up to caress her cheek.

'I know. And I don't want to keep going over old ground. It's just . . . when I think about the years that Eliza and Davey missed because neither one knew that the other was alive . . .'

'It's heartbreaking. But they made up for those missed years in the loving life they built together afterwards. That's what we have to focus on.'

There was a knock on the door. Esme poked her head in, eyes closed, 'Are you decent? I'm coming in.' She had a notebook and pen in hand.

'She means business,' Saoirse said, pulling the sheet up over herself.

'Look, we have a busy day ahead. Kate's birthday is tomorrow. We have a lot to organize. So promise me, no more drama, okay?'

Saoirse and Finn nodded.

'Good. Saoirse, you need to message Noah and gently let him know that Kate isn't ready to chat. I found her looking at photographs again, in the middle of the night. I tried to get her to take a proper look at Noah's photograph, but she was adamant that she didn't want to discuss him any further. Try to word it so that he knows the door is slightly ajar. Maybe Kate will change her mind.'

Saoirse sighed, disappointed that her aunt had let fear win. 'I'll word it carefully. I hope you've not forgotten that you have an appointment at the opticians today,' Saoirse reminded her.

'I know, twelve p.m. – I'll take the bus.'

Saoirse chewed her bottom lip as she tried to summon the courage to tell Esme something else she'd organized. 'Last night, Finn and I went for a drink in the Rum Bum bar after our meal. And I got talking to Rene – remember that waitress who served us the other day?'

'Oh, I liked her. A nice no-nonsense young woman.'

Saoirse grinned, 'I'm glad you liked her. Because as well as waitressing, she cleans for two families in the area. Long story short, I called them to double-check they were happy with Rene – glowing references, I promise you – so I've booked her to do some light housework for you twice a week. Two hours each day, cleaning, shopping, whatever you need. And before you say no, I've already paid her in advance for three months.'

Saoirse held her breath as Esme considered this. Saoirse's plan was that Esme wouldn't refuse the arrangement once the money had changed hands. Rene had also promised to respect Esme's position in the house. She'd told Saoirse that her mother was territorial at home, so she understood the nuance of the situation.

Esme made a face and sighed. Saoirse steeled herself for an onslaught of questions and objections.

Instead, Esme pulled her into her arms and embraced her warmly. 'You are the kindest girl. How lucky we are to have you looking after us. Thank you.'

'You won't cancel her the second I return to Ireland?' Saoirse asked suspiciously.

'I most certainly will not. I know I need some help, and I'm not too proud to accept it when it's been so generously given.' Esme cleared her throat as her voice cracked dangerously at the end, then went straight to business. 'Now back to Kate's birthday. I'm taking Kate to a hair salon in Hamilton tomorrow morning. Then we'll go directly to the hotel at two p.m.'

'Perfect. That gives us plenty of time to ensure we have everything sorted before you arrive. We'll make an early start of it,' Saoirse replied.

'What can I do to help?' Finn asked.

'I'm glad you asked,' Esme replied cheekily. 'I've written down the address of the bakery in Hamilton where we need to pick up the cake. Can you take that job on, please? It will be ready to collect any time after ten o'clock. And I also want you to take all our bags to the hotel, if you don't mind. I'll pack one for Kate and myself. Remember, not a word to Kate. She doesn't know she's staying over-night. Saoirse, I'm leaving the videographer to you. Double-check he has set the video as we've asked.'

'Consider me at your disposal,' Finn said. 'Happy to chip in and do everything you've asked.'

'Thank you, child,' Esme said warmly. She ticked off a few more items on her list, muttering to herself as she double-checked her plans.

Then an idea struck Saoirse, making her bounce up and down on her bed. 'That song Kate mentioned that Eliza sang to her, the "I love you truly" one – wouldn't it be nice to have that play in the background of the video? I can ask the videographer to add it in.'

'Such a thoughtful idea. I love it!' Esme said.

The hairs stood on Saoirse's arms as she thought about the surprise they had planned for their beloved Kate. 'I hope she won't get too much shock at everything.'

'I'd say after yesterday's shenanigans, we'd better ensure she's sitting down,' Finn said, with a quick shrug.

'I want this to be an afternoon she'll never forget, for

all the right reasons,' Esme said. 'Right, let's go have breakfast before Kate comes looking for us.'

Saoirse and Finn threw on shorts and a T-shirt each, then joined the aunts in the dining room.

'You're up early,' Saoirse said in surprise when she saw Kate was dressed and ready for her day. 'It's not even eight a.m.!'

'Sleep evaded me last night,' Kate replied. 'You two look happy. Good.' She said this with a slight wink.

'We are,' Saoirse said, beaming lovingly at Finn.

'Before you start breakfast, can you come with me for a minute, Saoirse?' Kate asked, standing up from the table.

'Sure,' Saoirse said. 'I'll have a coffee, please, Finn. Think I need a caffeine hit.'

'She was back on the Rum Swizzles again last night,' Finn said to Esme, who groaned in response.

Saoirse followed her aunt as she slowly ambled towards the third bedroom in the cottage.

'Top shelf of the wardrobe, there's a large box,' Kate said, pointing up at the shelf in question. 'Will you get it down for me, please?'

Saoirse did as Kate asked and placed it on the bed between them. It was cream, with a large black silk bow tied around its middle.

'This looks fancy!' Saoirse said.

'Open it,' Kate instructed.

Untying the black silk bow, Saoirse lifted the lid. Peering in, Kate carefully moved aside layers of white tissue paper to reveal a folded wedding dress.

'This is Eliza's wedding dress. Her third one, but the only one that actually made it as far as any vows,' Kate said with a chuckle.

'I hope I don't need three,' Saoirse said, laughing. 'I can't believe you've kept it all this time!'

She reached in gingerly and gently stroked the material, trying to imagine how Eliza must have felt on her wedding day. Saoirse had never given Kate's mother a thought up until this visit. She was a ghost of her aunt's past. But the more Kate shared, the more Saoirse felt a connection to Eliza, a woman she'd never even met. Her story resonated with Saoirse, and she found herself caring deeply about what happened to the young woman who bravely left her hometown of Donegal to follow her heart and head for adventure.

'Eliza waited a long time to wear this dress, didn't she?'

'She did. But the wait was worth it for my mom and dad. They loved each other, just as you and Finn do. And I want to tell you that I've been watching how that young man of yours conducts himself. I like what I see. I've got a good feeling about him.'

Saoirse basked in the glowing compliments to Finn. It meant a great deal to her that her aunts and Finn get on. And she could see a bond fast forming between them. 'I'm so happy you like him. And the feeling is mutual, he couldn't stop talking about you last night. You've got a new fan.'

'Well, I'm very loveable,' Kate joked. 'Now, back to Eliza's dress. Or rather, yours now.' She picked the dress up and handed it to Saoirse. 'You can tailor it, of course, but I think it will fit you just fine.'

Tears sprang into Saoirse's eyes as she cradled the dress carefully. 'I can't take this from you,' she said, holding them back. 'It's too precious.'

'Yes, you can. I've always thought that you were like

Mom. I know that's silly – you're not even blood-related – but you have a way about you that reminds me of her. And there's a lot of love in this dress. I think Eliza would be chuffed to see you walk down the aisle wearing it.'

Saoirse lifted the dress up and held it against herself, the silk skirt cascading to the floor below.

'If I can be as happy with Finn as Eliza was with Davey, I'll be a lucky woman. Aunt Kate, I'd be honoured to wear it on my wedding day. It won't be for at least a year though. Finn and I have agreed to enjoy our engagement before we rush into planning a wedding.'

'That's smart,' Kate said approvingly.

'Aunt Kate, I don't know how to thank you.'

'Be happy; that's all I ask.' Brisk again, Kate added as she turned for the door, 'Put the dress away now, and let's go back to the others. There's something I want to talk to you all about.'

FORTY-FOUR

Kate

Palm Tree Cottage, Horseshoe Bay, Bermuda

'Yesterday was quite a day,' Kate said to them all, once they were back together in the dining room.

Esme, Saoirse and Finn acknowledged this understatement with a ripple of laughter.

'The reason I didn't sleep much last night was because I couldn't stop thinking about how everything I believed to be true about my life appeared to be based on an untruth,' she continued. 'I felt bewildered and betrayed. I know you may not understand, but it's how I felt.'

'Betrayed by who, love?' Esme asked tentatively.

'Everyone. According to that DNA site, I have a brother. So someone has lied to me, kept that information from me.'

'You're worried that Eliza hid it?' Saoirse asked disbelievingly.

'No. Not Mom. She would have told me if she knew I had a brother.' Kate was confident of this at least.

'Then who? Your aunts?' Saoirse asked. 'I wouldn't put anything past that Hanora one.'

'Maybe,' Kate admitted. 'And that's assuming this isn't a scam, which still feels likely to me. Every second day I get a text message with a new attempt to de-fraud.'

A murmur of non-committal sounds echoed back to her.

'You all think this Noah man is my baby brother Richie?' Kate asked dubiously. Her breath quickened.

Saoirse looked at Esme, then Finn, before answering slowly, 'Yes, we do.'

Kate felt her body recoil from their words. Because, if they were right, then that opened up so many possibilities, which terrified her.

'What frightens you most about this?' Esme asked gently.

'If Richie survived the *Athenia*, then maybe Mammy and Daddy did too. And if that was the case, why didn't they come looking for me?' Saying it aloud sent her spiralling towards a chasm filled with fear and pain. But facing this, whatever it was, could not be worse than how she'd felt ever since the email arrived from this Noah.

'That said, something Finn mentioned yesterday struck a nerve, as I tossed and turned last night. I'll never have a night's sleep again if I don't find out the truth,' she took a deep breath. 'So, Saoirse, I need you to call this Noah.'

Kate almost enjoyed the shock on each of their faces.

'Now?' Esme asked, looking slightly startled at the change in Kate's stance.

'Yes, now. I don't know if I want to speak to him myself until I have all the facts.'

With a shaking hand, Saoirse picked up her phone and dutifully walked out into the garden.

'I'll make some tea,' Esme said brightly.

It was the longest ten minutes of Kate's life. She watched Saoirse pace around the garden and sit at the patio table and chairs until finally, she came back, jittery. Kate reached out to clasp Esme's hand as she looked to the ashen-faced Saoirse.

'I've spoken to Noah. He's a nice man and I believe him to be genuine in all he's shared with me. Like you, Aunt Kate, he's reeling with the shock of your connection,' Saoirse started gently. 'Noah was adopted when he was a baby. He's lived in America for most of his life,' Saoirse paused before she next spoke, her words thick with emotion. 'Aunt Kate, he *was* on the *Athenia* when it went down.'

Pain twisted Kate's stomach. Time stood still then reversed backwards, free-falling, bringing her all the way back to 1939 and her little baby brother, playing peekaboo on her knee.

'There's no doubt that Noah is your brother Richie,' Saoirse confirmed.

'And Mammy and Daddy?' Kate whispered. She sucked in a sharp breath and closed her eyes as Saoirse spoke.

'He knows little about how he ended up in the care of a Jewish family, who went on to adopt him. His adoptive mother was also on the *Athenia* and she told him that he was placed in her arms on the lifeboat. A steward discovered him when he heard an infant's cry. Richie had been underneath two bodies, a man and a woman.'

'Mammy and Daddy,' Kate sobbed.

'He stayed with that family, and they ended up on a

rescue ship called the *Knute Nelson* that took everyone to Galway.'

Kate couldn't take it in; she kept shaking her head, clutching her chest, then shaking her head again.

'He didn't know he had a sister, or that his parents were Mary and Diarmuid MacShane. Or that once he was a baby called Richie.'

Kate began to properly cry then, wracking sobs that shook her small frame. She clutched her head, pulling at her hair in agony and regret. She pushed arms of comfort away, because nobody could help her as she tried to make sense of this discovery.

Kate had no idea how long they sat watching her grieve, but eventually, when her sorrow quelled, Saoirse continued, 'Noah has asked me to say to you, that he would very much like to meet you.'

Kate thought of all those who had gone before her. Her mammy and daddy. Matthew. Eliza and Davey, her mom and dad. All had endured a long and twisting road to find their way in life. And all the while her baby brother had been out there, following that path on his own.

All doubt and fear disappeared. She was his big sister and it was time she acted as such. She sat up straight, wiping the tears from her cheeks.

FORTY-FIVE

Kate

Hamilton Princess Hotel, Hamilton, Bermuda

'I don't think we're allowed up here,' Kate said, as Esme led her down the grand hallway in the hotel.

'Hush now with your worrying. Here we are. Knock on that door,' Esme insisted.

Kate heard a squeal of excitement from the other side of the door when she rapped it as instructed.

Saoirse and Finn opened the door together, stepping back to let Kate and Esme enter the room, holding each other's hands. Thanks to their pampering at the salon, they both looked even more elegant than usual, both with their coiffed hair and subtle make-up. And Esme now sported a pair of red square glasses that suited her perfectly.

'Happy Birthday, Aunt Kate!' Saoirse and Finn cried out. 'Surprise!'

'I knew you were up to something,' Kate said, beaming. 'But I'm still not sure we are allowed to be in here? It looks fancy.'

'This penthouse suite is our room for the night,' Esme said. 'My gift to you. Because you deserve somewhere fit for the queen you are.' Esme leaned down and lightly kissed Kate on the lips.

'And we have a suite too, down the hall!' Saoirse exclaimed. 'Come on, I'll bring you for the tour.'

The living area, in muted creams, boasted comfortable sofas and chairs, with a large smart TV. A long dining-room table was set, and champagne was on ice. It had a wrap-around balcony with panoramic views of Hamilton Harbour. Two bedrooms had their own bathroom with a vast soaker bathtub. Finn told Kate that there were ninety balloons, in gold and silver shades, tied in bunches around the room, and a custom-made banner with a photograph of Kate sat above the door to her balcony.

'I don't know what to say. I've never seen a more beautiful suite. I don't think I ever want to leave it. Thank you!' Kate walked around the suite, touching everything as she moved, her eyes bright with wonder. The sound of champagne corks popping made them all cheer as Finn poured a glass for them all.

'Take a seat,' Saoirse said, directing Kate and Esme to the large sofa in front of the TV. Finn passed the drinks around.

'I'm overwhelmed,' Kate said. 'You've all gone to so much trouble.'

'Afternoon tea will be delivered to the suite soon, too,' Esme said.

'Thank goodness. I'm famished. I've not had a cup of

tea since breakfast,' Kate said, rubbing her small tummy with a smile.

'We have gifts for you to unwrap in a bit, but we also made you something. I hope you like it, my darling,' Esme said.

Saoirse got up and hit play on the TV, which came straight to life with a photograph of Kate, aged five years old, her blonde hair tied into two pigtails, sitting on her bicycle. The words *This is your life, Kate McDaid* flashed on to the screen.

'That's me!' Kate exclaimed. 'Look at me on that bike. Dad bought it for me a few days after we arrived in Boston. A welcome home gift, he called it. I was never off it.'

The videographer had done an incredible job, intertwining music and newspaper headlines between photographs of Kate's life. Saoirse explained that they had not managed to get any images of Mary and Diarmuid MacShane, but they did have the photo of her grandparents and one of Diarmuid as a young boy with his sisters.

'I'm going to keep looking for a photograph of Mary and Diarmuid. If one exists, I promise you I'll hunt it down. I'm on a mission!' Saoirse declared.

'I don't doubt you will succeed too,' Kate said, smiling at her. 'I can't take it in. You're so clever finding that photograph. Gosh, doesn't my grandmother look cross,' Kate pointed to her dour-faced grandmother, as that particular photo flashed up on screen. 'Maybe that's who Hanora took after.' She cackled laughter at her own joke.

'Take it all in. We can watch it as often as you like, my darling,' Esme said, beaming with delight at Kate's enthusiastic reaction.

The SS *Athenia* came on screen next, with stills taken

from photographs in the media, ending with the iconic image of Mrs Montague in her boiler suit beside Eliza and Kate.

Kate clapped her hands together, 'Dear Mrs Montague. Oh, how my mom loved her. She was wonderful.'

Kate's eyes brimmed with tears as she laughed with each changing snap. There were several photographs from their short month in Bermuda, in 1939, including many with Matthew.

When a picture of a sleeping Kate, cradled in Eliza's arms, came on screen, the music changed to the haunting melody of 'I Love You Truly', sung by Elsa Barker. Kate put her hands over her face, and, for a moment, it was almost all too much for her. But then she took her hands down and sang every lyric, word for word, in time to the music.

'Gone is the sorry, gone doubt and fear, for you love me truly, truly dear,' she finished. 'It's as if Eliza is here with me, and how apt those words are now,' Kate said, but then she broke into a fit of giggles when an image of her teenage self, complete with braces and a dodgy perm, filled the screen.

Next came a baby photograph of Richie, alongside a picture of five-year-old Kate.

'We couldn't exclude him, so Saoirse made the photographs of you both into a collage. It's clever, isn't it?' Esme said.

Kate could only nod. She watched the images fade, and two final photographs appeared in their place. It was a second collage, this time of them as they were now – Noah, in his tweed suit, and Kate, sitting in the sunshine on her patio.

'Brother and sister, side by side,' Kate said in wonder. 'And one day soon hopefully I'll meet him in person. Am I dreaming? If I am, please never wake me up. I have a brother!'

'I know, my darling. I am so happy for you.' Esme pulled her into her arms, and the two women held each other in joy at this new-found miracle.

'I thought life could not surprise me any more,' Kate said, taking another sip of her champagne. 'But it feels good to be proved wrong. Tell me again what he said to you, Saoirse, when you sent him our travel plans.'

'He said that you had made him the happiest man alive. And that he would count down the days until you arrived in New York. From what I can gather, his family are all excited to meet you too.'

Kate put her hands on her face, feeling the lines on her cheeks beneath her fingertips. Roadmaps to a life lived well. She thought about that little girl in the photograph, who fearlessly rode her bicycle around her neighbourhood in Boston. Feeling the wind whip through her hair, and the air squeezing out of her lungs as she pushed herself to go faster and faster, until she could almost fly. Kate sighed in pleasure, as excitement coursed its way through her body. Turning ninety today, she felt younger than she had done for over a decade.

'I think I'd like a bicycle,' she said to Esme, who quickly tried to talk her out of that new idea.

Finn got up and quietly left the room.

'Don't be cross, but we do have one more surprise,' Esme said when Finn returned a few moments later, leaving the door to their suite slightly ajar.

She helped Kate to her feet, turning her to face the

doorway. Then, a couple walked in. As if he were suddenly transported from the TV screen, there was Noah, wearing the same suit and dickie bow, his wife Leah by his side.

Silence filled the room as everyone watched Noah move closer, finally stopping in front of Kate.

'When I heard it was your birthday, I had to come to give you my best wishes in person.' Noah said, his voice gruff with emotion. 'Happy birthday, big sister.'

'Is it really you, Richie?' Kate asked.

'I'm Noah now, but I'm so happy to meet you that I'll gladly change my name if you want me to,' he chuckled.

They looked at each other hesitantly.

'I thought I had forgotten what Mammy and Daddy looked like until now,' Kate said, reaching up to touch Noah's face. 'You have Daddy's eyes, and mine too. But your nose and mouth are all Mammy's. Saoirse said she was sorry she couldn't find a photograph of Mary and Diarmuid, but she's done much better than that.'

Noah reached up to clasp Kate's hand. He couldn't take his eyes off her, as if she'd put a spell on him.

'Richie . . . Noah, you've not only brought my baby brother back to me, you've brought Mammy and Daddy back too,' Kate said.

A sob came from Leah. Esme walked over to her and put a gentle arm around her shoulders.

'I wish I could remember them,' Noah said sadly.

Kate took his hand and said, 'I'll help you. I'll tell you everything that I know.'

'I'd like that,' Noah agreed, then he laughed as he looked around the room, saying, 'All this time, I didn't know where I was originally from. But I've been Irish all along! I can't believe it.'

They all laughed along with him for a moment.

Kate watched Saoirse lean into Finn, who wrapped his arms around her. Esme stood by her side, as she'd done for decades. And now, before her, she'd found her baby brother again. Everything turned out exactly as it was meant to.

The room quietened again when they heard a sob escape Kate. 'The last time I held you, you were only six months old. I didn't know that it would be the last time. I didn't know . . .'

'You can hold me again now; I'd like that.' Noah replied, wiping tears away with the back of his hand.

Kate opened her arms wide and Noah clung to her. Eighty-five years of love poured into their warm and loving embrace.

EPILOGUE

Eliza

May 1991
Boston, USA

Eliza walked out to the porch, carrying a small bag. She carefully took a seat on the swing Davey had built for them decades before. It was more of a daybed really, with a large seat hanging on four ropes, and plenty of room to curl up on with a good book. Or each other, of course.

Eliza settled in against the soft pillows and used her legs to kickstart a gentle sway back and forth. That was usually Davey's job, but he was gone now. She looked at the shallow dent in the space beside her, where her husband should be, and her throat tightened. Two weeks had passed since Davey had died – for the second and final time. Eliza had barely had a moment to catch her breath. First, the funeral, then dealing with the inevitable paperwork that knocked on your door after a loved one died. And finally, packing away Davey's things this week.

Well, not quite all of them.

Eliza breathed in the musky aroma of Davey's after-shave. It lingered in the fabric of his favourite sweater that she now wore every evening. Eliza only allowed herself to pull it on once her day was over. She supposed that soon his scent would wear away, but she didn't think she needed to worry about that. Eliza had a feeling that her time in this world was nearly at an end, anyway. She'd be with Davey again soon. This morning, as the dawn broke, she had even seen him at the end of her bed, waiting for her.

'Need anything, Mom?' Kate asked as she joined her on the porch.

'Nothing at all. I'm good,' Eliza answered.

Having Kate and Esme here had been a blessing. They'd not left her side once since Davey died. They'd watched her closely at all times, ready to catch her should she fall.

'We thought we might go into town to see a movie if you fancy it?' Kate asked. 'You can have the deciding vote what we go to see.'

'Let Esme choose. You get your own way too much,' Eliza said. 'But I'll stay here. I might go to bed soon anyway, I'm tired.'

Kate looked at her mother and frowned.

'Go. Have fun. And I'll see you in the morning,' Eliza reassured her.

'Okay, if you're sure,' Kate agreed, although with a reluctant tone in her voice.

Esme came bounding out at that moment, looking radiant in a bright orange sweater dress and trainers.

'Oh I like that colour on you! Esme, you brought sunshine into all our lives when you met Kate,' Eliza said, unexpectedly. If her time was as short as she suspected, she didn't want to leave anything unsaid. 'Thank you for that.' Eliza had always marvelled at her zest for life.

'That's a lovely thing to say. Thank you. But trust me, I can also bring the rain when I need to,' Esme said, winking.

'And the odd storm,' Kate said, then leaned down to kiss her mother's forehead. 'See you later, Mom.'

Eliza clasped her hand and whispered, 'I love you truly.'

Kate touched her mom's face, replying as she always did, 'Truly I do too.'

Then Esme and Kate walked out into the night air, their chatter echoing around Eliza.

Seeing her daughter settled and happy was a gift, and Eliza knew that she would leave Kate, secure in the knowledge that she was living a good life. Davey used to say that they needn't worry about their daughter, because she was a survivor, like Eliza was. She hoped that there would be no more tribulations for Kate to endure and test that theory.

Once she'd heard that they'd gone, Eliza finally opened the bag beside her, pulling out a sheath of pages. She'd written a letter earlier this evening but wanted to read it over one last time before sending it on its way. It was long overdue, a missive that Eliza had meant to write many times, but had always doubted herself.

But now Eliza was eighty-nine years old. There was no more time for procrastination or regrets. Putting her reading glasses on, Eliza began to read.

My dear Matthew,

Fifty years have passed since we last saw each other, and I'm an old woman now. I'm sure you would scarcely recognize me. When I catch myself in a passing mirror, even I am confused by the reflection I see. Because inside, I feel the same as I did on that day we met on the shores of Ballymastocker Bay. Do you remember?

I watched children chase the waves, and I envied them. Because they had their entire lives ahead of them, whereas I felt stuck. Locked in a world of grief and loss.

But then you said hello, and that small act changed everything.

When you asked me to marry you, you gave me a reason to move forward with my life. You promised me an adventure, although I don't think either of us could ever have predicted the magnitude of the one we had in store!

At first, I thought fate had conspired to put you in my path that day in Donegal so that I could save Kate on the Athenia *and become her mother. And oh, the joy of that girl. But you know that for yourself. I am so happy that you've reconnected – I know she is so very fond of you.*

Fate had a far bigger plan for all of us though, didn't it, when you brought me to Bermuda and led me to my first love? The impact you had on all our lives is hard to quantify. My family would not be as it is today if it had not been for you and your generosity of heart.

I travelled the world, as I promised you I would.

And Davey and I passed on our wanderlust to Kate. We have returned to Donegal many times to see our dear friends Larry and Eimear. Most recently to attend their grandson's wedding, who had a baby daughter last month, Saoirse. That's a pretty name, isn't it? It means freedom.

And that's what you gave to me, Matthew. That small world I had created for myself in Ireland, you found the key to unlock it and you set me free. I want you to know that I honoured that gift of freedom by making sure that I have lived my best life every day since I last saw you.

Kate I'm sure has told you this, but my beloved Davey died two weeks ago. During our fifty years together, we never spent a night apart. Our love for each other grew more profound with every passing year. I feel it's important to share that with you, so you know I didn't walk away from us for anything less than profound. Now that Davey's gone, a part of me has too. And until we are back together again, wherever that might be, I will have to live with an ache inside me.

There's one more thing that I've wanted to share with you for the longest time. In case there was ever any doubt, I need you to know that I loved you, Matthew. And I am certain that if Davey had not returned, you and I would have had a long and happy life together. I broke your heart when I chose Davey, I know that. But you need to know that a little of my heart also broke on that day.

My friends and family know Davey as the most important man in my life. But in my head, Matthew, you have always been the unsung hero. You were the one who first suggested the idea that we adopt Kate, and you were the first adopted father she knew, the father who brought joy back to her when she had lost everything, and everyone, else. You could have paid her horrid aunt to take her, but you recognized that her life would be better with me. For that, I have never forgotten you, and I have never stopped being grateful.

Matthew, you were a shelter in my turbulent storm, and a safe passage to calmer waters.

You were a friend.

You were a loving and kind man.

Know that, because of you, I have lived a great life full of wonder and joy.

And love. Always love.

With my eternal gratitude,

Eliza

AUTHOR'S NOTE

With each of my books, readers have come to expect a family saga filled with emotional twists, set between Ireland and an international destination. I like to transport readers to new places as I bring them on emotional journeys with my characters. I've picked incredible locations for *The Girl from Donegal* – from the wild Atlantic coast of Ireland to the majestic Canadian Rockies and then to the dazzling, tropical islands of Bermuda. But this time, I'm transporting readers not only to another place, but also to another time.

I've always read historical novels and adore how fictional accounts of real events can bring the past back to life. But I'd never planned to write one myself until a story took root in my imagination, growing stronger daily and leaving me with no choice but to write it.

It started when, a few years ago, I stumbled across a fascinating short account of a young woman from Northern Ireland who was bound for a new life in Bermuda with her fiancé, a British Admiral. She was due to set sail from Liverpool on board the SS *Athenia*, but a telegram from her mother stating an emergency at home made her cancel her plans. Less than 24 hours later, the SS *Athenia* was struck by a German torpedo and sunk, with 117 civilian passengers and crew killed. I thought this fateful story was charming, and as I knew little about the SS *Athenia*, I began researching its ill-fated journey on September 3, 1939. I then discovered that many of the survivors were rescued by a Norwegian freighter, Knute Nelson, and ended up in Galway. I stored the information away, thinking I might write a story about what happened to those survivors.

Shortly after that, I discovered that I had quite a few (distant) family members from Bermuda. This, coupled with the snippet I'd read about the woman heading to Bermuda on the SS *Athenia*, felt like a sign. Should I write about the ill-fated passage, but with Bermuda as the final destination for my characters? I began noodling ideas and asked myself, could I bring the past to life? The answer was apparent when Eliza's character came to me perfectly formed. But further noodling was needed to work out her story and what I wanted to achieve in writing this book.

Like so many others, world events have made me anxious and unsure over the past couple of years. So I turned to beloved and iconic romantic sagas as a balm, my joy and tears cathartic. I knew I wanted to write an unforgettable love story of the past and present, filled with satisfying surprises and reveals. A timeless saga, so it could be re-read many times. The kind of story that makes you gasp out loud, gives you hope and ultimately makes you drop everything so that you can curl up until you reach the final page.

That's when the idea of exploring two women, eight

decades apart, torn between their first and last loves, revealed itself to me. Eliza had been with me for some time, so her story unfolded with ease. In fact, my agent and editors all said when first reading Eliza's story, it was as if I'd channelled a character from the 1930s. And as I lost myself in that time, it did feel exactly like that. I turned to one of my childhood loves for Saoirse's storyline. For many years, I dreamt of running my own stables and of working on a ranch in Canada. Mr Bojangles, Saoirse's horse, was named after my own pony. Childhood dreams realised through writing Saoirse's storyline! Kate's character was a surprise for me. Her voice grew louder with each re-write until she shared centre stage with both Eliza and Saoirse. I hope you love my three leading ladies as much as I do, and I'd love to hear what you think of their great loves – Davey, Matthew, Finn, Riley, and Esme.

Donegal is one of my favourite places in Ireland, where I've had the most glorious holidays with my family. If you've not been there yet, add Ballymastocker Bay to your list.

In April 2022, I visited Bermuda for the first time. I had read so much about this tropical paradise that it felt like I was coming home. It's a beautiful archipelago, not just thanks to its breathtaking beaches, but also thanks to its people. This research trip took me to the Royal Naval Dockyard, the Commissioner's house, the pink sands of Horseshoe Bay, and the cobblestone streets of Hamilton and St George, so rich with history. And, purely in research interests (I'm good like that), I forced myself to drink a rum swizzle or two, as Saoirse and Esme do. Highly recommended!

The details of what took place on the SS *Athenia* are

a mix of actual events and gaps filled in from my imagination, so please forgive any inaccuracies. If you would like to read more about the sinking of the *Athenia*, or the Royal Navy in Bermuda, these are books that I found fascinating: *Athenia Torpedoed* by Francis M. Carroll, *A Night of Terror* by Max Caulfield, and *The Andrew and the Onions* by Ian Stranack.

I hope I've achieved my objective and readers will lose themselves in Eliza, Kate and Saoirse's stories, finding solace within the pages. And that *The Girl from Donegal* lingers and becomes a story that readers can keep in their hearts forever.

Much love,

Carmel

ACKNOWLEDGEMENTS

The Girl from Donegal is my first historical novel, and reader, I am hooked! What a joy it's been taking my characters from 1939 to now. Holding my hand along the way were my book village – the people who all play a part in helping me to get this novel ready for publication. In no particular order, sincere thanks to:

My agent, Rowan Lawton, for her guidance, friendship and support, and whose early response to Eliza, Kate and Saoirse's story gave me the confidence to carry on. Her assistant, Eleanor Lawlor, and the entire team at The Soho Agency, plus Abigail Koons at Park & Fine Literary and Media and Rich Green.

My publisher, Lynne Drew, and editor, Lucy Stewart, who both understood what I was trying to achieve with this story and pushed me to dig deeper, helping me polish *The Girl from Donegal* into the book it is today. There are so many others at HarperCollins UK and Ireland who have worked on and supported this book too, including Kimberley Young, Kate Elton, Susanna Peden, Sophie Raoufi, Sarah Shea, Claire Ward, Emily Langford, Conor Nagle, Patricia McVeigh, Tony Purdue, Jacqueline Murphy, Anne O'Brien and Sarah Bance.

The writing community who support and inspire me, and occasionally do so with a side order of gin, you are all legends – Caroline Grace-Cassidy, Alex Brown, Claudia Carroll, Vanessa O'Loughlin, Sheila O'Flanagan, Patricia Scanlan, Cathy Bramley, Milly Johnson, Katie Fforde, Melissa Hill, Debbie Johnson, Marian Keyes and many more.

The book retailers, media, bloggers, reviewers, libraries, book clubs and festivals, whose passion to put books into readers' laps helps authors, including me, every day. I started an online book club called The Curl Up with Carmel Book Club a few years ago. It's always fun talking books with the members there – come find us on Facebook if you'd like to join! And speaking of Facebook, I asked my readers there to help me come up with a name for Saoirse's stables in Donegal. Thank you Laura Kehoe, for suggesting Anam Cara Stables and Cottage, which means 'soul friend' and is the perfect choice.

Special mention to Catherine Ryan Howard and Hazel Gaynor, who listen, sympathise, cheer, stage interventions, talk me both off and *on* a ledge, and who make Westbury Day like Christmas every year! Because of you both, I cry a lot less and smile a lot more.

To all the branches of the O'Grady and Harrington family tree, thank you for your enduring love and support. The older I get, the more I appreciate and need you. As I always say, all that matters is family. Special shout out to my first reader, my mum, Tina. She is the only person

I allow to read my books before the final proofread version, other than my editors and agent.

There is nothing better than a friend, unless it's a friend with cake, rosé or chocolate – well let's just say, I have excellent friends! You all know who you are and I'm so grateful that you are in my corner.

As always, my final thanks goes to my H's – my children, Amelia and Nate, who fill my days with laughter and love; my stepdaughter, Eva, who we watch in awe as she makes her way out into the world; and George Bailey, our rescue cockerpoo who never leaves my side. Last but never least – Roger. As I wrote Eliza and Saoirse's love stories, unpacking their emotions as they chose between their first and last loves, there could only be one person that I dedicated it to. Roger, my constant, this book is for you. Thank you for making our love story so epic and for giving me lots of swoon-worthy moments. And most of all, thank you for being *my* last love.

READING GROUP QUESTIONS

1. *The Girl from Donegal* is first and foremost a story about great love. Did you relate to any of the love stories we see in the novel? Whose was your favourite?

2. The novel is also heartbreaking at times. Which part do you think moved you the most?

3. Of the three leading ladies – Eliza, Saoirse and Kate – which character did you most warm to? Why?

4. When we meet Eliza she is offered a life-changing opportunity, but it means leaving everything she has ever known behind. Did she make the right decision? Would you have taken the same brave step she did?

5. Did any of the events in the novel take you by surprise? Did you see the twists coming?

6. Both Saoirse and Eliza find themselves having to make a decision about who will be their last love. Do you think they both made the right decision?

7. The gorgeous settings are always such a huge part of Carmel's novels. What did you think of the places – and time periods – she takes us to in *The Girl from Donegal*?

8. What three words would you use to describe the novel? Have any parts of the novel really stayed with you since you closed the final page?